To Please Her

Praise for Elena Abbott

Pack of Her Own

"There are a lot of subtle and not so subtle messages about a trans experience, and I really liked all of the metaphors being weaved around each other. All of the characters have a lot to wrestle with, between internal struggles and fears about society and physical dangers. Supernatural characters always have to deal with the matter of secrecy, but this author adds a couple more layers to give the story a deeper than normal feel."—*The Lesbian Review*

"There's big series potential here, so I'm curious to see where it goes!"—*The Lesbrary*

Mate of Her Own

"One thing that Abbott does really well here is establish both internal and external conflict for Heather and V to work through. I liked the way the author played around with shifter tropes to tell a queer story, and I look forward to reading more of her work."—*The Smut Report*

By the Author

Pack of Her Own

Mate of Her Own

Hunt of Her Own

To Please Her

Visit us at www.boldstrokesbooks.com

TO PLEASE HER

by
Elena Abbott

2025

TO PLEASE HER

ISBN 13: 978-1-63679-849-3

This Trade Paperback Original Is Published By
Bold Strokes Books, Inc.
P.O. Box 249
Valley Falls, NY 12185

First Edition: May 2025

READER ADVISORY: HOMOPHOBIA AND TRANSPHOBIA

CREDITS
Editors: Jenny Harmon and Stacia Seaman
Production Design: Stacia Seaman
Cover Design by Tammy Seidick

Acknowledgments

It would take me a book just to acknowledge all of the people who made this novel happen and supported me through struggles not just in writing but in life as well. But hey, I'm gonna try anyway.

To Soph and Arra for always being there for me and putting up with a disaster lesbian such as myself. I owe you more than I could ever repay. And to Luna, for making sure I smile every day and being such an amazing friend.

To all the online friends I've made, I appreciate you so much. Autumn and Issy and TJ and everyone else, it's been a pleasure getting to know you all and learning what it's like to have a pack of my own. (wink wink)

To the folks at Bold Strokes, for giving a girl a chance. And to my readers and reviewers who keep coming back for more or decide that one of my books might be for them. I thank you so very much.

To all those looking for a little something more in their lives. Sometimes you run into it, sometimes it runs into you.

To Arra, Luna, and Soph. I'm so glad I ran into you.

TO PLEASE HER

Chapter One

I'm late, I'm late, I'm late," I muttered, as I ran down the street with coffee in hand, my ginger hair bouncing around behind me, my bangs in front of my eyes. The morning couldn't have gone worse. First my alarm not going off, then the buses running behind, and the line at the coffee shop being twice as long as usual. "Nothing is going right today!"

I sped around the corner, heading to the storefront of Oracle Books—which I had to open by myself in five minutes—when someone suddenly appeared in front of me. I had no chance to stop before plowing into the well-dressed woman. I could only watch as her own coffee cup, in excruciating slow motion, crumpled backward and spilled all down her cream-colored blouse.

"Oh shit!" The words were far too late to do anything to help the situation, and I stood frozen on the spot, staring at the woman who was looking down at her cup like she was surprised it was empty. Digging around in my purse, I pulled out a wad of napkins and offered them to her instead of dabbing at her chest. "I am so, so sorry."

She held up a hand imperiously and my mouth clamped shut. I let my eyes drift over her, from her expensive boots to gorgeously fitted pants, up to the stained blouse and dark overcoat, and finally to her face, which left me in awe. Her dark hair was cut short in an asymmetrical pixie and her gorgeous golden-brown eyes stared down at me like she owned everything she surveyed—including me.

"You really should watch where you're going."

I bristled at her attitude but couldn't really argue against it.

"I know, I'm so sorry, I was in a hurry," I said, "and I wasn't paying attention and I'm so, so sorry." I tried to look away, but her gaze held me captive until I couldn't help but keep staring. "I'll pay for the dry cleaning if that helps at all."

She shook her head, closing her eyes and releasing me from her hold. "That won't be necessary." I tried to refocus on her without getting lost in those eyes again. "I will handle it."

"Please, there has to be something I can do," I began. She waved her hand again, but this time her mouth was quirked up in the beginnings of a smile.

"Trust me, it's fine." She glanced down at her top. "Honestly, you probably did me a favor. This is one of my least favorite tops. It's really not my style, you see."

"So why wear it?"

"Pressure to be seen a certain way, I suppose," she said. "I'm certain you can relate."

My cheeks flushed with embarrassment, and I stared down at the ground. How did she know? Could she tell just by looking at me? Or had I forgotten something this morning? I started going over my routine in my head when her fingertips touched my chin and raised my head.

"Oh!" I gasped, pulling back quickly. That touch…unexpected, but definitely not unwanted.

"I'm sorry," she said quickly. She seemed sheepish about what she'd done. "I'm used to people talking to my face, not the ground." She let out a little laugh. "I'm Delilah, by the way."

I gave her a smile. "Sabrina." I opened my mouth to try and continue our conversation when my phone let out a shrill alarm. I almost dropped my own coffee as I scrabbled for the phone and swiped the alarm away. "And that's me being late! I have to go!"

I looked at the empty cup in her hand, looked at my own coffee, then shoved it into her free hand. "Here, I hope you like cream and sugar." I moved around her and headed for the bookstore before she could stop me and before I ended up putting my foot in my mouth, because it was only a matter of time before that happened. I mean, never mind that she knew what I was with only a glance, so I had to be doing something wrong, and I needed to open the bookstore, and I didn't know what my boss was going to say, and, and, and… My brain began skipping over that one word. I slammed the door shut behind me and leaned against it, breathing heavily.

I shivered in the darkness of the store, still feeling her fingers on my chin. As much as I wanted to focus on that and only that, I had a job to do. I set about opening the store, starting with the door and register so I could make sure anyone who came in was taken care of.

A half hour and only two customers later my manager came in, looked around the store, and said in her most annoying voice, "You were late, weren't you?"

I rolled my eyes. "Gee, thanks for announcing it, Cori."

She smiled and came around to my side of the counter. "Come on, it's not like you to not have this place looking pristine by now. It had to happen one of these days."

"I'm not exactly proud of it."

"Well, of course not. But it's not like I'm going to fire you on the spot or something."

I held a hand over my heart. "You're too kind."

She raised both her arms over her head like a queen. "Cower beneath my benevolence."

I bowed, all but falling to my knees in front of her. "Oh, wise and magnificent Cori, please forgive those who are lower than you."

Laughter filled the store, along with a smattering of applause, as we linked arms and bowed for our audience of three. I rang up their purchases and waved them all goodbye as Cori moved around the store, stocking and cleaning up and basically doing the work I'd missed out on by being a half hour late.

"So?" Cori asked after a while.

"So, what?"

"So why were you late?"

"Because none of your business."

She held a hand over her heart. "And I thought we were friends."

"We are."

"But you won't tell me."

"Nope."

"You're fired."

I stared at her for a long moment, then started to pack up my things.

"I was kidding!" She scrambled to stop me from walking out the door, her terrified look bringing me extreme pleasure. "I swear I was kidding. You can't leave me here all alone."

"Why not?"

"Because I said so."

"That's not a very good reason."

She gave me a big sigh. "Look, I just wanted to know why you were late this morning. Was it a rough night last night?"

I shook my head, deciding to stop giving her a hard time. "No. It was the same as any other, mostly. Drunk women, handsy dudes, repetitive music, and the smell of alcohol. The joys of the lounge."

"You know you have more going for you than busting your ass at two jobs every day, don't you?" She asked in that way that always made me want to believe what she was trying to tell me.

I shook my head. "I know and I appreciate it. I really do. I'm tired. I was up late and then this morning went all to hell. It's a mess."

I told her about my issues this morning and running headlong into Delilah. She laughed at all the appropriate times until I told her about Delilah touching my chin, then her smile turned sly.

"Really? She lifted your head?" she asked. "Like, you do talk to the floor too much."

"I mean, yeah. That's weird, right? I feel like that's weird."

"It's a little weird. But it's also a little sexy, if the look in your eyes means anything."

"Shut up."

"I don't think so. It's cute! It's an adorable meet-cute for you and her!"

"A meet-cute? Really? Do you think this is a romance novel? I'm probably never going to see her again, so there's no point in even considering it."

"But wouldn't it be amazing if you did?"

I didn't answer her. I knew the answer. So did she.

Yes. A million times yes.

But I had to stay logical, rational, for my own sanity. I didn't have the luxury of pining over every woman I had a crush on. I hadn't had luxuries like that since Mom's boyfriend walked out and she decided to take it out on me. I'd had to work, had to earn money to pay for my keep, as she liked to put it. Then when I came out as trans…

I shook my head to clear those thoughts. "I can't think that way," I told Cori.

"But wouldn't it be magical if you two met up somewhere else and got together and…I don't know, the thought gives me goosebumps."

"Sure," I agreed, "but the world isn't a magical place. I learned that a long time ago. It's full of hard work, blood, sweat, and tears. That's what life is for me at least, and I don't see that changing any time soon."

Cori gave a loud sigh. "You are far too much of a realist to be working here."

I gave her a wry smile. "I balance you out."

"Fair enough." She smiled back. She opened her mouth to say something but was cut off by the doorbell for the stockroom. "I should go get that."

"Yes, you should."

"This isn't over."

"Yes, it is."

She threw up her hands with another sigh, turned on her heel, and headed for the back. "Learn to live in romance, Sabrina Doyle!" she called back before she disappeared into the stockroom.

I shook my head at her parting words and got back to work. She was right in a lot of ways, but that didn't mean I could drop everything and be that person. But oh, if only I could.

And for the next few minutes, I allowed myself the dangerous practice of daydreaming.

CHAPTER TWO

I enjoyed my work at the bookstore. The busy times flew by, punctuated with the usually happy faces of customers who had found their next read—or several. The slow times I got to spend mostly by myself, restocking the shelves or checking out some new releases so I could give people better recommendations when they came in not knowing what they wanted.

Today, however, dragged worse than usual, with fewer customers than I normally got to interact with, and there was little to restock that Cori hadn't already taken care of. That left me stuck behind the till. I drummed my fingers on the counter and spent far too much time idly touching my chin and wondering why I could swear I still felt Delilah's fingers.

"You're doing it again," Cori commented as she approached from the rear of the store.

"Doing what?"

"You're touching your chin."

"So? Maybe I'm itchy."

"You've been itchy for the past four hours. If it's that bad you should see a doctor."

My embarrassment made itself known, the heat growing in my cheeks and working its way up. "I'm fine."

"Still thinking of your new crush?"

"I don't have a new crush."

She snorted. "Really? So, you aren't completely interested in this Delilah you ran into?"

"Yeah, right, like anything could possibly happen with the woman I spilt coffee on and will probably never see again."

"You need to give yourself a break."

"That's not something I can do."

"Well, then you need to learn to take time for yourself."

"I do! I play my video games sometimes, and I read a lot." I realized how pathetic I sounded as I spoke. "I do things."

"When was the last time you got out of your apartment for something besides work?"

"I…" I had to stop and actually think about it. "I grabbed groceries on my day off last week."

"Groceries," Cori said, clearly unimpressed.

"Yeah, groceries," I said, trying to put a little bit of steel in the words. "I'm an introvert. I don't like going out and doing things. It's not easy for me. So, I work, I scrimp, I save, and I will have a life when I'm ready."

She let out a long-suffering sigh. "I just don't want you to miss out on your life *today*, Sabrina."

"My life *today* doesn't necessarily include someone like Delilah."

"But there's no reason it can't."

I made a point of looking down at myself. "There's plenty of reasons that it can't."

She frowned. "You're beautiful, you know that."

I bit my lip. It was a common argument for us. She seemed to take a perverse pleasure in complimenting me, and I refuted them every time. But I didn't want to today. Today I actually wanted to believe it. Because then maybe I *could* have a life now, outside of working and scrimping and saving for the life I longed for.

"I wish I could be as confident as you are," I said softly.

Whatever she was going to say next was interrupted by the timely arrival of the mail, dropped off by an older gentleman. He had a large box in his hands along with a small stack of envelopes that I helped relieve him of before he abruptly left again without a word. I put the pile on the counter in front of Cori, who was more than happy to start going through it.

"Really?" she muttered, looking up and through the door as if she could glare at the mail carrier.

"What's wrong?"

"He dropped off next door's mail too."

"Again? That's like two weeks in a row." Next to the bookstore was an adult toy store, Vibe Check, that was managed by a lovely woman named Lexie. I loved the store, personally, and often found myself browsing for the odd toy or for a book a little more adult than what we sold here at Oracle.

"I'm pretty sure he's allergic to silicone toys or something," Cori said.

"You think he's afraid that Lexie will start pelting him with dildos?"

"I wouldn't put it past her."

The image of the short, plump woman who had a perpetual knowing smile on her face throwing multicolored dildos at the mail carrier made me smile as I gathered up the offending envelopes.

"I'll take them over on my lunch break."

"Tell Lexie I said hi."

"You got it, boss."

I left the bookstore with equal parts relief and regret. I knew Cori was only looking out for me. She'd known me for years, since I started my transition. She was the one who took a chance on me and gave me a job. She'd taught me more about being a full and functional person than my mother ever had. But I'd still let myself flounder, in a lot of ways. That was something difficult to break free from.

But now wasn't the time to worry about that. I wanted to go say hi to Lexie. I went into Vibe Check and the bell over the door tinkled cheerfully. The store was laid out in a large figure eight, with shelves along the walls displaying the toys and tester models, and the actual for sale toys underneath. There was a large display table in the center of the first circle, showing the latest models and best sellers. The rear circle held more shelves, which displayed anal toys for all to see. The store was clean, well-kept, and bright, a far cry from some other adult toy stores that felt seedier and made you feel like you were dirty just being there.

Lexie was behind the counter on the back end of the figure eight. She looked up as I entered, gave me a nod, and went back to whatever she was working on. I took a moment to browse for a bit, checking out their selection of books at the front of the store against the window. These were books you couldn't find at Oracle, even though I pressed Cori or the owner to bring them in. I guess they didn't want instruction manuals on shibari and other ways to tie up your lovers, or a book with tips on how to have a safe and healthy polyamorous relationship. Then again, a book on poly relationships might be one that they'd agree to bring in. I made a mental note to ask Cori about it.

Eventually, I made myself part from the books and wander to the back wall beside the desk where Lexie stood. This was where the real fun stuff was, the leather, the straps, the whips and chains. They all hung from hooks on the wall, and I was inextricably drawn to them like a moth to the flame. There were collars and leashes, cuffs of all colors and sizes, under-the-bed restraints, along with things like gags and hoods, and even a gorgeous velvet-seated queening chair sitting beside it all.

It was only here that I ever saw things like these, but I'd read enough erotica to have a basic understanding and a fascination with toys like these. I reached out and ran my fingers over the leather muzzle of a dog-like harness gag and reveled in the feel of the material against my fingertips. An image of wearing the harness flashed through my head for only a second, followed shortly by the image of Delilah strapping it on me. I pulled my hand back and shook my head.

"You come in here all the time and stare at that one," Lexie said. I jumped and turned toward her, but her head was still down in whatever she was working on. "When are you going to buy the thing? It might look good on you."

I faltered and took moment to find my words, then looked down at my feet. "Maybe someday…when I have someone to wear it with."

She met my eyes and smiled that warm smile of hers, and I wandered over to the desk. I handed her the mail and she stared for a moment before taking the envelopes.

"I swear, that mail carrier is scared of me."

"Cori says he might be allergic to silicone."

She looked confused for a moment. "So? It's not like I'm going to throw vibrators at him for coming in here."

I opened my mouth to agree with her, when the door to the back room opened and the woman I hadn't expected to ever see again walked out of my fantasies and into being. Delilah had replaced her stained blouse with a candy apple red tank top made of shiny vinyl. It fit her snugly and showed off her chest in a way that captured my gaze, until I realized what I was doing and forced myself to look at the floor before she could say something.

"Lexie, have you seen Brand? They were supposed to be here half an hour ago." She spoke to the other woman as if I wasn't there at all. I kept quiet, still staring at the floor and the tips of her boots.

"I haven't seen them," Lexie replied. "It's only been me for most of the day."

"Well, the class is ready to start, and I don't have my demo bunny."

"Demo bunny?" I repeated quietly. What was a demo bunny? Two strong fingers found my chin and forced my head up. I gasped, much like I had that morning, but I couldn't look away from Delilah and her stern eyes.

"What did I tell you about talking to the floor instead of to me?" Lexie looked between us like we were the most interesting thing to happen all day. "You two know each other?"

"We met early this morning."

Lexie laughed. "Is this who spilled coffee on your shirt?"

I wanted to hide my face in embarrassment, but I fought not to lower my chin as Delilah removed her fingers. I didn't look her in the eye, focusing instead on her nose, her mouth, her ears, anywhere but those amazing eyes that would suck me in. "It…it was an accident."

Delilah tapped my cheek with her hand in a *there, there* gesture. "I know, pet. I know."

Lexie laughed again, and I felt the delicious mix of embarrassment and arousal heat up my face even more. I was sure I was about to implode on the spot. "Sabrina here works at the bookstore next door," she told Delilah. "She was dropping off the mail."

"Was she now? Well, maybe this is fortuitous for me."

I cocked my head to the side a little, confused. "Fortuitous?"

"How would you like to make up for the little accident this morning?"

"I…I don't know…What do you mean?"

She caught my eye, and I fell deep into that beautiful gaze of hers. I was about ready to say yes to anything that she wanted, without a thought, without a fear. She reached out and shook my shoulder lightly, a confused look on her face. I realized then she'd been talking, and it hadn't registered in my head at all.

"I'm sorry," I managed to squeak out. "What were you saying?"

The way she smirked did things to me that would be inappropriate to talk about at Sunday brunch. "I was asking you if you wanted to help me out with my class."

I opened my mouth to answer but closed it abruptly, unable to get anything out. Instead I managed to nod several times, still unsure what exactly I was agreeing to.

"Perfect!" She grabbed my hand and pulled me to the door to the back room. "It won't be hard, I promise. All you have to do is listen to me and follow my directions, okay?"

I nodded again, feeling that was safer than opening my mouth and saying something stupid.

"Oh, we should go over safewords. You know what a safeword is?" I nodded once more, suddenly more comfortable with where the conversation was going. "Good. We'll go simple and use green, yellow, and red. Does that make sense to you?"

I'd read enough erotica to know what a safeword was, and the traffic lights were a basic example that worked well. Green meant things were awesome, yellow meant to slow down. Red was stop. Full stop. It worked for all parties involved in a scene—dominant, submissive, somewhere in between. Of course, some of those books overlooked or omitted safewords altogether. Those books were a little less comfortable to read, and I often didn't finish them.

"I've...never had a safeword before."

Delilah paused. "You've played with rope before?"

I let out a small sigh. Rope. I could do rope. It took a moment to remember that she'd asked me a question. "I've, um, I've read a lot about it."

"Instructional or fantasy?"

I glanced away in the hopes that she wouldn't see the embarrassment on my face. "Fantasy."

I looked back up and she smiled. "Then you're going to love this."

I couldn't help but match her smile. It was infectious, really. And comforting to me. I wanted to make her smile like that more. She had a hold over me that I didn't understand, but with the safewords she was allowing me some agency of my own.

She stopped with her hand on the doorknob, looking at me over her shoulder. "I need you to say something, pet. I want your consent for this."

I swallowed the dryness in my throat. "Okay. I want to do this. For you. Whatever it is."

She grinned and opened the door, then ushered me into the back room.

CHAPTER THREE

The back room was a warehouse space, large enough for storage and also a classroom area. Boxes were stacked along one wall, the back wall had a large roll-up door and a man door beside it, and the other wall had a small office and what looked like a single stall bathroom leading off it. The floor was covered in soft mats that sank slightly under my feet. I followed Delilah across the mats, focused solely on her as she reached down and took off her boots, then placed them to the side. I did the same with my shoes before turning around and realizing that we weren't alone.

About a dozen people were congregating near a long table against the wall beside the door we'd come through. They were milling about, chatting amiably, until we turned to face them. Then all their attention was on us. I noticed most of them were holding long lengths of colorful rope, and I lowered my gaze to the floor.

Right. Rope class. I tried hard not to shy away as Delilah took a step toward the crowd.

"Good afternoon, everyone," Delilah said, clapping her hands once. She gained everyone's attention and left me relatively unnoticed. "Thank you for your patience. We had a bit of a staffing issue, but my friend Sabrina here was kind enough to step in and clear it up." She turned and gave me a smile that sent all the heat in my body to two places, my face and my groin. I was so glad my underwear was tight enough no one could see what was trying to stand up and say hello.

"So, today we will be going over some basic rope work. We'll start with simple column ties and several knots before moving on to a couple of easy harnesses and how they can work in conjunction with each other." Delilah looked around the room at her students. I avoided looking at them for fear of drawing undue attention to myself.

I focused on my breathing. Rope class. I could do this. I could handle this. It would be like a scene in one of my books. I'm pretty sure at least one had a rope class in it. I closed my eyes and tried to think of one for only a moment before I felt a soft hand touch my cheek. I opened them to see Delilah in front of me, a length of rope dangling from her other hand.

"Pet." I focused on Delilah and tried to forget about the others in the room the moment she said the word. I didn't know when I decided I was going to answer to the pet name, but clearly, I was. "Give me your wrists."

I held out my arms to her, and she draped the rope over both of my wrists.

"This is a basic wrap," Delilah announced to the room at large. "It's useful for wrists, ankles, wrists-to-ankles, and anything else your devious minds can come up with." She wrapped the rope a couple times around my wrists, then paused. "It can even be loosened mid-scene without freeing your partner, allowing for longer play and hopefully not needing to use your safety shears."

I closed my eyes and focused solely on the feeling of the rope as she continued to wrap it around my wrists. The feeling was charging my brain, my body, with an energy I hadn't felt in…hell, I hadn't ever felt quite like this before.

As she cinched my wrists together, my lips parted, and I let out a loud moan that had the room chuckling. Delilah gave me a wicked smile and pulled a little tighter, forcing me a step closer to her.

"At this point," she said to the crowd around us, "if you have a long enough piece of rope to have something left over, it allows you some control over your toy's movement." She pulled on the long end of the rope, and I stumbled forward on the mat, right into her other hand. She caressed my cheek, and I moaned again, my eyes fluttering closed as I sank into the feeling of being touched, of being bound, of being owned. "Good pet," she said as she patted my cheek. Those words echoed in my head.

Then, just like that, I fell. Not literally. I was still standing on the mat as Delilah moved around me with a length of rope, showing off another tie that I couldn't name or even pay full attention too. No, I fell into a foggy nothingness where I felt only the rope on my skin, pulled taut around my shoulders, on my chest, under my breasts. I'd envied the characters in my books when they fell into what was called subspace. I never thought I'd experience it myself, but wow, did I fall hard into it.

My eyes remained closed as I followed Delilah's directions as she moved and posed me to her liking. I let out a soft hiss as the rope tightened through my legs and framed what I hadn't had surgically removed yet. But even that wasn't enough to break me out of the fog that had taken over my mind. It felt like floating, weightlessness releasing me from a world that was full of fear and anxiety and pain. Everything I usually felt, all the emotions I normally kept bottled up because I couldn't explain or recognize them, drifted away into nothingness. A tear slipped down my face, but I was too well tangled in the rope to wipe it away. A soft finger touched my face, and I let out a little gasp.

"Okay there, pet?" Delilah's voice was soft in my ear.

It took a moment to find my voice, find the word I wanted to give her. "G-green," I said and could see her smile in my mind as she again patted my cheek.

"Good girl," she said. "Now, on your knees."

A whimper slipped out of my mouth, and I dropped onto my knees immediately. A hand touched my shoulder, slightly moving the rope that ran over it. I opened my eyes and looked at Delilah, basking in her smile as she spoke quietly.

"Sit tight, pet. I'm going to help the others with their ropes. Are you okay with that?"

I nodded and closed my eyes again, falling once more into that fogginess of subspace. The sounds of the room around me were little more than murmurs until I heard Delilah speak. Her words came out clear, and I felt myself inching my head in her general direction every time she spoke.

The ropes around me rubbed softly over my blouse, and the restraint felt delightful. It was better than I'd ever imagined before. I don't know how long I knelt on the mat, waiting for Delilah to return. Eventually the room grew quiet, and the shuffling of feet disappeared until only one set of footsteps remained.

"Open your eyes, pet," Delilah said.

I did and squinted against the light. Delilah was squatting in front of me, and that damned smile of hers made me wonder if I was getting more. She maneuvered herself beside me and sat on her butt with her legs bent in front of her. I turned to look at her as she wrapped an arm around my shoulders, her fingers once more fiddling with the rope.

"Thank you."

I blinked. "For what?" My voice was raw and lower than I liked.

"For helping me." She reached over and fiddled with a line of rope that went beneath my breasts. "For agreeing to do this with me. You were amazing for me today."

I felt myself coming down from the immense high that I'd been floating in. I blinked a few times and watched Delilah as I tried to find my voice again. "I...I owed you."

She seemed to be watching me closely. "Is that the only reason you agreed?"

I struggled a little against the ropes, my wrists tied to the harness in front of me. I knew I couldn't have a rational conversation with her like this. There was too much chance I would slip into that fogginess again.

As much as I didn't want to, I asked, "Can you take this off?"

She scooted over until she was behind me. A second later the ropes loosened, and I felt them getting pulled as she started to undo her work. She moved around me, doing her best not to make me move as she removed the rope, until she sat in front of me and took my wrists in her hands and untied the knot that had held them together since near the beginning of the class.

I looked down at my wrists, at the rope marks pressed into my skin and I trembled. I loved the marks, I loved how they looked, how they felt, how they made me feel. I had always been interested in this type of play, but how quickly I'd sunk into the brain fog surprised even me.

"How are you doing?" she asked, as she set all the rope aside but kept her hands around my wrists and pulled me in close to her.

I let out a long breath. "Good. I'm doing good." I looked at our hands between us. I could feel the soft pads of her fingertips tracing the marks on my wrists. "And no, that's not the only reason I agreed to this."

"Then, if I may ask, why did you agree?"

I shook my head slowly. "I don't know. Because you asked. Because *you* were the one who asked."

"Is that right?" She let out a low laugh. "That's interesting."

I blinked up at her and caught the look on her face. It wasn't one I recognized or could describe. But the way she was looking at me made me feel like I'd caught the attention of a fierce predator who saw me as nothing but prey. It made me feel wanted, like I thought I had been back before I came out. Before I realized who I really was.

But as much as I desired to fall into that feeling, to wrap it around myself and take comfort, I knew I couldn't. The high of the bondage was wearing off and reality was returning like a chokehold around my throat. I looked around the room for a clock of some sort, before I remembered that hey, I had a phone in my pocket. But I didn't want to pull my wrists out of Delilah's hands. I shook my head.

"I think there's a lot going on in that head of yours," Delilah said, which drew my attention once again.

"Oh, there usually is."

"You hid it well during the class."

"My brain shut up the moment you wrapped the rope around my wrist."

She smiled widely. "Isn't that one of the wonderful parts of submission? To put aside the world, even for a few moments, and simply be?"

I shrugged. I felt a little uncomfortable about how much I wanted to feel that way again. "It's a nice feeling, but it's a lie."

"A lie?"

"It's the part the stories don't tell you. It's a beautiful respite in the moment, but coming back to the world…nothing goes away. Nothing changes. There's still bills to pay, work to be done, and life to suffer through." I looked away, knowing I should shut up now before I put my foot too far in my mouth, but I couldn't. "It's not real, and to fall into the trap of thinking it is can be so damned dangerous."

"That's…pretty cynical."

I flinched at her tone and refused to meet her eyes. "You're right. It is. I'm sorry."

"Don't be sorry. It sounds like you're trying to convince yourself."

I pulled one of my hands free and wiped it across my face, trying to force myself to recover from everything we'd done. "Maybe I am," I admitted. "I've been known to be a bit of a pessimist."

"I can see that. More's the pity."

"Why?"

"Because a beautiful woman like you shouldn't have had a life where she ends up being that pessimistic."

I did my best not to scoff at her use of the word "beautiful." As much as I didn't believe it, I wanted to believe her. She reminded me a bit of Cori, in that way. She seemed to sincerely believe what she was saying and made me want to believe it too.

Either that or I had a crush so big I didn't care if I was being led on. It could honestly go either way.

I reluctantly pulled my hand out of her grasp and kept my eyes on the mats around us as I stood and collected my shoes. I was pulling them on when Delilah sat down near me and began to pull on her boots. I don't know what came over me, but when I had my shoes on, I turned and knelt before her. I helped her pull her boots on and tied them for her. I glanced up at her face to find her watching me carefully, gently, as if afraid to make a sudden movement or I might bolt. And to be fair, I might have at that point.

"You are an interesting creature, Sabrina," she said softly as I helped her to her feet.

"I'm really not," I replied. I wasn't, really. There was very little interesting about me. I tried very hard to keep it that way.

I let her take the lead as we left the little warehouse area and went back out into the store proper. Lexie was still there, poring over whatever book was on the counter. She looked like she hadn't moved in…however long we'd been back there. She looked up as we walked toward the desk.

"All done back there?"

Delilah nodded. "Just needs a little cleanup. I'll take care of it in a bit."

Lexie's attention turned to me, and she gave me a sly smile. "So? How was it?"

I wanted to absolutely die on the spot. Instead I looked away, unable to find the words to tell her how much I'd loved what we'd done back there, especially in front of other people.

"She performed wonderfully," Delilah said. She clapped me on the back with a cheerfulness I couldn't match. "So well that I want you to comp her something from the store, whatever she wants."

Lexie's eyebrows rose. "Really? You sure?"

I stared at Delilah, wondering exactly who she was that she could ask such a thing. Did she own the store or something? My eyes caught on the gag harness I'd been admiring before all of this happened and I licked my lips, wondering how far I could push this.

Then my phone started to vibrate in my pocket, and I groaned. I pulled it out and found a missed call from the bookstore, and I turned away from the ladies.

"I'll have to take you up on that later," I said quickly. "I have to get back to work."

Delilah looked almost…disappointed, as I turned away from her. I wanted to stay. Dear Goddess, I wanted to stay. But I had a job, and I was expected to do it. I was already late coming back from lunch, and I hadn't even eaten anything. I shook my head and opened the door, probably a little harder than I had to, the bells above the door tinkled so loudly.

Outside I took in a deep gulp of fresh air. My mind cleared a little to think about something other than Delilah. I had no doubt that she would be on my mind for a long time coming, but the further I kept from her, the more I could think clearly again. Not that I didn't want to see her again. In fact, I'd have loved to see more of her, maybe wearing something a little more interesting than that vinyl tank top and…

"Shut up, Sabrina," I muttered. I took another deep breath and turned to head back to the bookstore. I took another moment outside the door and prepared myself to get the third degree from Cori the moment I entered the store. "I have a job to do," I reminded myself softly. "Work comes first."

Words to live by, according to my mother. It could have been a family motto. The simple thought of my mother, of my family, made my chest feel like it was being compressed, like someone was sitting on me. I forced myself to take a breath, to try to keep the anxiety at bay, as I recited the coping statements my therapist had tried to drill into my head.

I am enough.

I am not my past.

I am learning to love myself.

Corny, probably, but the words repeated in my head with my breathing exercises helped keep the anxiety down enough that I could function. I opened the door to the bookstore and stepped in, ready to weather whatever punishment might come from being late.

"Sabrina! There you are, I was getting worried."

I did my best not to have a negative reaction to Cori's exclamation and instead meekly lowered my head. "I'm so sorry," I told her, "I didn't mean to be late. I got…distracted."

I started to head past the front desk, but Cori's hand shot out and took my arm in a firm grip. As much as I wanted to kind of hide in the stockroom for a few minutes, to take the time to get my head on straight, she clearly wanted to do this now.

"This isn't like you, Sabrina," she said, her tone not unkind. "Late this morning, then late from lunch. Is there something going on?"

I shook my head. "I had a…an interesting lunch break, that's all. I'm really sorry I'm late. It won't happen again."

She seemed about to say something more when her eyes widened, and a wicked grin split her lips. I followed her gaze to my wrist, still with the rope marks pressed into it. I pulled my arm away and did my best to hide my wrists behind my back, but knew it was too late.

"An interesting lunch break?" She raised an eyebrow. "Do tell."

I shook my head again. "There's nothing to tell. I…I just helped someone with something, and it ran a little later than I meant it to. No big deal."

"No big deal?" She squealed. "What are you talking about? You come back here with fucking rope marks on your wrists and say it's no big deal? Are you high?"

"Cori!" I snapped, looking around the store. The place looked empty, but there might've been someone lurking in the back rows who could overhear everything. "Keep your voice down!"

"Relax, there's no one here. I've only had a couple customers while you were gone. Now spill, what the hell did you get up to?"

I clenched my fists in petulant anger but knew she was just…Cori. There was little chance of getting away with not telling her everything.

"I went next door to drop off the mail. Delilah was there." Cori squealed again, and I gave her a dirty look that was totally ruined by the fierce blush heating up my face. "She needed someone to help her demonstrate some ties for her rope class, and I owed her for the coffee mishap this morning. So I spent my lunch break getting tied up."

Cori's eyes went wider and wider as I spoke, like she couldn't believe what I was saying. "Are you kidding me?"

I shook my head. "No, why?"

"I mean this is like something out of a fucking novel! You ran into this beautiful woman twice in one day and you did something like rope play together? That's pretty heavy stuff."

I shrugged. "I guess. I didn't really think about it."

"And you trusted her not to hurt you?"

"She wouldn't have hurt me."

"How do you know? You don't know her."

"She gave me a safeword. She was really nice about it all, gave me clear instructions and everything." I hesitated to keep talking, but once the words started they didn't seem to want to stay in. "And it was easy. And nice. And so fucking hot and sexy and it was a dream come true that…that will probably never happen again, and I should relegate it to a happy memory and get on with my life."

Cori blinked, snapping her head back like I'd given her whiplash. "Wow, that was a complete one-eighty in a single sentence. You don't know that she won't want to play with you again."

I scoffed, but there was little scorn in it. It felt more pathetic than anything else. "Why would she? She doesn't know me. I don't know her. I don't even know if I'll see her again."

"That's what you said this morning, and yet you ran into her this afternoon."

"That was a fluke. I guarantee I won't see her again."

Cori smiled that irritating smile of hers. "Well, now you're definitely going to run into her again."

"Shut up."

Her smile widened. "Make me."

I resisted the urge to throw a book or two at her. "Go on your break, I'll take care of the store."

"You just want me gone so you don't have to talk about *Delilah*." She said her name with such an air of importance I wanted to stomp my foot on the floor and yell at her. But I was in my thirties. Temper tantrums are only for people in their twenties.

"Just go so you'll be back before I have to leave to get ready for my other job."

She grinned and stepped out from behind the counter, ushering me into the spot she'd vacated. "All right, I'll stop bugging you. But honestly, Sabrina, maybe you should think about getting everything you want, instead of staying in your rut."

"I'm not in a rut," I said, refusing to believe she was right. "I'm focused."

"Focused on avoiding life."

"Stop pretending to be my life coach and go away." The words came out a little harsher than I meant them to, but Cori seemed to take it in stride. She laughed and waved as she headed out the door and I settled behind the counter. I pulled out one of the new lesbian romance novels we had gotten in that week. "You won't judge me," I muttered to the book, a sapphic shifter novel called *The Last Caspian* by Taryn J. Dallas. "Will you?"

The book did not reply, and I gave it a grateful little nod before opening it up and beginning to read, keeping an ear out for the door as I sank into a world of tiger shapeshifters and sexy geneticists.

CHAPTER FOUR

I only had to suffer Cori's incessant haranguing for a couple more hours before I finished my shift at the bookstore. I knew she was coming from a place of caring and love, but it was hard to hear that the way I chose to live my life was wrong and I needed to do something to change it. I thought I'd been doing pretty good—as far as a trans woman in this world can, sometimes.

I worked hard and focused on what I wanted, and for the past few years that had been saving money so I could afford my surgeries. Maybe I was a little closed off to all else, but I guess I didn't know how not to be. I'd been told from a young age that work was the most important thing in life, that making money took precedence over all else. I never had a job that gave me the kind of financial security most people dream of, so working more than one at a time was sometimes needed. Hell, I hadn't even finished high school because I was expected to hold working to a higher importance than school.

I guess I didn't know any other way to be, but damned if I didn't want something else now. *Someone* else now. I hadn't felt this way in a long time, since I came to realize who I really was and came out as transgender.

My mother wasn't pleased. Of course she wasn't. I was throwing away my life. Hurting everyone who loved me. I reasoned that if they didn't love me for being my authentic self, then they never truly loved me at all. They loved a shadow, a ghost, a mask that I wore to earn their requited love.

I lost my family, I lost my girlfriend—my fiancée, I lost what friends I had. I could survive all of that, I was sure. But then I lost my job. A job I'd been at for a while, one I was comfortable at, seemingly well-respected, and they kicked me to the curb shortly after I came out. That had been the hardest blow to take, in some ways.

These thoughts and more were a barrage on my mind as I slipped off the bus and walked the block to my apartment building. It was a tall building, nondescript in a beige kind of color with black steel balconies jutting out from the side. I knew there were something like twenty floors, but the higher you went, the more you started to pay for the view. I swiped my fob and stepped into the building, then forwent my usual exercise of walking up the stairs in favor of the elevator to take me to the third floor. I wasn't in the mood to climb the steps today.

I reached out to unlock my door, saw the mostly faded rope marks around my wrist, and felt a pining for something new. Something different than what I was used to. But I shook my head and let myself into my small apartment.

Inside the studio apartment, I looked around and tried to find some sort of feeling of coming home, but there was nothing there. This wasn't a home. It was a room. A room with a bed, a television, a tiny galley kitchen with limited counter space, no closet space, and a bathroom that was thankfully behind its own door. I couldn't say when I'd started to hate living here, but the feeling was creeping up on me as I once again glanced at my wrists and saw the rope marks. The idea of having something more flashed through my head, but I pushed it back.

I'd have more later. Right now I had what I needed, and that was a roof over my head that didn't involve living with my mother, wherever she was, and money in the bank.

And with those melancholy thoughts, I closed and locked the door behind me and headed for my bed. I had a couple of hours before I had to be at work—again. I threw myself on the queen mattress and let out a long groan that made me feel better for only a moment before my traitorous mind decided to review what had happened between Delilah and me at lunch.

I could still feel the ropes being pulled against my skin as she had created the harnesses across my chest and down my back. I shuddered to think that it might never happen again. But did that mean I wanted to hunt Delilah down and beg her to do it again? Not a chance. I wasn't that pathetic. Like I told Cori, I would probably never see her again— despite that she seemed to have something to do with Vibe Check. I wondered if she worked there and I'd never met her before, or if it was a one-time class she put on or something.

Then I wondered what it'd be like to take her clothes off and taste her, looking up at those golden eyes as I worked my mouth between her thighs, licking my tongue up her clit—

"Fuck!" I shouted to the empty room. I rubbed my hands over my face and sat up, unable to even relax now. I didn't want to go to my second job this pent up and stressed out. But I really didn't want to do…that, either. The idea of touching myself wasn't appealing. Not only did I plan on removing that part of my anatomy when I finally got some answers after jumping through the hoops of the Canadian health system, but since starting on my hormones, even trying to get a quick fix always seemed to leave me wanting more instead of feeling satisfied.

I sighed. No, the only thing that was going to help was compartmentalization. I focused on relegating Delilah to the farthest recesses of my mind so I could focus on how my life really was, not the dream she'd infected me with. With a groan I got up off the bed and headed for the bathroom. I needed a shower—a cold one at that, and then I had to prepare myself to head back to work.

An hour and a half later, clean and bright and wearing a pair of pleather leggings and a tight black T-shirt that showed off my tits, I walked into the Emerald Lounge. The lounge was something of an upscale bar that prioritized socialization over pounding, loud music and club dancing. There was a stage in the corner for live music, where we hosted local bands and sometimes bigger numbers at least once a week. The area in front of the stage had a number of tables that could be moved out of the way to create standing or dancing space when needed. Booths and couches took up the rest of the room past the tables to the bar, which was long and encompassed most of the rear wall. There was a small kitchen in the back that served an array of tapas plates for hungry loungers.

I nodded to the woman behind the bar, who glanced up and gave me a small smile before returning to serving drinks. Moments before I was to begin my shift I headed into the back, moving past the kitchen to a small hallway that led to a stock room and the office, which had its door closed. I knocked, got a loud grunt in reply, and opened the door. I stopped dead in my tracks a moment later. I'd expected a whole other person than the one who was currently lounging behind the desk. She held a glass of amber liquid to her mouth, and her eyes widened when she saw me.

"Delilah?"

"Sabrina?"

I absently rubbed at one wrist as I took another step into the office to clear the doorway, staring at the woman who I was trying so hard not to let further into my brain. She still wore that red top from earlier, and as she spun the chair and leaned back, she lifted her legs to let her boots rest on the desk. She gave me a wide smile.

"What are you doing here? Are you stalking me or something?" I demanded.

She snorted. "I should be asking you that! Running into me on the street, then coming into my places of business. I think if anyone is stalking, it's you."

"I'm not stalking you! You just end up everywhere I need to be!"

"Need to be? Including the private office of an upscale lounge?"

"I…I work here!"

She laughed at the slight hesitation in my words, and I tried not to let her see how that laugh affected me. There was nothing mean about her laugh, only a joyous sound I wanted to bottle and sell so I didn't have to work two jobs. She reached under a thick leather book on the desk and picked up a sheet of paper.

"So, you're the Sabrina on the schedule," she said. "I was laughing a little how often that name seemed to be coming up for me today. I didn't realize it would be you."

I shook my head. "I still don't know what you're doing here."

"She owns the place." A new voice interrupted our conversation. I turned around and found Tiffani, the lounge's owner and my boss, stepping up behind me. Her blond hair was tied back in her usual tight bun, and she looked a little more perturbed than I usually saw her, her green eyes narrowed at Delilah sitting behind her desk. She wore a T-shirt with the lounge's name emblazoned on the front and black jeans that were tight on her legs. "She's the co-owner. Also, my sister."

I stared between the two of them as Tiffani came into the office and snatched the schedule from Delilah's hand, then playfully kicked the rolling chair so Delilah rolled away from the desk.

"Sisters?" I echoed, not seeing the resemblance.

"Half-sister." They said it in unison, with a tone that said that they had to explain that all the time.

"She helped me open the lounge," Tiffani said, "but she's been more of a *silent* partner."

Delilah held up her hands. "Hey, I just came in to check on things. No harm in that, is there?"

Tiffani crossed her arms over her chest. "There is when you start trying to bang my employees."

"Hey!" Delilah said.

"I'm not—" I started but cut myself off when I remembered what we'd done that afternoon. Sure, there was no actual intercourse, but in some ways what we'd done could be considered more intimate than a simple one-night stand. I shook my head again. "I'm not sleeping with her!"

"Easy, pet," Delilah said, "before you say something we both might regret."

Tiffani looked between the two of us. "You've met." It wasn't a question.

"Earlier today. We seem to keep running into each other," Delilah told her sister.

My mind was still on the rope class that afternoon, and I could only nod in agreement.

"Please, Lilah, please do not corrupt my staff. Sabrina's a good worker, I don't need her to be wandering around like a zombie pining after you."

"I wouldn't—" I started, but quickly remembered I'd spent most of the afternoon at the bookstore and at home with my mind on her, so it wasn't out of the realm of possibility. I shook my head and tried to stand a little taller, certain I could handle myself.

"You make me sound like a predator. You're going to scare the poor girl away."

Again I opened my mouth to argue, but I realized this was a disagreement between them. A common conversation, I guessed, as they bickered back and forth while I stood near the doorway. It felt like it happened whenever the sisters were together, and I should either buckle up for the ride or run away while I still could. But I didn't want to run. I wanted to be close to Delilah. It was overriding everything I thought I knew, and I wanted her to send me into bliss like she had before.

"You really can't keep your hands off people, can you?"

"There was no hand touching anything! I was sitting behind the desk. How am I supposed to put my hands on her from there?"

Tiffani rolled her eyes. "Oh, knowing how you operate, I'm sure you have a lasso of rope in your back pocket or something."

At the mention of rope, I flushed with embarrassment and glanced away from Delilah, who sputtered indignantly. "Hey, everything we did was completely consensual. I'm not some terrible predatory wannabe domme."

Tiffani's look sharpened as she glanced between the two of us. She let out a long sigh. "Fine. You two do what you want, but not here, please. I don't need the health department on my ass."

I blanched. "I wouldn't—"

"Oh, honey, it's not you I'm worried about." Tiffani's voice was harsher than I'd heard it before, and Delilah noticed too. Instead of replying, she was up and out of the chair, her face tense with an anger I hadn't seen before. Something Tiffani said had struck a nerve, clearly, and I watched Delilah storm past me without a second glance and leave the room.

"Shit," Tiffani swore, staring after her.

I looked between the open door and my boss. "What was…"

Tiffani shook her head and took a seat in the vacated chair, pulling it back up to the desk. "Don't worry about her, she'll cool down soon."

"I don't understand."

"It's okay. Just a bit of sibling rivalry."

"I feel like I'm missing a story here."

Tiffani sighed. "It's not you, I promise. She…she stole my girlfriend once, and I guess I've given her a hard time about it ever since."

"What happened?"

"I came in after close one night because I forgot something and found Lilah and my girlfriend having fun on the bar. I still don't know where she pulled the rope from." She sighed again and shook her head. "She wasn't a very good girlfriend, and she probably came on to Lilah, but it still hit hard, you know?"

I nodded like I knew what she was talking about when really I had no idea what that was like.

"Anyway, that was clearly the end of that relationship, and Lilah was beside herself with guilt. Promised me it would never happen again. But I guess I can't really let her forget it. I haven't."

I was an only child, so I really couldn't relate to the sibling rivalry, but I knew what it was like to be unable to forget something. During the rougher times, I still thought about my ex-girlfriend wanting nothing more to do with me the moment I told her who I really was. I told myself I was better off, and I'm sure Tiffani said the same thing, but the hurt was still there.

"Why are you telling me this?" I asked softly. It wasn't that I didn't appreciate the story, but I wasn't anyone special to either of them.

"Because I see how she looks at you," Tiffani said. "Like she wants to own you. But she's left her fair share of broken-hearted girls behind her, and I don't want you to be the next one."

I took a moment to think about her warning. Did she mean that Delilah had relationships that didn't work out, or was it more of a one-night thing where she didn't spend more than one with a particular girl? And if something did happen between us, could I protect myself well enough not to become the next broken-hearted girl that she left behind?

"Thanks for the warning," I said after a long moment.

Tiffani nodded. "How comfortable are you on the bar?"

I jumped at the sudden change in topic and barely managed a quick shrug. "I'm okay but need to work on speed over anything else."

"Good. If it stays slow tonight, I'll have you behind the bar. If we pick up too much, let me know and I'll take over and you can serve. Sound good?"

I nodded, finally getting the information I'd come in here for in the first place. "Sounds good. I'll see you out there."

She waved a hand dismissively and I left the office, feeling more confused and unsure of myself than normal. I set up behind the bar, greeted the other bartender, then started taking orders and mixing drinks as needed.

Hours passed and the lounge didn't get much busier than it had been when I walked in. A number of the booths were filled, and some of the stools at the bar were occupied, but for a Tuesday night, things were pretty dead.

It was coming near the end of my shift as I restocked one of the fridges on the end of the bar near the door to the kitchen, when someone took a seat right near me.

"How can I help you?" I said automatically, without looking up to properly greet the newcomer. I rose and turned to find myself pinned by the golden-brown gaze of Delilah as she seemed to take a moment to size me up, not unlike how she'd looked at me that afternoon. You know, before asking me to let her tie me up with a bunch of rope for a class of strangers. The mere thought of which sent a shock of pleasure coursing through me.

"Whiskey," she purred, smiling sweetly. "Neat, please."

I gave a short, sharp nod and pulled myself away from her gaze to start making the drink. I fumbled around with the glass, nearly dropped the bottle of whiskey on myself twice, but finally got her drink made all while under the scrutinizing glare of those sharp eyes.

"Thank you, pet."

I couldn't say if it was a term of endearment or a pet name solely for me or if she called others *pet*, but I hoped it was only for me.

"You—I mean—you're welcome," I said, trying hard to focus on finding my words, but I was feeling flustered. I remembered what Tiffani said about her sister, and the information was warring in my head with how I felt. How Delilah made me feel.

She gave me a look like she knew exactly what I was thinking and sighed. "My sister warned you away from me, didn't she?"

"She...she might have." I shrugged like it was no big deal. "I was only half listening."

"I don't believe that for one second," she replied. "You probably hung on her every word, like you do with me."

"I do not!"

She laughed. "Easy, pet. You're so much fun to tease."

I crossed my arms and tried to find some steel in my spine. "It's, um, it's not like I fall to my knees every time a beautiful woman tells me to."

"Are you calling me beautiful, or my sister?"

"Can't it be both?"

She chuckled. "Smooth, very smooth."

"Thank you."

She took a sip of her whiskey, and I watched as her lips parted slightly against the glass, letting the amber liquid slide home. I wanted to know what it'd be like to kiss those lips. Would they be as soft as they looked? Would she be as domineering in a single kiss as she was that afternoon, when she was draping rope over my body? I had to take a deeper breath simply watching her as my mind ran away with the idea of having those lips on my body, kissing and nibbling.

She was watching me as I watched her, and I swear she knew exactly what I was thinking. She lowered the glass and licked at her upper lip to catch the remnants of her whiskey. I wanted to stay neutral, focused on my job and not on Delilah, but she made it nearly impossible, and I couldn't figure out why. Obviously she knew the effect she had on me and reveled in it.

"So," she said, watching me closely. "Tell me more about Sabrina. I'm sure there's plenty of story to tell."

I shook my head immediately and felt heat start to creep up my face. I didn't like being the center of attention, scrutinized for everything I did or said. I was more of a behind the scenes kind of person, the shadow who got things done but wasn't celebrated for it.

"There's no story. I'm just...me. That's it."

"Now, that I don't believe for a second. Everybody has a story."

"Well, apparently I'm not everybody, because there's no story." What was I supposed to tell her? I lived a boring life, or so I'd been told time and again by Cori. I didn't need to tell her the sob story about losing my family, my fiancée, my life, because I came out as who I really was. Would she look at me differently if she knew I was trans? Did she already suspect? Did it matter? I truly didn't want it to. Here at the lounge the only person who knew for sure was Tiffani, because I'd told her. No one else had said anything, even though I knew I didn't always do the best job of passing.

"Come on, Sabrina. I only know the CliffsNotes about you. You work in a bookstore and a lounge—two very different places, by the way. You get lost in your head when interesting things start to happen to you, and you wonderfully fall to your knees when told to in a firm tone."

The heat in my cheeks intensified and I had to glance away from her. I looked down the bar, hoping that it was oddly busy and I needed to help my co-worker, but she was chatting away with several of the patrons in her corner of the bar, and no one seemed to be waiting for any drinks.

"Maybe that was just for you," I said softly, tucking a strand of hair behind my ear as I stared at the bar between us. I didn't feel like getting caught in those eyes again. She took another sip of her whiskey, and I tried to remember what Tiffani had said about her sister. Why the hell was Delilah so damned interested in me? "It's not like I'd do it for just anybody, but you had me all wrapped up in rope, and it...made sense to do it."

"Maybe you'd enjoy doing it again some time?"

"Is this you propositioning me?"

She laughed. "It might be, yes."

"Why?"

"Because you intrigue me."

"That's not the first time you've said something like that."

She shrugged. "No, but I have to admit that today was the first time I played with someone without having...you know, *played* with them before."

"I feel honored."

"You should." She shook her head. "I don't even know why I asked you this afternoon. It was a moment that might not have worked out so well, but I swear you took to it like a duck to water. I was very grateful."

I glanced away. "It's not like I didn't enjoy it."

"So there's no reason we shouldn't do it again. Privately."

I blinked and took a deep breath. I wanted to agree. I wanted to agree so damned badly. But I was pretty sure I wasn't the kind of person who could only handle a single night, and if Tiffani was right, that's all Delilah was looking for from me. One night together. And then what? How did people ever go back to normal after that?

"Lilah."

Tiffani's appearance at the end of the bar prevented me from replying. Delilah glared daggers at her sister but got up and finished her drink in one swift movement.

"Don't go anywhere, pet. I'll be right back."

I couldn't even bring myself to nod but looked between the two sisters. Tiffani looked pissed at her sister, while Delilah didn't seem too happy with Tiffani either. I really hoped they weren't fighting about me. I would never live it down.

Together the sisters disappeared to the back room. I bussed Delilah's glass, staying near the end of the bar and waiting for her to come back. But by the end of my shift at one in the morning, she never had.

CHAPTER FIVE

After a restless night of sleep where Delilah took a starring role in many a dream, I returned to my regularly scheduled life of working without having a sexy woman requesting that I let her tie me up. I was early enough to the bookstore that I made up for missing the time yesterday, and I was able to get the store ready to open in record time. When Cori finally came in after I'd opened, there was little she could complain about. She gave me a big smile as she came in the door and looked about ready to gossip, but I shut it down quickly by refusing to talk about my night. I didn't need to tell her that Delilah was involved with the lounge as well as Vibe Check. Or that she seemed oddly interested in me.

Yesterday was yesterday. It was best to leave it in the past, no matter how much I didn't want to.

No matter how hard she tried, Cori couldn't pry anything from me. And I was proud of myself for not giving into her. She didn't need to know I saw Delilah again, or that she propositioned me and left without me giving her an answer. Instead of focusing on all that, I tried to rein in my overactive imagination and settle into my work, cleaning up and restocking the shelves near the back as I avoided Cori's questions.

By the time the mail arrived in the early afternoon, we'd moved past talking about Delilah and on to Cori's post-divorce life and her attempts to get back on the horse of dating—and which apps she was preferring at the moment.

"I mean, it's like there's a giant pond of people ripe for the catching!" she crowed, flashing her phone at me. "I don't even have to say that I want something long term to have a good night. Honestly, why would I want something long term when I just got out of a fifteen-year marriage?"

I shrugged, unsure of where to go with this. "I guess some people still want that companionship? Maybe? It's not like I have a lot of experience." I'd only had two girlfriends in the past, and I had planned to marry the second until she broke it off.

We were interrupted by the door opening and the mailman arriving. He dropped off a handful of envelopes on the counter in front of Cori, then exited as quickly as he'd come in, unaware that we were both staring after him.

"He reminds me a lot of my ex-husband," Cori said as she started going through the mail. "He was a prude too." She held up a couple of envelopes. "Messed up the mail again."

"You know, you could talk to the post office about it, get him assigned to a different route or something."

There was a sparkle in her eye that made me a little uncomfortable. "But then how will you run into the woman you're pining after?"

I shook my head. "I really don't want to talk about it."

"Okay, now I know something happened yesterday after you left here. You were completely enamored with her when I got back from lunch."

"I know, I know. But that was yesterday. Today is different. And I don't need you beating me over the head about it!"

Her smile and humor faded as I snapped. She glanced away for a moment, and I felt like shit for making her feel like she couldn't even look at me. What was she thinking? She liked to gossip, liked to tease and poke and prod. I'd never had an issue with it—no, that's not true. I'd never told her I'd had an issue with it. It never seemed important enough to do so. But her teasing had never been about something I wanted so damned badly but was so terrified to even consider.

"I get it," she said softly. She looked up but refused to meet my eyes. She grabbed the envelopes and plastered on a smile that looked fake, then stepped out from behind the counter.

"I'm going to head over and drop this off before getting something to eat," she said, her cheerfulness not quite where it was a moment ago. "Do you want anything?"

I shook my head, not daring to speak and make things worse. She moved around me and headed out the door without another word, and I didn't take a breath until it shut behind her.

"Damn it," I said as I took her place behind the counter. Cori was my best friend. My closest friend. She was also my manager and boss, so already there were times when things seemed a little complicated between us. But I never wanted to hurt her. She was the way she was, and it was something I could always handle. Because she allowed me to be who I was. She was the first person who really knew me to give me a chance. I didn't want to ruin all that because I couldn't handle her teasing me about my crush.

I should've told her about last night, come clean about Delilah and her role at the Emerald Lounge. It wasn't even that big a deal. It was the thought of Delilah and what she might represent that made me not want to talk about it. I didn't want anything to get my hopes up that something might happen between us. I mean, she never even came back last night. Clearly something else had popped up that was more important. Maybe another girl. Someone more than me, better than me. More…intriguing than me, to use her word.

I shook my head. That was the reason I didn't want to think about it. I knew that I would fall into a depressive spiral if I even considered the idea that there might have been something more between me and Delilah. It had happened before, with a crush I'd developed not long after I came out. It didn't end well, and I was not in a good place for a long while. It was then that I decided to focus on work, focus on my goals, my needs. But now it always happened when I thought about things that were so clearly out of my reach. And Delilah was. I doubted I could be anything for her but another one-night stand, like Tiffani had said.

Of course, that was when the optimistic side of my brain, the one I usually ignored, piped up. It was wondering if we could handle that. To have one amazing, fantastic night with this woman whom I had been so quick to become attracted to. No one had wanted me since my last girlfriend—my fiancée—found out I wasn't the man she'd been prepared to be with for the rest of her life.

"Okay," I said aloud. "We're not thinking about this anymore. It's not gonna happen. She borrowed my body for an hour yesterday, and that was that. Nothing more is going to happen."

I let out a noise somewhere between a chuckle and a sob, then shook myself and closed my eyes for a long moment. I was not going to have a breakdown at work. I wouldn't allow it. Every time I thought about my past life, it was always hard. I didn't regret coming out. I didn't regret working toward being my real self. But I did regret the things I lost because of it, at least mostly. I missed having a partner and coming home to someone who seemed to care about me.

"And I will have that later," I told myself firmly, ignoring the wavering in my tone that usually preceded the slow, annoying tears that came with thoughts like these. I wasn't going to allow those tears to fall.

I heard the front door open and kept my head down, trying to school my face into something mostly neutral if nothing else.

"Good afternoon," I said without looking up. "Thanks for coming to Oracle Books."

The customer didn't say anything, but I heard their footsteps on the hardwood floor. My mind stayed aware of them as I tried to pull myself together well enough to look up, but it was taking longer than I liked. Finally the footsteps stopped, and I frowned. It sounded like they were right in front of the counter. Wouldn't they want to browse first?

"What have I told you about looking at the floor, pet?" Delilah's voice shocked me enough to make me wrench my head up to stare at her.

"Delilah?" I gasped and looked around even though I knew there was no one else in the store except the two of us. "What are you doing here?"

"Aww, is my pet not happy to see me?"

I stared at her, focusing on those lips that I wanted on mine so damned badly. All my thoughts from earlier were beating at the walls in my mind, desperate for me to pay attention to them and refuse to let myself become putty in her hands. Because that's where I was headed. The moment I saw her, I was ready to fall to my knees. How pathetic was that?

"It's not that."

"Then what is it?"

I clenched my teeth, knowing I should be honest but at the same time knowing that there was no way I could tell her everything that was going through my head.

"You didn't come back last night." The words slipped out of my mouth, accusatory and riding the border into anger. I didn't realize how much that had hurt, actually, until that moment. "I waited, but I had to head home. You never came back."

It was her turn to look away, and she actually looked apologetic. "I remember. And I'm sorry. There was an...emergency that I had to attend to. By the time I got back to the lounge, you were already gone."

"The last bus comes right after one," I explained. "If I miss it, I have to find another way home."

"I would have offered to drive you."

"I didn't know that in the moment, did I? I don't know where I stand with you. What I'm even doing right now with this conversation."

"What do you mean?"

"You make it hard to think straight."

"Good thing you aren't straight, then."

Heat crept up my face. "You know what I mean."

"I do. I also know what you're thinking."

"Oh, you do, do you?" I said as I shook my head. This would be interesting. "Please, do tell."

"Well, you were thinking you weren't going to see me again. And to make that happen you were going to try avoiding the places I'd be. Vibe Check is easy, it's not like you work there, but the lounge is another matter. Am I close so far?"

I didn't reply, but it was surprising how well she was reading my mind.

"Someone like you," she said, "is repressed." I opened my mouth to argue, but no sound came out, and she continued. "It's not a bad thing, like you might think. It's safe. It's comfortable. But yesterday you agreed to do something completely out of your comfort zone for a complete stranger. That tells me that maybe you're not entirely happy with your comfort zone. That maybe you want something else, something more." She smiled widely at me. "I'm here to offer that to you."

I let out a little scoff and immediately regretted it as she narrowed her eyes.

"You think I'm lying to you?"

I shook my head. "I think that there's far more to your offer than you or I realize."

"Ah, here's the pessimism I was expecting," she said. She moved closer to the counter and put her palms flat on it. "What I am offering is a mutually beneficial opportunity. Do I need to spell it out for you?"

I gritted my teeth. She was playing with me, and worse, she was enjoying it. Hell, so was I.

"Please," I said, "I like to know details."

"It's simple, really. I do classes like you participated in yesterday when I'm in town, and my usual demo bunny happens to be sick this time around. That's why I needed you yesterday. I am offering the opportunity to do it again, this evening, for my intermediate rope class. It will be similar to yesterday, only with some more intricate ties and knots and harnesses." She grinned. "You might enjoy it."

Remembering how much I'd enjoyed playing with her yesterday, I was certain I would. And there was a huge part of me that was chomping at the bit to say yes. Tie me up again. I want to be used like that. But having Delilah there, now, and having time to consider the offer before we immediately had to go with it was making my brain do flip-flops between what I wanted and what I thought I wanted.

This was way out of my comfort zone, as she put it. But I'd be lying if I said it wasn't something I wanted to do. That this beautiful woman was standing in front of me offering to do something like this with me again was absurd, wasn't it? This didn't happen to people. Cori would be having a field day if she were there, talking about romance novels and meet-cutes and how they happened in real life. Which they really didn't. Not like this. I had to remember that. I had to remember that it wasn't always simple like that.

Why couldn't I throw caution to the wind and let myself do this? Fall into that wonderful fuzziness that I'd felt yesterday and let someone else take control of things for once in my life? The answer was simple—because I couldn't let someone else take control of my life. That's where the fear was coming from. Losing control. I'd been in my rut for so long, focused on what I felt like I needed, there was no room for anything else. But maybe there could be.

"Why me?" I asked her, moving a step back from the counter and crossing my arms over my chest. I tried to make it look casual, but I knew it came across as defensive.

"Because you—"

"Don't say that I intrigue you. I want a real answer."

Delilah laughed. "But you do intrigue me. Someone so closed off to things, and yet you decided to have fun with me yesterday. Like you couldn't say no to me."

I scowled. "I seem to have some trouble saying no to you. Some might think you're taking advantage of me."

She put a hand over her heart, her smile fading. "I would never take advantage of someone like that. I swear to you. I've had people fall to their knees around me before. I've played with people before. I love my lifestyle, but I have never, *never* taken advantage of someone who didn't want to play."

"Sorry," I said softly, "I didn't mean to accuse you of anything."

I let out a sigh and shook my head. "I don't understand your interest in me. I mean, I'm just me. There's not an interesting bone in my body."

"Well, that's not true. I could tell that from the moment you ran into me and spilled coffee all over that god-awful blouse."

"All I did was tell you my name and run away from you."

"And I spent the rest of the morning wondering who you were when you weren't running into people with coffee in your hand." She shrugged. "And I liked your taste in coffee."

I looked down at the floor. "But I'm…"

"If you say something disparaging about yourself right now, I promise there will be some punishment to go with tying you up this evening."

"I haven't said yes yet."

"You haven't said no either."

"What makes you think I won't?"

"Let's call it a hunch, shall we?"

I paused to avoid replying too quickly. She damned well could read my mind or something. Read me like a fucking book. Except that I wasn't going to insult myself before, when she cut me off. I was going to tell her the truth. She needed to know the truth before we could do anything else. At least, she needed to hear it from me.

"I don't know if you understand what you're asking of me," I told her softly, refusing to look up at her face. "You don't know who I am."

"How does anyone get to know anyone else? By talking to them, by doing things with them. Learning about each other."

"But is that something you actually want to do, or do you only want a single night of play?"

That seemed to stump her for a moment. Silence followed my words long enough that I glanced up for only a second, to make sure she hadn't disappeared.

"I am offering an evening of fun, being tied up in front of a small crowd of people. If you don't want to do it, I'll find someone else." She sighed. "It won't be as fun without you, but I'm not going to force you to do something you don't want to do."

"And afterward? What then?"

She shrugged. "What about it? If you need help getting home or somewhere else, I can take you if you need a ride."

"No, I mean…what about us? After we, you know."

A look flashed across her face, something almost like panic, but it was there and gone in less than a second. It was her turn to glance away from me, though. "Well," she said in a soft voice. "I suppose we'll see where things go."

I started to say something else, but I stopped. She'd made her position clear. Just because I wanted a guarantee that we would continue to play didn't mean she was able to give it. Hell, this evening might not turn out well, or anything we might do afterward. There were no promises to be had, and I couldn't force that kind of thing out of her. That wouldn't be right.

"I'm sorry," I said. "I shouldn't have asked that. It was too much."

"I'm sure my sister told you what I'm like," she said, still not looking right at me. "That I'm a one-night kind of woman?"

"She might have mentioned that."

"Well, let me make things perfectly clear." She lifted her head, her look hardening. "I am not looking for a relationship. I tried that before, years ago, and it didn't work for me. If something happens between us, then great. That's amazing. I promise you a night you'll never forget. Afterward, well, there's no reason we can't still be friends."

I needed to keep that in mind. I wanted to play—I wanted to be with her. But on her terms. Because I would never want her to do something she wasn't comfortable with.

"I think I'd like that."

She let out a long breath, as if she were expecting me to argue with her. "Thank you for understanding."

"Well, since you were honest with me, can I be honest with you?"

"Pet, you can tell me anything you want." She gave me a wide smile, like she appreciated the change in topic.

Despite her smile, I still had to take a couple of breaths before the words would come out. "I'm scared."

"Of what? You didn't seem frightened yesterday."

"Yesterday was very…spur of the moment. I didn't have time to think, never mind fear anything. But today, you're giving me notice, which gives me time to think. Which gives me time to overthink. Which gives me time to panic."

"Ah, so I should have sprung it on you."

"I mean, did you even know I wasn't working the lounge tonight?"

"I checked the schedule, otherwise it wouldn't have worked out."

I shook my head. "I keep getting off topic."

"You do seem a bit all over the place."

"Welcome to my life." I shook my head again, starting to feel like a damned bobblehead. "Look, I have to spit it out, okay? I'm trans."

She blinked. "Okay. Is…is that an issue?"

My mouth gaped open. "Um, I don't know. I was kind of asking you."

"Are you asking if I have a problem with trans people?"

"I…I mean…I guess so?" I covered my face with my hands. "This conversation is not going the way I wanted it to."

Delilah laughed. "Clearly not."

"You have no intention of putting me out of my misery here, do you?"

It was her turn to shake her head. "Not a chance, pet. I do love to see you squirm."

"Look, I'm…I'm just letting you know. Because it's been an issue in the past. *I* was an issue in the past."

"Oh, pet, you are not an issue. There is nothing wrong with you."

I bit my tongue from replying *says you*, and instead I watched her closely, waiting for the inevitable changes to come from her knowing my truth.

But it didn't come. She smiled at me, warm and inviting, no different than how she'd smiled at me yesterday when she was tying me up, no different than when she'd walked into the bookstore a bit ago. There was no difference.

"Besides," she said after a moment of silence, "it's not like I didn't notice something different about you yesterday."

"What do you mean?"

"We did a crotch rope with the last harness yesterday, remember? I figured either you were packing a strap-on—doubtful for a pretty little femme like you—or you were trans."

I thought back to the day before, remembering how she'd pulled the rope between my legs and subtly framed what was still there. I hadn't considered anything about it at the time, but now it seemed glaringly obvious. I couldn't keep the mortification off my face and felt it heat up so much I had to look away again, unable to meet her eyes.

"I'm sorry, I should have told you before we—"

"It's okay, pet, trust me. I have no problem with you being who you are. In fact, I kind of admire you a little."

"Admire me?" I laughed scornfully. "Why on earth would you do that?"

"Because you are a hell of a lot stronger than you seem to think you are."

I scoffed. "Yeah, right."

"Hey!" she said, and I flinched. "I have been exceedingly honest with you since the moment we met. I have given you no reason to believe what I said was a lie. Even if you refuse to believe it. You are working toward being the person you truly are, and that takes a kind of strength that few people know or can handle. I know it doesn't always feel like it, and everyone has their bad days, but you need to understand the strength it takes to tell society to fuck off and be who you really are despite what others may say or tell you."

I hung my head, feeling the truth in her words and in her anger. "I—I'm sorry. I just…"

"It doesn't feel like it's enough, does it?"

"How do you know that?"

"You're not the only one who hasn't felt like enough in your life. At least you've stepped up to make what you need a reality."

That made me look at her again, and I saw the pain that was etched across her face. It wasn't there long, but I knew what I saw. It helped. Not seeing her in pain but knowing that maybe she wasn't perfect. Maybe her life wasn't perfect. She'd seemed so composed, so confident, like nothing could hurt her. But she was human—like the rest of us.

Somehow it made me want her more.

"Okay," I said.

She cocked her head slightly. "Okay?"

"I'll work with you tonight. I'll be your demo bunny."

"Wonderful! I promise you'll enjoy it."

"I probably will, but take it easy on me, all right? It's my second time."

She laughed at that. "Don't worry, I know how to ease little subs like you into these things."

My face heated again at her words in time for the door of the shop to open and Cori walked in. She took one look at my face, then focused on Delilah, a sly grin on her face. In her hands were a couple wrapped sandwiches from a nearby deli.

"Hey, Sabrina," she said, drawing out the words slowly, "want to introduce me to your friend here?"

I swore if my face got any hotter I was going to spontaneously combust. I gave her what I thought was a glare, something she merely cracked a wide smile at, and replied, "Cori, this is Delilah. Delilah, this is my manager, Cori. Who is back from her lunch much earlier than expected."

Delilah turned to Cori and held out a hand. "Nice to meet you, Cori."

"And you," Cori said, taking it.

Delilah glanced back to me. "I should get back to work. Thanks for chatting with me, Sabrina. I'll see you tonight at Vibe Check, seven o'clock. All right?"

I nodded. "Seven. I got it."

"Wonderful. Thank you again, *pet*."

The emphasis on that damned word made Cori's eyebrows shoot up almost to her hairline, her eyes going wide. Delilah didn't seem to notice as she stepped past Cori and headed out the door. Cori's eyes were shining as she watched Delilah leave, then turned back to me with the biggest shit-eating grin I'd ever seen.

"Did she just call you *pet*?"

I sighed and lowered my forehead to the counter, tempted to slam it down a couple of times. It was going to be a long few hours until tonight.

CHAPTER SIX

I floated.

My body was lying facedown on the soft mats, my chest and abdomen wrapped in an intricate series of ropes that Delilah had promised to take a picture of before setting me free. My wrists were tied together behind my back, my ankles and knees and thighs tied together too. And then my wrist ties were tied to my ankles, forcing me to curl up in a hog-tie position. A blindfold covered my eyes, leaving me in pitch darkness.

But none of that mattered.

I was free. My mind floated in a peaceful bliss, a hazy kind of universe that made everything else seem so unimportant. I wasn't worried about money. I wasn't hating my apartment. I wasn't lamenting my body, the circumstances of my birth. I just...was.

If I focused enough, I could make out the sound of people chatting, others practicing their rope ties and harnesses. I could make out Delilah's voice amongst them, always polite, always enthusiastic about what they were doing. If I had to follow anything in the real world, it was that voice.

I lost track of time, but it felt like all too soon when I heard Delilah's voice speak over the rest of the sound of the room.

"And that's all the time we have, everyone. Take your time to come down, ease your partners out of the rope, make sure they come back to reality softly." She let out a soft laugh that was echoed by the participants of her class. "I'm here if you have any questions, and don't be afraid to browse the store before you go." More laughter. "And feel free to pet the demo bunny on your way out."

I heard the words, but they didn't really register as I fell into that sweet nothingness again. I squirmed a little as there was a smattering of soft touches around my head and shoulders, the ropes creaking slightly as I did. I swore I could hear Delilah's laugh in the background, but that could have come from my mind. I'd heard her laugh so many times now, I almost had the sound memorized.

Finally, there was a soft touch on my cheek. Someone's palm caressed my skin, and I shivered in the best of ways and let out a little gasp.

"It's all right, pet." Delilah's voice cut through the emptiness, louder than anything else that made it through. Of course it did. I belonged to her. That's where my mind had gone and stayed and erected a nice summer home. I was hers. All hers.

The ropes behind me tightened for a moment before loosening, and my body protested the change in position. I couldn't have been hog-tied for more than twenty minutes, I figured, but I hadn't noticed the aching in my joints and muscles while in that fugue state. Now, coming out of it enough to pay attention to Delilah, I was feeling everything—and it was not fun.

As more of the ropes disappeared, I whimpered, in equal parts disappointment and relief. Her idea of intermediate rope play had been a little much for me, if I was being honest, but there was no way I was going to tap out of this. I wanted it too damned much.

Finally, I was left in only the body harness, the rope still tight through my crotch and across my chest. Delilah helped me sit up, and I moaned as the ropes rubbed in the right ways and almost sent me back into that blissful fogginess.

"Easy there, pet," Delilah murmured in my ear and I took a deep breath. "Come back to me. Come on back." I focused on her words, on my breathing, until I felt like I could stay in the present moment. I nodded slightly and felt her hands on my face as she slowly removed the blindfold.

I didn't want to open my eyes, but I did. And immediately closed them again against the brightness of the back room. It took a few minutes of squinting until I could see properly, my first sight being Delilah kneeling in front of me, watching me so closely. Her face was only a few inches from mine, her lips close enough that if I moved forward I could kiss her and know what it was like to kiss someone who accepted who I was.

But I didn't. That would be too far. I was her demo bunny, not her girlfriend.

More than anything else, that thought brought reality crashing down around me. I wanted to be hers, but she didn't want that. She had no problem borrowing me, but it wasn't for good. It wasn't for more than one night. And I had to be able to live with that.

"I'm good," I said, opening my eyes and staring into hers. "I'm okay."

"Lost you to subspace again, did I?" she said softly with a chuckle.

"Do you blame me?"

"Not at all, pet, not at all."

Her hands flitted over the ropes still on my body, adjusting here, tugging there. It was like she was trying to make it perfect, even if the only people left were me and her. I reached out and took her hand without thinking, entwining our fingers for a moment. She looked surprised but didn't pull away as I brought her hand to my mouth and kissed her knuckles gently. I watched her face, waiting for any sort of negative reaction, but her eyes closed for a brief second as if she too enjoyed it before she took control and gently pulled her hand back.

"Thank you, pet."

"Thank you, Mi—" I cut myself off before I could finish the word *Mistress*. But she noticed it anyway, giving me a look I couldn't read. Was she interested? Hopeful? Or was she as afraid as I was that I was falling too fast? I shook my head slowly, glancing away from her. "Thank you, Delilah."

"Are you ready to be untied?" she asked.

I shook a little at the thought. "No, no, I'm not. But I guess the class is over, huh?"

"That it is, pet." She patted my cheek softly and I nuzzled into her palm. "Good girl. You did so well tonight."

I gave her a tiny shrug. "I only did what I was told."

"There's more to it than that and you know it." She was right, but at the moment my brain wasn't firing on all cylinders. My first instinct was to minimize my role in things. It was her work, her tying me up, telling me what to do or how to move. I was nothing but a participant. A very, very willing participant. "Now, how are you feeling?"

"A bit sore, my joints ache a little but it's a good ache. Will probably hurt more tomorrow." I gave her the report, simple and clean. "But all in all, I wouldn't trade the experience for anything."

She grinned. "That's one of the best compliments I can get from a demo bunny. Thank you."

"It's me that should be thanking you. For yesterday. For tonight. I've always been interested, always been…a bit submissive, even in my regular life and not just the bedroom. But I've never gotten to partake until now, and it has been absolutely amazing."

She held a hand over her heart and made a pleased noise. "I'm glad your first—and second—experiences were such good ones. It doesn't always end up that way for some people." She stood and held out her hands. I let her pull me to my feet, moaning slightly as the ropes went taut in certain areas.

"What was your first time like?" I asked, curious and wanting to know more about her.

"Certainly not like this," she replied with a smile. She gave my cheek a soft pat. "And that's all I'm going to say about that."

She moved around behind me. The ropes hugging my body began to loosen, and I tried not to fidget as she worked. I didn't want her to let me go. I didn't want to feel…naked, while being entirely clothed. There was something about the rope that I couldn't describe, but it felt like it belonged. Like it was supposed to be there.

I let out a shaky breath.

"All right there, pet?"

I nodded but didn't reply. I didn't trust my words. Our conversation from earlier in the day was still bouncing around my head. One night only. That's what Tiffani had said, and Delilah had only confirmed it. Could I handle that? Could I live with a single night together?

I rolled my eyes at my own insecurity. People did one-night stands all the time. They didn't have to lead to a relationship or anything like that. Hell, I probably wasn't in the best place for a relationship anyway. I had plans. I had *a* plan. A relationship would probably get in the way, if that was even something that could be offered. Never mind that even if this somehow led to some sort of relationship with Delilah, how secure would it be, considering it was based on presumably hot, kinky sex. You needed more than that. Mutual respect, caring, communication, all sort of other things went into a relationship—things I wasn't practiced at, wasn't sure I could even pull off.

But one night of bliss? I wanted to say I could handle that. I wanted to be able to. I wouldn't let it change my goals, change my mind. A fun night between two consenting adults. What could go wrong?

"Okay, pet, you're all good."

Delilah's voice broke me from my thoughts. I looked down, sad to see the beautiful rope harness missing from my body. I sniffled, feeling the onset of tears threatening to take over my face. I wanted more. I wanted *her*.

Fuck.

"Thank you," I managed to say without breaking down. It was a close thing, though.

"Are you okay?"

Curse her and her ability to read my mind. I sniffled and closed my eyes. I worked to hold back the waterworks. "I'm all right," I whispered, barely loud enough to hear. I shook my head and tried again. "I'm all right." It was louder this time, a little more believable.

She moved to the front of me and took my wrists in her hands. She looked them over, looking for any damage that her ropes might have done. I didn't feel any aftereffects, save for missing the restriction.

"Everything looks okay," she reported. "Are you feeling any pain or stinging, burning, anything like that? I'd hate to have given you rope burn or something."

I shook my head. "Nope, I'm all right."

She patted me on the cheek again. "Good girl."

I shivered but tried to stand a little taller, more presentable for her. She eyed me up and down. "Are you cold, pet?"

I started to say no, then shivered again. It took a moment, but I realized that my limbs were feeling cold, like I couldn't get them to warm up naturally, even underneath my leggings and tunic-length top. I rubbed at my arms and nodded. "I don't know why," I told her. "I don't usually get cold like this."

"It happens sometimes, when the rush of hormones and adrenaline and everything starts to fade after a scene like we had. You might start having some negative thoughts, some troubles concentrating, craving carbs. It's all symptoms of subdrop."

I shook my head. A few books I'd read dealt with subdrop, though not many. This didn't sound like any that I'd read about. "That doesn't make sense. Subdrop happens like...hours later. Even days. I shouldn't be feeling it this soon."

She shrugged. "Everyone's different. You might get it early. Hold on a moment." She turned and headed for the small office and disappeared through the doorway. She reappeared a moment later carrying a heavy dark purple sweater. "Here, put this on. It's really warm."

I stared at it for a second before taking it. I glanced at her, and she nodded encouragingly. When in Rome, I guess. I'd never had a girl give me their sweater before. I pulled it over my head, twisting inside a little to fit my arms and head through the holes. I breathed in and got a face full of Delilah's scent and tried really hard not to prance in place in excitement. When I got the sweater situated, Delilah stepped close and wrapped her arms around me in a tight hug. I melted into her embrace with a soft groan.

"Is that better, pet? Warmer? More comfortable?"

I nodded against her shoulder, not wanting this hug to end. Her arms felt like they belonged around me, giving me a similar feeling to the restriction of the ropes that she'd bound me with. All too soon it was over, and she took a step back, looking me up and down.

"Are you ready to get out of here?"

I wrapped my arms around myself, taking in the scent and warmth of her sweater. "O-okay. I think so."

She took my hand gently, and we left the back room and entered the store proper. I saw Lexie wandering the store as she stopped here and there to talk to some of the people I recognized from the beginning of the class. Another woman I didn't recognize was behind the till, currently ringing up a couple hanks of rope for another pair of intermediate rope play enthusiasts from the class.

We were passing the racks of BDSM gear when Delilah stopped suddenly. "Damn," she breathed. "Hold tight here, pet. I forgot something in the back." She let me go and headed back through the doorway.

I felt her absence far too keenly for comfort and shook my head. The effects this woman was having on me were kind of frightening. I tried to pull my attention away and onto something else, and as I looked around my gaze fell on that same leather gag harness I'd been admiring the day before. I reached out and caressed the leather puppy-ear pieces that stuck up from the top strap and suddenly got the image in my mind of wearing this at Delilah's feet. The ball gag forcing my mouth open behind the leather muzzle, the ears sticking up from my head. Her pet, in more than just name. I shivered, even in the warm sweater, and pulled my hand back.

I started breathing a little deeper and tried to keep myself calm as my mind tried to go down a road I wasn't sure I should travel. I looked at the other items hanging from the racks: a plush-looking leather collar that looked like it might fit, with a large O-ring in the front for attachments. Leather and steel wrist and ankle cuffs. A box showing off a model in a tight, shiny latex hood. I could feel my heart beating rapidly as my breathing came a little quicker, my mind bombarding me with images of playing with different toys, all at the behest of my Mistress. Delilah.

"Are you okay?"

I spun around at the voice, almost knocking into the queening chair that jutted out from against the wall. I refused to allow my mind to even consider that piece of equipment and instead focused on Lexie, who was holding a hand over her mouth as if to keep in her laughter.

"I'm okay," I said. "Just a little…overwhelmed."

She gave me a small smile. "Delilah does have that effect on people. She's kind of like a hurricane, sweeping people along with her."

"I am starting to notice this," I said.

"Well, do what you can not to get all spun around, you hear?"

I stared at her. Was Lexie warning me away from Delilah? "What do you mean?"

"You're a sweet girl, Sabrina. I'd hate to see you get hurt."

I opened my mouth to reply, but Lexie was quick to walk away as the door to the back room opened and Delilah stepped out. She held what looked like a small backpack, and my purse.

"Oh, shit," I said as she handed me my bag. "Yeah, it would've been bad to forget this. Thank you."

"You're very welcome, pet." She looked past me, at the wall of toys I'd been admiring. "Anything here catch your interest?"

I glanced at the harness gag again, then quickly looked away. But not fast enough. I saw the grin that spread over her visage, and she moved forward and pulled the harness off its hook.

"Is my pet interested in being a pet?" she asked, her voice low as if to keep the conversation between us. My blush returned with little fanfare but plenty of embarrassment and I started to shake my head, but I didn't want to lie to her.

"Yes, some day," I said. I couldn't meet her eyes lest she see how much I wanted to be *her* pet.

Luckily, she seemed to take pity on me and put the harness back on its hook. "I'll keep that in mind."

With her back to me, I managed to put myself back together a little.

"Are you ready to go?" I asked as Delilah turned around.

"Ready when you are, pet."

I stumbled a little and she caught me by the arm, then led me to the front door. She held it open for me and we exited into the cool night air.

Chapter Seven

Delilah's car was rather nice, if a little low to the ground. It made it awkward to get into, but the leather seat was comfy and apparently had a heating option—I didn't even know that was a thing. She turned it on for me, and between her sweater and the seat, I was starting to feel overheated, and not in the good way.

Still, the heat helped my body relax more than I thought it could as Delilah took the wheel and followed her phone's directions to take me home. My mind, meanwhile, was wild with thoughts of me and Delilah, sometimes playing with each other and sometimes me simply submitting to whatever she wanted. It was printed into my head, like I couldn't shake it. I wanted it so damned badly. *Needed* it.

But then Lexie and Tiffani's words would echo through my mind, reminding me that I'd only met this woman yesterday and there were things I didn't know about her. Even by her own admission, I could only count on a single night with her. I wanted to be able to handle that, but I wasn't sure I could.

And besides, how could I be sure she even wanted me? Sure, she seemed to enjoy tying me up, but having a night together was a very different thing. Or maybe it wasn't for her. Maybe it was even more simple. I didn't know. I had no idea what the hell I was doing, what I was thinking. Nothing in my life had prepared me for what I wanted from Delilah.

I was overthinking things. Complicating things. As I always did. All I had to do was ask the question. The worst she could say was *no*.

"We're getting close," she said softly and pulled me from my jumble of thoughts. "Which building is yours?"

I looked out the window and pointed to the beige and metal

monstrosity that housed my tiny apartment. A wild thought touched my brain, wondering what she would think of my one-room home.

"There's usually plenty of street parking," I told her, having to raise my voice a little over the sound of the engine and Delilah's music. "Or there's visitor parking right beside the building."

A female singer's voice drifted through the speakers, lamenting about being unable to talk to girls, as Delilah pulled into the parking lot and the first available empty visitor spot. We were silent together for a long moment, the only sounds between us the rumble of the engine and the music. I watched Delilah out of the corner of my eye, wondering what the right decision was. Did I invite her up, or did we go our separate ways? I didn't want her to go. I didn't want to not be with her. But would I survive the aftermath?

"I—" I began.

"So—" she said at the same time.

We glanced at each other, both seemingly speechless, and shared a little laugh. It broke the tension that had built during the ride, and I let out a long breath.

"Thank you," I said.

She waved her hand. "No problem. You've done so much for me, giving you a ride is the least I could do."

"That's not what I mean." I wrapped my arms around my torso and refused to look her in the eye. "I-I mean of course, thanks for the ride, but also everything else." I bit my tongue hard, trying to stop myself from feeling flustered and get the words out properly. My mother would have killed me hearing how much I was fumbling around Delilah.

Stop choking on your words and speak properly! Her shrill tone echoed through my mind.

"Are you okay, pet? We can take a minute here, if you need. There's no rush."

She reached between us and turned down the music a little—it was another female singer asking her lover twenty questions about their questionable activities.

I shook my head. "I…I'm fine." I took another deep breath and let it out, trying to calm the pounding of my heart, the bleariness in my head. I let my breath go in a long exhale, thinking about my tense muscles relaxing enough that I could speak normally. "I'm…I'm trying to thank you for showing me this…these new experiences. The rope, the care, the fun. I…It's been an amazing ride."

"There's no reason it has to end here," she said over the sound of the music. "If you don't want it to, that is."

I turned to look at her, forgetting to breathe for a moment. When my lungs decided to work again, I half choked on the air I tried to gulp down and ended up coughing, covering my mouth with my hand so as not to look completely inept and out of my league around this beautiful woman.

"Easy there, pet. Are you okay? I know subdrop doesn't go away that quickly. Are you still cold? Feeling disoriented?"

I started to shake my head, then nodded instead. I hoped that was the reason for feeling so…infinitely not okay. Maybe it wasn't only my brain being hard-wired to question everything when someone showed any sort of interest in me.

Everything in my life came with a cost. Maybe this didn't have to.

"I'm sorry."

"Don't be. It happens." She turned the key, shutting off the engine. "Come on. I'll help you get home."

"You don't have to—" I started to argue, but she already had the door open and was climbing out of the car. I scrambled to get my seat belt off and open my door in time for her to get there and offer me her arm. My legs were wobbly enough that I needed her help to get out of the car, clutching my purse in my other hand. Her strong grip on me was comforting, and I shivered, but for the first time since we'd ended the class earlier, I wasn't really that cold. I leaned into her, knowing I was doing too much but unable to stop myself. She closed the door behind me, and the car made that little beeping noise to say it was locked as she played with the fob.

"All right, pet?" She pulled her backpack on.

I clutched at her arm. "Just a little unsteady."

"It's okay. Lean on me."

I managed to pull my keys out of my purse as we made slow progress up to the door. I swiped my fob, the doors parted before us, and Delilah stepped through with the regal air of someone who owned everything she surveyed—and for some reason had chosen to own me as well.

We waited for the elevator in silence, me clutching Delilah's arm as if she were a safety line. We didn't have long to wait. The doors slid open, and Delilah pulled me into the elevator. The doors closed behind us, and without warning, Delilah spun me around so I was in front of her. She pushed me against the wall and trapped me with her arms as her head dipped low and her lips stopped less than an inch from mine. I stared at her, my breath coming hard and fast, as her eyes met mine. She smiled.

"Are you going to let me kiss you, my pet?" Her voice was low—her timbre sent a burst of welcome heat rushing down to my core. I couldn't speak, but I managed to nod—once—before her lips were crushed against mine and I moaned into her mouth. She took control by pressing her tongue against my mouth until I opened and let her explore as she liked. It took a few seconds for me to put any form of steel into my backbone, and I tried to give as good as I got.

Then, as quick as it had started, Delilah pulled away with a wide smirk. I almost fell to my knees, my legs were so wobbly, as she merely wiped her mouth daintily. "What floor, pet?"

I stared at her, breathing heavily. "T-three," I managed to say. I wanted to beg her to kiss me again, rather than think about what floor my apartment was on. She reached out and hit the button, and the elevator started moving with a lurch. I barely stayed standing upright.

I tried to regain some semblance of stability, finding my feet as the elevator came to a stop. The elevator dinged and the door slid open to reveal the familiar hallway. Delilah held out her hand and I took it without hesitation and led the way slowly down to my apartment. Her hand was warm in mine, and it was taking everything in me not to stop and bring it to my lips. I needed her to kiss me again.

But I pushed that aside and got to my door in one piece. I unlocked it and pushed it open, stepping into the tiny apartment and feeling a moment of shame that this was where I'd taken her. She deserved better. She deserved five-star accommodations, not a tiny studio apartment where you could see pretty much everything as you walked in. At least it was relatively clean—I'd had time to putter between my bookstore shift and joining Delilah at Vibe Check. And I'd had nothing else to focus on.

She let go of my hand, then looked around with a small smile as she closed the door tight behind her.

"It's…it's not much," I said, looking away. Her fingers grasped my chin, directing my gaze to her face.

"Don't do that, pet. It's a home. It serves its purpose." Still holding my chin, she leaned down and pressed her lips against mine again. I fell into the bliss of the kiss, but unlike the ferocity of the one in the elevator, this was more tender, caring, and I felt myself fighting not to cry again. Gah! Emotions were always worse on estradiol.

"Would you like anything? Can I get you anything?" I asked after we parted once more. I didn't want her to leave. I needed her to stay.

"Just a water, if you will, pet," she said. "And one for yourself. You need to stay hydrated." She gently released my chin, and I turned to the galley kitchen.

She smacked me lightly on my ass as I moved to get her water, and I squeaked loudly, which made her laugh. I retrieved two bottles of water from the fridge and brought them back.

"So, um, this is my place," I said in perhaps the most pathetic voice ever. Whatever strength she'd said she saw in me had clearly flown the coop. "It's not much—"

She cut off my words by pressing another kiss to my lips, and I almost dropped the bottles. It didn't last as long as the others, but it still had the same effect on me. I needed her. I wanted to be hers.

"Do I need to kiss you every time you start to say something disparaging?"

I managed to crack a smile. "I mean, wouldn't that be incentive to continue?"

She tapped my cheek with her fingers. "Brat."

I shook my head. I knew what that word meant in the lifestyle, and I was fairly certain there were very few brattish qualities in me. She took the bottle of water from me, opened it, then offered it back to me and took the other one.

"Drink, pet. You're still feeling disoriented, aren't you?"

I took a sip of my water, the coolness of the liquid sliding down my throat. If I was still feeling disoriented, I couldn't say if it was from the subdrop or if it was Delilah herself with her whiplash kisses and domineering personality. I wasn't exactly feeling normal, so she had a point.

"How can I help you?" she asked.

I stared at her for a long moment. It was my job to serve her, not the other way around. Clearly, she was reading my mind again, because she cut me off before I could argue.

"I'm not talking about serving you," she said quickly. "I'm talking about taking care of my pet. Which you are, right now, my pet, and it is my responsibility to take care of you. A broken toy isn't nearly as fun to play with."

Her use of the word *toy* sent another wave of heat through me, right down to my girlcock, which was already straining against my underwear from the kisses she'd bestowed upon me. Right now, I didn't care. I wanted her. Now.

"Kiss me again," I said softly, almost pleadingly. She smiled and I raised my head a little so I could look at her. She leaned down and we kissed again, softly this time. We were of the same height, but her boots put her a few inches taller than me. It was a feeling I'd never had before, being shorter than the person kissing me. It was different. It was nice. She took control of the kiss—of course she did. She raised her hands and tucked them into my hair. I had just pressed my tongue against her lips, asking permission when her grip tightened and suddenly my head was pulled backward roughly. A loud moan ripped from my throat as the pain in my head quickly fed into pleasure, and I knew I was a goner. I'd do anything she wanted. Not that I wasn't already inclined to do so anyway.

"Tell me what you want, pet." Delilah's voice drifted over me as I tried to keep my head still. The grip she had in my hair was like iron, and my head was pulled back so I was looking at the ceiling. "Tell me what you need."

I gasped as she tightened her grip, and I let out a yelp of pain. "You, Mistress!" I cried out. "I need you!"

She released my hair, and I let my head fall forward until I was looking at the floor between us. What was she going to say? What was she going to do? I didn't know, and I didn't want to look at her to discover the wrong answer.

Chapter Eight

My mind raced with the possibilities until strong fingers lifted my chin and I was met with Delilah's hard stare.

"You want me to be your Mistress?" She smiled like a satisfied cat who had caught and now intended to play with her prey. "Then get on your knees."

I fell to my knees immediately, landing on the soft carpet. I looked up to find her staring down at me, that smile still on her lips. Then she moved, walking over to my bed and sitting primly on it, crossing one leg over the other. She slipped her backpack onto her lap, then looked back to me.

"Well? I'm waiting."

I had a second of indecision, unsure what she was waiting for, then I started to crawl over to her. My knees weren't happy with me for it, but I didn't care. I stopped at her feet and looked up at her. Her backpack was set aside, unzipped, and I wondered what was in there that she had plans for. Her strong hands forced me to face forward, then up, as she loomed over me. She leaned down, planting a soft kiss on my forehead, then leaned further to put her lips by my ear.

"What a good girl you are." Her words sent a tingle down my spine, but her hands held me tight in their grip. "Eyes on me, pet. Keep your head up, your eyes on me."

I nodded, not trusting my ability to speak. I kept my head up, watching her as she straightened up and met my eye.

"Good girl. Now, untie my boots."

It was hard, trying to keep my head up and looking her in the eye as my hands wandered down her pant leg to her ankle boots. I glanced down for a second, to guide my hands, and one of her hands smacked my cheek lightly.

"Eyes up, pet."

I swallowed the lump in my throat. "Y-yes, Mistress."

I found the laces by touch alone, my fingers following the strands and loops. Of course she tied her boots in, like, double bows or something. I tried to find the ends of the laces, fumbling around as the smile on her face only grew more feral. I don't know how I managed to make it work, but slowly I found the right strands and pulled, untying the laces and easing the boot off. I forced myself to keep my head up as I moved my hands to her other boot, finding the laces easier this time around. The boot slipped off after a moment and I set them both aside, careful to keep my eyes on my Mistress.

"Good girl. Now stand up for me."

I did so, climbing to my feet without breaking eye contact—which was difficult. Her hands moved with me at first, then fell away as I looked down on her. I forced myself not to look away.

"Good girl. Now strip." I almost fell over in my rush to pull the sweater off, then my tunic over my head. I tossed them to the side, then started pulling down my leggings. I craned my head up to keep my eyes on Delilah, undressing by feel as she watched me with that damned smile on her face. I made quick work of my underwear and socks, then reached around behind me to unhook my bra. It got stuck and I fiddled for a moment, trying so hard not to look away from her. I wanted to please her. Needed to please her. Another moment of fiddling and the bra fell away too, leaving me staring at my Mistress, fully nude.

"Now," she said, drawing a finger down her chin as if thinking hard. "What do I do with such a pretty girl like you?"

Use me. Ruin me. Destroy me. I wanted to suggest anything and everything, whatever would make her happy. But she hadn't given me permission to speak. All I could do was stand there and watch her as she stood up from the bed and moved in my direction. I followed her movement until she stepped up beside me, then past. I wasn't sure if I should spin to keep her in my sight, but she didn't tell me to so I stood still, waiting. She eventually reappeared on my other side, and I resumed focusing on her face as much as I could, no matter how much I wanted to drop my gaze.

"You really are a beautiful pet." The compliment was hard to take, and again I felt the urge to look down, but her finger found my chin and kept it up as if she knew what was coming. "Yes, pet, I called you beautiful. You can take the compliment."

"Yes, Mistress."

She leaned in and pressed her lips against mine. They were soft, sure, and only there for a second as she backed away. "You taste good, pet."

She ran her finger down my throat, toward my chest. My breathing hitched as her hand caressed my breast and a moan slipped out of my mouth. She laughed and brought her other hand up, giving my other breast the same treatment. I closed my eyes for only a second, and there was another hard tap on my cheek.

"Eyes on me, pet."

"Yes, Mistress." I forced my eyes open, focusing on her once more.

Her hands cupped my breasts, thumbs playing with my nipples as I moaned again, unable to stop myself. They were so sensitive, a relatively new sensation, one I'd only barely managed to discover by myself. It made me even more desperate for her. Slowly her hands started to move down, flitting over my stomach, down to my hips, where they caressed the skin. I quivered under her touch but kept my eyes on her to see if she was paying attention to what she was doing to me.

"You are gorgeous, pet."

"I—" I started to argue on impulse but stopped myself. She let out a small laugh.

"Very good girl," she said softly as she bent her knees and moved her hands farther down.

Her hands touched my thighs, thicker than they used to be thanks to the hormones. Every time the pads of Delilah's fingers made contact, I felt goosebumps rising in their wake. I wasn't used to being touched like this. It's not like I never touched myself, marvelled at how soft my skin had become, wondered about a day when I would no longer need to worry about shaving. This was different, though. This was someone who knew their way around my body, despite never having seen it before. It was like she was in my head, knowing exactly what to do to extract the responses she desired from me. I forced myself to keep my head straight, my eyes on her.

I didn't want to disappoint my Mistress.

Then her hands found my girlcock, and I let out a desperate cry as her fingers caressed me in a way that my clumsy attempts to pleasure myself never managed to make feel so damned good. One of her hands moved down, lightly scraping her nails along the skin and making me shiver with pleasure. I barely managed to keep my feet as I watched her wrap both hands around my girlcock and start slowly pumping. I moaned again, unable to keep my mouth shut, and she looked up at me with a wide grin.

"Very good, pet," she said. "So responsive to me. So needy too." She leaned forward and I felt more than saw her lean forward and run her tongue up the tip of my girlcock. I cried out again, almost falling to my knees from the sudden sensation as she leaned back and looked up at me. "And you taste absolutely divine here too."

"Thank you, Mistress." It felt like the right thing to say at that moment.

Delilah laughed again and stood up, her hands flying over my body, retracing their steps back up to my chin. One hand rested over my throat, as if she were thinking of squeezing, and my breath started to come harder. Her other hand caressed my cheek, then moved to the back of my head, tangling deep in my hair.

"Bed, pet," she said, but I stayed frozen in her hands. "Now." With the hand in my hair she pulled back sharply until I gasped, then pushed hard enough that I went stumbling to the bed. I caught myself on my arms, narrowly avoided tripping over her boots, then turned and sat on the bed beside her backpack. I wanted to know what was inside, but I had a feeling I'd find out soon enough.

I heard Delilah laughing and looked up to see her already halfway out of her button-down shirt. Her jeans were next, followed by her bra and underwear. In less time than it took me she was naked and sauntering back toward me as my eyes took in her beauty. She was toned, showing a care for her body that I certainly could learn from. She had a large tattoo on her right hip that looked like a bouquet of roses and lilies in various colors stretching from the front to the back. Above and around the bouquet were a number of different color butterflies, all sizes, that looked like they were fluttering above the flowers, waiting to land and pollinate. She followed my gaze to the tattoo as I studied it, and she cracked a grin.

"Do you like what you see, pet?"

I managed to nod in response. Her naked body took my breath away. "Yes, Mistress." The words tumbled out before I had a chance to think about it. An automatic response now.

She moved to the bed, picking up her backpack and reaching inside. She pinned me with her gaze. "Are you ready for this?"

I nodded. I didn't know what *this* was, but I was ready. I wanted her. Needed her. And damned if I was even going to think of telling her *no*. She pulled a rather large, dark silicone dildo out of the bag. It took my breath away. It was probably a good twelve inches or so, bulbous and round, with a flared base to fit in a strap. I stared at it for a long moment, then looked at her. She looked so serious, watching me with those golden eyes.

Then she started laughing again. Doubled over, laughing up a storm, and I stared at her, trying to understand.

"Oh, pet, we're not going to start with this monster. It's only for girls who are practiced in this kind of play." She put the monster dildo back into her bag and started rummaging around, then pulled out a much smaller dildo, probably half the length with a slight curve near the end of it. It was pink and shiny and clean, and I couldn't help but think about where she was going to put it. "Now, I want to ask, have you done anal before?" I shook my head. It was something I'd wanted in the past, but my exes certainly had no interest in being with someone who wanted *that*. "Thank you for being honest. Okay, so you have your safewords. You do remember them, right?"

I forced my head up and down in a nod, unable to find my voice to answer her.

"Let me hear you say it, pet."

"The traffic lights, Mistress," I said, finally finding my voice. "Green, yellow, red."

"Very good. If things get too much, we can slow down or stop if you need to, all right?"

"Yes, Mistress."

"Excellent," she said, reaching into the bag again and pulling out what looked like a pair of underwear with straps. "Now, I need to get ready. Would you like to assist?" I was nodding before she even finished the question. "Then come. On your knees."

I got off the bed and fell to my knees beside Delilah. Immediately, she put her bag in my hand and allowed me to hold it for her. In my other hand she placed the smaller dildo, and I stared at it, wondering what it was going to feel like. She pulled on the underwear, then adjusted the straps until she was satisfied. She took the dildo from me and fed it through the ring in the middle of her harness and I stared at it, thrusting out into midair.

"Pet," she said, drawing my attention upward. "Where are you at right now?"

"G-green, Mistress." I managed to get the words out through a rather dry throat.

"Good girl." I earned a soft pat on the head for that one. She reached into the bag once more and pulled out what I recognized as a bottle of lube and handed it to me. I thought for a moment to set the bag and the lube aside, to empty my hands in case she had need for them, but I didn't dare without her permission. "Now, pet, I want your mouth on me."

I froze up, staring at the dildo jutting out from her harness. How did I…I'd never done anything like this before. Sure, put it in my mouth. That sounded so easy. But what then? What came next?

I looked up into Delilah's face, her eyes, and she gave me a knowing smile. Like she knew I could do this. Like she wanted me to show her that I could step outside my comfort zone. Further outside it, anyway. Still clutching the bag and the bottle, I scooted forward on my knees until I was right in front of the strap.

"Lick it," Delilah said, "start with your tongue, pet. Then take me in your mouth. I want to feel it."

I took a breath. Took a second one, then a third. I leaned forward and ran my tongue over the silicone. It was…rather tasteless. Plastic, mostly, and a little bit of what I thought might be sweat from Delilah's hand. I licked up the tip, then leaned in further and took her strap into my mouth.

"Good girl." I heard Delilah say as I let my hands fall to my sides, dropping her bag, dropping the bottle of lube. I maneuvered my way closer to her and took her deeper into my mouth. It wasn't very large, but I still had little idea what I was doing. My lips closed around the dildo, and I sucked, then ran my tongue over the smooth silicone again and again. But I couldn't understand how she could feel it. It felt like it wasn't deep enough.

Suddenly, fingers reached into my hair and tightened their grip hard enough that I cried out against the dildo. Then Delilah pulled me forward and shoved the dildo deep into the back of my throat. I started to gag and panic and pull back, but her grip was strong.

"Swallow," she said, and I tried to get my throat to work, but it didn't seem to want to listen. "Swallow for me, my good girl." I continued to gag for a few more seconds before she pulled my head back enough that I could breathe again, but not enough to get the dildo out of my mouth—which I was kind of desperate for at this point. But my Mistress was making it clear that she controlled my head, my mouth, all of me. And she wouldn't let me forget it.

"Very good, pet," she said softly after loosening her grip in my hair. I continued to take the dildo into my mouth, as deep as I could without gagging again, but I tried to prepare myself for the possibility of her forcing me again. "Now, pick up that lube."

I started to pull back from the dildo, but her hand forced me to stay on it as I scrabbled around on the floor for the bottle I'd dropped. I picked it up without looking and lifted it to her like an offering while I continued to bob my head back and forth while wrapping my tongue around the dildo like she could feel it.

"Pour some on the dildo," she commanded. I faltered, glancing up at her through my eyelashes. "Don't give me that look, pet. It's flavored. You might enjoy it."

I could take a step back. Say *yellow* and pause the game. Even if my mouth was full of the dildo, I was sure she would understand what I was saying. I trusted her to understand what I said whether that was *green, red,* or *yellow.* But I didn't want to use my safewords. I'd asked her to be my Mistress. To take me any way she wanted. And that's what she was doing. It wasn't too much for me. I wouldn't let it be.

I flipped open the bottle with a flick of my thumb, drizzling it onto the dildo right in front of my mouth. Her fingers tightened in my hair again and I braced myself for another forced gagging, but this time the pressure was gentle, urging me forward more than forcing me. My tongue touched the lube, and I was surprised at the taste of strawberries as I used my tongue and my lips to try to coat the entire toy.

"Don't be afraid to use too much." Delilah's voice was soft above me. "It's going in your tight little pussy next."

I flinched as the top of the dildo caught my upper jaw and bounced off the roof of my mouth embarrassingly. I tried to pull away, but her fingers kept me in place.

"Easy, pet. We don't want to bite down, even if it's not the real thing."

The thought of taking the real thing at her command sent a blast of warmth coursing through me that settled down in my core and made me harder than ever. If Delilah commanded it, I'd do anything. I was way too far gone to even consider refusing. I worked my mouth on the dildo more, pouring more lube on it and soaking it with both lube and my saliva. Finally she pulled my head back, and it came out of my mouth with a little popping noise that seemed to please her when she chuckled at it.

"Very good, pet," she said, rubbing her fingers in my hair like you would a puppy. If I had a tail it'd be wagging nonstop right now. She took the lube from me with her other hand and smiled down at me. "Now, be a dear and go bend over your bed for me?" Her voice rose at the end as if it were a question, but I knew it wasn't. It wasn't even a suggestion. It was a command, and I was going to obey.

I crawled the short distance back to the bed and pulled myself up, bending over at the waist and letting my chest and stomach lie on the clean sheets. I spread my legs a little to retain balance, then rested my head on the bed as well, letting out a long breath as I waited. Fear flitted through my mind. I was scared of not being good enough, of not taking this well enough. I wanted to impress her. I wanted her to want me again, more than tonight. I knew that wasn't likely, but my mind was set on the idea, and damn it, I was going to do my best to make sure I gave her everything she could want.

I heard her move closer to me. Her hands touched my ass cheeks and rubbed them sensually as I moaned at the touch. It disappeared only for a second before her hand smacked my right ass cheek and I yelped loudly, almost pulling myself off the bed at the sudden pain. I was in a better place for the second smack on my other cheek, and I sucked in a deep breath. My girlcock strained against the bed, bent over as I was, but the pain from that only served to magnify every other touch my Mistress was giving me.

Her hand touched my back, caressing the skin between my shoulder blades and lower. "Easy, pet. I need you to relax and to focus on breathing, all right? I'm going to put some fingers inside you now."

A cold dribble of lube found its way into my ass crack, followed swiftly by Delilah's exploratory fingers. I told myself to relax, to enjoy the ride, to focus on breathing, as she moved around my tight hole. There was slight pain as she pressed her finger into my hole, moving slowly, never rushing. I gasped and cried out as she made it to her first knuckle, crooking her finger slightly to explore the unplumbed depth. I moaned as her other hand gathered more lube around the hole to push deeper.

"How are you doing, pet?"

It took a moment to find my voice. "G-green, Mistress."

What had started as a flash of pain had diminished and now felt amazingly good. The stretching sensation of having something inside me was intoxicating, and as I focused on keeping my breathing steady I couldn't help but wonder why I'd never thought to play with myself like this before. I felt her move her finger in and out slowly. She lubed up my hole further, and the stimulation resonated right down in my girlcock. I was certain she'd made it two knuckles deep at this point. I felt her lean over me, pressing her breasts to my back.

"I'm going to add another finger now, pet. Tell me if it's too much."

"Yes, Mistress." The words came out almost as a sigh as I breathed out and she pushed her second finger slowly into me. I gasped and moaned, and she pressed into me, her thumb massaging the perineum as she did so. The stretch was a bit uncomfortable, but it didn't last long as she collected more lube and started to fuck my hole a little faster.

"That's it, pet. Take me into you," Delilah was saying as she pushed those two fingers deeper and deeper. "I'm going to add a third, okay?"

I opened my mouth to agree, but all that came out was another moan as her fingers curled inside me and touched something that sent stars through my vision in the best of ways. If this was what a couple of fingers felt like, what the hell was her dildo going to do to me?

"Are you ready for the main course, pet?"

I didn't know how much better it could get after three fingers, but I moaned enthusiastically. I felt empty as Delilah pulled her fingers out of me and watched as she grabbed the pillows from the end of the bed and brought them back to me.

"Lift those gorgeous hips of yours for me, pet."

I did as she asked, adjusting as she placed the pillows underneath me, which gave me a different angle for her to work with. "Perfect. Just like that."

I was so fucking far gone that I would have done anything at that point, and as I felt the thicker tip of the dildo caress the skin of my ass cheeks, I levered myself back impatiently. I wanted that full feeling again. That stretched feeling. The pleasure that came with knowing that my Mistress was inside me. It wasn't long before I felt a bit more lube sliding down my crack, and I wondered if maybe there was such a thing as too much, but that didn't last long.

"Relax," Delilah said, as I felt the tip pressing into me, as if she sought permission to go further. I took a deep breath and let it out. She didn't force herself into me but slid in smoothly. I did my best to relax and take the thick shaft. It stretched me more than her fingers had and reached deeper into me too. As she pressed herself into me up to the hilt, my breath left me in a stuttered moan.

"There's my good girl."

I swear I blacked out for a second, because the next thing I knew she was sliding in and out of me with more force than she'd used with her fingers. I could feel every slight movement of her hips as she thrust into me. She filled me up and pushed in to the hilt of her strap as if she could feel it when she did. And she probably could. I wanted to turn around, to bring her pleasure too, but that thought was fleeting as my mind went blank with the pleasure of being railed like this. The sounds coming out of my mouth filled the room. I didn't even know I could make sounds like that.

"Very good, pet. You're doing so well." Her voice hitched a little as the words wormed their way into my brain, and I moaned at the praise and tried to raise my hips a little, desperate to bring her deeper into me. I was hers. Her hole. Her fuck toy. She was everything to me, and I belonged to her.

I could hear Delilah over the sounds I was making as she thrust a little faster and pushed as deep as she could go. The thought that she was getting off on this as much as I was sent pleasure coursing through me more than even the act of getting fucked. It was a full-body experience, starting from my head and reaching my toes, culminating in my core and around my girlcock. I reached down between the pillows, ready to start touching myself, when there was a hard, quick slap to my rear. I howled with the suddenness of the pain as Delilah reached out and grabbed my long hair and pulled my head up hard.

"Did I say you could touch yourself?" The words were rhetorical, but I managed to shake my head anyway. She let go of my hair and I flopped back down to the bed. "You'll come when I tell you to come. Understand, pet?"

"Yes, Mistress!" I cried out. I pulled my hands away and raised them above my head in an attempt to avoid temptation.

"That's right, pet. Feel how deep I am inside you. I can feel you getting looser every time I thrust my cock deep into your tight little hole." Delilah grunted as she bottomed out, and I couldn't help the moan that dropped from my mouth. Even without direct physical stimulation, I could feel my girlcock leaking onto the pillows, and I groaned and ached to be touched down there.

"Does my pet need to come? I can feel how you're clenching

around me every time I thrust. I love seeing you like this. Pressed face-first into your bed, nothing but a hungry hole wanting to be filled."

The waves of pleasure washed over me, cresting and falling away over and over again until I was rocking back and forth, trying to take her deeper.

"Come for me, pet," she said, her own voice breathy with need. "Be a good girl and scream my name while you come for me."

It was as if her permission was what I needed to push me over the edge. The wave finally gave that final push and tumbled forward as I screamed Delilah's name into the air around us. My girlcock leaked everything it had in it out onto the bed, soaking the sheets and pillows beneath me, as my Mistress echoed my cry. The sound of her getting off to this only intensified the orgasm, and I cried out again.

"M-Mistress! Delilah! Oh fuck!"

With one final thrust she all but collapsed on top of me, her body covering my back and pressing me to the bed. We lay there for a long moment, connected by skin and by a silicone dildo buried deep in my ass. I felt her breath on my back, felt her body moving up and down as she breathed in and out. Sweat dripped off both of us, like a sweet caress that ran in rivulets down my body.

"What a good pet." Delilah's words were barely audible over the heavy beating of my heart. "I loved hearing my name come off your lips."

"I...I live to please, Mistress," I managed to say, brain fuzzy from everything. There was nothing going on up there, only a pleasant, numb feeling that filled me from head to toe. It was like nothing I'd experienced before.

I never wanted the feeling to end.

CHAPTER NINE

I don't know how long it was that we lay there together, basking in each other and the post-orgasm glow. Slowly, Delilah pushed herself off me, and I felt the dildo still inside me adjust as she moved. I let out little gasps of moans, already feeling like I could almost go again despite the world-shattering orgasms we'd shared.

"I'm going to pull out of you now," Delilah said, and I managed to nod. I felt her sliding out of my hole until finally the tip was gone and I felt empty once more. There was an aching in the general area, but it still felt so damned good I wanted more, even if I didn't think I could take it. "You handled that so well, pet. So well."

I felt unable to form words. I tried to push myself up so I could assist my Mistress in whatever she needed, but my arms felt like limp noodles, and I was barely able to get them under me, never mind push. My whole body felt limp, and I didn't want to move more than I absolutely needed to. My eyes fluttered closed for only a second, and when I opened them again, Delilah had disappeared and I could hear water running in the bathroom. I tried to get my body to move and managed to wiggle around a little bit, then forced myself to my feet.

"Easy, pet." Delilah's voice froze me in place. "Just relax. You don't have to get up." She had returned from the bathroom, the strap-on harness gone and one of my washcloths in her hand. She stepped up to me and pushed me back down onto the bed, bending me over again. "Just relax now, pet. You did so well for me tonight."

My heart beat for the praise that she whispered to me as she wiped my body down with the wet washcloth. The warmth of it gave me a soft feeling in my stomach, a need to be cuddled and held by this amazing woman. She cleaned me up in quick, smooth strokes and ran her other hand over my back as she kept telling me what a good girl I was. When she finished, she grabbed both my legs as if I weighed nothing and levered me fully onto the bed, letting me roll across the mattress as I let out a soft breath of comfort and warmth.

"How are you feeling, pet?" she asked softly, and I felt part of the bed dip as she sat down.

"So good," I whispered, my eyes only half open. Her hands caressed my skin, moving in comforting circles on my back. I wiggled closer to her and lifted my arm to wrap around her. She tensed up underneath it, like she wasn't expecting the touch, but relaxed quickly. I wondered why she'd frozen up, but as quickly as the thought came it disappeared into the fog that still wrapped its way around my brain.

"Do you need anything? Water? Food? To talk about what we did?"

I listened to her words and frowned, trying to get my brain to work properly to understand what she was asking. Aftercare, I realized. She was going through the steps of it, like she had at Vibe Check. I wondered if I could tell her that I wanted more, but as I opened my mouth to speak, a massive yawn caught me off guard and almost made me choke.

Delilah sat for a few minutes, letting me cuddle against her skin, but before long she extracted herself and stood. She turned around and softly patted my face. She said something that I couldn't make out, then disappeared back into the bathroom. Feeling a bit better, I managed to push myself up and toward the edge of the bed, where I let myself flop onto the floor on my knees as I examined the mess I'd made. The pillows had survived with a minimum of mess, but the edge of the bed was pretty soaked in what had come out of me. I grimaced and turned, staying on my knees as I fetched a towel from a basket of clean clothes that I hadn't gotten around to putting away yet. I stretched the towel over the offending spot and hoped that would be enough to invite Delilah back into my bed. I pulled the pillows off the bed and replaced them with an extra pair I'd had from when I shared a bed with someone else years ago.

I heard the toilet flush and Delilah returned. She paused right out of the doorway as if surprised to see me on my knees.

"Oh pet, you didn't have to get up," she said quickly as she came to stand beside me. "You should be resting. We went rather hard for your first time."

I quivered a little merely thinking about what we'd done, and the truth was I did feel a little exhausted, but I wasn't about to let her go. Not a damned chance.

I looked up into her eyes. "I want to please you," I told her, my voice far stronger than I'd expected.

Her eyes met mine with a look that I couldn't read. "Tonight was for you, pet. You wanted me, and you got me."

"I…I did. And I loved it. But I want to bring you pleasure too. I want to serve you. Service you."

She stared at me for a long moment, and I couldn't tell what she was thinking. Did I overstep? Push her too far? I had to remember that safewords went both ways. If this was too much for her, she could end things, and I wouldn't argue. I wouldn't blame her. But I wanted to reciprocate. To give as good as I got, in any way that I could.

I waited for the potential dismissal, the negative answer, even the use of a safeword. But it didn't come. Instead she held out her hands to me, palm up. I glanced from her hands to her face, trying to read the intent, but took her hands anyway. She helped me to my feet, then drew me in closer to her and wrapped her arms around me.

"Thank you," she said so softly I wasn't sure I was supposed to hear it. She pulled back slightly until we could look at each other. I resisted the urge to lower my gaze, despite wanting to feel her fingers again. She looked me up and down, then nodded sharply, like she'd come to a decision. She lifted her hand from me and snapped her fingers, then pointed downward immediately, and I fell to my knees in front of her. She smiled and moved around me, settling herself on the edge of the bed beside the towel that covered the mess I'd made. "Come here, pet," she said, patting her leg as if I truly were her pet and she wanted my attention.

I crawled over to her, only a few feet, and rested my head against her thigh. It was soft and warm, and I could almost feel myself ready to fall asleep pressed against her like this. But I had other plans. I looked up into Delilah's eyes, asking permission to do something that I felt I couldn't even articulate. And she hadn't given me permission to speak.

A hand grasped my hair once more, and Delilah's voice sounded in my ears. "Well? What are you waiting for?"

Courage. Confidence. Hell, I'd even take a little bit of daring with the position I was in. I hadn't done this in eight or nine years, and even back then I don't think it was my greatest skill. But I'd begged to please her. I wanted this. I hoped not to disappoint.

I let Delilah's hand guide me forward, taking a breath and breathing out against the bundle of nerves that sat above her wet and glistening pussy. I leaned forward and planted a soft kiss on the hood, trying to coax it forth, wanting to please her so badly.

"Easy, pet." Delilah's voice floated down to me. "You need some build-up before you go after the goal." I eased back a little and tried to think straight, the smell of her making me feel intoxicated. I pressed a kiss to her thigh, then mirrored it on the other side, then back again. I trailed kisses up both sides until I reached the apex and let myself draw an exploratory tongue up her labia.

Her taste was amazing, like rich fall air with a hint of the sweetness of a red apple. I lapped at her again, then a third time, desperate for more of the taste. Her hand in my hair gripped a little tighter, not enough to pull me away but enough that I knew she was there.

"That's it, pet. Get in there and taste me."

I needed no further urging. I thrust my tongue inside her, reaching as far as it could go before licking up and down as best I could. I felt movement near the top of my mouth, like a part of her was awakening from my ministrations. I lifted one of my hands tentatively, waiting for her to demand I continue with only my mouth. But when she didn't, I brought my fingers to play over the hood of her clitoris, applying pressure gently. I heard her gasp of pleasure, and I smiled against her, proud of knowing that I had made her feel that way, if only for a second.

"Do you like eating my pussy, pet?" she asked suddenly, the words sending a rush of pure pleasure through me like a vibrator against my girlcock. "Do you like pleasuring your Mistress?"

I hummed and moved my tongue move up and down inside her, taking in more of her taste. It had changed slightly, an added tartness to the taste like my favorite green apples coating my tongue.

"Take my clit into your mouth," Delilah said, her hand still resting in my hair. Her thighs twitched as I pulled my tongue out of her and moved up slightly, finding the engorged clitoris and taking it into my mouth as she'd requested. "Gently now, pet. Suck on it. Tease it. But I better not feel teeth."

I did my best to follow her directions. I focused on her clit, wrapping my lips around it and sucking gently. She moaned and a thrill ran through me. I wanted to be the one to make her make that sound again. I let loose the suction only long enough to lave my tongue over it, earning a quake from the thighs on either side of my head. She gasped again as I resumed suction and those thighs clamped around my head, dampening all sound.

"Use your fingers, pet." Delilah's voice was muffled by her thighs, but I did as she requested immediately. "I want you inside me."

I focused my mouth on her clit as my fingers pressed into her, collecting some of her arousal to make the entry as smooth as possible. I was glad I kept my nails cut short, otherwise I'd risk hurting her—something I had no wish to do. I slipped two fingers into her and explored deeper than my tongue could have reached, all the while coaxing more moans and gasps from my Mistress.

"Yes," Delilah hissed. "Yes, pet. Just like that. Keep sucking. Keep touching me."

I used the tip of my tongue across her clit and tried to split my focus between my mouth and my hand, but it was difficult. I slipped my fingers out more than once as I was thrusting, trying to bring her pleasure. Finally, buried to my knuckles inside her, I added a third finger that stretched her slightly, and she moaned louder than before.

"Don't stop!" The words were louder than anything I'd heard her say all night. "Don't you dare fucking stop, Sabrina."

I almost did stop, hearing my name drop from her lips, but instead I focused and doubled down on the intensity. I curled my fingers to massage against a slightly rough spot I'd found inside her as I used tongue and lips on her clit until she was nearly bucking off the bed and almost throwing me off her. Her thighs clamped tighter and tighter until I thought my head was going to pop off my body.

"Sabrina!" she cried again and grabbed my head in both hands, pressing me tight against her. Together we rode out her orgasm, my lungs straining to get a breath of fresh air and my arm cramping a little from the awkward angle of my fingers inside her. But it was worth it. It was worth every little pain, every fear, every bit of worry that I wouldn't be able to do this. It was all worth it to have her come undone by my hand—and mouth.

Slowly she relaxed, her thighs first, then the hands in my hair. I gasped in an ungainly breath as I moved back from her, my face covered in her sweet juices. They coated my face, and I couldn't help but smile as I looked up at her once more. Her eyes were closed, a slight smile on her lips, and she looked absolutely ravished, her hair a mess like she'd tangled her other hand in it while I serviced her. She opened her eyes, looking down to find me staring at her, trying to convey my devotion to her with nothing more than a look.

If this was going to be our only night together, I wanted her to know how much I loved it.

I licked at my lips, tasting her on me. One of her hands came down to pat me lightly on the cheek. "Very good, pet. Lacking some finesse, but you could be very good with some practice."

I resisted the urge to beg her to let me practice on her, then replied, "I wish to serve, Mistress."

"And you did. And you did." She giggled and flopped back onto the bed. Taking a chance, I climbed onto the bed next to her, wrapping my arm around her and pulling her in close. I knew I probably should have gotten up and cleaned myself up, but I wanted to be near her more. In her post-orgasm haze she seemed to accept my snuggling and pressed even closer to me, even deigning to lift my arm and plant a soft kiss on my hand. "You did so well tonight, Sabrina."

With her use of my name again I felt a hint of panic roll through me. Was I not her pet anymore? Was it over now that she'd had her fill of me? I pushed those thoughts away. I'd deal with them in the morning. Right now was for cuddling with my Mistress—even if she was simply Delilah from now on. Delilah was enough for me. I wondered how I could show her that.

I passed out with that thought in my head, curled up with Delilah.

When I woke it was still dark out, the only light filtering into the apartment coming from the streetlights outside—and even then, not much of that. I heard a rustling around and realized that my arms were empty. That wasn't overly surprising, as that's how I usually woke up, but tonight I'd had a guest. Where was Delilah?

"Mis..." I started to say aloud, then shook my head. "Delilah?" Her name filled the room, and the rustling sound stopped. "Are you okay?"

It was taking too long for my eyes to adjust to the darkness as her voice floated back to me in the near-pitch black. "Go back to sleep, Sabrina. Everything's fine."

I took a moment to focus on the sounds that had started up again, a sinking feeling in my stomach. "Are you...leaving?"

I could finally see a figure in the darkness, standing frozen near the foot of the bed. She looked half-dressed, holding what I assumed was her shirt in one hand. I couldn't tell what direction she was looking, but I was certain her eyes were on me.

"I should...I should go." She sounded as uncertain as I usually did.

"You don't have to," I said earnestly. "You're more than welcome to stay. I can sleep on the floor, if you like."

She let out a soft chuckle. "No, Sabrina. I'm not going to kick you out of your bed."

I reached for my phone where I normally kept it on the bedside table—but it wasn't there. I frowned, realizing it was probably in my pants on the floor somewhere. "What time is it?"

"A little before one. You didn't sleep long."

"Did you sleep?"

The longer the conversation went on, the more I could make out in the darkness. I didn't want her to leave, and I had the feeling that she didn't want to either. But something was telling her she should.

"Yeah, yeah, I had a bit." I saw her shake her head. "But I should go home. And you should get some sleep so you're not late for work in the morning."

It was my turn to shake my head. "Fuck work. Stay with me."

"Sabrina, I—"

"Please, Delilah." I hated how much pleading there was in my tone. There was no way she'd miss it. "Stay with me."

She was quiet and still for a very long moment in which all the possible outcomes flitted through my head. Would she laugh at me? Get mad at me? Would she hate me for asking or would she think I was pathetic for needing her so badly?

Or would she stay?

"Sabrina," she began. "I don't...I'm not really the *stay the night* type."

"Oh. Okay." I nodded slowly, trying to make it look like I understood. After all that we did last night, she didn't want to stay? "Did...did I do something wrong?"

"No, Sabrina, darling, you were perfect for me." I heard her draw in a long breath. "You really...you really want me to stay?"

"A thousand times, yes," I said without hesitation. That seemed to make her pause for another long moment, and I tried not to torture myself thinking about what I might have said wrong again.

"Okay," she said finally, but her voice wasn't the strong, sultry tone it usually was. This seemed almost...pensive. Worried. "I'll stay."

Chapter Ten

I woke once more to sunlight streaming through my balcony door and my usual alarm, muffled but still loud enough to wake the dead. I groaned and started to move to turn it off when I realized I wasn't alone. Delilah was still beside me, her breathing steady, her eyes closed. One arm was thrown over me carelessly, and it tightened slightly around my stomach as I tried to move.

Damn it. Now I really didn't want to move, but I wanted to shut the damned alarm off. I slowly managed to extricate myself from her arm and slipped off the bed to search the floor for the offending phone. I found it in my leggings, still on the floor where I'd left them last night, beside Delilah's sweater and the rest of my clothing. I stopped the alarm and turned back to see Delilah watching me with sleepy, hooded eyes, and I froze under her gaze.

"Sorry," I said quietly, glancing at my phone. It was a little after six thirty in the morning. "I get up at this time for work usually."

She shook her head stiffly, rolling her shoulders and stretching a little as she did. "Don't apologize, Sabrina."

I couldn't help frowning at the use of my name. Where was the term of endearment? Did she not want to call me *pet* anymore? Or did I screw something up last night?

I think she noticed, because her gaze sharpened a little and she had a slight frown of her own. "Are you okay?"

"Yes, Mis—" I cut myself off, but I could see her frown deepen when she realized what I was about to say. "Yes, I'm okay, Delilah."

Truth was, I wasn't okay. I was pining for her already, for her touch, for her handling of me the previous night. Even the rope that we'd played with, I was almost longing for again. I knew I was naturally submissive, but it seemed a little excessive that I couldn't stop thinking about what we'd done together and was craving more. I wanted her even more now than I had the night before.

She smiled at my words, though, her expression softening and then going somewhat blank. I couldn't tell what she was thinking, but I hoped it was nothing bad about our experience together. She slid to the edge of the bed and stood, in all her naked glory, and stretched out further. I couldn't help but stare at her as she did. How had I managed to hook such a gorgeous person? By spilling coffee on her, clearly. Had that really only been a couple of days ago?

"I should probably get going anyway," she said, her expression still hard to read. "I have an appointment later this morning, and I need to get back to shower and change."

"I—" I started to tell her that she could use my shower, have some of my clothes, but I stopped. I didn't want to embarrass myself further as the memory of her words yesterday filled my head. One night only was what she said she could give. And she had. Hell, she'd given me more than that. I'd had an afternoon, an evening, and a night with her. I couldn't ask her for more. "Can we…" I drifted off, trying to find the right words.

Delilah held up her hand to stop me even though I couldn't figure out what I wanted to say. "Don't, Sabrina. Please don't. We had a wonderful time. I will remember it, that's for sure. But you knew what this was going into it."

The words hurt, but I did my best not to let it show. I failed at that, but at least I tried. I shook my head. "I don't mean that. I wasn't going to beg for more."

She tilted her head as if curious now, her expression opening up a little more. "Oh? Then what were you going to say?"

I licked dry lips, trying to find the right words. "I still want to be friends. Plain and simple, my life is more interesting with you in it. I don't want to lose that. Even if we can't…I mean, I'll always be a willing demo bunny for you."

She actually smiled this time, the first I'd seen all morning, and she moved toward me and gave me a quick hug. "Thank you."

"For what?"

"Understanding."

I didn't understand. She'd given me the best night of my life. She'd introduced me to this range of new experiences that I'd only ever read and dreamed about. Submission. Being owned. And most of all, her wanting me as I am. She saw me for who I really was.

I wanted her so damned badly, but that's where the dream would end. There was no way I would ever seek to pressure or coerce her into doing something she didn't want to do. She had her hang-ups at the idea of a relationship or anything like it, and I had to respect it. I didn't have to like it, but I did respect it. And her.

But all of that went unsaid as I hugged her back, getting aroused again by pressing our naked bodies together. All too soon she let go, however, and I knew that there was little chance for fun this morning. I started cleaning up my clothes as she went searching for her own. The next time I turned to look at her, she already had her jeans on and was fastening her bra around her chest. I slipped on a pair of loose sweatpants and a T-shirt in the time it took her to finish getting dressed and make sure her toys had returned to the backpack. I kind of wanted to look at that monster dildo again, just for fun, but now wasn't the time.

"Thank you," I said softly as I turned to face her. "For everything."

"You're very welcome," she replied with a soft smile. She swung her backpack up to her shoulder and headed to the door when I noticed a small scrap of clothing that had been on the floor behind her.

"Mis—Delilah," I said quickly, going and picking up her underwear from last night. "You forgot—"

She came back over to me and pressed a kiss to my lips that shunted all thoughts of language out of my head. I stood there and let myself be devoured, unable to think, unable to move, her underwear dangling from my fingers.

"Keep them," she said as she leaned back, leaving me shell-shocked. "A souvenir. A reminder of your first time."

My mouth floundered like a fish on dry land as I tried to find words, and she gave me a sly smile like she knew exactly the effect she had on me. She was headed out the door and gone. The apartment door shut with a heavy thud, and I found myself on the floor on my knees, doing my best not to cry.

Fuck. I had it bad for her. And who could blame me? Eight years since my last sexual encounter, and that was when I was still pretending to be a man. My first time being fucked as my true self, to be affirmed for who and what I am. I loved every moment of it, and it was all connected to Delilah. She'd given me this gift that I could never properly thank her for, then just walked out of my apartment like...like...

"Like I'm not enough," I whispered to the silent air around me. *No. I am enough.* We had an understanding. She'd told me it could only be one night. It wasn't personal. I was the one who had to go and develop a crush on her.

This wasn't merely a crush. Not after what we'd shared. I was falling for her, and so quickly it was almost frightening. I'd never had this reaction to either of my exes, but Delilah was bringing something out of me that made me want more. It was not a simple crush, but I couldn't let myself think of it as more than that. The moment I did, I wouldn't be able to handle only having the one night with her. I had to remember what this was, for both of us. A good night. A fun time. An introduction to a lifestyle for me, one that I found myself craving now.

I let out a giggle that helped hold back the tears. She'd ruined me for other women, at least that's how it felt. How was I ever supposed to be with someone else if they didn't fuck me like Delilah had, being so kind and caring while at the same time tearing into me and using me for her own pleasure as much as she granted me my own?

I looked down at the underwear still in my hand. It was a simple pair of black boy shorts, similar to the harness she'd used. I wondered how many other women had pairs of Delilah's underwear, souvenirs of their nights together. I didn't care about the number, but I could certainly use some support in trying to make sure I didn't let her rejection destroy me. Not like before, when I lost everything.

But was it a rejection? Not exactly. We both went into it knowing that it was only for the night. Yes, I wanted more, but that was a me problem. She told me exactly what I could expect. I had to be okay with that.

I wiped at my eyes, ineffectively irritating them over getting rid of the chance of tears falling. I don't even know why I did it. I sniffled, allowing myself a single moment of feeling sorry for myself, before I stood up and placed Delilah's boy shorts on my dresser. I didn't know what else to do with them, to be sure. But for now, they were up there, and I could ignore them while I got ready for work.

I caught a glimpse of myself in the bathroom mirror and grimaced. My hair was a rat's nest, my face was a mess with the remnants of Delilah's orgasm still around my mouth and nose, and what little makeup I'd worn to the rope class was mostly worn off with small streaks and bits of it still on my face. I ran the shower hotter than normal and used the pain of it to distract from my thoughts of Delilah and how much I wanted to beg her to take me again.

I scrubbed my face extra hard until I started to feel clean again. I went through the usual routine, taking care around my ass when I went to wash it. It was sore from last night—understandably, I supposed. Good thing I was on my feet for most of the day. I didn't know if I'd be able to sit down for an extended period comfortably. Every time my brain tried to drift back to thinking about Delilah, I forced it to think about something else: the bookstore, new books coming in, a video game I hadn't picked up to play yet. Whatever I could think of.

Out of the shower, I dressed in clothes a little more comfortable than what I normally wore to the bookstore. Soft, easy leggings were paired with a T-shirt when I stopped, looking at the floor by the bed. Delilah's sweater was still there. We'd forgotten it this morning.

I knew it was a bad idea, but I slipped the sweater on over my T-shirt and breathed in deeply the scent of her, now a slowly fading memory. I closed my eyes for a moment, remembering, before I sighed and started to take the sweater off again. I had my hands on the hem when I stopped. I wanted to wear it. I wanted to keep it on. If I ran into Delilah I'd give it back, no problem. Until then, well, it was soft and smelled like her.

Oh, this was a bad idea.

But I ignored the part of my brain that said that, and I went to grab my phone and my purse. I was ready to go in record time, surprised that I was running early after everything that morning, when I realized I'd missed eating breakfast. Well, I wasn't hungry anyway. I'd have a larger lunch, maybe. Still, to be on the safe side, I threw a granola bar into my purse to bring with me. Lastly, I took my morning medications—I didn't want to forget those and let my levels get all out of whack.

That thought reminded me of my goal, and the reason why I couldn't let myself pine over Delilah. I had things to do, money to make, and surgeries to pay for. That was the goal, and I was going to focus on that instead of on the golden-eyed beauty who rocked my fucking world for a night.

I found myself heading to the door almost an hour before I normally left for work. I couldn't be in the apartment anymore. I was trying hard not to think about Delilah, despite having her scent on me from her sweater. I shook my head and put in a pair of headphones. And then I turned up the volume on the orchestral video game music playlist that I'd carefully curated until I couldn't hear anything else around me. I wanted to drown out the thoughts in my head—that's how I was going to cope for now.

I stopped off at the coffee shop down the street from Oracle Books, the same one I'd stopped at on Tuesday morning. I got the same drink as I had that morning, this time not racing the clock to get to work on time. Hell, I was almost an hour early and even had time to pick up a donut from the coffee shop and put it in my purse for later.

This morning I did not run into a beautiful dominant woman outside the bookstore, nor spill my coffee on anyone. A step in the right direction, I supposed. If I had another meet-cute like that, I'd be wondering what kind of author would use the same trope in a story more than once. Then I reminded myself that I didn't live in a damned novel and trudged my way to the bookstore, unlocking the door and letting myself in. I locked the door behind me, stashed my purse behind the counter, then went around and started dealing with making the store spotless for when I opened. I kept my headphones in and enjoyed my music as I cleaned the shelves, replaced books, organized, and made the place as clean as I could. I worked right through until it was time to unlock the doors, my phone blaring another alarm in my ears.

Cori was the first person to come into the store, a half hour after I opened, as always. I'd finished my coffee and was about to take a bite of the vanilla icing sprinkle donut to cheer myself up when she came through the door. She gave the place a once-over, then looked at me curiously.

"I know you're good at your job," she began, "but the place looks really good this morning. Did you come in early or something?"

I shrugged. "I had time to kill."

She frowned, and I took the time to eat my donut as she tried to think of what to say next. "Nice sweater. I don't think I've seen it before."

"It's, um, it's new," I said, feeling the heat rising to my cheeks. Stupid words. Stupid blushing.

"It doesn't look new. Unless you picked it up at a second-hand store, which is totally cool, by the way, I don't judge."

"I mean, it's not new, new. It's been in my closet a while—I just haven't worn it in forever." Why was I lying to her? Why couldn't I say that it belonged to Delilah? Was I really being that secretive? We usually told each other everything. I lived vicariously through her and vice versa. I didn't like to keep things from her. She was my best friend, after all.

How sad was that? Best friends with my boss? Ugh.

Cori didn't ask how my night was and didn't ask about the rope class I'd told her I'd agreed to help with. In fact, she seemed to avoid any mention of Delilah at all. Not that I wasn't grateful. I was trying hard not to think about Delilah myself.

With Cori there, I put my focus on the store, putting together a mock-up for a display we wanted to put up for the weekend. It was a quiet Thursday morning, but I tried to fill my time with something to do to keep my mind from wandering to places I didn't want it to go. In the early afternoon when the mail arrived—of course mixed up with next door's—I hesitated. Cori seemed to understand without me having to say anything, and she offered to take the mail over. But I didn't want to seem like I was avoiding Delilah. I'd been honest with her when I said I wanted to at least be friends, even if we couldn't be more.

"Okay, something's going on with you," Cori said as I tried to wrestle the mail from her iron grasp. "You're a great worker and wonderful company, but today you've been acting like a woman possessed with cleaning and working and getting shit done. What's going on?"

"Nothing," I said. "I need to focus on working right now, you know? I have my goals, and I want to reach them."

"I'm not firing you any time soon, so you don't have to go all mega maid on the store."

"I'm…" I let out a long sigh. I was going to tell her sooner or later, might as well be sooner. "I need to get my mind off something."

"Something, or *someone*?"

"Someone, all right? Happy now?"

She shook her head. "No. I want you to be happy, and all I see is you hurting. What's going on?"

I let go of the mail and ran my hand across my face. As much as I didn't want to think about it, maybe it would be better to put it out there. Air it out, get it out of my system.

"Delilah and I…" I began. "We…we slept together last night."

Cori pumped her fist and let out a whoop that filled the store, and I hissed at her to keep it down, despite there being no customers. "I knew it! I knew you two were gonna get together. I mean, who calls another person *pet* and then doesn't get with them?"

I held up a hand to stop her from talking over me. "Yes, we had a good night. A really, really good night. But that's all it was. One night."

"What do you mean?"

"One night only," I said. "No encores, no repeats. That's what Delilah wanted."

Cori looked at me skeptically. "But that's not what you want. You're not a one-night kind of woman, why would you agree to that?"

"Because it's what she wanted, and I wanted her." I shrugged, then realized how I'd said that and hated myself for sounding so damned crass. "I mean, I'm attracted to her, okay? Clearly. I want a relationship or something, you know, however that works these days, it's not like I have experience. But she doesn't want a relationship, and I am okay with that. I need to be okay with that."

"But if you're trying so hard not to think of her, you aren't okay with that."

"Obviously! I mean, she fucked me last night and it was amazing and affirming and wonderful, and I want more from her, but that's not an option. What am I supposed to do? Beg her to go out with me? I'm not that pathetic, especially when it's something she doesn't want."

Cori was quiet for a long moment, a thoughtful look on her face. That wasn't a look I saw often. She tended to run her mouth quicker than her brain could catch up. "So, if you're trying not to think about her, then why take the mail over?"

"Because I can't let the idea of seeing her stop me from living my life. I've been taking the mail over to Vibe Check almost every day for the past few weeks. If she's there, I'll say hi. Be friendly. But I won't know if I can do that if I don't try."

She gave me a strange look. "You're a lot stronger than you give yourself credit for. You know that, don't you?"

I scoffed. "I'm just trying to get through my life. I picked hard mode for some reason, and it's not always been kind to me." I shook my head. "Now, are you going to let me take the mail and go for lunch, or do you really want to go first, and I'll go later?"

She handed me the mail without argument. "Don't do anything stupid."

"I won't," I promised, and headed out the door.

CHAPTER ELEVEN

Vibe Check was busier today than I usually got a chance to see it during the afternoon. There were at least half a dozen customers inside, perusing the shelves and chattering in their small groups as I moved toward the back of the store. Lexie was currently ringing up some items for two young women. I ended up near the bondage gear as usual while I waited for Lexie to finish up. I looked for the puppy ball gag harness that I liked, but its hook was noticeably empty. I felt sad that it wasn't still here. I knew that Lexie would probably order one in for me if I asked nicely, but there had been something comforting about getting to look at it every time I came in that made me feel...good.

Lexie finished up with the current customers, then held up a hand to me as if telling me to wait as another approached the desk. I could be patient, despite the beating of my heart telling me that if Delilah came through that door to the back room, I wasn't going to be okay. But she didn't. The door remained shut.

There was a second staff member wandering the store. It was the same woman from last night, and she looked my way and smiled. I fought not to let the embarrassment show on my face, wondering if it was an open secret now that Delilah and I had been together. I tried to push that thought away but failed abysmally.

"Fuck." The word escaped with a long sigh of breath. I shook my head slowly. I wasn't going to let myself fear like that. I had to be stronger. I wasn't going to keep pining over someone who didn't want me.

Finally, Lexie was free at the counter, and I headed over, offering her the mail I was still clutching in my hand. Lexie glanced around the store and found her co-worker. She gestured to the counter and stepped out from behind it as the other woman hurried forward and took her spot.

"Don't often see two people here during the day," I commented.

"She's relatively new, and I wanted her to have a daytime shift. A good day for it too."

"Sure looks like it. You seem busy enough to warrant two people."

She looked around the store, still with a handful of people browsing.

"You're not wrong." She turned back to me and gestured, moving our conversation near the door that led to the back. "I have a question for you."

That was surprising. "Go ahead," I said warily, wondering if she knew about last night.

"Have you seen Delilah since last night?"

I tried my best not to flinch but failed. "She...er...she stayed with me the night."

"Okay, so you saw her this morning?"

"She left around seven. Said she had an appointment or something."

"And you haven't seen her since?"

"No, why?"

Lexie's brows furrows. "She cancelled her class for this evening. Sent me an email about it and posted on the group chat. No one's heard from her since."

I opened my mouth a few times but wasn't sure what to say. What could I say? Did she think I had something to do with Delilah going off the grid?

"I didn't—"

"I know you didn't. I'm not blaming you for anything, dear." She shook her head. "It's that she schedules these classes whenever she's in town, and it isn't often she misses one without good reason. And she didn't give a reason."

"In town? What do you mean?"

"She didn't tell you?"

"Tell me what?"

Lexie looked almost sad, like she didn't want to be the bearer of bad news. "Delilah doesn't live here, Sabrina. She lives out in Toronto, works for her parents there. She's only in town for a few weeks every year."

The news shouldn't have hit me as hard as it did. I refused to let this break me, though. I thought maybe we'd started something with an expiry date. But nothing was being started. Because she didn't want me like that. But hearing Lexie's words felt like someone had kicked me in the stomach. She never intended to stick around.

"I'll, um, I'll keep an eye out for her," I said. I felt my heart breaking soundly into a dozen pieces. "I'm sure she's just…worn out or something."

"Yeah," Lexie replied, though she didn't sound like she believe it. "Sure, something like that. Thanks, Sabrina."

I left the shop as quickly as I could, my breathing coming harder and harder as I power-walked my way past the bookstore and further down the street.

What the hell was wrong with me? I had about finished deciding that I wasn't going to pine over this woman. I had my own shit to deal with. So what if she wasn't in town for long? It didn't affect me. She didn't want anything more than a little fun with me, and that's what we had. It was over now.

So why the hell did it hurt so much?

"Nope. Nope not caring about it," I said to myself as I headed as far away from the bookstore and Vibe Check as I could to find somewhere to eat. Sure, it was a cheap fast-food place, but the burger was good, and the fries were better, and I drowned my sorrow in sugar-free cola. And I worked on my poker face to show Cori when I returned to the bookstore.

Maybe I'd perfected it, or she decided to take pity on me, but when I returned, Cori didn't ask a million questions. She didn't pry about Delilah and what we did last night or how I felt. It might have helped that we had a rush of customers that kept us busy from about the time I got back to when my shift ended. No space to talk about the racy stuff when a five-year-old is clamoring for the latest *Good Egg* book.

I returned to my apartment to rest, because I had a shift at the lounge later. What time I had between jobs was spent mostly on my bed. I lay curled up in Delilah's sweater, fighting a losing war against remembering how she'd played my body like an instrument just last night. I wondered where she was, what she was doing, and if I was going to see her tonight. I doffed the sweater but kept it nearby as I changed into a tighter pair of leggings and a short black dress with cap sleeves that showed off my cleavage. I put the sweater back on before I left.

I was not looking forward to potentially running into Delilah, but if I did I was going to show her that I hadn't fallen apart without her.

The bartender gave me a smile as I slipped past a small crowd that was lingering near the entrance. Tables were a hot commodity tonight, it seemed, with everyone and their friend trying to find somewhere to sit and enjoy their drinks and company. I made it to the back without being accosted which, sad to say, was surprising, and headed for the office.

Tiffani glanced up from some paperwork and took a moment to focus on me, then gave me a small smile.

"Good evening," she said. "How was your day off?"

"Very enjoyable, thank you," I said before I had a chance to think about my answer. At least I didn't blurt out that I'd had sex with her sister. That might've been awkward.

"I'm going to have you waitressing tonight, if that's okay. I've got the bar covered, and I have a couple others helping you on the floor. It's busier than I anticipated, so I want you to clean up as you go as much as you can, to make room at the tables."

"No problem." I knew my job.

"We've got a band coming in tomorrow for some live music, so we'll have the tables moved for the dance floor after we close tonight." She looked down at a sheet in front of her. "But I don't know if you need to worry about that too much, since you're off before we shut down for the night. Just keep it in mind."

"Got it."

"That's about it for tonight," she mused, then looked up at me with a frown. "I don't know why I'm asking you this, but you might have an answer for me: Have you seen Delilah?"

I froze. Why was everyone asking me that today? I felt the heat creeping up my face and looked down at the floor for a second, trying to school my reaction to the unexpected question.

"Not since this morning."

Tiffani's gaze sharpened. "When this morning?"

"She left my place around seven." It was the truth. There was no point in lying.

"She stayed the night with you?"

"We were…together last night. Yes, she stayed."

Tiffani made a surprised sound, her eyes widening. "She doesn't usually do that with her…um…"

"Her toys?" I offered, probably less delicately than I should've. "Why are you asking about Delilah?"

"She was supposed to come in and look over the books with me this afternoon," she replied, giving me an appraising look like she hadn't really seen me before. "Are you okay? I know she can be a lot sometimes."

"I'm here and I'm ready to do my job," I said with as much confidence as I could muster. Would I rather be at home curled up in this sweater remembering what we'd done? Sure, but I had a job to do. And money to make.

"Good, then get that sweater off and get out there." She glanced back down at her paperwork. "And be careful out there. If you need anything, my door is open."

I slipped into the small locker room beside the office and hung up the sweater and my purse. I took a deep breath, then another, and tried to put Delilah's disappearance out of my head. That was two places where she'd been expected that she'd ghosted today. I hadn't seen or heard from her at all either, not since that morning. I wondered what she was doing.

The upside to the lounge being busy meant that time flew by. I cleaned tables as I went and replaced the rag on my short apron throughout the night as needed. My feet were sore by midnight, and I was all but exhausted, but it'd been a good night. The other servers were good at their job and fun to work with. I grabbed a handful of bottles from one of the tables and carried them to the recycle bin at one end of the bar, then dumped them in.

I was wiping my hands clean at the small sink at the back of the bar when I heard someone clear their throat. My heart leapt as I turned around, foolishly hoping to see Delilah, but it was only another impatient customer, demanding he be served while both bartenders were busy. I smiled at him and got him his beer anyway, then moved out from behind the bar and back onto the floor.

By the time one o'clock came around, I was dead on my feet, but I felt pretty good about myself. I hadn't let myself fall apart. I'd remembered my focus, and it wasn't Delilah. Things were going back to normal, like I hadn't met her at all.

For some reason, that thought didn't cheer me up as much as I wanted it to.

Tiffani caught up with me as I exited the locker room, ready to head for the bus stop nearby. She gave me a once-over, then smiled. "You're really doing okay, aren't you?"

I shrugged, somehow knowing exactly what she was talking about. "I respect her decision. I may not entirely like it, but I'm not going to push her boundaries. I wouldn't be able to live with myself if I did that."

"I'm glad. I'm also glad you're not falling apart over her. She has enough people who do that already."

"I need to go. I can't miss this bus."

"Yeah, get out of here." She moved out of my way, and I started to walk past her. "But hey. If you hear from Delilah, let me know, will you?"

"Yeah, of course." I paused for a moment, curiosity getting the better of me. "Does she do this often? Disappear, I mean."

"What do you mean?"

"Well, Lexie at Vibe Check said she was supposed to be in today too but never showed. Like she ghosted everyone."

Tiffani frowned. "No. No, this doesn't happen. I don't know what's going on."

"I hope she's okay."

"Me too." She shook her head. "But you should go. I'll see you tomorrow night?"

"As always." I headed for the lounge proper and exited into the night. As I rode a practically empty bus home, my mind of course returned to Delilah. What was going on with her? Why had she up and disappeared?

Worse, was it something I did?

CHAPTER TWELVE

Friday morning came and went with little fanfare. I took my lunch early, before the mail arrived, because I got hungry. I was not going out of my way to avoid running into Delilah. At least, that's what I told myself.

By the time I returned from lunch, the store was hopping. At least four people were in line at the counter, Cori working hard to ring them up, while another half dozen or more were perusing the shelves. I pushed away the thoughts I was still having about Delilah and got to work. I offered aid where I could and chatted to the customers waiting in line to make sure no one had a bad time at the store. I was able to find a few of them more books to read, or at least recommendations for what they might read next, and I was especially happy to sell a copy of *The Last Caspian* to a young woman who had shyly admitted to looking for sapphic romance. I left her with a small list of other books to check out. She left me with a smile and a promise to check out the books, and I felt really good about my job—a nice change of pace to how I'd been feeling since yesterday morning.

Together Cori and I cleared the store of customers. When the rush had died down, Cori leaned against the counter, muttering something to herself, as I moved around and replaced books that had been bought or left off the shelves for whatever reason. It didn't take long to clean up, thanks to the work we put in when we weren't busy, but Cori seemed oddly irate.

"You okay there?" I asked her.

She shook her head. "I don't know what it is about Fridays. Maybe 'cause it's the last day of the week or something, but I'm exhausted. Don't you feel that way? Doing two jobs and all?"

I shrugged. "I guess so, but I don't really think about it. My work is a means to an end, so I bear it."

"I still don't know how you manage to do it."

"I have a goal. I have priorities, and two jobs will let me reach that goal faster than only one. Never mind we live in a capitalist dystopia as it is, so having as much money as possible is never a bad thing."

She snorted. "Yeah, yeah, I can see that. I just get tired. I must be getting old."

"You? Old? Never."

She chucked my shoulder lightly with her fist. "Flatterer."

"I call it like I see it."

"Yeah?" She gave me a shit-eating grin, and somehow, I knew what was coming. "So, what did you call Delilah?"

Cori wanted to play games? Fine. I could play games too.

"Mistress."

Cori's mouth dropped open and I barked out a loud laugh. I was so glad there was no one else in the store to hear it. It wasn't very ladylike.

"You brat," she exclaimed, slapping my arm again, this time a little harder.

"You asked."

"I meant because you were so sure you weren't going to get with her when we talked the last couple days! You brat!"

I let the laughter drift out of me, enjoying the moment of levity after feeling so tense for the last day or two.

"What can I say? It happened and it was wonderful."

"You seem happier about it than yesterday."

"I've had time to sit with it. I'm okay."

"That's good to hear."

"But I don't think I'm much of a one-night person," I told her, wanting to be honest. "I think if I do find someone, sometime, I want to be with them more than just once. Does that make any sense? I feel like I'm not making sense."

"I get what you're trying to say. And it's okay. Not everyone is made for one-night stands. That's nothing to be ashamed of." She gave me another smile. "But it was worth it, wasn't it?"

I couldn't keep my face from breaking out into a wide smile, even showing my teeth. "So fucking worth it."

We shared smiles for a long moment before Cori took a step

forward and wrapped her arms around me in a soft hug. We parted a second later and I stared at her.

"What was that for?"

"Because I think it's been about seven years since I saw you smile like that."

I stuck out my tongue at her, but that didn't do anything to stop a pleased sound from coming out of my throat.

"All right," she said, clapping her hands. "It looks like things have calmed down here, so I'm going to go get some lunch. Will you be good by yourself?"

I ran my hands over my cheeks, ineffectively trying to hide the awkwardness that made me blush. "I'm good. You go."

She stepped out from behind the counter and headed for the door. "I'm just going to grab food and come back in case it gets busy again, okay? I won't be long."

I nodded, not pointing out that she deserved her full break as much as anyone did, but instead grateful for the potential help, or at least company. She left and I took my position behind the counter, pulling out yet another book to read as I waited for something interesting to happen. I didn't have to wait long.

It was maybe five, ten minutes after Cori left that the door opened once again. I looked up from my book and watched as a couple of people filed in.

"Good afternoon," I called out. "Welcome to Oracle Books."

My greeting seemed to go unheard by the first two young women, who moved together immediately into the sci-fi/fantasy section and started talking in low, hushed tones while showing each other books from the shelf. The third person was Lexie, and I watched her walk toward the counter, unable to keep the surprise from my face.

"Hey, Lexie," I said. "Haven't seen you out of the store for a while. What brings you here?"

She shook her head slowly. "Nothing good. I'm wondering if you've seen Delilah since she left your place."

"No, I haven't," I replied, then added, "But her sister is looking for her too."

"Tiffani?" Lexie asked and I nodded. "Good. It's not just me, then."

"What's going on?"

"That's what I would like to know. She cancelled her class this afternoon with a poorly written message to me at like five in the morning. I don't know what's going on with her, but I've never seen her act like this."

"Maybe she went back to Toronto? I mean, she was only visiting, wasn't she?"

"Yes," Lexie said. "But I don't think that she did that without telling me, or her sister. Especially if she had a class. You've probably noticed that she takes what she does seriously. She wouldn't cancel everything at the drop of a hat."

I frowned. I looked away from Lexie at the other women who were perusing the books. I watched them for a moment, trying to figure out what I wanted to say.

"I hope it wasn't anything I did."

"Sabrina," Lexie said, her voice sharp. "You can't think like that. Delilah can make her own choices, her own decisions. Unless you've kidnapped her, you are not responsible for what she's chosen to do."

I looked back at Lexie, hoping to convey something that told her I was listening, but I was having troubles believing her. There were two people close to Delilah who kept coming to me to figure out where she went or what she'd been doing. Whatever she was going through, I couldn't shake the feeling that it had something to do with me. I tried to think about what I might've done that would have triggered behaviour like this, but I couldn't think of anything. And honestly, I thought, was it really my fault? Or was I blaming myself because that's what I was used to doing?

Delilah was a grown-ass adult. I knew better than most that grown-ass adults didn't always make the smartest decisions, but something about Delilah suddenly being lumped in with those seemed wrong. But even if it did stem from me, there was little I could do about it unless she reached out. I wanted to see her again, wanted to talk to her again, even if she was going to yell at me for whatever had gone wrong that made her hide away from her friends for whatever reason.

Or maybe I was overthinking this entirely and she had gone back to Toronto to be with her parents. I wondered what she did for them, what kind of company they ran. The way Lexie talked about it, they sounded like important people in whatever circles they ran in. I wondered if that was the reason for Delilah disappearing like she had. I wasn't the only one in the world who didn't have a close relationship with her parents, but at least I didn't work or live with my mom.

Either way, I was trying hard not to let myself fall into the trap of blaming myself for whatever was happening with her. I didn't ask her to disappear and eschew her responsibilities.

Lexie sighed as she turned away from me. "If you do see her, let me know? I kind of want to yell at her a little."

"At this point, so do I," I said.

"Good. We can go up one side of her and down the other."

We both chuckled at that as the other women who had come in approached the counter with their purchases. Lexie nodded to them, then to me. "Thanks, Sabrina."

I gave her a bit of a wave as she headed for the door, and I started ringing up books. My mind was definitely still on Delilah, though. Always on Delilah.

Wherever she was, whatever was going on with her, I hoped she was okay.

CHAPTER THIRTEEN

Friday night was usually the lounge's busiest night, and tonight was no different. I was on the floor with several other servers, while Tiffani was behind the bar with another bartender. They were slinging drinks as quickly as they could. I did my best to avoid conversations with anyone else, focusing on my work and getting as much for tips as I could manage from the ever-growing crowd. It was hard to hear over the live music, but the singer—a young woman named Beth McCarthy—was definitely a big hit. There were a few times I found myself stopping and singing along with the music, recognizing a song or two from Delilah's car when she drove me home the other night. I let out a little chuckle about that when I realized it, then got back to work.

By the time one in the morning rolled around, there had been no word, no sign of Delilah still, and Tiffani was beyond worried. I couldn't say if she blamed me for something, but she kept shooting me glances like I might know more than I let on. But I didn't. I had no idea what was going on.

That didn't stop the thoughts of Delilah keeping me awake through the night. What little sleep I got was short and choppy, and even though I didn't have to work at the bookstore that morning, I found myself waking up early, as though I did.

I rubbed my hands over my face, trying to either beg myself to fall back to sleep or wipe the dregs of tiredness from my eyes. I wasn't sure which way I was leaning. But it seemed like being awake was the direction I was headed, and I rolled off the bed to head to the tiny bathroom. I did my business, then hopped in the shower, making it cool enough not to overheat. I liked colder showers, personally. And with Delilah still on my mind, that wasn't a bad thing.

Though now my thoughts were more worrisome than the sexy-time memories that I enjoyed. What the hell was going on with her that she needed all her friends to come to me to check on her? And where the hell was she?

I tried to put it out of my mind. Yet with each passing moment I was worrying more and more. I'd call her, but I didn't even have her phone number. And she'd been ignoring everyone else, so why did I think she'd answer my call?

"If she wanted to talk to me, she'd find a way," I told myself softly. She found me at my work the other day, and she knew where I lived. If I could do something to help and she reached out, I'd be there with bells on, but until then I had no idea what I could do.

So, I spent my time off at home, booting up my PlayStation and flipping through games for far too long, unable to keep my interest on anything in particular. It was annoying, but there was a part of me that wanted to go out. Wanted to find something to do outside my tiny apartment. I didn't want to be there. Not alone. But what if she did come find me? What if she came looking for me to explain why she had gone off the grid?

"For fuck's sake, stop thinking of her," I chastised myself. But that didn't help. It only made me think of her more.

By the time I left for work at the lounge, my mind was firmly entrenched in Delilah territory. I could barely keep my mind off her. I walked into the Emerald Lounge and found myself wishing that Delilah would be in the office, her feet up on the desk like the first night we'd seen each other there. I wanted to ask her so many questions, I wanted to be there if she had a problem. I wanted to help this woman who had introduced me to a life that I never thought I could have.

I wanted another night with her, and another, and another. Those were dangerous thoughts.

But alas, Delilah did not greet me when I opened the office door. No one did. Which made sense. Tiffani was busy on the bar with another bartender, both of them knee deep in dealing with customers. I hit the locker room and dropped off my things, then headed out to the floor, flagging Tiffani down to see where she needed me.

I started bussing the few tables that needed cleaning, then started taking orders and bringing people their drinks. The crowd was rowdy tonight, louder than usual, though that might've been a symptom of my mood in even being there. The more I thought about Delilah and our night together, the more I didn't want to be working but instead tracking her down and indulging in another night.

It was nearing midnight, and I knew I wasn't doing too well at my job. There was too much going on in my head, and my heart wasn't in it. That didn't mean I wasn't doing my job, but I was maybe a little shorter with people than usual, or less attentive than I should have been. I could almost feel Tiffani's gaze across the bar several times, like she was watching me a little closer than the others. I could only guess what for, but either she noticed I was going through the motions, or she thought I knew more about Delilah than I was saying. And I wished I did.

I was about to leave the bar with a tray of drinks when I saw Tiffani's face drop as she glanced toward the door. I followed her gaze, interested in what had caused such a reaction from my boss while she was working.

Delilah was moving through the crowd of people near the bar, barely being touched as the patrons seemed to part before her. She looked amazing, and I almost lost my grip on my tray as I stared at her. She was wearing tight, leather-looking pants with a pair of boots that went up to her knees, giving her a height that let her tower over a good chunk of the crowd. She was wearing that candy apple red top that I'd first seen at Vibe Check the other day, the first time we played together. Her makeup was applied perfectly, heavier than I remembered seeing her in before, like she was trying to make an impression. And she certainly was making one. On me.

I expected her gaze to sweep the club, perhaps looking for her sister, perhaps an empty table, but it didn't. Instead, it fell on me, and only me, as she sauntered forward. It took Tiffani three calls of her name before she turned her eyes to her sister. Her wicked smile disappeared as I watched Tiffani nod toward the door to the back with a gesture that clearly said *we need to talk*. Oh, to be a fly on the wall for that conversation.

I managed not to spill the drinks on myself as I moved away from the bar and did my job, trying hard to put Delilah out of my mind. I couldn't help but think how hot she looked. And the way her gaze had fallen on me? I almost melted into a puddle then and there. I greeted a group of men who had taken one of the larger booths in my section, taking some drink orders and trying not to overthink why Delilah's attention had seemed to be solely on me until Tiffani drew it elsewhere.

I brought out their drinks, serving the table as they laughed and shouted at each other. They were celebrating something, though I couldn't seem to get a straight idea of what. They made it hard to even listen to the music our house DJ—a cute young woman named Aurora—was spinning. One of them came a little too close to me for comfort and I scooted away, stepping farther from him as I brought my tray between us like a shield. I moved away from the group the next second, trying to make it look like I'd done the movement on purpose and wasn't trying to keep a group of drunken business-boys away from me. I still needed the tips, after all.

I hovered by the door that led to the back, passing by it as much as I could, waiting for Delilah to reappear. I still did my job, but my attention was on that damned door so much that I had to tell myself to come to my senses and focus on what I was doing before I spilt something down someone's back. Even the bartender, after preparing a few drinks for my tray, was quick to tell me to pay better attention to what I was doing. I returned to the floor, focused on not pining after Delilah. That was my mistake.

I was passing by the table of business-boys, heading back to the bar, when something hard and firm smacked my ass. I jumped, letting out a gasp of surprise, and the tray fell from my hands, scattering several empty beer bottles and a couple glasses I had bussed onto the floor. I spun toward the asshole who had decided to touch me. He stood at least a head taller than me and didn't look sorry in the least. He laughed, his buddies laughed, and it took everything in me not to deck him in his cocky-looking mouth.

"C'mon, baby," he said. His voice gnawed on my nerves as I faced him. "Lighten up. You've got a great ass."

I gave him a smile that bared teeth. I purposefully deepened my voice, going lower than I had even used before I came out. "I've got a lot more than that, baby."

His face ran the gamut of emotions from surprise to horror to disgust, as his buddies laughed even louder, but this time at him. He snarled and raised a hand, his fist closed, like he was about to hit me. I braced myself for the attack, but the blow never fell.

"Back. The. Fuck. Off."

Delilah was there, seeming a little unsteady on her feet, but her eyes were boring into the man's skull like she could kill him with a look. She held his arm back in an iron grip, straining against him for a second as he tried to pull away from her.

"What the fuck, lady?" He gasped, looking like he was in pain. I saw Delilah's fingers digging into his wrist, her nails piercing skin.

"Get the fuck out of here. You and your friends are no longer welcome," she snarled.

"I was only going to teach this freak a lesson!" he shouted, well over the music, and the crowd of people who hadn't already noticed what was going on were clearly in on it now. I felt my face heat with shame, and I looked away, my hands clenching so hard my fingers started to ache.

Delilah pushed him back against the table, spilling their drinks all over and rousing a chorus of shouts from the other men.

"She's mine!" Her words came out more as a growl than anything else, but I heard them loud and clear. I froze in place, mind reeling. "Now get the fuck out of my club!"

At this point the bouncer, who normally blended in with the crowd well enough that he wasn't noticed, appeared at Delilah's side. With Tiffani, who showed up behind me, the two of them walked the men out of the club as the crowd continued to stare at me and Delilah. For her part, Delilah looked almost flustered but managed to turn to face me. She wobbled a little on her heels and I wondered what was going on with her. Then I noticed the smell.

The stench of whiskey drifted off her like she'd been bathing in the stuff. Had she been drinking nonstop since she got there? Or was she already inebriated when she came in? I shook my head, telling myself it wasn't my problem. And I forced myself to forget that she'd called me hers.

"I'll get this cleaned up," I said, not looking her in the eye. "I'm sorry to be trouble."

I expected something from her. Anger, maybe. Drunken yelling. Even a bit of caring. But instead she nodded and turned away, heading for an empty table that was along the far wall, where she sat and held her head in her hands, like she needed to get away from me. I didn't really blame her. There were plenty of times I wanted to get away from myself.

I picked up the tray and any intact bottles and glasses as Tiffani and the bouncer returned. The bouncer took up a position nearby, steering people away from the mess as I went to drop off the tray and grab a broom to finish sweeping up the pieces. Tiffani gave me a look like she wanted to talk to me, but instead she looked over at the booth where Delilah was sitting and went to join her.

I tried to put it from my mind and continued working, knowing that if I was going to make it through the night, I had to stay away from Delilah.

There was no other choice.

CHAPTER FOURTEEN

By the time I finished cleaning the mess, Tiffani had disappeared into the back once more, and I shrugged and got back to work. I didn't have much longer left of the night, and if Tiffani wasn't going to say anything to me, I figured I'd get back to it.

It wasn't until I went too close to Delilah's table that she flagged me down and my traitorous feet brought me to her right away.

"Whiskey," she said. "Neat. Bring the bottle."

I stared at her for a moment, not moving. "Don't you think you've had enough?"

"What are you trying to say?" Her eyes narrowed as they watched me, her voice still as cold as it was when she'd been protecting me from the young man.

"Nothing," I said, then left to get her drink. I didn't think she needed more whiskey, but what was I going to do? Technically she was my boss. I couldn't not do it. I went behind the bar and grabbed a glass and a bottle of the whiskey I knew she liked because it's what she drank before. A hand grabbed my arm and made me spin, almost losing my grip on the bottle. Tiffani stood there, holding on to me.

"What are you doing?"

"It's for Delilah."

"And you jumped at the chance to take it to her?"

I shrugged. "She's a paying customer and my boss at the same time. Am I not supposed to serve her?"

She took the bottle from me and poured about half a glass of whiskey. "Give her this. After that all she gets is water. Understood?"

I didn't want to get into a thing between the sisters. "And if she asks for something more?"

"Come get me. I have some work in the back, but I'll be done soon, and I'll take care of her. Whatever you do, don't let her leave here under her own power, understood?"

I nodded, then thought to ask, "Where has she been? Did she tell you?"

"That's nothing you need to worry about, Sabrina. Go take her the drink." She looked around the lounge, as if trying to decide something. "Then head home, if you want to. I know you're off soon anyway. After that altercation, you must be feeling a little out of it."

I shook my head this time. "No, I'm fine. I want to stay." Needed to stay was more like it. I needed the money. I needed the full shift. And mostly I needed to stay for Delilah.

"All right, but be careful, please."

"I will," I said, and she let me go, allowing me to collect the glass and take it to Delilah. I placed the glass in front of her and she stared at it for a long moment, then looked at me, anger flickering across her face.

"Where's the bottle?"

"Your sister wouldn't let me bring it."

"Since when do you listen to her over me?"

I frowned at her. "She's my boss as much as you are. Besides, you've already had too much."

"Who the hell are you to tell me I've had too much?" Delilah snapped and I flinched. This was hitting too close to home. Too close to what I grew up with.

"Nobody," I told her. "I'm nobody." I turned and walked away, refusing to spin back around despite hearing her call my name. What the hell was she playing at? I mean, I know I told her I wanted to stay friends, but I felt like this was pushing it. And what the hell was that growl with the guy? She'd really called me hers. Did she mean that? It had sounded like she did.

Fuck. I couldn't get it out of my head. The way she spoke to him. The way she said I was hers. I could barely pay attention to what I was doing. Her voice kept playing in my head over and over and over again.

She's mine!

I shook my head, returned to the bar, and stayed behind the counter for a moment. I closed my eyes and focused on my breathing. I was stronger than this. I know I'd been pining for her for the last two days, but even I was worth more than being treated like she was treating me. I was worth more than being yelled at like this.

I managed to ignore Delilah for the next fifteen minutes, but eventually I returned to check on her. She was still glaring daggers at anyone who approached, and her glass was empty. I took it away without a word.

"Another," she said through clenched teeth as I started to walk away. "Please," she added after the fact, like she thought that was going to help matters. I headed back to the bar and grabbed a taller glass, filling it almost to the brim with cool tap water. I took it to her table and set it in front of her. She stared at it like it offended her.

"Drink it." I said.

"This isn't what I asked for."

"It's all you're getting." I could do this. I could stand my ground with her.

I hoped.

She took a sip of water and grimaced. "Fuck that," she spat. "Get me a fucking whiskey."

"No."

She screwed up her face, and I swear I could almost see tears threatening to fall.

"Damn it, Sabrina! You're just like her!" She ignored the water and pushed herself out of the booth, barely catching herself to avoid falling on the floor. I took a step back, aware of how close we were now.

"What are you talking about?"

"Nothing!" she snapped. "Never mind. Just…just get out of my way." She reached into her jacket pocket, and I heard the jingle of keys. I froze, knowing there was no way I could let her get into a car in the state she was in now. She pulled them out and I recognized them as the same ones she'd used when she drove me home. She was focused on keeping her feet, and before I could think better of it, I reached out and plucked them out of her hand.

"No," I said, trying to keep my voice firm.

She glared at me. "Give me back my keys."

"You're in no condition to drive."

"Fuck off, give me my keys."

"That's really not going to happen here."

"Give me my keys, Sabrina."

I shook my head. "No." The word came out far more firmly than I was certainly feeling at the moment.

She took a step forward, then another, until she was well within my personal space. I put my hands behind my back, keeping the keys from her. She leaned forward, putting her lips near my ear as if she had a secret to share with me.

"I am your Mistress," she said, her voice reminiscent of how she had spoken to me the other night. "Give. Me. The. Keys."

What the actual fuck? Did she really think that bringing that up now would get her what she wanted? Sure, she was my Mistress for one night, but that's all she wanted. That's all she could give me. Now she was only a friend, and quickly losing that that title too.

"You were my Mistress," I hissed at her. "Now you're a spoiled bitch who can't get what she wants."

As much as I wanted her, pined for her, I wasn't about to let her treat me that way. Other people in my life had tried, and I wouldn't let them either. Why would Delilah be any different?

She tried to grab for the keys, but her movements were easily telegraphed and sloppy, nothing like the smooth allure that she usually exuded. I stepped away from her, then turned and headed for the bar. I looked back only once, but she didn't follow me. She'd sat back down in her booth and was staring after me.

I put the keys behind the bar, then filled another glass with water. I turned around and went to take it out to her but found her booth empty. I looked around, desperate to find her, to make sure she was okay. I caught sight of her through the crowd, heading sloppily to the exit. The crowd parted before her as she did, but this time it was less because of her confidence and swagger and more because she looked like shit, and no one wanted to touch her.

I set the water down on a table, ignoring the people sitting at it, and hurried after her. I didn't want her to get in trouble. I didn't want her to go and do something stupid either.

She was outside on the street, kind of swaying from side to side as she looked around. She looked more confused than anything, as if she were trying to figure out what to do but her brain wasn't firing on all cylinders.

"Delilah," I said as I moved up beside her. She immediately took a step back from me, anger flickering across her face.

"What do you want? Here to yell at me more? Call me pathetic? Make me feel like I'm nothing?"

I slowly shook my head, trying to figure out why she'd even think that of me at all. When had I ever done something like that?

"No, Delilah. Why would I do that?"

She shook her head, then looked like she was about to throw up from the movement.

"What do you want, Sabrina?"

"I want to help you."

"Then give me my keys back."

I reluctantly pulled my phone from the pocket of my little half-apron. "You know I can't do that. Even if I didn't know you, even if I didn't care, I still couldn't do that." I showed her the phone. "I'm going to call you an Uber. It can take you home."

She snorted. "I don't have a home here."

"Then to your hotel, or wherever."

"What the hell do you care?"

"Because I care about you! I'm tired of this attitude. I'm trying to fucking help you, Delilah."

She stared at me for a minute, like she was trying to understand what I was saying.

"I'm fine on my own."

"That's pretty clearly not true."

She turned away from me. "Leave me alone."

"I'm not going to do that." I fiddled with my phone, opening the app to order a ride. "Now, tell me where your hotel is."

"I don't want to go back there."

I faltered. She sounded so...hurt. Had I done that? Had I hurt her?

"Just...just stay right here," I told her. "Please, stay, okay? I'll be right back."

"With my keys?"

"No, not with your keys."

She let out a sigh. "Fine."

Hoping that she'd actually listen to me, I turned and ran back into the lounge, ignoring a stare from the bouncer as I did. I needed to grab my things, then get back to her. It was the best idea I had and the only way I could think of to take care of her.

I wanted to take care of her.

CHAPTER FIFTEEN

I grabbed my things from my locker, throwing on the sweater I'd borrowed from Delilah that I couldn't stop wearing. I slammed the locker shut and all but ran out of the room. I'd almost made it to back out into the lounge proper when someone else stepped into my path. I managed to stop and not run headfirst into Tiffani, who was blocking the door.

"Are you leaving?" she asked, eyeing me up and down.

I tried to avoid her suspicious gaze and failed. "Yeah. I need to get out of here."

"Hoping to catch an early bus?"

"With any luck. Or I can order a ride if I have to."

"Where's my sister?"

I shrugged. "I left her at the table. She wouldn't drink the water I gave her, yelled at me a few times, and I walked away."

She gave me a look like she didn't know whether or not to believe me. Why the hell wasn't I telling her the truth? I could tell her that Delilah was outside, looking for a way home. I couldn't remember the last time I had lied about something so much, first to Cori to avoid her third degree, now to Tiffani.

I wanted to help. I wanted to help Delilah, to take care of her. And I was afraid that Tiffani would try to stop me, refuse to let me do it, and take over. Which wasn't the worst idea ever. I was way out of my league here.

I almost told Tiffani that Delilah was outside, but I could see the anger boiling beneath the surface in her and knew I couldn't. Delilah deserved to be cared for, not yelled at. Whatever was going on with her, she didn't deserve to be punished. I knew that far too well, having grown up with my mother.

"I took her keys away," I said after a moment of withering under her glare. "They're on the back of the bar where we normally keep them. I didn't want her to try to drive home like she is."

Tiffani's face softened a little. "Thank you. I appreciate you looking after her."

"What is going on with her?"

She shook her head. "It's not my place to say," she sighed. "Even if I knew. I haven't seen her like this since…" She drifted off, her eyes looking into the distance. "It's been a while, anyway. She's usually so much more controlled, confident, sure of herself. She doesn't get drunk like this." She moved to the side, gesturing to the door. "Go home, Sabrina. Have a good night. I'll take care of my sister."

I nodded before I said something stupid and she found out what I was planning. Hell, I wasn't entirely certain this was a good idea, after all. I didn't even know if Delilah was still outside, waiting for me.

But I hoped she was.

I hurried out of the lounge and back onto the street. I stopped dead in the middle of the sidewalk. Delilah was gone. I looked up and down the sidewalk, but there was no sign of her. She'd disappeared. I sighed. Of course she was gone. Probably for good. It wasn't like she'd showed any sign of actually wanting to be around me. Except when that guy was going to hit me.

The scene played over in my head. His fist raised, Delilah stepping in to stop him. She claimed that I was hers to everyone around! Her growled and angry words made me feel…amazing.

"Hey."

I spun around at the word, called out from behind me. Delilah was leaning against the side of the club, somewhat hidden in shadows. She looked like she was going to be sick, but her eyes were focused on me.

I hurried over to her, resisted the urge to wrap my arms around her, then pulled out my phone. "I thought you were gone."

She shrugged slowly. "Nowhere to go."

"You could have caught a cab and gone back to your hotel."

"I told you, I don't want to go back there."

"Okay. Where do you want to go?"

"I don't know."

I held my breath for a moment, trying not to push her too far too fast. "Do you want to come to my place?"

She caught my eye and gave me one of her sly smiles, but there was something off about it. "Are you trying to take advantage of me in my inebriated state, Sabrina?"

"N-no!" I shook my head and held up my hands. "I want you to have a safe place to rest. You need to rest, Delilah, to sleep it off. And if you don't want to go to the hotel, I could always go tell Tiffani that you need a ride somewhere. I'm sure she'll help you."

Delilah's face went white as the words hit her. I figured there was no way that she'd want to spend the night with Tiffani, but it was still a bit of a crapshoot.

"Fine," she said finally. "Take me home."

I punched my address into the rideshare app, hoping she meant my home and not hers. The car would be there in a few minutes. It was going to cost me a bit more than I would've liked—stupid surge pricing, but tonight it was well worth it.

I thought about trying to make small talk while we waited for the car but decided against it. She seemed off in her own world as it was. I didn't want to interrupt her thoughts. Maybe she was sobering up already, maybe she wasn't even as drunk as I had thought. Either way, I was going to damned well take care of her.

The car pulled up and the driver looked at her with suspicion. I was certain he didn't want her throwing up all over his vehicle, and I tried to assure him she wouldn't. It didn't take long before we were in front of my apartment, and I thanked him and got out to assist a now half-asleep Delilah out of her seat and headed for the front door. The elevator ride up to my apartment was not nearly as sexy as the one we'd shared the other day. Instead Delilah leaned heavily on my shoulder, breathing deeply as if she were concentrating on staying upright. Her hand drifted over the sweater, and she looked up blearily.

"Isn't this mine?"

Embarrassment heated my cheeks as I mumbled something about it being comfortable. I was saved from more questions as the doors slid open and I helped her down the hallway to my apartment. I opened the door and got her inside, taking her immediately over to my bed and settling her down on it. I untied and removed her boots, and she let me without a word, her eyes half-closed as she watched me. I hesitated after the boots and socks were off, setting them to the side. Did she want me to continue? Should I?

She wasn't giving me any hints.

"Do you…" I began. "I can help you undress, if you like."

She shook her head. "I'll be fine."

I nodded and went back to the door, taking off my own shoes before heading for the bathroom. I did my business, then took a moment to use a wipe to take off the minimal makeup I had on. Stupid, Sabrina, I thought as I cleaned myself up. Asking to undress her? Who the hell does that? What kind of creep was I?

I spent longer than normal in there, berating myself for being a twatwaffle and losing my senses whenever it came to Delilah. She was hurting, she was drunk, she was clearly not completely in control of herself. There was no way I was going to do anything to take advantage of her when she was like this. Not a fucking chance. I wanted to help. To take care of her.

By the time I left the bathroom, I heard a soft snoring sound and checked the bed. Delilah was curled up under my blanket and passed out on my bed. She was lying across almost the whole thing, and the blanket moved slightly with her heavy breathing. I took a breath of my own before I turned away and headed into the kitchen. I leaned against the counter for a moment and felt unsure of what I was doing. I opened the fridge and pulled out a bottle of water, then grabbed a bottle of painkillers from a cupboard and moved quietly to the bed. I left both bottles on the bedside table, for when she awoke.

I stood there and stared at her for longer than was strictly necessary. "Fucking stop being a creep!" I whispered. I smacked myself on the forehead for good measure as I forced myself to turn away and moved around the apartment as quietly as I could. I changed into a pair of pajama shorts and a tee that hadn't seen the light of day in some time. I usually slept naked, but as I looked over at the second-hand recliner that sat near the television, I knew I was going to want clothes for tonight.

I wasn't a stranger to sleeping on the recliner. I'd fallen asleep a number of times during long gaming hours or even stretches of zoning out while binging a TV show. But this was the first time I'd sleep in it because someone else had taken my bed. I picked up the throw blanket that lived on the recliner and sat down, then flinched as it creaked a little. I waited to hear the soft snoring before I started moving again. I didn't want to wake her.

I pulled the lever on the side to put the footrest out and lay back until I was almost horizontal, then pulled the throw blanket over top of me. It wasn't the most comfortable, and there was an odd piece of the recliner that jutted into my back, but after a few minutes of adjusting, it was comfortable enough. I called out in a soft voice to my home assistant device to turn off the lights, and the apartment plunged into darkness. The sliver of a moon shining through my balcony doors provided the only light.

With Delilah asleep and me in the recliner, trying to sleep, there was nothing to stop the onslaught of thoughts that decided to take this moment to besiege me. There were the questions first: Why was Delilah drunk tonight? What was going on with her? Why had she disappeared for a couple days? What was I doing letting her stay here for the night when she'd made it perfectly clear that we'd had our one night together and there was going to be nothing more between us no matter how much I wanted it? That last pile of the word-vomit seemed the most prominent in my head, as I tried not to think of myself as a creep for all but forcing her to come to my place instead of taking her back to her hotel.

"I should have taken her back to the hotel," I told myself. I shook my head as I tried to relax enough to get some measure of sleep in the chair.

Or I should have let Tiffani take care of it. Tiffani was her sister, after all; weren't they supposed to take care of each other? I had no experience with healthy sibling relationships, as I didn't have siblings and lost the whole rest of my family when I came out. Good riddance.

Of course my mind slipped that way. It wasn't bad enough that I had Delilah in my bed a few feet away, but now I was in self-pity mode, as my mind reconsidered for the umpteen millionth time the intelligence of coming out to my family. I mean, they were going to find out sometime, and at least I was honest with them from the start. It didn't make things easier, but it did mean I knew that I could never count on them to help me with what I needed as I started to transition.

Cori was the first person I met that didn't care. She saw me as a real person, not something to be mocked, studied, or feared. I remembered the elation when she offered me a job at the bookstore. Someone saw me for me, not what I showed on the outside. Delilah was the same. She'd noticed while playing with me but hadn't said a thing. It hadn't changed how she acted around me, how she treated me. Me telling her hadn't made her change anything, that I knew of. But what if that wasn't true? Maybe that's what all this was about.

"No," I whispered harshly in the quiet of the night. "She isn't like that." I refused to let my mind go off on some tangent assuming that Delilah's problem stemmed from me and what we did together. Not a fucking chance. "Just get some fucking sleep," I hissed at myself.

Despite the vehemence with which I told myself to go the fuck to sleep, it was still some time before my brain slowed down enough to listen. Whatever was going on with her, whatever we were going to do about it, talk about it, whatever, all of that could wait until morning. I needed to sleep. I needed to do more than sleep. I needed to keep Delilah out of my head. Just because she was in my apartment didn't mean anything was going to happen, and damn it, my brain drifted back to her again.

I took a deep breath and let it out, focused on trying to get my brain to quiet down, my body to relax. *It's only another night.* Another night for me to relax and fall asleep. Even if Delilah was in my bed...

Chapter Sixteen

Sunday is my fun day. And by fun, I mean *stay at home and try not to let the boredom overcome me* day. Most Sundays I was free from both jobs, so I had the day to myself. That meant playing video games, catching up on TV shows and movies, running errands, or catching up on sleep all day.

I opened my eyes and immediately squinted against the intrusion of sunlight through the balcony door. I groaned and stretched—the recliner was not the most comfortable bed. I glanced over at the actual bed. Delilah had barely moved in the night, still sprawled over most of the bed, under the blanket. She snored a little louder than she had last night, but it didn't bother me. It was kind of cute, actually.

I eased the recliner back into a sitting position as quietly as I could and stretched my arms out as a wave of fatigue slammed into me. Clearly I didn't sleep well. I couldn't remember dreaming, which was out of the ordinary. But with how long it took me to fall asleep, it was no wonder it wasn't very deep. I couldn't keep my mind off my guest.

I slipped off the chair and turned around, sliding the door to the balcony open enough for me to step outside. It was a little box, basically, the railing bolted to the side of the building. It was enough space for a small barbecue and a deck chair, which was what I sat down in as I enjoyed the wind that was blowing a little too strongly for most people's tastes. The sun was intermittent, with large clouds dotting the sky and offering some glorious shade. I was not a direct sunlight kind of person. I tended to burn something fierce.

How long was she going to sleep? I didn't know. Would she remember last night when she awoke? I couldn't say for certain on that one either. I had so many questions, wanted to know so much information, but the only person who could give me that was the woman in question, and I didn't want to wake her simply to sate my curiosity. There had to be a reason, a good one, that she agreed to wait for me last night. There had to be a good reason for everything she did last night.

I tried to pull my mind away from her and focused on what I had in the house. Delilah was likely to be hungover when she woke up. I didn't have any experience when it came to drinking a lot because I didn't do it, but I knew enough that she'd probably be hungry. I didn't have much to work with, having planned to go grocery shopping today or soon, anyway.

There was a Tim Hortons not too far away, but that meant leaving her in my apartment alone. Was that a good idea? It wasn't that I didn't trust her, but I didn't want her to wake up and be alone in a strange place. I rubbed a hand across my face. Fuck, I was overthinking things massively, like I always did.

Okay, focus on being a good host. She was still asleep, so I could probably slip out to get her coffee or something. I'd leave a note, I decided, in case she woke up. I didn't know how she took her coffee, but she seemed to like mine, so I'd get her the same thing. Maybe a couple pastries? Donuts? Donuts sounded better to me. That would work.

I quietly slipped back into the apartment and closed the sliding door behind me. It squeaked a little and I glanced at the bed, but Delilah was still asleep. I moved around the room as quietly as I could and wished, not for the first time, that I had a separate bedroom or something, so I didn't risk waking her up. I collected the leggings I'd been wearing the night before and changed out of my pajama shorts, then grabbed Delilah's sweater and pulled it on over my shirt. That was good enough to run to the store.

I ran my fingers through my hair and adjusted my bangs to the side, so they stopped getting in my eyes. I reminded myself yet again that I needed to get that fixed sometime soon. I wasn't a fan of going to the salon. I was usually lucky in hairdressers, but sometimes I got one that didn't quite…get me.

I pushed those thoughts to the side and collected my purse and keys, then checked to make sure I had my phone and cards on me. With one last double-check that Delilah was still asleep, I headed out of my apartment and took care to close the door as softly as I could manage.

It took a little more than a half hour to walk to the store and back, laden with random things I thought sounded good and that Delilah might like. I opened the door and pushed my way back into the apartment, then paused for a minute to listen for her soft snoring, but there was no sound that I could hear. I began to panic a little, then hurried to drop off my goods on the counter before I turned to the bed.

Delilah was sitting up, her upper body unclothed and uncovered, holding the bottle of water I'd left for her to her lips as she sipped slowly at it. The rest of her was still covered by my blanket. I looked away, unable to meet her eyes.

"It's not like you haven't seen them before," she said dryly. "You can look at my breasts."

"I-I didn't want you to think I-I was taking advantage."

"Sabrina, you're far too much of a bottom to ever consider taking advantage of me."

Mortification rolled over me, and I stared down at the carpet under my feet. "I...I mean..."

"Look at me," she said, and I knew a command when I heard one. At least coming from her. I looked up and met her eyes, then watched as she took another sip of water. "I know you were looking after me. You don't have anything to feel bad about."

I tried to take in her words and use them to stop my overthinking before it could pick up momentum.

"Did you go out?" she asked softly, her eyes flickering toward the kitchen.

"Oh!" I spun back to the counter and grabbed a cup of coffee first and brought it over to her. "You said you didn't mind my taste in coffee, so I got you the same. And I got you a sandwich." I looked into the bag in my hand and grimaced. "Well, a few sandwiches. I...uh...didn't know what you liked."

She smiled and took the coffee, then placed it on the bedside table beside the bottle of water and the painkillers. Then she took the bag from me and placed it on her lap.

"You're too cute, you know that, don't you?"

I shook my head immediately. "I...I didn't know what you'd want, and I panicked a little, so I got one of everything."

"You didn't have to do that for me."

"I know. I wanted to."

She sighed. "Damn it, Sabrina, you really are the perfect little sub, aren't you?"

I froze at her words, unsure of what to even say to that. I knew I was naturally submissive, had known it for a long time. But to have her just…point it out like that, without comment, without inflection…I didn't know what to do with the sentence. She pulled a couple of sandwiches out of the bag and glanced at the scrawled writing on them. I picked one up, a ham and cheese on white, not toasted, with no tomatoes, and kept it in my hand as I watched her. She chuckled at me but continued her perusal until she found something that she seemed to like.

"I've…um, got donuts in the other bag," I managed to tell her, and she smiled at me. "And Timbits too." Timbits, basically little round mini-donuts, were cheap and delicious and I'd gotten a box of twenty of the best flavors.

"Are you trying to impress me? Because if this is your idea of breakfast in bed, I'm going to need to work out more."

"Oh, I, uh, it's not, um…"

Delilah laughed and it curled around me and made me want her even more. "Sit and eat with me," she said softly, and I plopped down on the bed with sandwich in hand, then realised I'd left my coffee in the kitchen. She laughed again when my face heated in embarrassment as I stood and went to collect my drink, then returned to the bed, taking a spot a good couple feet or so away from her. To give her some space, especially after last night. Though she seemed to be doing pretty well for how drunk she had been.

She took a bite of her sandwich and gave a little groan that told me that clearly I'd chosen something correctly. She polished it off in record time, before I was barely halfway through my own. I sipped at my coffee and fought the urge to grimace at the taste. Tim Hortons was not my go-to coffee shop, but it was quick and easy and convenient. She pulled the bag up to her again and started searching through it. She pulled out another sandwich, this one turkey and swiss, I thought, and shrugged her shoulders, then started unwrapping it. She finished the second sandwich as I was done with my ham and cheese, then took a long drink of her coffee.

I cleaned up the garbage and returned to the bed, where Delilah was nursing her coffee. Her eyes were on mine as I sat back down, unsure of what to do or say at that point.

"So…I…um…" I cleared my throat and looked away, unable to meet her eye. "What…what happened last night?"

She took a longer drink of her coffee, probably almost draining the whole thing in a couple swigs. Then she let out a long sigh. "I guess we need to have a conversation, don't we?"

"Well, yeah. And about the last few days too. I've had your people coming to me, wondering where the hell you were."

It was her turn to look away from me, and it was strange to see her looking so vulnerable. "I'm sorry about that, Sabrina. I didn't think they'd...they'd do that. I needed...some time alone."

"I can understand that. I've had times when I wanted to disappear, too." I understood that more than she probably realized. "But I'm surprised you cancelled your classes and everything. Lexie was really worried about you."

"I know. I'll talk to her, I promise. And I'll make sure no one bugs you again."

"Don't worry about it, I didn't mind that. I was worried about you too."

She closed her eyes and glanced down, and I swear I could see her eyes start to fill with tears. "Damn it, Sabrina."

I didn't know what to do. Did I try to comfort her? Did I touch her? Did I move away? Move closer? Instead I ended up opening my mouth. "Did I...did I do something wrong that night? Was it something I did?"

She looked up sharply, and I was right about the tears starting. A couple of them fell, but there was nothing but ferocity on her face.

"No, Sabrina. You did absolutely nothing wrong that night. Or any night that I've been with you. Fuck, you've been perfect. More than perfect." She let out another sigh. "It was me, I fucked up. I fucked up and I couldn't make it make sense in my head."

"What do you mean?"

"I spent the night with you," she said, then quickly shook her head. "I don't mean that how it sounds, I promise. I mean that I never spend the night. It...it always complicates things."

I felt a lump in my throat and tried to clear it with a light cough, but it was going nowhere. "But I begged you to stay."

"And honestly, a part of me was going to say no. But a larger part of me wanted to say yes, so I did."

"But that's what's causing your issues?"

"It's what triggered them."

"Do you want to tell me about them?"

"No, but I think I should. You should know what happened. What's wrong with me."

I shook my head. "There's nothing wrong with you. You're perfect."

She barked out a laugh. "I wish that were true. But I'm not, Sabrina. I'm really not."

"Tell me, please," I said. "Help me understand what's happening. Why you showed up at the lounge drunk last night."

"That...that was a mistake. One I can't take back."

"But why did it happen?"

"Because I was in love, once."

I blinked at her. Out of all the answers I could have gotten, that was not one I expected.

"I don't understand," I said.

"If I recall correctly, and I might be wrong because last night is a little blurry, I think I told you that you were...*like her*."

I did remember her saying that. I nodded.

"Well, that wasn't a slip of the tongue. It was the truth. Not about how you act or how you are. You are so different from her, which is a good thing. But how I feel about you? I haven't felt that since her. In that, you're just like her."

"How you feel?"

"It was over a decade ago. I was twenty-three and had started coming into my own as a domme. I knew what I wanted. I knew what I liked, and I met the perfect little submissive who seemed to want me and what I offered as much as I wanted to give it." She said the words like they didn't affect her, but I could see the hurt on her face, the pain of the memories her words were giving rise to. "I fell in love. I thought she did the same."

"But she didn't."

She shook her head. "No. Not even close. She wanted me for what I could do for her. Whenever the real me came out, the rest of me that wasn't the domme, she wanted nothing to do with it. I thought she'd change—I thought she could be different. But she didn't."

"What happened?"

"What else? She left. Took her things and I never saw her again." She sniffled, and I watched more tears fall down her cheeks. "She left and took my heart with her."

"And you never got close to a partner again."

"No. I played, because the need to do so never left, but I could never bring myself to get too attached. I learned to give women what they wanted—what they needed. I learned to please them, and please myself while I did so." She glanced away from me. "And then there was you."

"What about me? Why am I so special?"

"Because you were the first one who wanted to reciprocate. I've had women go down on me, desire to serve me, don't get me wrong. But you...you didn't want it for yourself. You wanted it for me. To please me, to service me. I wasn't a means to an end for you. And that's something I hadn't felt in a very long time."

"Is that why you stayed?"

"I didn't want to leave you, but I was going to. Until you begged me to stay." She looked me in the eyes. "I couldn't say no to you."

"So why did you disappear?"

"Because I didn't know how to handle it. I hadn't felt this way about anyone in so long. I thought if I ignored it, it'd go away. I was afraid to see you again, to bump into you, so I didn't leave the hotel room. I didn't talk to anyone beyond what I had to in order to cancel the classes I had scheduled. That was a number of refunds, I'll tell you. I'm so glad Lexie is good at her job."

"You made Lexie cancel everything?" I said.

"I knew Lexie would call everyone. I turned off my phone, hunkered down in my room, ordered too much room service when I got hungry, and tried to sleep and eat off my feelings."

"I take it that didn't work."

She laughed again. "Not a chance. So I tried something else."

"Whiskey."

"If I couldn't sleep or eat enough to forget, I figured I'd drink. But then they stopped bringing it to my room, so I went to the lounge."

"And you protected me."

"Of course I did. Like I told that asshole, you're mine."

Her words did something to me. I moved a little closer to her and reached out to take her hand and hold tightly to it. I felt my heart swell, my mind want to know more, and my body want to be even closer to her. I wanted to be hers. In every way that mattered. I needed it, so badly.

And that's what scared me the most. How much I desired to be hers. How much I seemed to need it. Whatever power she had over me was dulling everything I thought I knew about my life. I had my goals. I had my path. I needed to focus on that, not Delilah. And besides, after last night, after her disappearance, who could say that it wouldn't happen again?

And truthfully, I never wanted to be the one to break her heart.

"You protected me," I said again, then glanced away from her but still held her hand. "And then you demanded I bring you more to drink."

"I know. I know I hurt you, and I'm sorry. I'm so sorry, Sabrina. I wasn't thinking clearly. I was drunk, and I was so terrible to you."

"You did hurt me, Delilah. You really did. I was trying to take care of you because I care about you. I know I didn't understand what you were going through, but you could have come to me. I would have helped. And I think you knew that."

"I did, I really did. But I thought if I stayed away from you, I would be okay. It would pass. I didn't even think you were working last night, which is stupid. Busiest night of the week, of course you were working. I was willing to deal with my sister in order to get another drink, no problem. But you? I didn't want to hurt you."

"What did Tiffani say to you?"

She grimaced, glancing away again. "She told me to stay away from you," she said quietly enough I had to lean in to hear her properly. "She was afraid I'd hurt you. And I did."

"And yet you waited for me outside. After everything you said and did, you waited for me."

"I had nowhere to go. And I didn't want to go back to the hotel. I'd been in there for days—I couldn't do it. And you were so…so nice. You weren't thinking of yourself, only of me. Of taking care of me."

It was my turn to shake my head. "I'm not that angelic. There were plenty of thoughts of myself. Whether I should do it or not. What might happen if I did. But none of that mattered. I wanted to keep you safe. And yes, take care of you. Because I caught feelings when I wasn't supposed to."

Her head shot up and she looked at me, almost confused. "What do you mean?"

"I mean I've had a crush on you since we met. The moment you put your fingers under my chin, I was yours." I shook my head. "I didn't even know you, and I felt that. It scared me. It still scares me. How could I feel something so strongly for someone I only just met?"

She shook her head slowly, as if unable to believe what she was hearing. "I mean, I guess it's not unheard of—the idea of love at first sight is a thing—but I didn't realize you felt so strongly."

"I tried not to. I tried really hard, because you said we could only have one night."

She sighed again. "Shit. Yeah, about that…"

I held up my other hand. "Don't. If you're going to tell me something different now, you better be serious. I'm not someone you can just play around with."

"I wouldn't dream of it," she insisted. "I promise, Sabrina. I have that rule because I didn't want to fall for someone. I didn't want to catch feelings, as you so aptly put it. I've kept everyone at arm's length. Sure, I played with a lot of girls, and I can tell you that some of them at least would have loved to have me stay the night, but I never did. They'd have loved more than one night together, but I never wanted more than that. I couldn't handle more than that."

I pulled my hand back from hers, crossing my arms over my chest. "And I'm to believe you think I'm different? You have no idea how much I want to say *yes I am, take me.* But I can't say that, because what if I hurt you? What if you hurt me?"

"I promise you I will do whatever I can not to hurt you. I don't want to hurt you, Sabrina," she said. "And I think the fact that you're even asking makes you different already. No one else has ever thought about it."

"You never gave them the chance to."

"True, true." She shook her head and looked away again. "I don't know how to say this, Sabrina. I'm not great at feelings. Not like this. Lust, sex, sensuality, I've got in the bag. Real feelings, attachment, even infatuation…it's not something I deal with."

"I'm not here to fix you, Delilah. I'm a person with my own dreams, my own goals. Yes, I like you. A lot. I love what we've done together and will never forget it. But I can't be the one who puts who I am aside for someone else. I can't do it."

"Oh, Sabrina, I would never ask you to do that. I don't want you to *fix* me. That's for me to do. But with you, I want a chance to try."

"Try what?"

"I want to try to have a relationship. With you."

I blinked. "I'm sorry, what?"

CHAPTER SEVENTEEN

I want to try to have a relationship. With you."
Her words rang in my ears. They were words I never expected to hear from…well…anyone, really. Blame it on the pessimistic part of my brain that usually seemed in control, but being who I am had caused more people to run away from me than flock to me. But now here was a woman who seemed to want to be with me, and it was hard to believe.

"I don't understand. What is it about me that makes me so different?"

"Because you *are* different. Different than all of the other women I've played with. A lot of them never bothered to offer to please me. They got what they wanted, and bam, they were done. Some of them wanted me to stay the night, but it wasn't the same as when you did it. And you didn't fall to your knees in front of me, begging to be used. When I asked you to the rope class the first time, you took to it immediately, but the second? You asked questions, you tried to get to know me better, to let me get to know you. No one's ever really done that before."

"You mean none of your other toys wanted to know who was beneath the domme?"

She flinched at my use of the word *toys* but managed to keep her composure. "They were more than toys. Everyone has been more than just a toy to me."

"You're right, we are more than toys," I said. "I'm sorry. It's kind of what I felt like, afterward. Like I was nothing but a toy."

"Don't apologize, Sabrina. It's my fault for making you feel that way in the first place. I never meant to make anyone feel like they were nothing but a toy for me. Unless that was the scene we were playing in, that is."

She looked like she was trying to give me one of her sly smiles, but there was something off about it. She was being vulnerable and clearly wasn't used to it.

"I did want to be more than that to you. I *do* want to be more than that to you."

"I want that too, Sabrina. I really do," Delilah said.

"And the fact that you're leaving town in a couple weeks?"

She frowned. "Who said I—" She cut herself off. "Oh, Lexie, probably. Yeah, I…uh…yes, I live in Toronto. But if you're game and this works out, maybe we can figure something out."

"We barely know each other," I said softly. "And you're asking me to have what will essentially become a long-distance relationship with you? I can't up and leave my jobs for you."

She shook her head once more. "I'm not asking you to, I promise." She looked almost pensive for a long moment. "It's been a very long time since I knew exactly what I wanted, Sabrina. And you're it. But if you don't want this, you want to try pushing away whatever this is between us, then so be it. It'll hurt, but it's nothing I haven't felt before."

I flinched at her words. "You're already skipping to the breakup?"

"You can't tell me your brain wasn't headed in that direction."

"How did you know?" It took effort to stop my brain from catastrophizing and overthinking, something I'd been struggling with since this conversation began.

"I saw it on your face, darling." She smiled at me. "Your thoughts flicker across it, for anyone to read if they know how."

"And you're already so good at reading me?"

"It's a skill I've developed, more or less. You need to be able to read people when you play with them. Some things aren't as easy as simply using a safeword."

"I get that. I'm not sure how happy I am that you can read me like that, but it makes sense."

"I only ever use my abilities for good," she said solemnly, a hand over her heart. It made me laugh, and she cracked a smile.

"So you're asking if I want a relationship with you," I said, trying to get us back on track.

"I want a relationship with you."

"And what's to stop you from doing the same thing you did yesterday? The same thing you did this week?" I shook my head. "You can't disappear on me, Delilah. I know that I'm inclined to do it too, but I don't want to hurt you like that. Can I trust you to do the same for me? And last night, you hurt me. You and I both know it. What's to say you won't do that again?"

"I don't do that normally, Sabrina. I want you to know that. I can hold my liquor, when I drink, which isn't even as often as you might think. Last night was a mistake in a lot of ways. I treated you like shit. I—"

"You pulled the mistress card on me," I interrupted her.

Her eyes went wide. "I did?" She glanced away. "Oh fuck, I did, didn't I? Fuck, I can't believe I did that. I am so sorry, Sabrina."

"You keep apologizing."

"Because I don't know how else to tell you that I fucked up, and I am so sorry for it."

I shook my head again. "I don't expect you to be perfect, Delilah. But I don't want to get hurt."

"I won't. I swear to you, I won't hurt you. Please, give me a chance."

Fuck. She was putting the choice on me. Of course she was. It wasn't like she'd come here, demanding to date me. That wasn't her. She was a domme, and a fantastic one at that, but she still cared enough about a person's autonomy to never override that, especially outside of a scene. Still, I didn't feel like I was confident enough to be able to make this decision. I'd been by myself for so long, I didn't know how to have a relationship like this. And I couldn't forget about what had happened the last few days. It wasn't that simple.

But here was Delilah, pouring her heart out to me, asking me to take a chance on her. And by the Goddess, I wanted to do so. That annoying pessimistic side of me was certain this was a bad idea, that this would blow up in my face. And there was still a chance it might. But I wanted to try. I needed to try.

"Fine," I said finally. "Okay. But we start slowly."

Delilah sat up straight, cocking her head a little. Surprise flickered across her face, and it made me happy that I could at least read her a little like she did me.

"Wait, yes? You're saying yes?"

"Yes, I'm saying yes."

She reached forward and grabbed both my hands, holding them tightly in hers. "Really?"

I laughed and shook her off. "Yes!"

She leaned forward and captured my lips with hers, pressing herself against me. I was far too aware of the fact that her upper body, at least, was naked and her breasts were pressed against the sweater I'd all but stolen from her. I fell into her touch, into her kiss, and pressed myself back against her. Warning klaxons went off in my brain, reminding me that I'd told her that we'd start slowly. Kissing like this wasn't slow.

Neither was what we did the other night.

Her tongue pressed against my lips, and I opened for her, letting her explore as she wished. I didn't want it to end. I wanted to live like this. I wanted to die like this. It would be the best way to go.

But eventually, she backed off, licking her lips as I stared at her, mouth agape, barely able to form coherent thoughts.

"Did I, um, hear you say something about going slow?"

I waited for my brain to reboot before I answered. "Yes. Yes, I think we should take things slow. I want to date you. I want to get to know the woman under the domme." Her joyous smile melted my heart, and I moved a little closer to her. "But you know, I don't mind kissing. That we can do now."

We came together again, more forcefully this time, and we took turns tasting each other. It lasted long enough that my lungs were burning, and we were forced to part, only slightly, to gather our breath. Our foreheads pressed together softly as we both gasped for air, our eyes meeting as if we could peer into each other's souls. Her golden-brown eyes were still an enigma to me, but she smiled as if she could read everything in my hazel ones. And she probably could.

"So…I guess that means I don't get to tie you down and have my way with you?"

My face flared with embarrassment, and I broke eye contact with her. "No," I managed to squeak, then cleared my throat and tried to put some backbone into my voice. "I mean, not yet. I want to go on a date with you. I want you to…to woo me." I looked around the room, trying to avoid that gaze of hers that could send all of my convictions out the window with a simple glance. "And besides, I don't have any rope. I don't know what you'd tie me down with."

She grabbed my chin and forced my face back to hers, giving me another soft kiss. "Oh, *pet*, I'd say I'm motivated enough to find whatever I needed to tie you down around here somewhere. Do you believe me?"

I let out little mewling sounds of pleasure with her fingers on my chin, around my jaw, pressing in ever so slightly as if reminding me of who I belonged to.

"I want to hear you say it, pet."

"Y-yes, Mistress." I felt a wave of warm relaxation flow through me as the words slipped out of my mouth. It had been so hard, trying not to call her that before. My mind had already decided for me, days ago, that this woman was mine, and I belonged to her.

"Good, pet," she said. "Now, is there anything I should know about planning a date for you?"

My mouth loosened as if it was going to drop open, but her fingers held firm as she watched my face intently. It was like she could read every thought I had in my eyes.

"I…I don't know. I haven't—I haven't been on a date in years. Since before I…before I…" I couldn't even finish that sentence. My mind was torn between trying to show me scenes of a life, long past, and memories of what we'd done the other night and wanting more of it.

Why the fuck had I said I wanted to go slow? Too late to take it back now.

"Surprise me," I whispered, my turn to watch her face for reactions. "Care for me. Want me. That's what I want."

"I think I can handle that." She finally released my chin, and I reflexively pulled back a little, but not too far. I did look away from her, the eye contact having caused a little more anxiety than I would've liked. But it was Delilah. I loved it anyway. "Now, why don't you busy yourself unpacking the rest of our breakfast while I get dressed?"

I jumped up from the bed and hurried back into the kitchen, listening as Delilah got off the bed and started finding her clothes from last night.

"If you like, I can let you borrow something," I called out to her, unsure if she wanted to wear the same clothes that still probably reeked of whiskey.

"Does that mean I get to raid your drawers?" She laughed and I blushed yet again. How was I going to survive her if she could make me react so damned easily all the time?

"I mean…if you want to. I don't have, I mean, I don't mind." My voice grew ever quieter as I tried to tell her yes, I wanted her to raid my drawers. Except the top drawer of my dresser. I froze with the box of donuts in my hand. "Wait!"

I dropped the donuts on the counter and hurried over to the dresser, not really noticing that Delilah was almost entirely naked, having only her panties on. She was looking down into the top drawer of my dresser, a playful smile on her lips.

"So, you do have some toys to play with."

I resisted the urge to slam the drawer in her face.

"I never said I didn't have some...some toys."

She reached into the drawer and drew out a pair of nipple clamps, attached by a chain. They dangled from her finger, and I felt like I was going to combust right there.

"A fine choice, my pet." She looked over at me with a glint in her eyes that told me I was in the best kind of danger. "Perhaps we'll get to play with these?"

As calmly as I could—which wasn't very—I took the clamps back from her and put them in the drawer with the rest of my small selection of toys. "Date first," I said, surprised at the firmness in my tone. "Then we'll see where it goes."

She pouted but allowed me to close the drawer. I pulled open a couple of other ones, selecting a pair of leggings and a T-shirt that I thought might fit her. She was close to my height, but her body was much leaner than mine, which meant the shirt looked a little overlarge but not bad. The leggings fit better, a pair I hadn't worn in a while and realized I might've grown out of. I needed to get back into some sort of exercise routine. I'd been slacking off too much lately.

With that thought, and with Delilah dressed in my clothes and me secretly trying not to rip them off her again, we went to the kitchen and selected a donut each, then took a long moment of silence to eat the pastry goodness. It was a surprisingly domestic moment, and one I was kind of falling in love with.

Then I had to ruin it.

"You need to talk to your sister."

She glanced at me, the last bit of donut dangling from her fingers before she had a chance to put it in her mouth. "I'm sorry, what?"

"And Lexie," I added. "Tiffani and Lexie, at the very least." I hesitated for a moment, worried about what she might say. Would she get mad at me for sticking my nose where it didn't really belong?

She popped the bite of donut into her mouth and chewed thoughtfully before replying.

"I know," she said. "And I hold myself accountable for my disappearance. I don't blame you, Sabrina. And neither should they. I've got some bridges to mend from the sound of it. Cancelling classes in quick succession like that wasn't the smartest thing I've ever done."

I reached around her and took the box of donut holes and the rest of the donuts and put them in the fridge, though not before Delilah managed to snag another donut. She seemed happy to munch on it as I puttered around the kitchen, a pent-up energy coursing through me that I didn't know how to deal with. Every time I moved past her there was a simple brush of limbs, or her hand somehow found a way to touch some part of me, and it made me want more. Stupid brain, telling us to take it slow. The last thing I wanted to do was take it slow.

"So, you've got some work to do today," I said softly, joining her by the counter as she finished eating.

She sighed. "I know. I need to go see my sister." She looked me up and down, then gave me a small smile. "I don't suppose you want to come with me?"

Hell, yes I wanted to go with her. I didn't want to leave her side for a moment. But I also didn't want to make waves between Delilah and her sister. Tiffani already looked at me like she didn't quite trust me around Delilah. When she found out I'd lied to her about leaving Delilah at the bar last night, how mad was she going to be?

"I would," I said finally. "I really would love to, but I think you might need to talk to Tiffani on your own. She might not be happy with me that I lied to her last night."

"You lied to her?"

"I told her I left you in your booth when I went home. I didn't want her to come out and drive you away when I was trying to take care of you. She seems…a little protective of you."

"We have a tough history," she admitted. "I'll try to keep you out of it, I promise. I don't want to risk your job or anything."

"That's appreciated." I pulled out my phone. "Do you need a ride somewhere?"

She shook her head. "I've got it." She snatched my phone from my hand anyway and started poking at it. "But I think I need to give you my number so I can give you the details of that date, right?"

It took me a moment to reach out as she handed the phone back to me, our fingers brushing and the wash of desire rolling through me. Slow, I reminded myself, we're taking it slow. As if she were reading my mind once more, she leaned forward and kissed me, and I melted into her once more. When she pulled away, I followed.

"I'll text you," she said quietly, putting a hand on my shoulder to stop me from plowing into her lips first. "We'll have our date. I promise."

"Okay," I managed, pulling myself back before I could embarrass myself further. We stared at each other awkwardly for a long moment. "I guess, um, you're headed out, then…"

"I need to get the car keys back from my sister."

I rubbed a hand at the back of my neck. "Yeah, sorry about that."

She shook her head. "You did the right thing. I was in no condition to drive last night. I don't intend to do that again anytime soon."

I walked her to the door. She put on her boots, which I gracelessly fell to my knees to help her lace up. She looked a little funny in knee-high boots in a pair of my leggings that were a little big on her. But she stood straight and confident and pulled off the look with ease. Goddess, I was so fucked. Not literally, not right now, but metaphorically. If this was just the beginning, I was a goner.

"I'll text you, okay?" she said again and I nodded, then she turned and opened the door. Before she could leave, I grabbed her arm and planted a kiss on her cheek, if nothing else to say goodbye when my words clearly weren't working. Her smile was dazzling, but it didn't stop her from heading down the hallway to the elevator. I considered going after her, walking with her, but shook my head. Instead I watched from the doorway until she gave a little wave from inside the elevator and the doors closed.

"Fuck," I swore as I safely returned to my apartment and closed the door behind me. I stared at the mess in the kitchen from our impromptu breakfast, already missing her presence. "I'm hopeless. Utterly hopeless."

CHAPTER EIGHTEEN

The week was far too long. Delilah and I talked whenever we saw each other, texted when we didn't, and I spent most of the days with a smile on my face and my phone in my hand. Even getting grilled by Cori couldn't bring down my mood, which was a nice change of pace. Things were going well. We hadn't had our date yet, but then that was difficult with schedules like ours. She and her usual rope bunny had to make up for the classes they'd missed, which Delilah seemed happy to do.

I didn't miss getting to help, not at all.

At least that's what I kept telling myself.

I was not above pining for her, clearly, but I also told myself I couldn't lose myself in her entirely. I still had my goals, my jobs, my life. I had to make it clear to her that those weren't changing any time soon. Not without a damned good reason.

I was afraid of it, changing for her. Changing my life for her, changing who I was for her. I'd almost done it long ago, with my ex-fiancée. It would have been so easy, to be the same person I was, to not be true to myself. I would have hated every moment of it, but I would have had a safer life, an easier life.

I wouldn't let myself fall under Delilah's sway just to have an easier life.

It was Friday night, and I was about to leave the lounge when Tiffani came up to me, her arms crossed over her chest. I still didn't know what she and Delilah had talked about last weekend, but things seemed better between the sisters, and so far Tiffani hadn't gotten overly mad at me about pining over Delilah. She did give me a funny look when she'd caught us kissing in the office the other day, but she'd been tight-lipped in her admonishments.

"I've had a request from my sister," she began, her eyes giving nothing away about whether she was angry with me or only a little perturbed. "She wants you to have the night off tomorrow. Something about a promise she made?"

I stared at her for a long moment, then realized what she must've been getting at. "Delilah and I...we're going on a date."

"A date? Lilah?" She shook her head. "You're kidding me, right?"

I shook my head. "No. We're going on a date."

"Is this about what I saw the other day? What happened last weekend? I know she went home with you."

I couldn't keep myself from frowning. "She told you that?"

"She asked me not to be mad at you for lying."

"And?"

"And I wasn't going to lose a good server and bartender because you wanted to take care of my sister, no matter how misguided it was."

"I care about her," I told her. "A lot. I asked her to take me on a date, and I'm guessing she picked tomorrow."

"You're guessing?"

I shrugged. "She wanted to keep it a surprise."

It was her turn to shake her head, her posture becoming less defensive. "Sounds like her." She shook her head. "So you're really going to date my sister."

"That's the plan."

"I didn't know she even knew what a date was."

I opened my mouth to defend Delilah, but honestly, I was kind of surprised too. "She wants to try something new with me. And I'm all for it."

She uncrossed her arms and gave me a look I couldn't read. "Just...treat her well, okay? Please don't break her heart."

I nodded and she walked away, letting me leave the back. Tiffani was so worried about Delilah, but honestly, it was my own heart I was more worried about.

I left the lounge to head home, watching the bus drive by right as I exited the doors. I cursed my stupid luck and started pulling up the rideshare app again. I wondered how much it was going to cost me this time, when a car pulled up in front of the lounge. I smiled as the window rolled down and Delilah glanced at me from the driver's side.

"Need a ride, good-looking?" she drawled, her arm stretched across the back of the passenger seat. I leaned over through the window.

"Fancy meeting you here."

"Well, I was in the neighborhood, figured I'd stop by."

"Really? Just in time to pick up little old me?"

Her look turned almost sheepish. "Or I may have been waiting nearby for an excuse to come pick you up."

"You rigged the bus to come ten minutes early?"

She laughed. "No! But it was fortuitous, wasn't it?"

I laughed with her and opened the door, settling in the passenger seat. Delilah pulled out into traffic, and I settled in comfortably.

"You're not wearing my sweater tonight," she commented.

"It had to get washed sometime."

"I guess so. I thought it looked good on you."

"It only fit because it's oversized on you."

"And it fit you wonderfully. It's yours, for as long as you want it."

I grinned. "I might need you to wear it for a while, get that scent back going for it."

"Oh? You like that, do you?" I nodded vehemently. "I'll keep that in mind. Maybe there'll be more things of mine you can wear."

I refused to let my brain run wild on that throwaway comment and glanced at her as she steered her way through the traffic. I gave her a sly smile.

"I'll happily wear whatever you want me to, Mistress."

I watched her hands grip the wheel a little tighter and reveled in the fact that I could work her up like she did to me. I glanced out the window, watching the buildings zip by as Delilah drove me home. She parked in the visitor lot, in the same spot as she did last week. She let the car idle for a moment and we sat in comfortable silence.

"So, you asked Tiffani if I could have the night off tomorrow?"

I swore I could see her face reddening a bit, and I loved it.

"I know I promised not to interfere with your jobs or anything," she said quietly, "but I could only get the reservation for tomorrow night. I hope that's okay."

I giggled. "Of course it's okay. I can miss a night here and there."

She let out a long breath. "Good. Good. I was afraid you might be upset with me."

"No way." I took one of her hands, holding it tightly. "I can't wait to see what you have in store for me."

She gave me a dazzling smile. "I think you'll love it."

"So are you going to give me a hint of what we're doing tomorrow?"

She shook her head. "Not a chance. I want to surprise you." She turned to look at me. "Is that all right?"

"More than all right."

"Good. Then do something for me when I pick you up tomorrow?"

"Anything."

"Wear something really nice."

I panicked for a quick second as I considered my wardrobe. "How nice are we talking?"

"Fancy nice. I don't want to give too much away."

I chuckled. "There's not a lot of fancy places around here, I think I could guess where you're taking me."

"But do you really want to? Or would you rather enjoy the surprise?"

"You have me there."

"I think, after tomorrow night, I could have you anywhere."

I flinched at her words, and my fingers tightened around her hand. She laughed, low and sultry, and I tried to push down the humiliation as I cursed myself for letting my arousal show far too easily. She knew how to play me like an instrument, and I loved every moment of it.

"Tomorrow is not the only date we're going to go on, thank you. I'm not that easy."

"I never thought you were easy at all."

"Really? Even when I fell to my knees at your command?"

"That doesn't mean you're easy. It means you know what you want and decided to take it."

I shook my head. "Sometimes I feel like I haven't known what I wanted in a long time."

"You give yourself too little credit, darling. You're a lot stronger than you think."

I shook my head. "I'm just trying to live my life."

"And I admire you for it."

I did my best to hide the scoff that came out of my mouth. It was an involuntary action, one I'd perfected when I was younger when people would compliment me. It was something I never got used to, something my mother made sure wouldn't stick to me. Heaven forbid I have greater self-esteem than she did.

"What was that, pet?"

Damn it. She'd heard it.

"Nothing," I said quickly. "I…nothing."

"Do you think I'm lying to you?" She tried to meet my eyes, but I looked away.

"No. No I don't think you are."

"But you don't believe me."

"I didn't say that."

"Then why scoff?"

"Because I'm not that special."

"You are to me."

There was nothing I could say to that. I tried to let go of her hand, but she held on tightly for a moment longer before letting me pull away.

"I'm sorry," I said softly.

"Don't apologize."

"I'll try not to."

I looked up and she gave me another one of those smiles of hers.

"Are you going to be okay tonight, pet?"

"I will."

"Good. Get some rest. I'll pick you up tomorrow at seven, all right?"

"Seven. I'll be ready," I assured her.

We sat in the car for another minute, neither of us speaking. I felt like the words I wanted to say were too heavy for the moment and could break everything we were trying to build. I didn't want to take it slow. I didn't want to wait. I wanted to invite her up right now, screw taking our time. But I didn't say it. I let the silence linger until I opened the door and started to step out.

"Sabrina?" she asked quietly before I could lift myself out of the car. I turned to look at her once more. "Have a good night, all right? I hope you dream of me."

If words could make me melt, I would've been a puddle at her feet right then and there. It was honestly the sweetest thing that anyone had ever said to me. I nodded wordlessly to her, unsure of even what I could say for a response, then climbed out of the car. I looked back only once, feeling her eyes on me until I opened the inner door of the apartment building and was safely inside. Only then did I hear her rev up the engine and pull out of the parking lot. I turned around to watch her go, cursing myself a little as I did so.

"Fuck," I groaned. I glanced at the elevators, then at the door to the side marked Stairs. I took the door, pumping sore muscles into climbing the flights of steps instead of taking the easy way up. By the time I reached my floor I was panting and aching, and my mind was still on what I wanted Delilah to do to me if I'd invited her up.

I made it to my apartment and headed straight for the shower. This time I made it even colder than usual, to try and shock my system into thinking better thoughts. Well, maybe not better, but more wholesome? Isn't that how it's supposed to work? I didn't want to spend the rest of the night pining over what might have been.

With a wide yawn and my mind sufficiently subdued, I headed to bed. As I lay there, trying to sleep, there was one major thought in my mind: *Where the hell is she taking me tomorrow?*

CHAPTER NINETEEN

Most Saturdays I had work at the lounge to look forward to. Today there was nothing. I slept in peacefully, and by that I meant that I was up about two hours later than I normally got up to go to the bookstore, so that wasn't bad for me. I found myself spurred on by the knowledge of my date tonight, ready to go almost a full twelve hours early. But as I rubbed the sleep out of my face and felt the annoying stubble of a couple-days-old beard that grew slowly but surely even with my medications, I knew there was plenty to do to get ready.

Every trans woman's routine is different. Some are big into beauty regimens; I was not. Some are huge into making sure they're always clean-shaven; I was a little more lax about it. I used to try to make sure I shaved every day, but with the slow growth of hair I was only irritating my skin more than keeping myself clean-shaven. It was a frustrating, precarious balance, and one I honestly wished I could do without.

Makeup was another thing that I didn't do a lot of. Some trans women swear by it. I had trouble learning how to use it effectively. I knew the basics, however, of liner and shadow and mascara, and I could make something work.

I knew I didn't always pass, which was the goal of many trans women. I tried hard to, early on, believing that I had to. But over time, I got sick of the effort and not seeing the reward. After almost seven years on hormones, I didn't get misgendered often from simply looking at me. Most of what gave me away was my voice, but that was something I was still working on.

Today, though, I wanted to put in the extra effort. I wanted Delilah to see me at my best, most coifed, most put together. I wanted to impress her, to show her that she wasn't wrong in choosing me to try to have this relationship with, when honestly there were probably so many others she could have.

I shook my head, pressing my face into my pillow. That was not a good line of thought. I didn't owe her anything for choosing me. She said she liked me. I liked her. We'd both caught feelings at some point over the past two weeks, and now we were going to see where we could go with that. So why did I feel like I still wasn't good enough?

That was easy enough to answer: Because I didn't think I'd ever been good enough. But I wasn't going to let my mind slip down that particular, depressive rabbit hole as I got up and forced myself to focus on making some breakfast. Simple enough, a couple fried eggs on bread, throw on a little ketchup and there you go. Fried egg sandwiches, just like Mom used to make.

I spent the morning focusing on one thing or another, like cleaning up the apartment, reading, and playing a few video games. Whatever held my attention the longest. And whatever prevented me from panicking about the date that was still a few hours away was definitely a bonus.

As the time that Delilah said she'd pick me up got closer, I started to get more and more nervous. I hadn't been on a date in years. Almost a decade, if I really thought about it. Was I going to do it right? What was she going to expect from me? I had to remind myself that she hadn't actually dated in years either, and that we were hopefully going to be on the same footing.

"Time to get ready," I told myself, hoping to break the cycle of worrying thoughts in my head. I shaved and showered, primped and preened, brushed out my hair and worked it up into a pair of space buns on top of my head. I glanced in the mirror and had that knee-jerk gut reaction of a guy looking back at me for only a second before it faded and I was able to see who I really was. I let out a deep breath to steady my nerves and pulled out my small collection of makeup. I carefully applied my eyeliner, then wiped it off and did it again. And again. And finally kept it after the fourth try of keeping it nice and neat. I did not attempt a wing tonight because I wasn't sure if that was the vibe we were going for. But I did accomplish the clean line, then moved on to some colorful shadow. I preferred color in my eyeshadow, so I did pink on the inner lid and dusted some purple to the outside, creating a bit of a gradient. Then a few swipes of the mascara wand and I felt like I was finished.

I looked at myself in the mirror and couldn't help but smile. It'd been a long time since I put effort in like this, and I enjoyed how much it paid off. I hoped that Delilah would like it, then told myself firmly that I was doing it for myself as much as for her, so what mattered was that *I* liked it.

I had to search through my wardrobe for the dress I wanted. I hadn't worn it since I tried it on in the store. A friend had invited me to their wedding but was quick to rescind the invitation when they found out I was planning to wear a dress. That friend certainly wasn't a friend anymore. But I still had the dress, and when I found it, I let out a soft sigh, glad that it was in one piece and seemed unscathed by the couple of years it'd been in there.

It was a gorgeous emerald green that brought out the red in my ginger hair when I wore it—at least that's what the woman at the store had told me. I assumed that meant it looked good. It was a long dress, falling to my ankles. Sleeveless, but not in a way that broadened the shoulders. The top half was lace and mesh but had a nude sheath underneath. It actually fit a little large on me, which made me surprisingly happy that my daily routines were helping me to slim down a little. The bottom of it flowed around my legs happily, and I resisted the urge to do a little twirl to see how far the skirt would flare out. I was not going to be stereotypical and do the whole *skirt-go-spinny* thing.

I spun. Once. Only once.

Okay, twice. With a little giggle.

I was going on a date with Delilah.

She was taking me on a *date*.

I glanced at the clock on my stove. Almost seven. Good timing. I didn't want to sit around waiting like this for a couple of hours. In a moment of giddiness I took a selfie, because it made sense. I wanted to see what I could do if I put effort in.

At seven on the dot the intercom buzzed. I wondered if Delilah had stood down there waiting or if she was lucky. I hit the button to let her into the building, then slipped my feet into a pair of flats before I went to stand by the door. Was that the right thing to do? Should I have gone down to her? I didn't know, but I had a feeling I was about to find out. A few moments later there was a polite tap on the door, and I swung it open.

Delilah stood there in a soft-looking black blazer over a red mesh shirt that was barely this side of decent. Her legs were covered by a pair of black leather pants that looked like they were damned well painted on, and I had to do my best not to swoon. I looked her up and down, reveling in her appearance and considering the idea of skipping the date and going straight to bed with her. But that wouldn't be taking it slow, I reminded myself.

When I met her eye, I realized she was doing the same thing to me. Looking at me like she wanted to swoon. Her lips turned up in a sly grin.

"Wow, Sabrina. You look amazing."

I glanced away, but it did nothing to stop the compliment from making the flush creep up my neck and into my cheeks. "I was about to say the same to you."

"I like that we're thinking the same thing." She held out her hand to me. "Are you ready to go?"

"I've never been more ready."

I grabbed my purse and took a moment to check it for everything that I might need. Phone, keys, wallet, the usual stuff. Delilah offered her hand, and I took it, letting her lead me out the door. I locked it behind me, and we headed for the elevator hand in hand.

The car ride was relatively short, only about ten minutes. We drove into the downtown core of the city, where I didn't normally go. I worked and lived on the other side of the river, and there was no reason for me to go downtown. But Delilah drove these streets like it was something she did every day. We pulled into the parking lot of the Holte Hotel, a high-end place that I'd never really seen before outside of ads on TV. I stared at the building, all lit up for the night, as we pulled up to the front doors and Delilah put the car in park. I turned to look at her.

"Here? We're going here?"

She glanced my way. "Is there a problem?"

I shook my head, not wanting to ruin whatever she had planned. I knew there was a restaurant here, pretty much the fanciest place in the city. The restaurant was on the top floor of the hotel, and it apparently rotated slowly, giving the patrons a sweeping view of the city and the river valley.

She got out of the car, handed her keys to a valet, then came around and helped me find my footing on the asphalt. She led the way into the hotel like she knew exactly where she was going, heading toward the elevator bank without stopping and without taking her hand out of mine.

"Are we…are we really going to…to eat here?" I couldn't remember the name of the restaurant from the ads.

"I thought it might be a nice place to eat," she said softly, smiling at me. "You wanted a memorable date, didn't you?"

My mouth dropped open a little as we stepped onto the elevator. "I mean, yes, but I wasn't expecting this."

"Surprise."

I let out a little laugh. "That it is."

My stomach lurched a little as the elevator rose higher and higher. Was this too much for me? Was she trying to show off to me? I had expected maybe a nicer restaurant than something like a basic steakhouse, not one of the most expensive in the city. But it was too late to think about that now, as the elevator came to a stop and the doors opened onto a small lobby-like area. Delilah gave me a reassuring smile and pulled me out of the elevator, my wobbly legs only barely keeping me upright. This was too much. Too much for me. I didn't belong in a place like this.

"Madam." A man at a small podium looked up as we approached. "And madam, can I help you?"

"Yes, thank you," Delilah said, ever so politely, the sly grin being replaced by something far more…uptight. Like she was something of a different person up here. "We have a reservation tonight, under Holte."

He took a second to check a thick book that lay on the podium and looked up suddenly, his eyebrows raising so high they almost hid under his hair. "Of course, Ms. Holte, your table is ready for you."

I frowned, but Delilah didn't let go of my hand as we were led into the restaurant, around a number of other tables, and seated in a plush, luxurious booth along the glass wall. Delilah thanked the host and slipped him something, then waited until he left before ushering me into one side of the booth. She sat opposite me, fingering the menu that was already laid out on the table as if they were waiting for us. And I guessed they were.

"Are you okay, Sabrina?" Delilah asked softly, reaching across the table. I tentatively reached for her with one of my hands. The table was hard beneath me, proving that this wasn't a fantasy or a dream. I took her hand and held it tight, then closed my eyes and took a deep breath.

"I wasn't…I mean, I didn't know…" I shook my head and took a moment to try and find my words. "Did he…did he call you Ms. Holte?"

To my surprise, I watched Delilah avert her eyes from me. It was such a cute gesture that I couldn't help but smile a little at it. I wondered if I looked half as good when I did it.

"Yes, he did."

I shook my head. "Are you sure it's okay to use someone else's name just to get into a fancy restaurant like this? Aren't you worried about getting caught?"

She gave me a look like she couldn't understand what I was saying, then she started to chuckle. The chuckle turned into a full-throated laugh, one that was surprisingly loud for the quiet restaurant. I looked around to see the reaction of the staff and other diners and realized that the tables nearest to us were all empty, all with little placards on them declaring that they'd been reserved. It almost gave us a buffer, allowing Delilah to laugh as loud as she wanted without attracting undue attention.

"Delilah?" I demanded, a little miffed at her laughing at me.

"Oh, Sabrina," she wheezed. "You're so...so cute."

The way she said it put my hackles up, and I crossed my arms over my chest.

"It's a valid concern," I told her. "I don't want to get kicked out."

"Oh, pet, they won't kick us out. Not without a damned good reason."

"But the name! The reservation?" I tried to catch her eye. "I don't want us to get in trouble."

She wiped delicately around her eyes, and I noticed her immaculate eyeliner, thinner and better applied than mine, with a subtle wing on the end. Damn, I wish I could have pulled that off. She probably managed it first try. She settled more on her side of the booth, reaching out with her other hand until she was holding both of mine over the table.

"Sabrina, darling, my pet, I'm not pretending to be someone to get this reservation."

"But that name..." I shook my head. "That name he called you. That's the name of the hotel." She smiled encouragingly as the thoughts worked in my head. "Holte. The family that owns the Holte hotels. He called you Ms. Holte." I stared at her as if she had two heads. "You're a Holte? Like...one of those Holtes?"

She chuckled again. "My name is Delilah Holte, yes. My parents own this hotel, along with a number of others across the country. I work for them and get a number of perks doing so."

My mouth dropped open. "You're Delilah *Holte*?"

The laughter started to disappear from her face, and she let go of my hands. She pulled back, looking more embarrassed than I'd ever seen her. Damn it. I was making a big deal over nothing. I reached forward and grabbed one of her hands before she could completely back away.

"I'm sorry," I said quickly. "Even I know the name, which is surprising because if you hadn't noticed, I kind of live under a rock." She gave me a small smile and I pressed forward, wanting to bring back jovial Delilah over whoever this was. "You caught me off guard with your surprise. I didn't…I had no idea that…I didn't know, and I'm sorry for making a big deal of it."

She sighed. "I don't really go around announcing it. The few people I've…played with who knew who I was started to expect things. Like I'd dote on them for being with me. So I stopped generally using my last name until I needed to." She shrugged. "And tonight, I needed to, so I could wine and dine you."

"I'm so sorry." I couldn't apologize enough. "I appreciate this, I really do. It was more than I expected, far more than I had hoped for. I don't mean to sound ungrateful or anything like that." I sounded so pathetic, but I didn't know what else to say. I didn't want her to think I was judging her. I was the last person who should get to judge anyone.

Delilah's smile was small but genuine and she didn't try to pull her hand away again. She glanced at the simple menu, then to what looked like a small book of wines, then back to me. "Is this too much? I didn't really take into account how you might feel being here."

"No, I'm okay being here. I just wasn't expecting it." I glanced around again, taking a good look outside. The restaurant rotated almost imperceptibly. "This is amazing, really. I never thought I'd be here."

"I wanted to do something for you that others might overlook," she said softly. "It was something I could do that I hadn't done for anyone else before."

That made me smile. "You've never brought anyone else here?"

She shook her head. "Not since…not since my first girlfriend."

"I feel honored. Thank you, Delilah."

She smiled again. Her confidence returned, and I let out a tiny sigh of relief. I wanted to make her happy. And for some reason, she seemed to be happy with me. I didn't want to let that go.

I didn't want her to let me go.

CHAPTER TWENTY

"Wine?" Delilah asked, handing me the wine list. I stared at it for a moment before giving her a smile.

"You decide," I told her. "I'll take a glass of whatever you choose."

I'd never been to a restaurant with a dedicated wine list in its very own little book before. I wouldn't have a clue what any of them were. My expertise in wine came from the odd glass I managed at the lounge once in a while. I certainly didn't know enough about them to select one now.

I wondered what it'd be like to learn something like that.

The waiter took our drink orders. I asked for water, knowing that one glass of wine was going to be enough, and I wanted something else to drink. The waiter looked at me like he was surprised I asked for it, but nodded and ran away after Delilah ordered the wine.

"They bring you water no matter what," Delilah commented with a small smile. I tried to hide my embarrassment and buried my face in the menu. Not that I understood a word of it. My usual go-to was a burger and fries, but something told me they wouldn't have that here. And the prices...

"Wow." I stared at the over-fifty-dollar price tags for most of the entrees. I put a hand to my throat for a moment, feeling my pulse there pounding. This was way more than I was comfortable with.

"Are you okay, pet?"

I nodded automatically to Delilah's query. I wasn't sure how to tell her that I was overwhelmed. I didn't want her to think less of me or, worse, think she did anything wrong. This was a once in a lifetime opportunity for me to be here, and I couldn't get out of my head long enough to enjoy it.

Delilah had her menu closed and on the table in front of her. I kept looking at mine, trying to figure out what half the food was and hoping not to spend too much of Delilah's money. I didn't want her thinking I was going to take advantage of her. But that meant that everything was taking a bit longer, so even after the waiter returned with our wine—and my water—I still asked for some time with the menu. Delilah was amazingly patient with me as she watched me pore over that menu, going over the same page time and time again.

"Sabrina." Delilah reached over the table and put her finger on my menu and pushed it down to the table. "Are you having troubles deciding, darling? I can help you, if you'd like."

"I…" I didn't know what to say that wouldn't hurt her in some way. I didn't know what a mango chutney was, or what *au jus* meant. Words like *beurre noisette* were also confusing. I had no idea what these things were, but I didn't want her to think I didn't belong with her. I wanted to be with her.

"It's all right," she said softly. "I can help, if you'd like."

I glanced up at her. "I don't mean to be trouble, I'm sorry."

She shook her head. "Darling, you are absolutely no trouble at all. There's no need to apologize." She gave me that wide smile of hers, like she was saying that everything was perfect, even with me here. I let go of the menu. "Did you want me to help describe some of the dishes or simply order something for you?"

I started to ask if she'd describe the words I didn't know. But then there was the idea of her ordering for me. Her taking control of the decision. Helping me so I didn't have to panic, didn't have to fret. The kind of control that I could only pass off to someone I trusted. And I trusted Delilah.

"I'd appreciate…" I began, watching her closely as I spoke. "Could you order for me? I just don't know what most of this stuff is, never mind what I'd actually like of it."

"Are you okay if I ask you a few questions?"

"Yeah, I can handle questions."

"Well, first of all, I'm going to ask a simple one." She gave me a smile and held my eye. "Do you want to go somewhere else?" I started to respond but she held up her hand. "Take a moment to think about it. I won't be disappointed or feel anything bad toward you at all. I should've realized this place might be a bit much for you, but I got hooked on the idea of doing something for you that no one has ever done before. I'm sorry if that's hurt you in any way."

"Oh, Delilah, no, you haven't hurt me," I said right away. "Not at all. It's true I'm out of my element here, but isn't that what you've been doing for me since we met? Pushing me out of my comfort zone, getting me to try new things? I don't want our first date to crash and burn because my mind is a bit of a mess."

"Good. That's good." She glanced away, releasing me from her gaze. She picked up the menu in front of her. "Then in that case, how do you feel about mushrooms?"

We laughed together and got down to business, Delilah asking me numerous questions about what food I liked or didn't like, if I thought I could handle something or not, things like that. It was actually a lot of fun, and an interesting way for us to get to know each other. At least, when it came to food choices. She was knowledgeable about what the words that confused me were, and if not able to identify exactly what was in something, then at least give me an idea of what it contained.

We spent a good fifteen minutes or so going over that menu with a fine-toothed comb, both of us laughing as we finally put the menus down and the waiter returned.

Delilah did all the talking. She ordered the prawns baked in Pernod garlic butter as an appetizer, then ordered the Alberta bison tenderloin for herself and the slow roasted prime rib for me. I smiled at the waiter as I handed him back the menu, then finally took my first sip of wine. It was a dark red color, tasting of fruits that I'd probably never heard of before. It was surprisingly good, if a little dry for my liking, and I knew that if I had more than one glass I'd probably end up making some bad decisions.

Delilah matched me for my wine drinking, sipping carefully at her glass while we continued talking. She asked me, ever so politely, about my transition. I was only going to give her the CliffsNotes version of the story, but there was something in me that decided that I was going to tell all of it. Everything. I told her how my mother's boyfriend left when I was little, how my mother ended up blaming me for it and blaming me that she couldn't have another kid—like that would have made the man stay. I told her about my first girlfriend, then my fiancée, the one who tried to change me, tried to make a man out of me. I told her about coming out and losing everyone I knew and thought I loved. She went silent during that part, looking pensive and almost angry, but not at me. No, she was angry for me. Because my family, my friends, hadn't been there for me when I needed them most.

"It took me a while to really be able to even consider people as friends again, and even then it was pretty much only Cori," I told her, as I fingered the stem of the almost empty wine glass. I shook my head. "I had to do everything myself. Had no one around to hold my hand through everything. Hormones, legal name change, all of it." I grimaced and looked away from her, not wanting to see the usual pitying looks that people gave me when I told my story.

"No friends online to at least talk to? There's communities out there." It was a good question, but I hated the answer to it.

"No, I have never been good at being social, especially online. And it only got worse when I came out because I was scared of putting myself out there. I found communities, but all I did was lurk, because I felt I wasn't...good enough. Trans enough."

"Oh, darling, you are amazing simply as you are."

I glanced away and gave a small sniffle. I was not going to break down crying in front of her. Not tonight.

"So, what lies in the future for you?" she asked softly, holding out a hand to me. I took it, and was awed at how soft her skin was.

"My long-term goal is to afford my surgeries," I told her. "It's why I work two jobs. I'm saving up."

"But aren't you afraid of working too much?"

"Sometimes," I agreed. "But I don't really have anything else to do with my time, so might as well make it work for me."

Delilah started to say something, but the waiter chose that moment to return with our garlic prawns. I stared at the surprisingly large shrimp that still had the heads and tails attached and wondered exactly how to go about eating these things. For someone used to frozen grocery store shrimp, this was a new experience.

Delilah was patient with me yet again, showing me how to remove the head and tail to best effect and make the most out of the meal. The garlic butter was phenomenal with the prawns, and I could see why people raved about the food here. It was worth the cost.

"So, I've told you my life story." I gave Delilah a grin. "What about you?"

"I don't think I'm half as interesting as you."

"I beg to differ."

She laughed. "I could certainly make you beg."

I gritted my teeth in a vain attempt to stop the sweet feeling of arousal that swarmed up and heated my face. "I swear, you only like seeing me blush."

"It certainly is a highlight of my day."

I shook my head. "So, what do you do when you're not going around preying on innocent girls and asking to tie them up?"

"I've never *preyed* on anyone in my life," she replied with a smile. "But there are plenty of innocent girls who have fallen to their knees in front of me." She put a finger to her chin. "Kind of like you did, the first time I tied you up."

I pointed my fork at her. "You're avoiding the question."

She sighed. "You're right. I am." She shook her head. "I'm not good at talking about myself. Outside of, like, my expertise in BDSM and stuff like that. Or the boardroom."

"See? There's a hint right there. Boardroom. Tell me about that."

"I told you I work for my parents, right? Well, my dad has been grooming me for years to replace him eventually, you know, as parents are wont to do."

I really didn't know. My mother hadn't owned anything important enough to hand down to me. She didn't need to train me to replace her. Her thing was mostly alcohol and yelling.

"Do you like working for your parents?"

She started to nod, then stopped and looked around, as if expecting someone to be nearby, listening in to us. She leaned a little closer to me, bringing her awfully close to dipping her top into the remnants of the garlic prawns that we'd devoured.

"Honestly? No. I hate it. It's not what I want to do with my life at all. Not even a little bit. But it's what's expected of me, and so I go along with it. I mean, I really can't complain. I'm good at what I do, and it's great money, and it's secure, so it's not like I have to worry about losing my job any time soon—even when I make mistakes."

I tilted my head to the side a little. That sounded a little on the nose. "Is that why you're here? Because you made a mistake?"

She squirmed in her seat, and I quite enjoyed having this little bit of power over someone who seemed nigh untouchable—at least she had until the other night.

"I'm on vacation for a month. Came back here to check on my investments and spend some time with my sister." She rolled her eyes. "My father doesn't give a shit. Just waved me out the door."

"Wow, why? Are you okay?"

"I'm fine. I didn't approve of how one of our hotel managers was treating his staff. The sleazebag had it coming."

"What did you do?"

She shook her head. "I really don't want to go into detail. Suffice it to say, he no longer works for us, and I've done what I can to blacklist him from any other major hotel family in the country."

I looked at her with wider eyes than before. "Remind me never to get on your bad side," I said, only half joking.

"Darling, you could never be on my bad side."

"I'm sure I could manage a way to do it."

"Then I'll be sure to spank you until I feel better, how does that sound?"

I did my best not to start panting right at the table.

The waiter picked that moment to bring out our food. Our hands parted and I missed her touch something fierce as a plate was set in front of me. He offered refills on our wine, but I shook my head. So did Delilah, and I smiled. She wasn't looking for a repeat of the other night. He offered instead to refill our waters and we both took him up on that, then the conversation halted a little as we dug into our meals.

It was certainly the fanciest meal I'd ever eaten, and also one of the smallest. Robust plate sizes this restaurant was not known for, but the prime rib was absolutely delicious, and the sides were almost as good. Delilah tore into her meal too, possibly eating a little more daintily than I was, but at least I wasn't picking up the meat with my fork and using my teeth to rip it apart. I was part cavewoman, I decided, as the idea passed through my mind. But I was good. I cut my meat properly, even trying to keep my elbows off the table.

I was so not made for a place like this. Something Delilah seemed to be getting a kick out of every time I did something uncouth, if her smiles were any indication. Either that or she was thinking of dirty things to do to me as we ate, and that's why she was smiling so damned much.

"So," I said after a moment of cutting several pieces of roast on my plate, "you hate your job, like a lot of people do."

"*Hate* is a strong word. I used to love it. I loved doing the work, working for my parents, all of that kind of stuff. But over the past few years I haven't felt…felt the joy I used to feel about going to work in the morning. Enjoying my day. Celebrating the successes. Lately I've been thinking that Tiffani has the right idea."

"What do you mean?"

"She had the opportunity to work with them too. Hell, they wanted her more than they wanted me. But she refused. She came back here to live, to make a life of her own. And she's succeeded pretty well, if you ask me. She's never come running to them for help."

"I thought you both owned the lounge?"

"We do, but it has nothing to do with my parents. She reached out to me, and I decided I wanted to invest because I liked the idea of it. And I think it was a tiny bit of rebellion that I could handle at the time."

I ate another piece of roast and chewed slowly, thoughtfully. Despite how much of a dominant she was, there were still people that she wanted to please. I wondered if that's why she kept such an iron-clad control over her own life outside of her parents. When you didn't have the kind of autonomy you necessarily wanted, you looked for it anywhere you could. Was she doing that? Was that where her dominant streak came from?

It didn't matter. She was who she was, and I liked her for exactly that person.

"So, if I may ask, was getting into BDSM a tiny bit of rebellion against your parents too?"

Delilah chuckled as she finished chewing a piece of her tenderloin. "No," she admitted. "No, surprisingly that part of my lifestyle came first. My mother…my birth mother, I should specify, told me when I was young that I didn't owe anyone anything, that I could be as strong as I wanted to be, and to strive for what I wanted in life."

"Sounds like good advice to me," I replied.

"But she never got to see me grow up. She died when I was six."

"I'm so sorry."

"Thank you, Sabrina." She gave me a soft smile. "I never forgot what she told me. When I grew up and started to discover the things that I liked, I knew they were different than a lot of the other girls I knew. I knew I liked girls. I knew I liked control. And I knew I liked sex." She fiddled with her fork on the plate, pushing around what was left of her food. "I had a good friend when I was in university. I was there on my parents' dime, taking business management because of course I was going to succeed them in running the company." She rolled her eyes. "I asked her how she was paying for tuition. She'd cut off her family but also hadn't taken any student loans."

I put my chin in my hand, listening to her story intently.

"She was moonlighting as a dominatrix. Using that money to pay for school. It was a brilliant idea. One I wish I'd thought of before agreeing to whatever my parents wanted from me. But she taught me how to be a better dominant. More than tying people up and spanking them. I learned how to read people better, to know what they wanted before they could even get a word in edgewise. I learned, and I yearned

to have a life in that world. I even assisted at her dungeon a few times."
She smiled fondly, her eyes staring away into the memory. "We had
good times together. I lost contact with her after I met my…my ex.
She'd get jealous."

"The ex who made you give up relationships for good."

"The very same." She closed her eyes against the pain that flashed
across her face, and I longed to join her on the other side of the booth
and hold her against me. For both of us.

"Thank you."

She blinked. "Why?"

"For telling me about you. I know it can't be easy."

"You make it easy."

"And you flatter me far too easily."

"What can I say? You're easy to flatter." The heat that had receded
over the course of dinner came back full force. "And you blush so
beautifully whenever I compliment you."

I glanced away for only a second.

"And I can't wait to take you into my bed and ruin you," she said
in a softer voice, the words drifting to me over the table as I tried not to
react overtly to how much the mere idea turned me on.

We both passed on dessert and looked into each other's eyes over
the table as the waiter took our plates and told us the bill was covered.
I stared at Delilah, confused. She shrugged sheepishly and put a few
bills on the table.

"Is that okay?" Delilah asked softly.

"I'm…I don't know. I'm not used to…to any of this."

"Is there anything I can do to make you more comfortable?"

I looked away for only a moment, and in that time she got up from
the booth and came to my side. She stood in front of me, and I looked
up at her, towering above. It felt right. It felt like the position I should
be in. Fuck, I wanted her.

"Kiss me." The words dropped out of my mouth before I could
think about it.

She reacted like she didn't even have to consider it. She leaned
over, her eyes locked on mine, and drew me into a soft kiss. It was
surprisingly chaste and definitely not quite what I had been hoping for,
but it still pulled me up from my seat and into her arms.

"That's my good girl," she murmured against my lips and kissed
me again. I couldn't help but start to melt into her hold on me. When
we parted I had to catch my breath, breathing in deeply, in case she

decided to go for kiss number three. Unfortunately, I was spared that fate for now, as she collected her jacket and my purse, then held out her arm to me. "Shall we?"

I took my purse from her, and she led me back toward the lobby. She smiled at the host as we passed by his podium. He returned her smile and gave a wave that seemed a little more familiar than one would give to a passing customer. Of course she knew him. She owned the place—more or less.

"I have a request for you," Delilah said as we approached the elevator.

"Yes."

She chuckled that low, sultry chuckle of hers. "You haven't even heard what I wanted yet."

"I'll do anything," I said with feeling. "Anything you want, Mistress."

She stared at me for a long moment. "That's a dangerous thing to say to me."

"It's true."

"What happened to taking things slow?"

"Fuck slow."

She chuckled. "Come to my hotel room?"

I nodded before she'd even finished asking the question.

As we waited for the elevator Delilah wrapped her arm around my waist and pulled me in close. I let myself lean into her, reveled in her soft touch, her breath upon my neck, her hand softly rubbing at my hip. *I could get used to this.*

That was dangerous, though. Because if I got used to it, what wouldn't I do to keep it? How far would I go? How far would I let her push me? I didn't know, but there was a part of me that was all for finding out.

CHAPTER TWENTY-ONE

As the elevator doors closed behind us, I watched Delilah hit a button not for the ground floor. I glanced at her and saw the wicked smile on her face and felt my core begin to heat with need. She turned to me and pushed me roughly against the wall of the elevator and kissed me with wild abandon. I barely had a moment to catch my breath as she came in for a second kiss, and a third, like she was thirsty and my lips were the only water she wanted.

"Delilah." I moaned out loud, then shifted as the elevator slowed and came to a stop. Delilah was quick to back away as the door opened to admit a couple more passengers, who took one look at me and my dishevelled appearance and quickly looked away. Delilah only smirked at them.

A couple more floors passed as I tried to discreetly put myself back together, but I knew I still looked like I was interrupted halfway through sex. Still, I straightened my dress and fixed up my hair, using the mirrored finish of the elevator to guide me. Finally, the elevator slowed again, and the doors slid open. Delilah took my hand, and we exited—to the relief of the other couple, I'm sure.

She swiped her key card and opened a door down the hall from the elevator. She ushered me inside and I stopped a few steps in, gaping. It wasn't a hotel room like any I'd ever been in before. It was a suite, with multiple rooms and a hallway and a living area and a damned balcony. It looked more like a posh condo than a hotel room, and I turned around to look at Delilah as she closed the door behind me.

The next thing I knew I was up against the wall, Delilah's hands on my wrists, forcing them above my head as her body pressed into me. Her lips met mine as her knee found its way between my legs, rubbing against my girlcock. I moaned into her mouth, and she moved both my wrists to one hand in a movement I barely noticed with her devouring me. Then her free hand moved to my chest, caressing my breasts through the dress, giving them both ample attention as I moaned her name again and felt her laugh against me.

"Such a pretty little thing," she whispered in my ear, biting at my earlobe. "I can't wait to ruin you."

"P...please!" I begged her, almost bodily coming off the wall to press harder against her as if I could prove my want and need by getting closer.

"What do you want, pet? Tell me what you want."

I closed my eyes and tried to find my words as she kept playing with my nipples through the fabric of the dress. I gasped as she pinched one, hard, and squirmed against her hold.

"Come on, pet. Talk to me. Tell me what you want from me tonight."

I took a deep breath, fighting to speak through the stimulation pooling down in my center. I cried out as she doted on my other nipple, then dipped her head and ran her tongue along my neck. I moaned again as I felt teeth on my collarbone, right above where my dress came to an end.

"Please." The word was pulled out of me by a simple desire: I needed her. I needed to be hers. "Make me yours."

"You are mine, pet," she whispered in my ear. "All mine. Have been since that first coil of rope I wrapped around your body. Since I tightened it and pulled you to me, made you fall to your knees that first time. You've been mine since the moment you put my strap in your mouth, since you lubed it up with that pretty little tongue of yours. You were mine the moment you came with my strap in that hot, tight fuck hole of yours." She lifted her knee, pressing harder into my crotch, and I moaned again for her. Then I felt her free hand move up my body, from my chest to my throat. My breathing quickened as my thoughts ran rampant about what she could do to me in this position. I wanted her to tighten her hand around me, make it hard to breathe, to think, to focus on anything but her, mere centimeters away from me. "Is this what you want, my hot little hole? Me to control you? Everything about you? Your body, your orgasms, your very breathing?"

I nodded only because I didn't think I could make the words come out without begging and moaning for her to do it. I needed her to control me, to control everything. I wanted it. I wanted to be hers.

In a quick movement she spun me away from the wall, my back suddenly against her chest. One arm wrapped around me, her hand still on my throat, as her other hand gently caressed my cheek. She put pressure on my throat but not enough to really affect anything, and I moaned again, desperate for her to choke me.

"Ah, ah, ah, pet. Not that way." Her soft words drifted into my head. Her other hand trailed across my cheek until it was situated over my mouth. "I want you to take a deep breath and let it all out. Empty those lungs of yours."

I did as she commanded. I breathed in heavily through my nose, flinching at the noise it made, then let it all out through my mouth. The second it felt like I had no air left in me to let out, her hand clamped down over my mouth, her fingers pinching my nose at the same time. I was left in this weird, unbreathing space that sent shock waves of pleasure through me at the same time that a corner of my brain was starting to feel panic. This was something we hadn't done before. This was new. But Delilah was my Mistress. She wouldn't hurt me. She wouldn't let me be hurt.

I trusted her.

But after about fifteen seconds my lungs began to burn with the lack of air, my body flinching and bucking a little as I tried to find a way to breathe. It was an intoxicating mix of fear and overwhelming pleasure to have one of the most basic fundamentals of my life taken away from me, to be controlled by my Mistress.

I whined behind her hand, fidgeting and writhing under her grip until suddenly she removed her hand, and I gasped in a full breath of air as fast as I could. It was difficult to settle down my lungs as I focused on breathing as much as I could, so much I almost choked on it, but the moment I had finished breathing out she clamped her hand down again. I fell into that blissful state of mind where I was somehow still cognizant of what was happening but there was no dire need to do anything about it. I wanted to let it all happen, to let my Mistress control me as she would. She released and I breathed in deeply again without thinking about it, lungs aching after twice being deprived of air for too long.

"Good pet," she said. "You're such a good girl for me."

"Yes, Mistress," I managed to say through deep, gulping breaths of air. She didn't clamp down again, instead running her hand over my cheek again, then planting a kiss on the back of my neck.

"I want to keep you, you know that, pet? I want you with me at all times, always at my side, a collar around your neck to make sure everyone knows who exactly you belong to. Ready to fall to your knees when I snap my fingers." I gasped as her mouth found my neck and I felt her bite down, hard.

"Mistress!" I cried out, squirming as she held me tighter, her teeth clamping down as she sucked a bruise into my skin. I squirmed and bucked but she held on tight as I moaned and felt myself drop deeper and deeper into that bliss. Finally, when she released me, I let out another hiss of pain but was still held in her arms.

"Good pet. Now everyone can see that you're mine. My little hole, for me to use as I wish."

I moaned again at her words. Apparently I had a degradation fetish. Who knew? Not me.

"Now, I'm going to snap my fingers, pet. Do you remember what I want you to do?"

I nodded, unable to see her without turning around. Even in this mindless state I was in, I could remember what she'd said. She held out her hand over my shoulder so I could see it, then snapped loudly.

I fell to my knees immediately, landing on the plush carpet. My dress bunched up awkwardly, but I didn't care. I was on my knees for my Mistress, as she'd asked.

"What a good girl you are for me. Do you want to be my good girl?" I nodded as she moved around me, her hand touching my head softly. "Then will you do whatever I tell you to?" I nodded again, not so patiently waiting for her next command. "Then bark for me."

My mouth dropped open in surprise. "W-what?" I gasped.

"You're my good girl, aren't you? My good pet? Then I want you to bark for me."

She was asking me to bark like a dog? What the hell was that? Should I do it? Should I not do it? I was still trying to think it over when I heard a definitive *woof* slip out of my mouth.

I covered my mouth. Did I just do that?

"Very good, pet. Now do it again, but louder."

"Woof!" I barked louder. I stuck my tongue out and panted for good measure.

Delilah smiled down at me, running her hands over my head as she pulled the bobby pins out of my buns and let my hair fall free. Her nails scratching through my hair and a little behind my ears felt so fucking good.

"Good girl, Sabrina." She scratched behind my ear some more. "Again."

"Woof!"

"Again."

"Woof!"

"Good girl!" She laughed and stepped around me again, disappearing from view. I stayed on my knees, awaiting her next command.

"Come, pet."

I turned and started to crawl further into the room, following the sound of her voice. I had to hike up my dress until it was above my knees to move properly. The carpet dug into my skin a little, but the pain didn't bother me as I made my way slowly into the main room. Two couches sat perpendicular to each other, facing the far wall that had a large television mounted on it. It was the nicest hotel room I'd ever been in.

Delilah had taken a seat on the larger couch, her legs crossed at the knee, arms stretched out along the back. She wasn't even watching me as I crawled toward her, stopping in front of her with a quiet bark as if to tell her *hey, I'm here.*

She reached out a hand imperiously and I stared for a moment, unsure what to do. We were playing this game, but I didn't know the rules. I leaned forward and tentatively licked her hand. She gasped, then chuckled, and I couldn't help but share her smile as she looked at me.

"Very good, pet. Very good." She patted the couch beside her. "Up."

I climbed onto the couch, staying on my hands and knees. Delilah touched her hand to my cheek, her palm warm against my skin. I closed my eyes and leaned into it, rubbing my face against her as if to scent mark her. She reached further, using her short nails to scratch behind my ears and into my hair, everywhere she could reach. If I had a damned tail, it would've definitely been wagging.

She pulled my head down onto her lap, uncrossing her legs to allow me to lie on her thighs. I sighed in contentment and closed my eyes for a moment, allowing my thoughts to melt away as I focused solely on listening for her next command.

But there was a thought that stuck in the back of my brain, a reminder of what had destroyed her first relationship. One built solely on the love of the dominant, but not the submissive. I wasn't like that. I knew I wasn't like that. But did Delilah? How could I show her how much she meant to me? Even in a game like this?

"Such a good pet for me," Delilah was saying as she played with my hair. "So beautiful, so willing. What a good girl you are."

I moaned with the praise, moving my head so I could lick at her hand, but she forced my head back down and I went with it. I wanted to show her I cared for her too, but right now it felt so good for her to run her fingers over me.

"Speak, my good girl. I want to know how you're feeling."

I barked, softly, from my position on her thighs, my hands and knees curled up underneath me.

"No, pet. Use your words. Tell me if this is too much."

I barked again, shaking my head enough that she had to be able to feel it. I didn't want this game to end.

She laughed. "I guess that answers my question." Her hand paused in my hair for a moment, and I tilted my head to look up at her face, shadowed in the darkness of the room. "Or are you so deep in your puppy space that you don't really know what I'm asking for?"

I barked again, hoping she'd understand what I was saying. I mean, it was kind of futile, hoping she'd understand my barks, but I didn't want to speak. This was better than talking, than being nervous, anxious, about what to say and do. This was easy. This was beautiful. She was beautiful. And I wanted to please her.

I lifted my head, pushing myself to hands and knees once more, and nuzzled against her. I found her chest and pressed my cheek against her breasts. I continued travelling upward, rubbing myself against her, trying to show her how much I cared, how much I wanted to be with her, while still playing the game. I loved this game. I...I really liked her.

When I came to her head and face I found her eyes on me, watching intently. It was like she was waiting to see exactly what I was going to do. I wasn't even sure what I was going to do. What was the plan here? To show her I could be the perfect puppy girl for her? Or to show her how much I was enjoying getting to be her pet?

Then I licked her cheek. A big, sloppy, wet lick that made her pull back with a yelp and a wild laugh. She reached out and dug her fingers into my hair again, but instead of giving soft pets and scritches, she tightened her grip and pulled my head sharply away from her as she wiped her cheek with her other hand. I couldn't help the smile that found its way to my lips as she glared at me with no hint of real anger on her face.

"Did I give you permission to lick me, pet?"

I gave her two little barks, hoping she'd understand that two meant *no*.

"That's right. I didn't. I don't appreciate being drooled on by my pet."

I gave her what I hoped was a wicked grin, then surged forward, hoping to catch her off guard. I had my tongue sticking out of my mouth when her hand in my hair gripped tighter than before, pulling me back as her other hand shot forward and pinched my tongue between her thumb and forefinger.

"*Bad* girl," she said. She shook her head and pulled on my tongue a little as her other hand pulled my head backward. It was the strangest feeling, but the pain was quickly swallowed by the pleasure of her touching me, playing with me. "That was not code for *do it again*, pet."

She pulled both sides of my head harder and a loud moan slipped from my lips.

"That's right, pet. I control you. I own you, you understand?" I let out a soft bark of acquiescence. She released her grip on my tongue and hair. "Very good. Now, we're going to go to the bed, and you're going to be a good pet and crawl to the bedroom, understood?"

I barked once more, then awkwardly flopped off the couch back onto the carpeted floor. She stood up and took off her jacket, leaving it on the couch as she led the way down a small hallway. An open door at the end of the hall led to a bathroom much larger than the one in my apartment, but we turned through a doorway before that and entered a bedroom that was about the same size as my whole apartment. A massive king-size bed took up a good chunk of the room, the wooden headboard pushed against the far wall and both sides clear for tired sleepers to climb on.

I crawled to the bed and put a paw—I mean hand—on the mattress, ready to climb up when Delilah reached out and smacked my hand lightly.

"No. Bad pet." She shook her head. "Pets sleep on the floor."

I let out a pretty convincing whine, wondering if this was part of the game or something different.

"If you're going to be on the bed with me, you're going to have to stop being my puppy for the night. Can you handle that?"

I stared at her for a long moment. I didn't want to stop the game, but I didn't want to have to sleep on the floor either.

As if she could sense my difficulty deciding, she leaned down and placed a hand against my cheek. "I promise, this is not the last time you'll get to be my puppy."

I barked happily at her and tried to lick her again, but she pulled away too quickly, grinning at me.

"On your feet, Sabrina."

On shaky legs I managed to stand, my knees complaining about the new position when they'd just gotten used to the old one.

"Thank you, Mistress," I said, trying hard to convey everything that I felt about her into my words, my look, my gaze on her.

She smiled at me and held out her hand. I took it in mine and brought it to my lips, bestowing a kiss upon her knuckles. She looked almost surprised at that but recovered quickly and led me to the bed.

"Bend over the bed, pet."

I cocked my head to the side. "What? Why?"

She moved around me to an open suitcase that was sitting on one of those folding racks that were usually found in hotel room closets. She started rummaging around in it, and her voice drifted back to me.

"You were a bad girl, pet," she said with authority. "Bad girls get punished."

I whined again and she shot me a look that was purely sadistic pleasure, but I did what she'd demanded. I bent over the edge of the bed, my dress hiking up a little with the movement. I turned my head to watch Delilah as she returned with a thick leather paddle with a cut-out of a heart at the end of it. I looked away quickly, not wanting to see what she had planned for that.

"Hike up that dress, pet."

I kept my position and pulled the dress up until my panty-clad ass was revealed. I felt her hand on me, pulling down my underwear one side at a time until it was on the floor around my ankles.

"Now, I was going to forgive the lick to my face as simple young puppy exuberance," she said, running a hand up my thigh and letting it linger over my ass cheek. "But then you tried to do it again. And that I'm not going to stand for, understood?"

"Yes, Mistress." The words dropped from my mouth without my even thinking about them.

She laughed. "So eager to please. What a lovely pet you are." I felt her fingers on my backside and almost reared back to get her to touch me more. Her mere caress was intoxicating. "Now, pet, there is discipline. Ten strokes with the paddle, I think."

I gasped at the idea. Outside of childhood bullshit, I'd never been spanked before, never mind with a paddle. For the briefest second my safeword was on my tongue, but I didn't speak it. I wanted to know what this would feel like. I wanted her to enjoy herself. I wanted all of it.

"Are you ready, pet?" she asked.

"Yes, Mistress."

"Excellent. Then let's begin."

CHAPTER TWENTY-TWO

The first blow of the paddle made me cry out. The second made me whimper. The third made me moan. Delilah chuckled at each reaction, rubbing my skin between each hit as if her touch could soothe some of the pain away before the next blow came. And truly, it did. Each and every touch felt like a soothing balm against an ocean of intensity that was threatening to overwhelm me.

But there was something itching in the back of my head, something that wasn't letting me fall into that blissful fog that I remembered from the rope classes. No matter how much I tried, I couldn't help but think about Delilah's ex, and how she treated my Mistress. What was I giving back to her while we played? Was I just as bad, only taking from her and giving nothing that she needed?

After she reached five I felt the bed dip and turned my head to see her put a knee up to lean over me. She brushed my hair back with one hand, trailing her fingers down my neck.

"How are you feeling, pet?" she asked softly. The paddle dangled from her other hand. "Do you need to stop? I know this is new for you."

I took a deep breath, then a second one, trying to get my pleasure-addled brain to fire on all cylinders. Or at least more cylinders.

"Green." I wanted her to keep going. I needed more. And that thought pulled me out of the pleasure even more. If I was feeling like this, I could only wonder what she was feeling. Was it really not bugging her at all that I was only taking? Was I reminding her of her ex, or was I overthinking everything?

"Are you sure?"

I caught her eye and opened my mouth to say *yes, Mistress,* but there was something in her eyes that stopped me. She was still smiling, still seemed to be enjoying what she was doing, and I was glad for that. But the way her eyes crinkled in the corners—her brow furrowed slightly. It made me wonder exactly what was going through her head.

I had to be honest with her. I wanted to keep going, but the longer we paused, the more my mind kept slipping into that sullen possibility that I was only taking from her. I bit my tongue lightly for a moment, then forced the words out of my mouth.

"Yellow, Mistress."

She straightened a little, the smile fading into a concerned line as she dropped the paddle to the bed. "Are you all right, pet?"

I lifted myself up, letting my dress fall back to my ankles, then turned and sat on the bed beside her. I winced from the punishment on my ass, then I took her hands and put them in my lap and held them tenderly.

"Not entirely," I said. "But I'm more worried about you."

"Me? Why are you worried about me?" She let out a little laugh. "I'm good. I'm in my happy place."

"I'm…not. I mean I'm almost getting there, but I can't seem to shake some thoughts that are preventing it.'"

"Can I ask what thoughts?"

I couldn't meet her eyes. "That I'm no different than your ex. Taking from you and giving nothing back."

"Oh, Sabrina, no…"

"Yes. You're doing all these things and I'm loving it so much. But it feels so…one-sided."

"Pet, no, it's definitely not one-sided. I assure you of that." She reached out and put her hand to my cheek. "I promise, you are nothing like her. Simply worrying about it makes you different. You care, Sabrina, and I can't thank you enough for that."

I fell to my knees in front of her and I looked up into her face that was so soft with worry and care that I almost felt like crying. "But I'm not giving back. I don't understand."

"You do give back. Your trust in me, your desire, your submission. They're all gifts that you give me as we play. Gifts that you offer gladly, and I accept humbly—to a point."

She smiled at me that way that made me want to melt, and I turned my cheek into her hand and nuzzled her palm.

"I'm…I'm worried," I said softly.

"About what, pet?"

"That there's some comparison between me and your ex going on in your head."

She sighed. "I won't lie to you and say she isn't on my mind a little. She lives in the back of my brain, a little gremlin that tries to ruin my happiness when I'm feeling particularly happy with myself."

I stared at her. I had plenty of those gremlins of my own. "How do you not listen to her?"

"By feeling—knowing—that I'm stronger than her. That I deserve better, deserve more, than she ever gave me. It's not perfect, doesn't always work, but I manage most of the time."

We were quiet for a long moment, as if we were both lost in our thoughts. Despite her words I couldn't shake the feeling that I wasn't giving back enough, that I wasn't doing enough. That I was like her ex, no matter what she said. I didn't want that. I didn't want her to feel that way.

"I'm sorry," I said. "I'm sorry I stopped the play."

"Don't be sorry, pet. That's exactly what the safewords are for. To stop things if something isn't feeling right." She looked down into my eyes and I couldn't look away from her. "If anything, I should be apologizing to you."

"What? Why?"

"Because my past is taking away from your present. That thoughts of my ex are preventing you from reaching the bliss you deserve. And you do deserve it, Sabrina. You deserve all the happiness in the world."

It was a hard-fought battle not to scoff at that, but with her hand on my cheek and her eyes on mine, I wanted to believe her. I was tired of having a life filled with nothing but work, nothing but living in the past and looking toward a future that might never be.

"Thank you, Delilah."

She cocked her head to the side slightly. "Why, pet?"

"For everything. For tonight, for last week. Everything. I don't think I could ever thank you enough for what you've done for me."

"And what have I done for you?"

I took a moment before I could answer. "Taught me to live."

She pulled me into a hug, pressing my head against her chest as her chin rested on my head. I melted in her arms, wanting to stay like this forever. "You're very welcome. You're my beautiful, wonderful little pet."

I let out a small woof of acknowledgement and she chuckled.

She released me and I pulled back enough to see her face again. "You liked being my puppy, then?"

"But I think you knew that was going to happen, it's why you planned it."

She laughed. "You're giving me far too much credit. My only plan for tonight was to get you on your knees. Beyond that I've been making it up as I go."

"Really?"

"Really, pet. But I am very glad we found something you really enjoy."

"I…really liked the breath play too."

"That, I promise to keep in mind."

I took a deep breath. "We can get back to it, if you'd like." I gave her a smile. "I believe I still have some discipline coming for trying to lick your face."

It was her turn to crack a grin. "I think we might save that for a later day. I think I have a different plan in mind."

"Oh? Do tell."

She shook her head. "I wouldn't want to ruin the surprise, but it does involve getting you out of this beautiful dress of yours."

I got up from the floor and turned around. "Unzip me?" I was rewarded with a soft hum and the feeling of the zip on the dress being pulled down slowly but surely, the fabric parting between my shoulder blades all the way down to my waist. Soft fingers caressed my skin, and my heart fluttered with pleasure. I couldn't even fathom what might be going through her mind.

"Take it off, pet."

I let the dress fall to the floor, leaving me in the nude, my underwear still by the bed. I felt her nails gently scrape against me and gasped at the sensation. She reached around me, her arms wrapping tightly as I felt her lean forward, pressing herself into my back. Her lips found my shoulder, my collarbone, my neck, and she kissed a trail up to my ear.

"I have a question, pet. And I want an honest answer from you."

"Yes, Mistress."

She gently nibbled on my earlobe, tongue flicking against the small piercing, and I couldn't stop the moan that slipped out of my mouth.

"I want to know how you would like me to take you."

I froze up as her hands caressed the front of my body, running from my stomach down to my hips and waist, then back up to my breasts. I had trouble wrapping my brain around her question as she fondled my breasts, her fingers roaming over my hardening nipples.

For a second, I had the briefest thought of putting my girlcock to good use, but the idea brought with it a wave of nausea that I had to fight back before my Mistress noticed it. I was not about to let my bottom dysphoria ruin a good night. Instead I focused on her touching me, on how I would like her to continue touching me, and the new addition of exactly how I would like to be touching her.

I turned around in her arms, pressing myself against her as I leaned in and kissed her softly. "I want to please you," I said softly, my hands dropping to the hem of her top. She grabbed my wrists, halting my movement, as her eyes searched my face.

"You don't have to..." She trailed off when I shook my head.

"I want to. I'm not like her, and I want to prove that to you. I want to please you, pleasure you, give you everything that you might think you could never ask for." I stood on my tiptoes and leaned into her ear. "I want to give you what you desire, Mistress. What you *need*."

She let go of my wrists, but one hand came up and grabbed my chin hard, and she pulled my gaze back to her face.

"I will allow this, *pet*," she said coolly, her breath hitting my face as she spoke. "But know that you're getting mighty close to forgetting your place here."

I tried to shake my head, but she was holding me too tightly. "No, Mistress. My only wish is to please you. To serve you."

"Are you arguing with me, Sabrina?"

"No, Mistress."

"Then why do you keep talking when I haven't told you to speak?"

I clamped my lips shut before another word could be uttered. She held my chin in her hand for a moment longer, then gave me a soft, sensual kiss that drew another moan from between my clenched teeth. Then she pushed me, hard. I stumbled backward and hit the edge of the bed with the back of my knees, falling onto the blanket.

"Stay," she said in that commanding tone she'd used earlier. I lay on the bed, unmoving, but my eyes followed her as best I could in my periphery. She stripped off her shirt and pants, leaving them on the floor, then moved out of my line of sight. A moment later I heard her rummaging around in something, then the bed shifted as she climbed onto it. "You can move now, pet."

I turned to look at her, naked and crawling across the bed. I got to my knees, bowing my head but keeping my eyes on her as best I could in case another command was incoming. She didn't move to me but instead lay down near the head of the bed. Her legs trailed back toward me, and I delicately touched her ankle, running my hand up and down her soft skin.

"Up here, pet."

She patted the bed beside her, and I moved up slowly, running my hand up her leg and over her thigh and settled on her hip. She held out her hand and opened it, revealing a small, purple bullet vibe.

"Do I need to tell you how to use that, pet?" Her voice had a hint of laughter to it, and I shook my head quickly but didn't speak. She hadn't granted me permission to speak. "Then use those fingers of yours, your tongue, whatever you decide, and pleasure me." She dropped the vibe into my hands. "Oh, and you've got five minutes."

I stared at her. What was she talking about?

"Five minutes, pet. Your time already started."

I panicked and dropped the vibe to the bed. It started to roll away and I swept it back up quickly before climbing over Delilah's legs and positioning myself so I could use my fingers the way one of my exes had tried to teach me. Just like riding a bike, I thought quietly, aware that Delilah still hadn't given me permission to speak.

My fingers found her core and found it absolutely wet, like what we'd done before had already soaked her. I slipped my first finger in, then quickly added the second. I tried to remember how I had pleased her the last time, pushing my fingers deep inside her as I started the vibrator with my other hand and introduced it to Delilah's nipple. She bucked off the bed at the touch of it and I pulled back a little, teasing the tip, then reached over to the other to give it a fair turn.

"S-Sabrina," Delilah moaned.

I fought not to say something to her in response. I wanted her to know how good she was making me feel by letting me please her and serve her.

"More," she demanded.

I did my best to give her what she wanted. I kept my fingers inside her and moved with a rhythm that I tried to emulate with the vibrator against her nipples. I leaned over and took the closer of the two nipples into my mouth and gently ran my teeth over it. I pulled on it slightly, with more suction than bite. Delilah gasped beneath me and bucked her hips. I almost lost my fingering position, but I refocused my efforts down there and thrust deeper. I tried to find that spot that I knew would drive her even higher.

I glanced at the alarm clock that sat on the bedside table. Two minutes had passed already, and I was frantic to build her up to her orgasm in the three that were left.

I brought the vibe down to Delilah's labia, letting it buzz around the lips for a second before moving it up to Delilah's clit. She gasped and moaned as the vibrations hit her and I doubled my efforts with my fingers, slipping a third in as she grew wetter and wetter.

"Fuck yes!" Delilah's cry was loud enough that it probably made it through the walls of the hotel room, but she didn't seem to care as she bucked under my ministrations. Her reaction gave me more confidence in what I was doing, and I leaned down again to take her nipple into my mouth along with a small bit of her breast itself. I sucked long and hard enough to probably leave a hickey around her areola. She cried out again as I licked the nipple inside my mouth.

"Yes, yes, yes." The words slipped out of my Mistress as I left a trail of kisses down her breast and onto her abdomen. Between keeping the vibrator on her clit with the palm of my hand and having my fingers inside her there wasn't a good, flexible way I could assist down there, so as I reached her waist I started to head back up. I left wet kisses up the entire way as I nibbled lightly at her skin. I felt her clench around my fingers as I reached her collarbone and started to suck at a tender spot.

"Don't you dare!"

She breathed out and I faltered. I released her skin and hoped I hadn't left too much of a mark—though a part of me was excited about the idea of getting to mark my Mistress even in that tiny way. My eyes caught on the clock again as it turned to five minutes, and Delilah cried out one more time and her body trembled beneath me. Carefully, I eased the vibrator off her clit and she settled a little bit as I withdrew my fingers slowly, one at a time.

"Did I tell you to stop?" Her voice was light, breathy, and had a hint of annoyance to it. "Or did I tell you that you could try to mark me?"

I glanced at the clock, then back to her, in an attempt to make her understand without saying anything since she hadn't given me permission to speak. I hung my head at the chastisement and let the vibrator fall to the bed between us and my wet fingers settle on my leg. I wanted to lick my hand clean, but I also knew to wait to see what my Mistress had to say before I did anything else.

"I know you had your time limit, pet, but that didn't mean you had to stop." She sounded a little less annoyed now, as she pushed herself up into a sitting position on the bed. "But I suppose you did accomplish your task, didn't you? With only a few seconds to spare, at that."

Elation filled me and I felt myself sit a little taller, my back a little straighter. She looked me over with those golden eyes of hers and gave me a smile as she reached for the vibrator between us.

"However, you did try to mark me, without permission." She shook her head. "That might have cost you your reward, pet."

My head perked up at *reward*, but I had a feeling there was more to it than that. I started to speak but stopped quickly at the look Delilah gave me.

"Good pet. Pets only speak when they're given permission, don't they?"

I nodded and settled onto my knees on the bed, my paws— hands—in front of me. I tried to wait patiently while my Mistress came down from the high of her orgasm, tried to be her good pet and wait to see what this reward might be, if I'd earned it or not.

"Stay." There was no way I could move after that command.

She climbed off the bed, but this time I was able to watch her as she moved over to her suitcase and pulled out what looked like a long length of dark purple rope. She brought it back to the bed with her and snapped her fingers at me. I was already kneeling, so I gave her my attention, primed to move whichever way she wished.

"Sit up on your knees, pet, and put your wrists at your sides," Delilah commanded as she unfurled the rope, keeping a section taut between her hands. I sat up, my ass off my heels, but still putting my weight on my knees on the bed. It was a little unsteady, but my Mistress was quick to put her hand out and ensure I didn't fall over. Then she took the rope and started wrapping it around my hips with deft movements that spoke of years of practice. After the first couple rounds she wrapped more rope around my wrists and knotted them tightly, keeping my hands stuck to my hips. "Now, spread your legs, pet." I did the best I could, spreading my thighs enough that she could maneuver the rope between them and pull up, making me cry out as my girlcock was caught in the rope and pulled upward. She added a quick loop around it, which forced it to stay erect and left me panting with need.

Then she reached over on the bed and grabbed the forgotten vibrator.

"Your turn, pet," she said slyly, turning on the vibrator and bringing it to one of my nipples. I cried out wordlessly, my legs wobbling as I tried to keep myself up on my knees. She ran the vibrator over my other nipple, and I bit back the words that threatened to cause me to speak when my Mistress hadn't given me permission. Then she reached downward and tugged my girlcock to the side, tucking the vibrator between the rope and my skin.

I couldn't stop the moan that left my mouth as the powerful vibrations all but made me writhe on the bed and I saw Delilah's face above me, smiling widely.

"Now, pet. I'm going to make you a deal."

I stared at her as I tried to control my breathing against the pleasure that was building in my core and threatening to overcome all the thoughts in my head with a single, absolute need for her to touch me and use me and want me in whatever way she so fucking desired. I managed to clear my head to look her in the eyes again, waiting for her to tell me what this deal was.

"My beautiful pet," she said, running her fingers across my cheek in a moment that made me close my eyes and cherish the present. "You're going to be allowed to orgasm, I've decided." I glanced up at her, a little surprised. I hadn't really been thinking of my own orgasm tonight, focusing mostly on pleasing my Mistress. "But there's a catch."

I whined as she pressed a button on the vibrator and the power increased. She grinned, a hint of the sadist within peeking out from the look she gave me, and I shivered and cried out again as I tried to reach toward my girlcock but couldn't, my wrists tightly bound to either side of me.

"You've only got five minutes."

CHAPTER TWENTY-THREE

I awoke slowly, nestled into a bed that was far more comfortable than my usual one, with a pair of arms wrapped around me and a soft chest pressed against my back. I didn't roll over, instead letting out a soft breath and leaning back against Delilah as I brought my hands up to my face and rubbed a little of the sleep from my eyes. I caught sight of the rope marks on my wrists and smiled.

I hadn't made it in the five minutes she'd given me. But that was okay. There would be other nights, other challenges, other times I didn't almost give her a hickey when I hadn't been given permission to do so. Of course, that hadn't stopped her from sucking a second bruise into the side of my neck, something I would have to explain to Cori come Monday morning.

But I didn't mind. The thought of her marking me like that almost pushed me over that elusive edge that was difficult enough to reach anyway, even without some bondage to play into it.

At that thought, I glanced at my wrists again and ran a finger along my wrist to feel the rope mark that was almost entirely faded. I guess if they weren't fading that would be a bad thing, but damn, did I want them to stick around for longer. I didn't care about showing them off or anything, I loved the idea of being marked by my Mistress, of there being a show of ownership, a roadmap of what she'd done for me. To me.

Damn, I had it bad for her. And what really scared me was how attached to this I was getting. Was I going to find myself changing for her? I was afraid of that. I'd fought so damned hard to be the real me, I didn't want to be throwing it all away for someone who might not fully like who I was.

Of course, she hadn't given me reason to think that she didn't like me for exactly who I was. I didn't even know why the thought even crossed my mind at all. Duh, trauma. But fuck, I wished I could think straight instead of my mind going in so many different directions at once. But it was Delilah. There was no way I could think straight with her. She was intoxicating, amazing, terrifying in her ability to draw out the things I wanted to feel, to experience, and turn them into pleasure and pain and everything else.

I kind of wished I had my phone with me, but it was still in my purse back near the door to the room. Where I'd dropped it when Delilah pushed me against the wall. At least with it I'd be doomscrolling or something right now instead of overthinking all the potential good things going on in my life right now. I could do this. I could have a relationship with Delilah and not be forced to change who I was, change my goals. I could have both. I could have it all, I needed to remember that.

With my thoughts finally calmed enough to stop grilling me, I snuggled into Delilah's sleeping form and wrapped myself in her warmth. I felt her stir against me.

"Mm-hmm," Delilah moaned into me, and I shivered as her breath cascaded down my neck and back.

"Good morning, Mistress," I said softly, snuggled into her arms.

"Good morning to you, my pet."

I squirmed a little as her lips tickled the fine hairs on the back of my neck. She kissed me once, twice, three times, her arms wrapping tighter around me as I melted into her.

"I could definitely get used to this," Delilah murmured.

"Used to what?"

She shifted slightly. "To waking up like this. A beautiful woman, wrapped in my arms every morning, greeting the day by calling me *Mistress.*"

I felt that heady mix of arousal and embarrassment begin to take over my face as I squirmed a little against her. A flash of insecurity flitted through me, and I said the stupidest thing I could think of. "I'm sure you could have had plenty of beautiful woman who would be chomping at the bit to wake up next to you and call you Mistress."

I felt her tense against me, and I resisted the urge to smack myself in the forehead. *Stupid, Sabrina. Really fucking stupid.* She didn't need me to remind her of what she could have had all these years that she had been avoiding it. I'm sure that it was as on her mind as the idea of her wanting me seemed a little ludicrous to the eviler parts of my brain.

"I'm so—" I started to say but Delilah suddenly wrapped her arms around me tight and I lost the word before it could slip out.

"Don't apologize, pet. I always want to hear what's on your mind."

I managed to shake my head slightly. "But it's not always a good thing."

"I don't care, I'm not here only for the good. I want you to understand that I want to be here with you, no matter what goes through that head of yours. I want the only degrading to happen not from your head but from my mouth when we play together and I treat you like the little slut you are."

"Fuck," I groaned and eased myself back into her some more, definitely invading any sense of personal space she might have had.

"Oh, did my little whore get turned on when I called her a slut?"

I moaned again, those stupid thoughts in my brain fading away slowly as new ones formed. The idea of being her little slut, sucking her strap again, feeling her take me again like she did that first night. I pushed my ass against her again, almost trying to make her understand what I needed without saying it outright. I didn't want to use my words. I wanted that floaty feeling again, that bliss that came with knowing that I was serving and pleasing my Mistress however she wished, and the pleasure that came with that.

"Stay right here, my gorgeous slut. I'll be right back."

Before I could react, her arms were gone and I was suddenly alone in the bed. I rolled over to see my Mistress digging around in that backpack of hers again. My heart skipped a beat when she pulled out the harness and the same dildo she'd used that first night, along with the bottle of lube I remembered tasting. I swore I started panting right then, imagining her taking me in this bed as I cried out her name.

It didn't take her long to have the harness on and the dildo in place, and she returned to the bed with the lube in hand.

"On your knees, you needy little puppy. I promise to take care of you."

I whined and rolled to my knees immediately, the sound of her voice, the look in her eyes, all of it making me so wet and needy for her.

"I'm going to work you open first, slut," she said from behind me, and I felt the first dribbles of lube roll down my ass. "I'm going to make you nice and open for me, like the good little fuck hole that you are." I whined again as she pushed a single digit into me.

That simple action almost made me want to orgasm, and as she put another finger in a moment later I cried out wordlessly. It wasn't long before she added the third and there was nothing left of me but a quaking puddle on the bed, needing to be used.

"What a desperate, needy little puppy. Whining for me to use you, to fill you. To treat you like the dirty whore you are."

By the time she started to slip the dildo in I was ready for her to start railing me until I couldn't speak anymore. All I wanted to do was make incoherent sounds that may have come across vaguely as barks for my Mistress.

And bark I did.

"Good girl. Good puppy. All you need is some firm handling, don't you, my fucking sloppy pet?" I barked my affirmative to her as she thrust into me. "That's it, pet. Speak!"

I barked again.

"Good girl! Again!"

She reached that perfect spot inside me, and instead of barking I let out a kind of howl and my mind went completely blank.

Then my stomach dropped into a pit as I heard a new voice break through my moans and Delilah's grunts.

"Delilah!"

My Mistress froze halfway out of me, and I looked around wildly, trying to find the source of the voice. A man stood just inside the doorway to the room, clad in a smart-looking business suit. Heat flared through me in equal parts embarrassment and anger as I shouted, "Who the fuck are you? Get the fuck out of our room!"

"Dad?" she exclaimed with a screech, and I cried out as she pulled all the way out of me and I fell to the bed, my sphincter on fire, tears on my face. I heaved in a breath of air and tried to stop myself from crying, but I couldn't stop the tears and the pain.

"What do you mean, *dad*?" I shouted.

"Sabrina!" Delilah said, and I felt her hands on me as if checking me over.

"Delilah!" that voice shouted again, and I flinched from the anger apparent in it. "What the hell are you doing?"

"Dad!" Delilah again, shouting over the man's voice. "Get out of my bedroom!"

"It's not yours. It's the hotel's. And I own the hotel. And you are here on my dime, so I will not leave."

I buried my face in the pillow and tried to claw at the blankets beneath me to cover myself. Delilah's hands left me, and my heart sank as I managed to pull a sheet up to cover my upper body, but part of my legs and my crotch were still on display for a hot second.

"Finally," I heard her dad say. "At least you're with a man this time."

Rage flowed through me, and I pulled the sheet off, about ready to swing my legs off the bed and have a fucking go at this asshole. Delilah's hands reached out for me, grabbing my arm before I could climb off the bed.

"Sabrina! No! He's not worth it!"

"Fucking let go of me! You heard what he called me!"

"Sabrina!"

She pulled hard against me, trying to keep me on the bed. I managed to get up, but she pulled me back down.

"Please!" I'd never heard her sound like she was begging before, and it shocked me enough to make me stop trying to get up, but I kept a hard glare on the man in the doorway.

"Don't tell me you're one of those men who think—"

"Oh, fuck that!" I shouted and pulled against Delilah's grip again. *"Dad! Get out!"*

He looked between the two of us, anger clear on his face, but he seemed to be putting things together in his head and realizing that this wasn't the place to have this conversation.

"Living room, Delilah. Now."

"I'll be there in a minute."

I turned to look at her, uncomfortable with how subdued she sounded. "She's not going—"

"Sabrina!" she said quickly as her father turned back toward me, opening his mouth as if to say something more. "Dad! Just go, I'll be right out."

He spun on his heel and left the room. Delilah let go of me slowly, as if ready to grab me again if I decided to go after him. But the rush of adrenaline was starting to pound in my head, and I tried to focus on my breathing to calm things down some as I turned to address my girlfriend.

"What the actual fuck is going on?"

She shook her head. "I'm sorry. I'm so sorry. I'll explain everything later, I promise. Just stay here, okay? Rest, take it easy, I promise I won't let him hurt you again."

"Delilah…"

"No, Sabrina," she said, getting off the bed and slipping the dildo out of the harness, then grabbing one of the hotel's robes. "I need to get rid of him, and the sooner I talk to him, the faster I can make that happen."

"Delilah!" I heard her father yell from the living room.

"Coming!" she shouted back. She turned back to me, tying the robe shut. "Just stay here, okay? Please. Just stay here and I'll be back in a minute."

She left the room before I could reply. I took a deep breath and covered myself with the blanket, trying to calm myself enough that I could think clearly again. Then I heard Delilah's voice from the other room.

"What the fuck are you doing here?"

"You've been ignoring my phone calls for the last week. You made me come all this way to find you…to find you pulling this deviant bullshit that I have been warning you about for the past decade! You can't be doing all of this and expect to move up in our company. People talk! And they have no love for people who don't have their heads on straight!"

"What the fuck, Dad? Are you seriously giving me a lecture about my lifestyle now?"

I kept myself covered and closed my eyes, hoping this was all a bad dream.

"When else am I supposed to tell you what people are saying about you? You run away after losing that contract and I don't hear from you for weeks, then I find out you've been slumming it all the way out here?"

What? What was he talking about? I wanted to look to Delilah for her reaction, but I wasn't going to leave the bedroom.

"I have not been slumming it!" she yelled back. "And my coming out here had nothing to do with that contract. I came here for some time away! I told you that!"

"You told me that after you made a laughingstock of yourself firing that manager that you claimed was abusing his employees."

"He was!"

"You never brought any proof forward. You fired him without cause."

"I caught him doing it and fired him on the spot!"

"And he's contesting it in a legal case! One he'll likely win because you aren't there to defend your actions!"

"You could have called me!"

"I have been calling you for the past three days. You haven't answered once! I can't have my second in command pulling stunts like this anymore!" he shouted.

"Well, maybe I don't want to be your second in command anymore!"

There was a long moment of silence between the two of them and I resisted the urge to pull the blanket down and go find out if the man had left or not. But now that the adrenaline from the surprise had started to fade, I only felt tired, my body shaking as it tried to ignore the impulse to fight, flee, or freeze.

"There is a plane leaving for Toronto at quarter after four this afternoon. If you value your job at all, your place in the company, you will be on it."

I heard heavy footsteps walking away, loud even on the carpeted floor. How we'd missed them arriving I wasn't sure. I must've been moaning louder than I thought.

"Fucking hell," I heard Delilah groan a moment after the door to the hotel room slammed shut with an ominous thud.

I couldn't move. Could barely breathe. I kept myself under the blanket as I heard Delilah come back into the bedroom. I couldn't stop the tears from falling. I hurt. Everything in me hurt. Physically. Emotionally. It all hurt. What the fuck was happening?

"Sabrina?" Delilah's voice drifted to me through the blanket. "Sabrina? Are you okay?"

I didn't move. I didn't speak. What the hell was I going to say? *Sure, Delilah! Everything's peachy! Your dad walked in on you railing me, then called me a man because apparently he's not only homophobic but transphobic as well.*

"Sabrina, pet, I need you to talk to me."

I opened my mouth, but I couldn't find my words. My mind was swirling, half of it still in that blissful state of being from being used by my Mistress, the rest panicking over the aftermath.

"Sabrina, babe, please talk to me." I felt a weight drop down onto the bed. Delilah's hand touched me over the blanket, rubbing at my leg awkwardly. "I'm so sorry, Sabrina. I'm so very, very sorry."

The first sound ripped out of my throat. A strangled laugh. I coughed after it slipped out. I couldn't even get my voice to sound right for a few moments, every sound I made sounding too deep, too much like my old self.

"Sabrina, please." Her hand grasped the blanket and slowly started to pull. "Please, baby, I need you right now."

I pulled back on the blanket, refusing to let her uncover me. "Yeah." I coughed again. "You need me."

"Sabrina?"

"W-what the hell was that, Delilah?" I'd finally found my words.

"What?"

I pulled the blanket off my face. "I'm sorry, was the only thing covering my naked-ass body from your *father* muffling my voice? What. The. Hell. Was. That?"

"I'm so sorry Sabrina. I'm so very sorry."

"I don't want a sorry, I want to know what the fuck is going on!"

"I didn't know he would be here. I didn't know he was going to do this."

"I don't care, Delilah." I glared daggers at her back. The robe was gone, and she sat on the bed clad only in the strap-on harness. She wasn't even looking at me. "I want to know why the hell he did that! Why your father walked in on us and called me a fucking *man!*"

She flinched but still didn't turn to look at me. Her hand was still on my leg, but it had stopped moving and was more gripping me, like she needed something to hold on to.

"My father…he has what you might call boundary issues."

"Yeah, no shit!"

"Please, Sabrina, let me talk?"

I forced myself to keep my mouth shut before I could fling more sharp words at her.

"I am so sorry. I've been so stupid. I should've seen this coming." I watched as she shook her head, her shoulders slumped, head bowed. "I didn't think he'd…that he'd…fuck him, I can't believe he walked in on us like…like that."

I had to keep my mouth shut. I didn't want her to stop talking. I needed to know what the hell was going on, why I'd had to be so fucking embarrassed, and have a dildo ripped out of my ass.

"I knew he was trying to call me, trying to get a hold of me. But I didn't want to hear what he had to say. I didn't want to talk to him. You don't get it, Sabrina. He controls so much of my life, I couldn't let him take this from me. I wanted this time with you. All that I could manage to have. Because it's you."

"I don't understand. What do you mean?"

"I wanted my time with you, so I ignored his calls. I didn't know he'd come here. I didn't know he'd do this."

I did my best to push down the anger, the rage that I was feeling about being made a fucking fool of. I took a deep breath. "What does he want?"

"I need to go back to Toronto."

"Why?"

She shrugged without looking back at me. "I don't know. He never tells me anything. Especially these days." She let out a sad laugh. "All he does is tell me how my lifestyle disgusts him, how he can't stand that I'm a lesbian, that I like women. It's all either that or him telling me I'm not good enough to take over the company someday. I'm tired of it. Sick of it. I don't want to keep doing what he tells me." Her shoulders shook like she was on the verge of sobbing, and I longed to go to her, wrap her in my arms, but I was afraid of moving. Afraid that he might come back the moment I uncovered myself.

"Then don't." I tried to make my voice sound stronger than I felt. "You don't have to go. You don't have to take all that from him."

"But he's my father."

"So? My mother told me I was a monster and I was going to hell when I came out to her. I don't talk to her anymore. My ex-fiancée couldn't stand to be with someone who was more girl than she was. She's not in my life anymore either. I gave up so much to be the person I really am. You can—"

She shook her head. "I can't do that, Sabrina. I'm not you. I can't give up everything."

"Why not?"

"Because I don't know anything else!"

Now I did pull the blanket down and sit up. Her grip was still on my leg, but I reached out and put a hand on her bare shoulder.

"Delilah, it's okay not to know. It's okay to try to live your own life."

"I don't know how. I'm not as strong as you."

"You don't have to be. You only need to be as strong as you are."

She shuddered under my hand.

"You think too much of me, Sabrina."

"Don't do that. Don't belittle yourself, please." It was my turn to shake my head, not that she could see it with her back still to me. "You believe in me, don't you?"

This made her turn her head, looking at me for the first time since she sat down. "Yes. I do."

"Then believe me when I say you're strong enough to live your own life. You don't need your father."

She watched me for a long moment, then her hand loosened its grip on my leg, and she stood up. Her shoulders were slumped, like she was defeated. I didn't like the look on her. I hadn't seen her quite like this before. She pointed to the small closet along one wall.

"Your clothes that you lent me the other night are hanging in there. They're clean. I figure you might want to wear them instead of your dress today. I…um…I'll take you home, when you're ready."

"What about you?"

She shook her head and turned around to face me, her look just about breaking my heart. "What about me?"

"What are you going to do?"

"I'm going to pack. I'm going to go back to Toronto. But I'll drive you home."

My jaw dropped open. Just like that. There was no discussion, no negotiation. "And us? What about us?"

"I still want this relationship, Sabrina," she said, but there was nothing of what was usually in her voice. The sultriness that she usually spoke with, the hint of command, of dominance, all were gone. All I could hear was the weariness in her tone. "I already warned you it might have to be long distance. Yes, it's earlier than I wanted, but it was inevitable. I'll come back when I can, I promise. And we'll see where things go, you know? I'm not giving up on this so quickly."

"Aren't you?" I snapped, unable to hold my tongue any longer. "I thought you wanted this, but at the first sign of pushback from your father, you're caving in? You're not even going to try to do—I don't know, something…anything to stay with me? At least for a little longer?"

"Sabrina, please. We're both adults here. We both have separate lives. I want to make this work as much as you do, but I can't…I can't throw away everything I know."

I got up from the bed and grabbed my underwear from the floor, then my dress, and headed for the closet. As she said, my clothes were hanging up and I pulled them out and started to dress. My mind raced as I pulled the leggings on, trying to figure out where to go from here.

"Why don't you come with me?"

I paused with my head trapped in the T-shirt. I pulled it down and got my head through the hole. "I'm sorry, what?"

"Why don't you come to Toronto with me?"

I laughed. "I can't. I have a job. Two jobs. Both of which I have to be at tomorrow. And the next day. And the next. I can't just take off and disappear!"

"I'm not asking you to disappear. I want you to come with me. Take a week off. Surely you've got some vacation time or something? I want you to see where I live, where I work. I want to show you my side of things."

I shook my head. "You don't get it. I can't just up and leave!"

She glanced away for a second, then back to me. "What about next weekend?"

"What about it?"

"If I get you a flight for, like, Friday night or something, would you come to Toronto?"

"You want to fly me to Toronto for what? The weekend?"

"Yes."

I stared at her. "Does the concept of money not occur to you?"

"Money is meant to be spent. I have enough to cover you."

I shook my head. "I don't know if I'm comfortable with that."

"I'm not offering to do it every weekend or anything like that. I…I'm trying to show you that I'm in this. That I want to make it work. And if I need to get you the odd plane ticket to make that happen, then so be it."

I couldn't process what I was hearing. She was trying to tell me that she wanted to fly me across the country to spend two days with her. Who did that?

I shook my head again. "Delilah, this relationship isn't something you can throw money at."

"Why not? Why can't I treat my girlfriend to something like this? I want to be with you, Sabrina, and I want you to still have your life and me to have mine. I want to make this work, and this is a way to do it."

I resisted the urge to growl at her, to yell at her that she decided that I could make a spur of the moment trip work in my life, but she wasn't willing to refuse her father for even one more day with me. I wanted her here. I wanted to be with her so badly. But I couldn't give up everything for it. I'd given up everything before, when I came out. I couldn't do that again, not even for Delilah. I wished she would show that she was willing to give something up for me. That I was important enough to stand up to her father.

Instead, I sighed. She was asking for a weekend. I could do a weekend.

I threw my hands in the air. "Fine! Fine, we'll do it your way. I'll go to Toronto next weekend."

She gave a sharp nod, standing a little straighter. She got that fucking sexy look in her eyes that I wanted to see all the time as she watched me finish putting my shirt on. It was like agreeing to her ridiculous plan had brought her back to the woman I was starting to fall for. And damn it, I wanted to go to her and touch her and hold her and kiss her right now, but I was still angry. Angry that she would let something like her father get in the way of what we could have. Angry that the whole damned thing had happened. Angry at how embarrassed I still felt.

Delilah opened the other side of the closet and revealed a few hangers of her own clothes. I turned away and went to pick up my dress, folding it nicely and tucking it under my arm. While she was busy I left the bedroom on bare feet. I slipped out into the hallway and headed into the living room, where my purse and phone were. I hoped.

I grabbed the purse from the floor by my shoes at the front door, then figured I'd slip on the flats anyway and be ready to go. Delilah had offered to drive me home, but there was a part of me that didn't want to take her up on it. I didn't want that awkward drive. I didn't want some teary goodbye that would make good fodder for a romance novel.

I started pulling up the app for a rideshare when I realized that there was a perfectly good bus stop right outside the hotel that would take me home. But I didn't want to just up and disappear on her. I waited, patiently, on the couch where only last night I'd pretended to be a puppy and climbed up on and put my head in her lap. Fuck, that was less than twelve hours ago. How the hell had things gotten so fucked?

"Sabrina?" Delilah's voice preceded her as she appeared from the hallway. "I thought you might have left."

I shook my head. "I didn't want to leave without saying goodbye."

She gave me a small smile. "I'll grab the keys so I can drive you."

"Nah, I'll catch the bus."

She flinched. It was small, but I noticed it. "But I was going to do it for you."

"It's fine, Delilah. I'm going to head home now."

"Are you sure I can't drive you? Do anything else for you?"

I tried to match her smile, but I knew it wasn't good enough and gave up. "It's okay. I'll get home safe, I promise. I'll even let you know when I get there." I took her hand and raised it to my lips, giving her a soft kiss. "You have enough to deal with here. I don't know how long it takes you to pack all your stuff, and we used a lot of toys last night. Go take care of your things."

"Sabrina…"

"Don't. Please, Delilah. I can take care of myself."

"Okay," she said, her voice low and hurting. "I get it. I'll text you the details and talk to Tiffani and make sure you get the time you need to come visit me." She leaned forward and kissed my cheek. "We're going to make this work. I promise."

"I know. I trust you." It took a lot for me to say those three words. I trusted so few people. Cori, Tiffani, now Delilah. I turned and headed for the door, listening to her footsteps right behind me. "Thank you for the amazing night. And the pretty good start to the morning, anyway."

I glanced over my shoulder in time to see her face turn as red as mine usually did. "Sabrina, there is no way I can ever apologize enough for what happened this morning."

I put a hand on her arm. "I don't blame you. But I really don't want it to happen again."

"I'll make sure of it."

I turned and she took my arms, pulled me into her in a crushing hug, and pressed her lips to mine. I melted under that kiss, and a moan slipped out of my lips as her tongue prodded its way into my mouth. But I pulled back all too soon, knowing that if she lengthened the kiss, I was liable not to leave.

"I'll text you," I promised.

"I'll do the same."

We parted, but our hands stayed together for a long moment. I didn't want to stop touching her. But soon enough I pulled away, opened the door, and slipped out of the room as it shut behind me. I didn't turn around until I'd reached the elevator, and then only gave a glance, but the hallway remained empty. When I boarded the elevator and the doors slid shut behind me, I pressed the button for the ground floor and leaned my head against the cool mirror of the wall.

"Fuck."

Chapter Twenty-Four

A s fucked as my emotions were that morning, things didn't get much better over the course of the week. Delilah had left for Toronto that afternoon, and while we texted and shared the odd video call over the week, by the time Friday evening rolled around, I was desperate for her touch. I couldn't believe how much I missed her. I was barely able to function, especially by the end of the week. I went through the motions at the bookstore and at the lounge, with my mind firmly entrenched in Delilah-space the whole time.

It still stung that she didn't stay longer, that she so quickly folded to what her father wanted. But I understood. How long had I lived under the reign of my mother? A woman who cursed any and all feminine traits that I displayed even the tiniest bit of? It would take more than what happened Sunday morning for her to break away from the life she clearly didn't want. But hopefully not much more.

I'd had an earlier shift at the lounge to make sure I could make my flight, something Tiffani had eyed me funny for but never called out. I guess technically dating one of the owners did have its perks, but I wasn't sure how long it would be before I got called out on it by the other. But the only thing Tiffani had said to me regarding the relationship at this point was a reminder not to hurt Delilah. Which I would never want to do anyway.

When the shift ended, I caught a cab to the airport with my luggage in hand, a small suitcase that I'd packed between shifts. The flight was only about four hours, but with the time change, it was half past one in the morning by the time I headed for the airport exit in Toronto. And there was Delilah standing and waiting for me, an appropriate-looking chauffeur hat sitting askew on her head and a wide smile on her face.

"You're here!" she exclaimed, as she threw her arms wide and pulled me in close to her. I buried my face in her neck as we held each other, and I breathed in the scent that I'd been missing for the past week.

"Of course I'm here," I told her. "I said I would come."

"I know, I know, I'm just...I'm so happy to see you."

I pulled back a little to look at her. Her eyes looked shiny, the way they got before tears start to fall. Was she about to cry?

"Delilah?" I said her name softly, running a hand over her cheek. "What is it? What's wrong?"

She shook her head and gave me a wobbly smile. "Nothing's wrong, pet. I'm glad you're here."

I cocked my head to the side a little. "Was the week so bad?"

"It's not...I mean, my father..." She shook her head again. "I'm really glad you're here."

I gave her a soft kiss. "I am too."

The kiss seemed to spur her into activity as she reached for the handle of my suitcase and took it from me, then grabbed my hand and we headed for the doors together. She led me to the small car park near the entrance and to a reasonably sized SUV, ushering me into the passenger seat before hefting my small suitcase into the trunk. She started the engine and pulled out of the parking garage, finding her way into the city. She put one hand on my thigh, and I revelled in the warmth and safety at the soft touch. Damn it, I'd missed her touch so much.

But still, the nerves of the day mixed with working two jobs had taken their toll, and it wasn't long before I felt my eyelids getting heavy as Delilah made her way through the early-morning streets of Toronto. Still, her hand never strayed from my thigh, and its warmth, along with the smooth ride of the SUV, lulled me into a light doze.

"Pet." I jumped as Delilah's voice drew me back to consciousness. "We're here."

Here looked like another parking garage, one I suspected was underground. I unbuckled my seat belt, getting out of the SUV on wobbly legs. It took a moment to steady myself, and by then Delilah had my suitcase in one hand, the other offered to me, and she led the way to an elevator bank a few spots away.

I swayed a little on my feet as the elevator rose, passing floor after floor after floor until finally coming to a stop. I didn't even question it, just followed Delilah blindly out of the elevator and toward one of the few doors that lined the shorter than usual hallway. Finally letting go of my hand, she unlocked the door, swung it open, and ushered me inside.

"Home sweet home," she said softly, placing a hand on my shoulder. "I know you're tired, so let's get you cleaned up and into bed. How does that sound, pet?"

A part of me wanted to argue that I was good. That I was ready and willing and able to take whatever games she wanted to play. A part of me ached to be her pet in more than name right away, something I'd been dreaming about all week. But the rest of me knew she was right. I wasn't in any condition to play right now, not when I was liable to fall asleep on her.

Her apartment was, for lack of a better term, sparse. The front door opened onto a small hallway, with a closed door immediately to the left and a closet to the right. The hallway ended as we entered an open concept kitchen and dining and living area. There was a smaller area off to the side where the corner of the wall cut away and I saw a desk with a rather nice yet somewhat dusty computer. The whole place was very modern, all clean lines and sharp angles. There was little in the way of adornment throughout the open concept areas, the kitchen looking almost pristine, like it was rarely used. An island countertop separated the kitchen from the dining area that led into a large seating space with a big screen television mounted on the wall across from a couch that didn't look like the most comfortable place to sit.

Delilah stepped up behind me and wrapped her arms around my waist as I looked around. Her arms seemed to stiffen a little as I glanced at the bare walls, no signs of anything personal hanging from them. No art, no pictures, nothing.

"I don't spend a lot of time here outside of sleeping," she said in my ear, almost defensively. "I rarely get a chance to even use my office, I never work from home. I haven't really done anything with the apartment. Hell, it came mostly furnished like this."

I shook my head a little. "It's okay. It's a nice place."

She chuckled. "Wait until you see the bedroom. Now, that's where I put my time and energy."

On the wall beside the large, mounted television was another door that at first I thought was a storage space, but she led me forward, reached around me to open the door, and ushered me inside.

I stopped dead, staring at what was in front of me.

"That's a sex bed." The words dropped out of my mouth and my eyes were riveted to the dark wood of the queen-size bedframe that had so many tie off points my imagination went wild thinking of all the positions someone—namely me—could be restrained in. "That's a bed for sex."

Delilah beamed. "It's kind of my pride and joy."

"I don't blame you." I took a cautious step toward the bed, then another, and another. There was nothing tied to it right now, but I was treating it like it might very well come alive and devour me if I so much as looked away from it. I reached out and brushed my fingers along the polished hardwood that had steel bars running along the bottom of the frame. The four posts in the corners ran high up over the bed and were connected to each other, with metal loops riveted into the wood in case someone wanted to be suspended, I supposed. Or to be restrained on their feet, or on their knees, or whatever kinky way my Mistress decided to tie up her sweet little submissive.

I had to remind myself to take a breath and pulled my gaze away from the bed toward the other side of the room—which did not much help my ability to breathe when I saw a free-standing x-frame tucked in the far corner. Black leather padding covered some of the wood planking. Beside it sat what looked like the exact same type of queening chair that they sold at Vibe Check, and I wondered what I'd have to do to get Delilah to put my head underneath it as she sat on the cushion.

A dresser was pushed against the wall to the left, with a tall armoire next to it. I could only surmise what toys might be hiding in those drawers, behind those solid, dark doors. It sure as hell wasn't a portal to Narnia. No, it was a pathway to my darkest dreams and desires, the ones Delilah had opened me up to only a few weeks ago.

That thought sobered me up a little. I'd only known her for a few weeks, and I was already drooling over the possibility of being bound to an x-frame while she went to town on me with a paddle or flogger or whip? We hadn't even really talked about limits yet, and that was something hugely important in this kind of world, this kind of relationship. So far, we'd really been playing things by ear, testing the waters, even if it did get a little intense last weekend, but even that wasn't nearly as deep as we could swim in this ocean. The question was would I tread water, or would I risk being caught in the undertow?

"This is…"

"This is my home." Delilah finished my sentence, and I caught the vulnerability in her tone. I wondered how many times she had brought a prospective play partner back here only to have them balk at the kind of equipment she had. Delilah wore her interest in kink on her sleeve; she didn't try to hide it. I wished I could be that strong. I didn't want to include the public in the kind of play I wanted to do, but I wouldn't argue against doing something a little more...exhibitionist. More than just a rope class.

"I love it," I told her, giving her a wide smile. "This bed looks absolutely amazing. You can tie someone down so many different ways! Like you could keep someone tied at the foot of the bed or the head of the bed and use them as a pillow or—"

She laughed and held up her hand. "Slow, pet. Take it slow. I have to admit I like where your imagination is going. But we're not going to play tonight." I made a whining sound that brought a smile to her face. "It's past two in the morning, pet, and I have plans for you tomorrow."

"Oh, plans? What kind of plans? Do I get to know these plans?"

Delilah shook her head. "Nope. You get to be a very good pet and follow me wherever I feel like taking you like the good little puppy you are."

I tried to hold back the gasp of excitement I released at her words. My brain felt like it shut down for all of three seconds, having to reboot into a clearly *no smut allowed* mode before it could work properly again.

"Yeah? Does my puppy like that idea?" She ran a hand under my chin and began scratching softly around my jaw, and I closed my eyes, simply being in the moment and loving the attention. "It's been so long since I brought someone in here, I can't wait to show you all the delights I've planned."

It took me a moment to parse the words she'd said. "Wait, what? What do you mean?"

"What?"

"Been so long? You don't bring people back here?"

She chuckled and looked away, almost seeming sheepish. "No, not really. Before, when I played with people, it was usually toys, maybe some equipment at their place. Never much more than that."

"But the cross? The chair?"

"Neither have been used since...well...in a long time, since I stopped bringing people back here to play."

The room took on a new aura before my eyes. At first it had seemed like the perfect playroom for someone who enjoyed playing with their partners. But now, knowing that she hadn't had anyone in here in so long, it reminded me more of a tomb. A dead space with which she tortured herself so many nights with the memory of what could have been.

"Since your ex, right?" I asked softly.

She didn't reply, but there was a soft sound of affirmation that slipped her lips. I wrapped my arms around her to give her what comfort I could, knowing there was little I could say that would help.

"Thank you," I told her.

"For what?"

"For bringing me here. Showing me you."

She shrugged but returned the hug. "You showed me yours, only seemed fair to show you mine."

"It's more than that, and you know it."

"Yes, yes, I guess it is." She let out a long sigh. "Not many people get to see this far into me. They might know I'm kinky, but they never get to see the me beneath everything." She walked to the bed and picked up a cute, red and orange stuffed animal that had been tucked between the pillows. It took a moment for my brain to piece together that it was a small fox with a little crescent moon on one of its front paws. "No one ever stuck around long enough to get to know me. Until the point that I stopped trying." She shook her head and held the fox to her cheek for a moment. "Then there was you."

"I'm not that special."

"You are to me."

The undue praise made me a little uncomfortable. I wasn't that special, like I'd told her. I liked her. A lot. That was easily reason enough to get to know her. And the more I learned, the more I wanted to find out. Like the adorable fox that I wouldn't have guessed for a moment that she'd be cuddling right in front of me. I couldn't see her letting anyone else close enough to be this vulnerable.

I took a deep breath and gave her a wide smile. "So, we're not going to give this bed a test drive tonight?"

She laughed and shook her head. "Not tonight, pet. But if you're a good puppy for me tomorrow, you might get to see some of its features tomorrow night." I moaned a little in hopefulness. "Oh, did you like that, pet? I think that you did."

I was already nodding before she finished her sentence. Of course I liked it. There was no way I couldn't. But before I could say anything else, I let out a wide, jaw-cracking yawn, earning another smile from my Mistress.

"To bed, pet."

I was already stripping down to my underwear when I replied automatically. "Yes, Mistress." She set the fox down on the bed and began undressing as well, and together we climbed onto the bed. The mattress was soft, yet firm enough, and I felt Delilah wrap her arm around me, pressing tight against me. I relaxed against her, and it was barely a moment after my head hit the pillow that I closed my eyes and sleep engulfed me.

CHAPTER TWENTY-FIVE

I certainly didn't know what to expect from my Saturday. I got to wake up next to my Mistress again, which was the first step to a wonderful day, one I would cherish forever. We spent a good amount of time in bed, enough that I had started to wonder if this was her master—or Mistress—plan, to keep us warm and cuddled in bed all day. But eventually, around ten, she peeled herself off me and managed to run a shower for the both of us. I happily joined her.

She told me to dress comfortably, so I put on a pair of bike shorts under a long skirt to deal with possible chub rub and was thankful I'd worn my runners for the plane ride here. A flowy blouse completed the look with a thin cardigan over top, just in case. I'd left Delilah's sweater at home, freshly washed and hung up, and I kind of missed the smell of it already, but at least today I had the real thing to keep me company.

We traveled around the city in her SUV. We had breakfast at a cute place on Yonge Street, then went to the Royal Ontario Museum and spent the rest of the morning and some of the afternoon there, then had lunch nearby when we got hungry. It was a pleasant time and a surprisingly much needed break from my usual schedule of work, work, and more work. And from the smile that graced Delilah's face for the whole time, it looked like she needed this too.

She never did tell me about how her week went, even though I asked her. I wanted to know that everything was okay. I didn't want there to be complications with her family because I was her girlfriend. As much as I never wanted to meet the man again, really, I didn't want her to have the kind of relationship with her parents that I had with mine. Which was to say, none at all.

One of our last stops was a quaint bookstore that heavily promoted LGBTQ+ books, and I felt so at home there, I began to take mental notes of how we might bring the same kind of atmosphere to Oracle Books back home. As it was, I came away with a small stack of novels that I hadn't read—hadn't even heard of, and was more than happy to adopt.

We loaded our purchases into the back of Delilah's SUV and climbed in. She casually put her hand on my thigh again as she drove, and I let myself melt into the soft and easy gesture that felt like she was claiming me all over again. My stomach growled softly as we turned a corner and pulled into a small parking lot set between a number of stores, and I looked to her, wondering if we were going to eat something.

"One more stop, pet," she said softly, "then we can get some dinner, all right?"

I wasn't about to argue. Everywhere she'd taken me so far today had been amazing. I was sure this stop would be as well.

We walked past a few of the stores, some of them looking like they were getting ready to close in the early evening, and stopped in front of a window that had mannequins clad in racy lingerie. For a moment I thought she was bringing me to a lingerie shop, one that carried the kind of stuff that I'd only ever dreamed of being able to wear well. But as she opened the door to the side of the window for me, I realized this store was much more than mere lingerie.

It reminded me a lot of Vibe Check, only larger and more spacious, with a larger variety of toys and other offerings. To one side was a clothing area, filled with vinyl and leather and even some latex, all carefully spread out and presented to best avoid damaging the goods. A couple of dressing rooms stood off to the side, their patrons hidden by heavy velvet curtains for privacy. The middle of the store had display tables with all sorts of racy things on them, from dildos to rabbits, to plugs and vibrators. The far wall was also covered in similar toys, spread out across the whole wall. A section near the back wall held some of the more vanilla kink gear, some simple paddles and floggers, ready-to-use cuffs, and even a couple of gags. A couple of tables offered a number of books and a few movies to shoppers who were interested, though from the Clearance sign hanging from the table with the movies, it looked like they were phasing them out.

I took all of this in for a moment, then turned to find Delilah walking confidently toward the counter where two young women were chatting. The store was empty save for us. I quickly followed her, still astounded by how nice the store looked, and wondered how much Delilah had used this place as inspiration for Vibe Check.

"Hi, Ms. Delilah!" one of the women said as we approached. She brushed strands of pink hair back behind her ear as she turned to us. "Are you looking for anything in particular today?"

"Lola, my dear," Delilah said with a smile. "I'm looking for Randi, she said she'd be here tonight."

Lola was quick to reply. "She's in the back, I'll let her know you're here."

"Thank you, doll."

Lola's face flushed at the term, and I had to stop myself from giggling. Finally, someone who blushed as easily as I did. Delilah turned back to me and waved an arm around the store.

"Welcome to Randi's Adult World."

I stared blankly at her. "It's not called that."

"It's not," the other woman behind the counter said. Her tone was bored as she gave Delilah a look of exasperated amusement. Then she turned to me. "Welcome to Velvet Desires. I'm Nikki, that's Lola, and you are?"

"Sabrina," I said, and offered my hand. Nikki took it in a hearty shake.

"We don't get to see Delilah bring a lot of dates in here," Nikki said.

I blushed as Delilah wrapped an arm around my waist.

"She's my girlfriend."

Both women stopped moving and looked up at Delilah in surprise. I fidgeted slightly under the stares that lasted until a door along the back wall opened with enough force that all of us turned to look. A woman stepped out from the doorway, taller than the rest of us and wearing heavy boots and jean overalls over a purple plaid flannel shirt that was rolled up to her elbows. Her skin was covered in tattoos, and her dark purple hair had an undercut along the right side that revealed an ear covered in more piercings than I'd ever seen before.

"Girlfriend?" The woman's voice was deeper than I expected, but it came out smooth and without too much grit. "Delilah has a girlfriend?"

I turned my face into Delilah's shoulder to hide my awkward embarrassment.

"Yes, I have a girlfriend. It's not that big a thing," Delilah said as the newcomer, presumably Randi, walked up to us.

"Well, I never thought I'd live to see this day." Randi pushed past Delilah and grabbed my hand with rough, calloused fingers. "You're Sabrina? I never expected to get to actually meet you!"

I shook my head. "You make it sound like you knew about me."

"Delilah hasn't shut up about you all week! Are you kidding me? I thought she was making you up!"

Embarrassment flared in my cheeks hotter than ever as Delilah pried my hand out of Randi's and slapped the butch on the back.

"If you're all done giving us *both* a hard time, I believe I have something to pick up?" She gave Randi a stare that would have me on my knees in an instant. It did not have the same effect on Randi. She smiled and laughed, then gave me a wink.

"Well, if you're Delilah's girlfriend, let's take a look at you." She literally did a walk-around of my entire body, her eyes roaming up and down as I stood still, unsure if I should move or run away or grin and bear it. Surely if this was an issue, Delilah would say something? I shot her a look, but her eyes were on Randi, an appraising look in them.

"Well?" Delilah said, as Randi started a second loop around me. I crossed my arms and tried to look disapproving at both women, but they ignored me.

"I don't think I have anything off the rack that would work, but give me a couple months and some measurements, and it's doable." Randi tapped her chin adorably while she spoke.

"What's doable?" I asked but again was ignored.

"I expected as much," Delilah said, her fingers tapping her chin. "We can do the measurements now, if you're not busy."

Randi gestured to the door she'd come through. "Step into my office."

Delilah followed Randi to the door as I stood on my spot, still wondering what the hell was going on. I looked to Lola and Nikki, who both whispered, "Go!"

That got my feet moving, and I reached Delilah right before the door could close behind her. She looked at me with those eyes that made me want to do anything for her, and I could have melted into a puddle right there.

"Come along, pet."

I nodded and followed her through the doorway. We walked

down a short hall, past several closed doors, into a back warehouse space much like Vibe Check had. Except instead of exercise mats on the floor and extra stock on the shelving, this back room was chock full of amazing looking furniture and equipment and even clothing on racks that all looked like it was made right in house. Then I noticed the workbenches scattered around, one with a sewing machine, others with tools I didn't even pretend to recognize. There was a clear area with several pieces of lumber that looked almost like it was going to make an x-frame when it was entirely assembled. A spanking bench was being used as a flat surface for tools right beside where I assumed Randi must work on her bigger builds.

I wondered if she was the one who built Delilah's bed.

Speaking of Delilah, I turned back to her in time to see her stalk up to Randi like a wolf approaching cornered prey. Delilah reached out and grabbed Randi by the hair, pulling her head down and forward savagely into her face. For a second, I was prepared for a wave of jealousy to hit me, but it didn't. Instead there was a rush of heat down in my core as I watched my Mistress pull Randi close, and saw the way Randi's eyes went wide and her lips parted softly.

"I do believe you were making fun of me, out there," Delilah said in her *Mistress* voice, the one that made my knees quiver like they were doing now, and I wasn't even on the receiving end of it. "Is that any way to treat your Mistress, doll?"

My breathing hitched and I felt arousal begin to overtake me as my blush spread down from my face into my upper chest. Was Randi another one of Delilah's toys?

"No, Mistress." Randi's breathing came hot and heavy, the swagger she'd had in the other room long gone as she stared into Delilah's eyes. I moaned softly, biting my lip and shifting from foot to foot, wanting to quell the ache I was feeling.

"Was there any part of *I have a girlfriend* that you didn't believe, doll?" Delilah demanded.

"No, Mistress."

"Then what gave you the thought that you could make fun of me for it?"

"I wasn't thinking, Mistress."

"That's right, you weren't thinking." Delilah shook her head softly, but the savage grin on her face was one I was all too familiar with.

Randi's face was an open book, her eyes wide, lips parted, looking like she was wanting more. I was sure I looked the same way when

Delilah played with me. Then Randi's eyes flickered to me and her eyebrows furrowed.

"What? What is it, doll?"

"Your girlfriend, Mistress," Randi said breathlessly.

"Ah yes," Delilah said, as if faintly remembering I was there. For some reason that sent another rush of heat through me instead of anything like anger or jealousy. What the ever-loving shit was I into?

"Pet," she said, louder than she was speaking with Randi. "Come here, pet."

I did as she asked, stepping up beside her, already breathing through my mouth in wanting.

"Mistress," I said softly, keeping my eyes down and resisting the urge to get on my knees when she hadn't asked me to. Yet.

"You don't mind me playing with one of my favorite toys a little, do you, pet?"

I shook my head immediately. "No, Mistress."

"Would you like to kiss my little doll, pet?"

I glanced between the two of them, unsure of what the right answer was. It took a long moment to realize that the right answer was the one I felt most strongly, and that honestly, I did want to kiss Randi.

On one condition.

"With her consent, Mistress."

The smile Delilah gave me was brighter than a thousand lightbulbs, but she quickly schooled her face back into her Mistress mask. "Do you consent, doll?"

Randi nodded the best she could with Delilah's hand still clutching her hair. I stepped forward, drawing my hand down Randi's cheek, feeling the soft skin under my fingertips, and pressed my lips to hers.

It wasn't a long kiss, but it wasn't until we parted that we both realized that Delilah had released Randi's hair and taken a step back. I turned to look at Delilah, catching her gazing at us with an approving look.

"Holy shit," Randi managed to say after catching her breath. I gave her a smile and stepped back toward my Mistress. "Where the hell did you find this girl?"

"Would you believe she spilt coffee on me?"

Randi's eyes went wide. "I have to get in the way of more beautiful women with coffee, then."

We all laughed at that, and the sexual tension in the room subsided somewhat. I was still feeling the aftereffects of not only kissing Randi but doing so under the orders of my Mistress. It was something I never thought I'd ever do before, and when Delilah had asked me to kiss Randi, I couldn't even begin to describe the feelings that had roiled within me. Was I becoming a different person, being with my Mistress? Or was this who I was, and she was only bringing it out of me? Dear Goddess, I wished for the latter.

Delilah and Randi hugged and exchanged several soft words, and I looked around the work room a little more, being drawn to the leather clothing that was hanging from a rack nearby. I'd always been intrigued by the use of leather as fabric for clothing, and wondered how it would feel to have it over my body.

"Like what you see?" Randi's voice came from right behind me and I jumped a little. I spun and she was right there, beaming at me. "Sorry, didn't mean to scare you."

I shook my head. "No, no, I'm good. I was…admiring your work. Did you do all of this yourself?"

"I've been working on my craft a long time."

I looked around again. "I can tell. These look amazing."

She flushed faintly but kept up some of that swagger I remembered seeing in the other room. She gave me a brazen smile. "Most of what's around here is just examples of what I can do. A lot of my work I sadly never get to see again because they go off with their new owners."

"Were you the one who built Delilah's bed frame?" I asked, hoping to get the question that had been niggling in the back of my head answered.

"I did! To her specifications. We worked on it together." She glanced away for a moment as if embarrassed. "She also tested it with me."

I couldn't stop the smile that spread across my face.

"Don't tell anyone," Randi said quickly. "I'd totally lose my butch card if everyone knew I was such a bottom."

I wrapped my arms around her in a soft hug that she returned pretty quickly. "Don't worry, I won't tell a soul."

We parted with a kind of understanding of each other that honestly made me want to be friends with her. I'd never badly wanted a friend in my life, not like this. I thought I was doing well without friendship. But Delilah was truly showing me a different way of life, and now I found myself craving more.

"So," Randi said with a sly smile. "Something was said about getting measurements?"

I opened my mouth to tell her that I had no idea what was going on, I merely followed Delilah around, when my Mistress arrived at Randi's elbow.

"Measurements would be a good idea," Delilah said before I could answer. "And of course there's what we came here for…"

Randi laughed. "Let's get the measurements first."

She beckoned me over to the clear area by the pieces of the x-frame I'd noticed before and told me to undress. I took my blouse off no problem, I wasn't worried about that, but when it came to the skirt and bike shorts, I hesitated.

"Pet?" Delilah looked worried, and I shook my head. I could do this. I wasn't going to let my fear stop me from doing something I wanted to do. Not anymore.

I turned to Randi and caught her eye as she prepared a cloth measuring tape and a small notebook with my name written in neat lettering at the top of a page. "I'm, uh, I'm trans," I told her, looking away before I could witness her reaction. I shouldn't have looked away.

"Sabrina, darling," Randi said as she put a hand on my shoulder. "So am I."

I glanced up at her. "Really? When…I mean…I didn't…"

She laughed. "It's okay. I started when I was a teenager. My parents pushed hard to get me what I needed. They were so accepting of me."

I tried not to show the anger that rolled through me. "I…I didn't have that."

She wrapped her arms around me in a bigger hug than before, almost as if she were trying to make up for all the hugs I'd missed because of the mother I had. I told myself I was not going to cry. Though I might have almost shed a tear or two down my cheek.

"I'm okay," I said softly against her cheek. "But thank you for understanding."

"I totally get it. Are you comfortable with pulling off your skirt or did you want to leave it on?"

"Can you do the measurements with it on?"

"Not really, but I can try to make something work."

I shook my head. "No, I'm okay. I…I don't get out much and I don't exactly advertise it, you know?"

"I understand."

We parted and I pulled down my skirt, putting it to the side, then did the same with the bike shorts. "Okay, I'm ready."

It was over far quicker than I expected. Randi was quick and professional, taking each measurement and writing the number briskly on her notepad. Arms, legs, inseam, neck, forehead, and shoulders, Randi moved without hesitation until her pad was full of figures.

"And…done," she said after taking her measuring tape to my feet, recording separate measurements for each on length and width. I began to worry about what exactly she was measuring me for, but figured she was being thorough. I hoped she was being thorough. If she was to make something for me once, I wouldn't be surprised if Delilah came to her again and again, and she'd need all the measurements she could get.

"All well?" Delilah asked.

"We're good. Like I expected, I don't have anything ready-made that would work, but I can whip up something that you'll love in a few months."

"Do I get a say in this at all?" I asked, but already knew the answer. I started putting my clothes back on and Delilah made a sad sound about it, but I stuck out my tongue at her in response.

"Don't make me steal your tongue, pet."

I hung my head but couldn't douse my smile. "Yes, Mistress."

I finished dressing as Randi finished with her work and turned back to Delilah. "And you wanted your package?"

"Yes, please, doll."

Randi headed for one of the worktables and I noticed a small, carved wooden box sitting on the table. I longed to open it up and see what was inside, but Randi brought it to Delilah and my Mistress was quick to keep her back to me when she opened it as if to check what was inside. The moment I stepped forward to see what was in the box, Delilah snapped the box closed and gave Randi a hug.

"It's perfect. Thank you. I owe you so much."

Randi shook her head. "You owe me nothing, Mistress. Just don't forget about me."

"I never could."

"Me neither," I piped up, stepping up to Delilah's shoulder. "I'll make sure she doesn't forget."

It took longer than it should've to say goodbye and leave the store, getting looks from Lola and Nikki as we left. I kept trying to get a peek at the wooden box, but Delilah was keeping it well hidden from me, leaving it in the trunk only after I was in the passenger seat and buckled in, waiting for her.

"Are you going to tell me what that is?"

"Not yet."

"Do I get to know what it is at some point?"

"Yes."

"Not even a hint right now?"

"Nope."

I crossed my arms and pouted in my seat, and Delilah glanced over at me.

"You know, you're not being a very good pet right now."

"I want to know what's in the box."

"You'll simply have to be a good girl and wait until I decide to tell you." Delilah returned her attention to the road. "You want to be a good girl for me, don't you?"

"Yes, Mistress." I flushed and turned to look out the window.

"Good girls get rewarded."

"Yes, Mistress."

"You want to be rewarded, don't you?"

"Yes, Mistress."

"Very good, pet, very good." She put a hand on my thigh, and I revelled in the small touch that made me feel cared for. "Now, let's go get some dinner."

CHAPTER TWENTY-SIX

After the fun we had at the sex store, the restaurant was surprisingly tame. Not that I minded. There was a lot going on in my head that I needed to take the time to process. I mean, I wanted to know what was in that box of Delilah's but had to be patient and believe that she'd show me when the time was right. At least right for her, that is. Other than that, there was this new feeling inside me that had blossomed in the workroom watching Delilah play with Randi and realizing how much I wanted to be involved and a part of it. I'd never considered myself any sort of switch, I'm firmly a bottom, but damn it, I'd wanted so badly to be a participant in what was going on.

And I was. I kissed her. With her consent, of course, because everything in this world should run on consent. Sadly, it's oftentimes overlooked, but it really shouldn't be.

I enjoyed kissing her. There was a thrill about it, made all the more intense by the fact that I was doing something my Mistress had asked of me. It was fun, it was beautiful, it was sensual, and I had to admit Randi was an amazing kisser.

Would it be the same with anyone we played with? Would there be others to play with? Delilah knew a lot of people, I assumed. Had played with a lot of people. Would she want to play with other people? What if I couldn't give her what she wanted?

"Pet." Delilah's voice seemed rather distant, and it didn't really register as my brain started to slip down that particular rabbit hole.

What if I couldn't give her enough, and she had to find it elsewhere? I mean, I wasn't perfect. I couldn't give her everything. Could I handle her finding it elsewhere? Would I be able to help like I did tonight?

"Sabrina."

What if she didn't want me to help? What if she wanted to do it on her own? I wouldn't stop her. If I wasn't enough for her, I wouldn't want to prevent her from finding something else, but would it break my heart in the process?

"Sabrina!"

I jumped when fingers in front of my face snapped loudly, and I felt the immediate need to fall to my knees. I focused on that hand as my awareness of the world rushed back into my senses. I felt the plush cushion of a booth beneath me and my feet flat on the floor. I realized I was wringing my hands on the table in front of me. Delilah moved her hand back and forth across my field of vision, and I followed it as if it were a lifeline to the world of the living. I didn't want to sink into my thoughts again.

"S-sorry," I whispered, as I tried to focus past Delilah's hand and onto her face.

"Are you back with me, pet?"

I nodded, then looked around. We were in a restaurant, seated at a booth between what looked like a nuclear family having a late dinner out and an awkward first date where neither person knew what to say to the other. I couldn't remember even walking into the restaurant. Last I could recall, I was still sitting in the SUV, watching as Delilah pulled into a parking lot. Had I followed her in here like a good little pet? That seemed...worrisome, in some ways. I had to have been very, very out of it.

"Where did you go?" Delilah asked softly, reaching out and taking my hands in one of hers. "What's going on in that brain of yours?"

There was no point beating around the bush with her. She could read me as well as any book, and I didn't want to try to hide it from her anyway.

"I'm having some arguments in my head," I told her. I took comfort in having her hand around mine, and I managed to stop wringing them. "About what we did back in Randi's workshop."

"Was it too much? Did I push you too far?"

"No, no, it wasn't too much. I...I never thought I'd do something like that." I chuckled. "There's a lot of things I never thought I'd do that you've introduced into my life."

"Is this a bad thing?"

"Not at all. I mean, I feel a little weird about it, kissing someone else. With you right there, no less. Like if I did it without you there it'd be even worse, but I did it and you told me to and I had your permission, but apparently my brain still wants to overthink it to death, when honestly all I really want is to have enjoyed it and move on."

"Are you saying you'd like to play with other people more?"

I glanced away from her but kept my hands in hers. "Maybe? I don't know. It was really spur of the moment. I expected to feel jealous when you started…um…topping Randi. But I didn't. Like it was okay, because that's you, and clearly you had a thing going with her and I didn't want to interrupt or destroy that…if that makes any sense."

"That seems an interesting, but healthy, way of thinking about it."

"But then my brain took it further. I started worrying that I won't be enough for you, that you'll always be looking for someone else to play with because I can't give you everything you need, and I want to give you everything you need. And then I worry that—"

She raised her other hand, cutting me off. "Whoa, slow down, pet." She shook her head slowly. "I want to start off by saying that you give me everything I want and need, at least so far. If there comes a day when that changes, we will have a grown-up, adult conversation about the possibility of opening our relationship or however we want this to work. I don't know if that's something we need to discuss now, but if it'll put your mind at ease, I am willing to have this conversation."

"But I don't even know how to have this conversation. I don't know if I'm poly, or monogamous, or what. I don't have the experience in any of these things to figure it out."

"Hey." She rubbed my hands with the fingers of one hand and reached over the table with the other to cup my cheek softly. "Hey, we'll figure this out together, yeah? If this relationship is going to work, we need to be partners, you understand? I know with a dynamic like ours it's simple to fall back and simply let the dominant one take care of the decision making, but that doesn't always cut it."

"You mean we won't be twenty-four seven?"

She shook her head. "That takes a very particular set of skills and way of thinking from both parties to pull off well. I'm not saying we won't play around with our dynamic outside of the bedroom, as we've already done, but to be full-time like that is not something I think I can handle. At least not at this point."

"But poly…" I drifted off, unsure of what to say.

"We don't have to make that decision right now." She furrowed her brows and glanced away for a second as if trying to find the right words. "Did I go too far, telling you to kiss Randi? Please, tell me honestly."

"No, it's not that. It's definitely not that." I let my shoulders slump a little. "And yet it is. It's not that you told me to. It's not even that I did it. I think I'm getting upset with myself for not being upset with myself. Does that even make sense?"

It was Delilah's turn to chuckle. "It makes more sense than you probably think it does. It's you and your brain fighting against what's usually considered a societal norm. But you have practice doing that already. You live that life every day. But that doesn't mean it's easy to start kissing another woman in front of your girlfriend, even if she did consent to it."

Our conversation was interrupted by the arrival of our server, who was annoyingly chipper and talkative when all I wanted to do was get back to talking with Delilah in private. Still, we ordered drinks—a Diet Pepsi for me and a regular Pepsi for Delilah—and he said he'd return to take our orders in a little bit. We hadn't even opened the menus yet.

What his visit did do was break some of the tension that had been building between us. We both kind of let out a breath and chuckled about it, then opened our menus together and I tried to find something I felt like eating.

My brain was still trying to push me in the direction that I did something wrong, but I wasn't letting it take the wheel like that. Like Delilah had said, I was used to breaking societal norms. This was just another one. I wasn't going to let it bother me anymore.

"So, what are you thinking?" Delilah asked, glancing through her own menu. She looked up and gave me a sly grin. "Or would you like me to order for you again?"

I paused and honestly considered the idea for a long moment before I shook my head. "I think I'll manage this time. Though I can't say I didn't enjoy it last time."

"Well, if you do enjoy it, I promise it can happen again."

"I'd like that." I turned back to the menu, then sighed and closed it. "I'll probably get my usual. I'm not in the mood for anything special tonight."

Delilah frowned slightly. "Did I pick the wrong restaurant?"

"No, no, not at all. I'm…" I hesitated as I tried to find the right words. "I'd prefer to go back to your place instead of eating right now." I gave her a wink.

"You want to head back so you can find out what's in here." She lifted something off the bench beside her. It was the wooden box from Randi. She placed it on the table in front of her, keeping it far enough away I couldn't easily grab it.

I glared at her. "That's not the only reason I want to go back."

"But it is a reason," she teased.

"Of course it's a reason! I want to know what's in there! What dastardly, despicable, deplorable thing do you have in there? And is it for me?"

"Oh, it's for you, pet." Delilah smiled. "No need to fret about that."

"But what is it?"

She opened her mouth, but our drinks arrived, and the waiter took our orders without blinking an eye, though I noticed his eyes lingered on the box for a moment. He walked away and I focused on the box again, tempted to reach out and see if I could grab it. Then I looked up and met her eyes and realized she was watching me so closely there was no chance I could make it.

I crossed my arms over my chest and gave a playful pout that Delilah laughed off.

"Your little pouts aren't going to work on me, pet."

"No? What if I pout harder?"

"I don't think you can pout harder."

"Oh, I beg to differ." I stuck out my lip further and gave her the saddest puppy-dog eyes I could manage, but she only laughed.

"Nice try, pet."

"So you're really not going to open that box and let me see what's inside?"

She sighed, her fingers playing along the lid of the box as if she were thinking hard. "I wanted to save it for later tonight, you know."

"But you really want to give it to me now."

"Oh, pet, there's a lot of things that I want to give to you right now, but we're in public."

I glanced away, this time in pure arousal as images of what she might do flitted through my mind, but that didn't cause my interest in the box to wane. And of course, Delilah could see that all over my face. She sighed again and gave me a slight eye roll but turned the box around and pushed it across the table toward me.

I narrowed my eyes at her. Was this a test? Was I supposed to open it? Would I be punished if I did? My mind went wild with theories and possibilities.

"Go ahead, pet. Open it."

"But—"

"I will not confirm nor deny if there will be consequences, but it's clear you want to know what's inside something awful."

"Well, yeah, but not if there's a punishment." I hesitated a little. "I mean, depending on the punishment."

"My good little slut," Delilah said softly with a smile on her lips. "Open the box or push it back to me. Decide now."

I put my hand on the box and froze. The indecision was killing me. Did I push it back, or open it? "Aww, fuck it," I said, then lifted the small clasp and opened the lid slowly, carefully, as one did when opening the Ark of the Covenant.

Face-melting ghosts did not erupt from the box as I had anticipated for a hot second. Instead there was simply a bed of velvet, and something nestled in it.

"A...collar?" I gasped. Sitting on a bed of red velvet fabric was a black leather collar with a metal buckle that shone with rainbow colors. I reached out tentatively and touched the soft material, running a finger along it. I couldn't believe how buttery soft the leather was, an amazing texture against my finger. The outside had a not-too-small O-ring riveted into it, and I felt some odd stitching along the inside. "May I?" I asked, looking up at my Mistress. She smiled and I pulled it out of the box.

The stitching on the inside of the collar was a deep purple color, and I held it up to my face, reading the cursive words carefully. "Property of Mistress Delilah." I glanced at her again, unable to contain the grin on my face. "Really? You...you got this made for me?"

"I thought you might appreciate it. A little symbol of who you are to me, who we are to each other."

"Can I...can I wear it now?"

Delilah quirked an eyebrow. "Are you sure, pet?"

I nodded. "Why not?"

"We're in a rather public place."

I faltered. Would that be too much? To let everyone know that I belonged to her, whether they knew the meaning behind the collar or not. It was thin, more decorative than meant for heavy duty play, and I could easily pass it off as a unique choker or some such. Besides, wasn't it a stereotype for trans girls to wear things around their necks? Chokers and collars and the like? I was playing into that. Though it meant so much more.

But there was also Delilah to consider. Did she not want me to put it on in public? She didn't exactly hide how kinky she was from the outside world, but this might be a step too far. I started to put the collar back in the box, unsure of what I should do.

"Wait, pet," Delilah said softly, reaching out and pulling the box away. "I want nothing more than to see that collar adorning your pretty little throat. I only wanted you to understand that people might…look at you funny with a collar around your neck."

I gave her a small smile. "I've had people looking at me funny for most of my life. I'll survive." I looked at the collar in my hands and started to raise it to my throat, then stopped and looked to my Mistress. "Would you like to do the honors?"

"I thought you'd never ask." Delilah got up from her side of the booth and I scooted over to give her room beside me, then turned to her. I handed her the collar reverently and she took it with equal gravitas, her smile growing wider as she set the collar upon my throat. I gathered up my hair and lifted it to keep it out of the way as she expertly tightened the buckle at the back of my neck, then adjusted the collar slightly so the O-ring was hanging directly from the center of my throat. It was the perfect tightness, enough that I could feel it if I took in a deep breath, but it didn't stunt said breathing at all.

I couldn't help myself. I reached up and hung a finger in the O-ring, subtly testing how much it could be yanked before the collar might break. Delilah let out a laugh.

"It's sturdier than you might think. Randi is good at what she does."

"I'm sure she is."

"Is that innuendo, pet?"

"It might be."

Delilah pulled the box off the table and closed it, then tucked it between us on the bench. "It's too pretty to let get lost," she said softly, and I nodded my agreement. I loved that the O-ring made a soft clinking noise against its housing that connected it to the collar. I couldn't help but smile.

When our food arrived the server looked a little confused at the change in position but managed to pull himself together quickly and sorted out our meals. A burger and fries for me, simple enough, and a club sandwich and side salad for my Mistress. We began to eat in companionable silence, Delilah chuckling a little as I pulled the tomato and onion off the burger and set them to the side of the plate. I shrugged, but neither of us said anything about it.

"So how was your week?" Delilah asked softly between bites of her sandwich.

"You didn't hear enough about it from my constant text messages?" I laughed. I had sent her a barrage of messages almost every day, even if she was slow to reply. "I mean, besides Cori being super excited about my trip this weekend, and Tiffani being less so, my week was the same as usual."

"Yeah, I guess I did drop the news on my sister a little last minute, didn't I?"

"You were supposed to tell her last weekend, and you waited until Wednesday."

She chuckled. "I figured the later I asked, the less likely she could say no."

"That makes no sense."

"Yeah, I'm starting to realize that."

"So what about your week? You barely talked about what you were up to the whole time we spoke."

She took a bite of her sandwich, larger than her previous ones, and seemed to make a point of focusing on her chewing instead of answering the question. I didn't pry—yet, but I was getting the feeling there was something she wasn't telling me. But if it was about her work, then did it have anything to do with me? Did I have the right to grill her about what might have happened this week? I knew her father wasn't the nicest person, and he might've done something to punish her for last weekend. I could see someone like him doing that. But I wasn't sure I should push her to talk about it.

"I'm sorry," I said softly, glancing away from her. "I'm not meaning to bring up anything bad. I was curious, is all."

She shook her head and held up a finger as she finished chewing and swallowed her mouthful. "There's nothing to apologize for, pet." She let out a long sigh, drumming her fingers on the table for a second as she bit her lip. "It wasn't a great week. Honestly, only the thought of getting to see you was what kept me going. I looked forward to this weekend more than anything I've looked forward to in a long time."

"Yeah?" I asked and gave her a smile. "I appreciate that. But did you want to talk about what happened? I'm a good listener."

"I'm sure it would bore you," she replied. "It's boring work crap, and there's a bunch of things going on and my father is treating me like…like he always does. Like I'm not good enough." She shook her head and started to lift a forkful of salad to her mouth but seemed to change her mind at the last minute and put it back down. "He doesn't listen to a word I say. I keep trying to get him to update the way he runs the business, but he's so firmly entrenched in the way he does things, and it just isn't working anymore. It lets people like that asshole I fired abuse their positions. I wish…" She shook her head again and no more words followed.

"You wish?" I prompted.

"It's silly."

"You're a lot of things, Delilah," I said carefully. "But silly is not often one of them."

"I never wanted this as a career." The words were said barely louder than a whisper. "I had no intention of ever following in that man's footsteps."

"Your father?"

"I wanted my own life. My mother wanted me to have my own life. But then she was gone, Dad remarried, and the new heir apparent dropped off the grid as soon as she was eighteen."

"Tiffani?"

"Yeah. She was supposed to go to university and learn the business." She frowned, then pushed her plate away, the sandwich and salad only half finished. "But instead she got my freedom, and I got her cage."

"I'm sure it's not quite that simple."

"No, no, it's definitely not. And I don't hold it against her anymore. But I did for the longest time."

"Now you own the Emerald Lounge together."

"It was the first bit of rebellion I had against my father. Putting my own money into something that he couldn't touch. Couldn't control. It made me crave more. So then I bought Vibe Check too. And I started taking more time away from the company for my own pleasures. My own life. The one I wanted in the first place." She let out a long sigh. "You saw how that turned out last weekend."

I winced, vividly remembering the man who'd burst into the hotel room.

"But none of it matters. I'm stuck in what I'm doing. I'm stuck with a father who doesn't respect me at all no matter what I do. I try to be myself but also please him, and I can't do both, and it kills me. It really does."

We were both silent for a long moment. I could see the emotions flitting through Delilah's eyes, her mind in turmoil. I opened my mouth to ask a question I hoped I wouldn't regret asking.

"What do *you* want, Delilah?"

She looked at me with her trademark smirk, but there was something a little hollow about it. "You, pet. I want you."

I reached over, took her hand in mine, and placed it on my lap as I tried to keep her attention on me. "And you have me, Mistress." I touched the collar with my other hand. "For as long as you want me." I took a deep breath. "But I want to know what you want, outside of me, our relationship."

She clasped my hand hard, and I pulled her hand closer to me. "I want to just get to be. Be free to do what I want, with who I want, without worrying that he's going to show up and start yelling at me. I want my freedom from him, from the company, from them all." She laughed and shook her head. "I don't need the company. The conglomerate. The stupid chain of expensive, not worth the time or effort hotels that my father loves more than he ever loved me."

"So why don't you quit?"

She pulled her hand out of mine and turned back toward the table, but I could see the war of emotions on her face. And the fear.

"Because I don't think I know how. I don't know what to do without my job. It's all I've ever done, all I have."

I put my hand on her thigh. "Not anymore. You have me now. You can have a life outside your father. I'll be with you the whole way, I promise."

She clasped my hand in hers again, but didn't turn to look at me. "I don't know, Sabrina," she said softly. "I don't know how to do it."

"You don't have to do it now. Just remember that I'm here."

"What about when you aren't?"

"You think I'm going to walk away from this?"

She shrugged. "I don't know. I'm scared."

The vulnerability in her tone made me want to pull her in tight. So that's exactly what I did. She gasped as my arms wrapped around her and I pulled her in for a hug, resting my chin on her shoulder.

"I'm not going anywhere without you, Delilah," I whispered into her ear. "I came all the way here for you, and I'll do it again and again to be with you."

She turned to look at me. "Sabrina, I…I…"

I didn't get to hear what she thought as the server returned at the worst possible moment. He smiled like he hadn't just interrupted a tender moment between my Mistress and me and asked if we wanted dessert as he cleared the plates.

"No thank you," Delilah was quick to say, her voice back to normal. "Just the bill, please."

The moment spoiled, I pulled myself away from Delilah and settled back on the bench again. I took a long drink of my Diet Pepsi, giving myself a moment to control myself before I went haywire wondering exactly what Delilah was going to say.

After the bill came and Delilah insisted on paying, she finally turned fully to me with that sultry smile that I had dreamt about all week.

"So? Ready to head home?" she asked.

I hooked my finger in the O-ring again and gave her my best demure look. "I'm all yours, Mistress."

Chapter Twenty-Seven

I woke up on Delilah's sex bed, snuggled deep in the thick duvet and soft sheets and fluffy pillows. I let out a sound that was suspiciously purr-like and giggled. The bed was the most comfortable thing I'd ever slept on, and after the night we'd had, the sleep had been some of the deepest I could remember having. A tightness around my throat reminded me of the collar that I still wore—and had worn all night since the restaurant. Delilah had even led me around on a leash for a bit using it, something my knees got tired of before my floaty brain ever did.

I sighed and melted into the bed a little more before I realized I was alone. There was no Delilah behind me, or in front of me, or anywhere nearby.

I blinked and slowly came out of my sleepiness.

"Mistress?" I said softly but there was no reply. I looked around the room. Our clothes were still strewn about the floor, and some of the toys we'd used were there too. But my Mistress was nowhere to be found. I fingered the collar a little more, unsure of what I should do, then peeled back the covers and sat up. "Delilah?" I said a little louder, but still got no response.

I got out of bed and debated whether or not to put something else on or stay in my collar. I opted for the latter, hoping maybe to coerce her back into bed for a while. I checked the time on my phone, but it was only a little past nine. We had most of the day to spend together before I had to catch a plane again.

That thought was sobering. I didn't want to go back. I didn't want to leave her. If I could bring her with me, I totally would. Could I have a life here? Could I start over again in a new city, knowing only Delilah? The way I felt now, I was willing to try.

The door to the living room was open, and I could hear Delilah's voice coming from beyond it. It sounded like she was talking to herself, but I reasoned that she was probably on the phone. I got up and left the bedroom, following my Mistress's voice. Delilah was sitting on the couch in only a thin tank top, a laptop open in front of her on the coffee table, as she held her phone to her ear. She was speaking softly and nodding every once in a while, though I could see the frustration apparent on her face. I stepped past her and headed for the bathroom, doing my business and coming back into the living area, still skyclad save for the collar. I didn't think she noticed me at first, but without looking up from what she was doing she reached out with her free hand and snapped loudly, then pointed at the floor beside her feet.

I didn't hesitate.

I was across the room as quickly as I could and sank to my knees at her side as she continued her conversation. She didn't so much as look at me, but her hand rested on my head, and I let out a contented sigh.

"No, Dad," Delilah said into the phone, and I flinched a little between her tone and the revelation of who she was talking to. She patted my head a couple times in a soothing gesture, and I tried to take it into myself. He wasn't there, he wasn't going to barge in on us again. It was safe. Then her hand left to poke at something on her laptop and I sorely missed her touch. I let out a little whine, not loud enough to be picked up by the phone, and she replaced her hand a second later. "I understand. No, I'm telling you it's not a problem. I already took care of it on Friday." She let out a long sigh. "Yes, Dad. I get it. I'm not flaking on this. I got it done already. It doesn't need to be—no, but I—"

She pulled the phone away from her ear for a moment and I could almost make out the words coming from the other end of the line. Holy shit, he sounded pissed, like he had last weekend. She tightened her grasp on my hair for a second, as if trying to relieve some tension, and I let out a little moan as she pulled slightly. Then she put the phone back to her ear.

"Yes, I'm listening. I told you I took care of it already. No, there's no need to get someone else on it. I handled it already." Her hand gripped my hair harder, and I moaned again, but this time she didn't release. The tension stayed and I quivered under her touch. "I'm telling you I took care of it already. I don't care that you don't believe me!

Then stop treating me like a child!" With every exclamation her hand tightened harder and harder until it was starting to be too much. It was starting to hurt—and not in the good way.

"Fine! Fine, Dad. Okay. I'll come in and get the work done." She shook her head. "It's fine. I wasn't doing anything anyway." For the first time her eyes found mine and I almost recoiled from the anger I saw in them. Her hand was still gripping my hair tightly and I tried my best to stay still and hoped she wouldn't tighten her grasp anymore. She looked back at her computer.

"I'll be there in an hour or so. I said in an hour or so. Because I just woke up! I'm going to get some breakfast and see to some things! Things you don't need to know about. I am allowed to have a personal life, you know." She let out another long sigh and stomped one of her bare feet on the carpeted floor. "Fine! Enjoy your Sunday."

She threw the phone on the couch beside her. It bounced and landed on the floor, and she let out a frustrated snarl before she turned to me again. My head was tilted backward trying to ease the pain of her grip in my hair as my breathing came in short spurts, trying to get my brain to kick into the *pain is pleasure* protocol part of it. A few seconds passed before she seemed to realize what she was doing and quickly let go of me, and I swung my head forward in a gasp of pain and pleasure that shot through me.

"Oh, no, oh, Sabrina, I'm so sorry." She knelt on the floor in front of me, lifting my head with both hands and making me look at her. "Are you okay? I didn't mean to hurt you. I…I was petting you and it was keeping me calm and then I lost control over the stupid conversation. I'm so sorry."

I very slowly shook my head. "It's okay, Mistress," I said softly. I used the honorific to show her that I was okay with what happened, even if it wasn't the most fun. "I understand better than you might realize what that can be like."

She wrapped her arms around me and pulled me in tight against her. "I don't deserve you, my pet. You are truly amazing."

I shrugged as best I could in the tight hug. "I'm just me."

We held each other like that for a long minute and I laid my head on her shoulder. I breathed in the soft scent of her as I rubbed my cheek against her bare skin.

"Are you hungry, pet?" Delilah asked.

I nodded against her shoulder. "But it sounds like you have other things to do. From what I gathered from the phone call."

She snorted, then pulled away until she could look at me properly. "I've mentioned it before, but my dad has massive boundary issues."

"Considering the first time I met him he walked in on us having sex? Yeah, I'd say so."

"Well, despite telling him I was busy this weekend—because I am, with my beautiful girlfriend—he has decided that I need to go into the office and redo a report I made damned sure I finished perfectly for him on Friday to avoid this exact situation." She let out a frustrated huff. "I mean, he's such a fucking asshole. Plain and simple. He doesn't care about anyone but himself."

"You know you don't need to please him," I said carefully.

She gave me a bit of a shrug, like saying *what're you gonna do?* Then she stood up. "Do you want some breakfast?"

"What about the office?"

"I have time. And besides, I can always drag you with me, I only need my leash." She winked at that last bit, and I couldn't help but smile. Definitely one of the highlights of my night. One amongst many. She stood up and I started to do the same when she put her hand out. "Did I say my pet could stand?"

I shook my head and bit my lip, already feeling myself getting aroused from her tone of voice.

"Stay, puppy." Her command had me plopping back down on my ass on the carpet as she walked around the couch and headed into the kitchen. I stayed in my spot, but after a couple of moments shifted to find a more comfortable way to sit that didn't put as much pressure on my knees.

It wasn't long before there was something cooking in the kitchen, the smell of bacon and something else drifting to me on the other side of the couch. But being on the floor and stuck in the one spot meant I couldn't see over the couch, which meant I had no idea what she was cooking. Besides bacon—which was making my mouth water in non-sexual ways. I laid my head on my hands as I waited patiently for my Mistress to be finished.

I couldn't believe I was there right now. Doing this with her. Getting to be her pet, to play with her in all the sweet, spicy, kinky ways that she wanted. That I'd never known that *I* wanted so much. I mean, I'd read the books and imagined myself in the main character's shoes, but this was so much better. She'd introduced me to this whole new life, and things would never be the same. As I listened to her puttering around in the kitchen, I started to wonder whether it was too soon to tell her that I loved her.

Because it was more than like. It was more than the desire for her to be my dominant. I'd fallen for her. I'd fallen for her the night she protected me in the lounge, and everything else since then had cemented the feeling into me. I closed my eyes and let out a long breath. I wasn't stupid. I knew that there was a chance we wouldn't work out. Clearly if her father had anything to say about it, we wouldn't last long, but I was hopeful. I didn't want anything else. I wanted Delilah, fully and completely. Like I'd never wanted anyone before.

"Puppy!" Delilah called, breaking me from my reverie. "Come here, girl."

I got back onto my hands and knees and crawled as quickly as I could toward the kitchen. Delilah was setting a plate onto the four-seater table she had near the window, and I placed a paw—I mean, hand on the chair in front of the plate.

"No! Bad puppy." Delilah's slap was light on my paw, and I withdrew it. She picked up another plate from the island and brought it down to my level, waving it in front of my nose as if enticing me with it. She grinned as I followed it with my mouth, wondering what game we were playing. It was a plate of bacon pieces chopped up into some scrambled eggs that had a number of vegetables cooked into it, with some cheese on top. It looked delicious, though I normally ate my eggs with ketchup. As she put the plate on the floor, I started to wonder how I could communicate that to her without speaking.

I whined and nosed at the plate and moved it a little, then looked up at my Mistress as she was about to settle in the chair with her own breakfast.

"Puppies eat on the floor, princess." She grinned down at me. "Oh, I like that name for you. How would you like to be my princess?" I nodded, but still pawed lightly at the plate on the floor. "Hmm? Something wrong with your eggs, princess?"

I gazed pointedly at the refrigerator. Delilah looked back at it, then back to me, then went and opened it up. "Want something on it?" I barked the affirmative and she laughed. She slowly moved her hand over several bottles until it hovered over the ketchup, and I let out another bark. "Ah, I see. I think we can accommodate that this time."

I wasn't sure what she meant by this time, but I wasn't going to argue either. She poured some ketchup on my eggs—much less than I would've, but I wasn't going to be picky—then returned the bottle to the fridge.

"Eat up, princess."

It was demeaning. It was ridiculous. It was surprisingly difficult. Yet I managed to start eating up the eggs and bacon with small mouthfuls using only my mouth. Every once in a while the plate would move as I used my tongue to maneuver the eggs into my mouth. I got more ketchup and egg on my face than in my mouth sometimes, but I'm sure that was only adding to the pleasure my Mistress was getting from watching me. And she was watching me. More than she was eating her own breakfast. It was like she couldn't keep her eyes off me.

I managed to eat all the eggs, sitting back on my haunches for a moment to allow my stomach to digest properly instead of the awkward horizontal position I'd been in. Delilah looked down at me from the table and toed the plate closer to me.

"Lick it clean, princess."

I couldn't help but moan a little at the command in her voice. I was wearing her collar. She was my Mistress, my owner, and I was her pet. And it didn't even cross my mind for a second to question her command. When my stomach felt settled enough, I bent over and started licking the plate clean. A moment later a second plate touched the floor, and I started on that one too.

"Goddess, look at you," I heard Delilah say. "You're fucking perfect, you know that? My perfect little pet. What a good girl you are." She reached down and started scratching softly above my ear, and I leaned into the touch. We stayed like that for several minutes as I listened to Delilah softly enjoying me as she gave me the head pats and scritches reserved for good girls like me.

Then she sighed and stood from the chair, collected the plates, and placed them in the dishwasher. She returned to me and patted her thigh. "Come, princess, time to get dressed, sadly."

I gave her a little *woof* of encouragement and crawled along behind her back to the bedroom. When we reached her bed she turned and offered her hands to me, which I took gratefully, and she helped me to my feet. She hissed when she saw the marks on my knees from the carpet.

"I think we need to get you a pair of knee pads if we keep playing like this, pet," Delilah said, running a hand up and down my legs as if trying to brush the carpet marks off.

"Something cute?" I asked, knowing it wasn't likely to find *cute* knee pads at a hardware store.

"I'll see what Randi can cook up."

I giggled at the reminder of Randi and the kiss we'd shared last night, then leaned forward and gave my Mistress a quick kiss on the lips. "Thank you, Mistress."

She pulled me back into her and gave me a longer, fiercer kiss that melted me enough that when she let go I had to sit on the bed for a moment. She gave me that wicked smile of hers.

"Do have a seat for a moment, pet. Get your head on proper, then I'll show you where I work. Would you like that?" It sounded like a pretty innocent question, but the idea of seeing her father again gave me some pause. As if she could read my mind she added, "He won't be in today. It'll be okay."

I put my hand to my collar. "Is it okay if I still wear this?"

"You like it a lot, don't you?"

"I feel more comfortable with it on. Like something was always missing and now it's not anymore."

She beamed at me. "How are you so fucking perfect for me?"

I shrugged. "I'm just me," I said for the second time that morning.

We got dressed, me in a pair of leggings and a soft red maxi dress that had cap sleeves and nearly invisible pockets. Delilah put on a pair of black pants and a light-colored blouse that reminded me of the one she was wearing the first day we met. She looked unhappy to be in such clothes, and she was certainly right about the blouse when I spilt coffee on it, it didn't suit her. Neither did this one. It was like she was toning down who she was, and I hated that she felt the need to do that. She was amazing and I was in love with her. There was no way I wanted her to feel smaller than her great personality showed.

But I didn't say anything. Not this time. Maybe in the future we could talk about it, sooner rather than later. But it felt like as much as she spoke about wanting her own life at the restaurant last night, that was kind of her limit. I didn't want to bring up anything harsh or risk having an argument with her when I had to catch a flight that evening. I wanted the rest of the day to go peacefully, with being able to serve my Mistress.

We climbed into Delilah's SUV, and I spent the better part of an hour hoping and praying that this was going to be a relatively quick visit to the office. I mean, there were other things we could be doing than having to deal with work, even stuff that wasn't kinky sex. Another day of exploring would be nice, or going swimming, or relaxing at a park somewhere, anything other than having to go to work.

I was fiddling with my collar when Delilah pointed out the tall skyscraper that housed not only the hotel division of her father's empire but also several other companies including Holte Rental Management and Holte Security Group. He'd branched out, apparently, in the last decade of running things, though Delilah said she had only ever really overseen Holte Hotel Group. She didn't have anything to do with the other companies.

"Because honestly, landlords and security? Ugh. Not my cup of tea," she said as she pulled the vehicle into an underground parking lot, swiping a card to open the door as she passed. "And even if I wanted to deal with them, I couldn't. My father would never listen to me about how we could be less predatory in our business dealings or how to take better care of our clients. All he cares about is his bottom line—and it needs to be higher than everyone else's."

She griped about him for a few more minutes as she pulled into a spot that actually had a Reserved plaque on it.

"Are you allowed to park here?"

"It's my spot, why wouldn't I be?"

I looked to the right where the elevator bank was. "You get a spot within, like, five feet of the elevator?"

"There are some perks to my position."

I turned back to her and gave her a grin. "I think there's perks to plenty of positions."

She slapped my arm lightly. "Behave, pet, or I won't hesitate to put you over my knee."

"You say that like it'd be a punishment."

"Fine. Behave, or I *won't* put you over my knee."

I looked down demurely. "Yes, Mistress."

We got out and headed for the elevator bank, Delilah swiping her card again to go to one of the higher floors. The elevator took its sweet time heading up, but thankfully we were alone on it. One of the good things about it being a Sunday, I supposed.

The doors finally opened onto a glassed-in hallway that had large boardrooms dotting either side and in front, making it feel almost like you were walking through a display case of corporate capitalism in action. I could imagine more than one hot and heavy power meeting going on in those rooms, with the women being silenced and talked over while a man at the head of the table slammed his hand down multiple times to intimidate anyone who would dare speak against him.

Or maybe I'd seen too many movies or read too many books with scenes like that.

I played with my collar some more as I followed Delilah through the maze of offices and other rooms until we reached what looked like a corner office, the door sitting ajar.

"That's not right," Delilah said softly, staring at the door. I stared too, wondering what she meant. Was the door not supposed to be open?

"What's wrong?" I whispered.

"Just...stay behind me, okay?"

"O-okay."

I did as directed. I stayed near Delilah's back as she stopped for a long moment, then quickly pushed the door open and stormed into her office. I did my best to stay on her heels, but she stopped suddenly only a few feet into the room, and I barely managed to hold myself back from bumping into her.

"Dad?" Delilah's voice was tight with anger. "What the hell are you doing in my office?"

I moved around her to see what she was seeing. Her father, the man I remembered far too vividly from last weekend, was seated on a couch that sat with its back to the large window showing off the city skyline behind it. He reclined on the leather sofa, his feet up on a crisp black glass coffee table that sat in front of the couch.

"It's about time you got here." His gaze flicked from Delilah to me, and his frown deepened. "And you brought one of your toys, wonderful."

Already the man was getting my back up, but I took a deep breath. This was Delilah's fight, not mine. I'd probably only make things worse. I did back her up by crossing my arms over my chest and glaring at him.

"She's not a *toy*," Delilah snapped. "She's my girlfriend, you asshole."

His gaze darkened. "I am still your father and your boss. You will not refer to me that way."

"So sorry, Daddy dearest, for calling you what you are. Please, pray tell what I can do for you today."

"You said you'd be here in an hour. It's been two."

"I had company."

"I don't care."

Delilah threw up her hands. "Of course you don't care!"

"I told you I needed that report—"

"You don't need it until tomorrow!" Delilah yelled. "And besides, I did it on Friday. You know it, I know it. Half the office knows it. There was literally no reason to call me in here today except to exercise your bullshit control over me and my life!"

He sat up, putting his feet on the ground, and I could see him gripping the couch tightly in his hands.

"You don't talk to me like that, daughter." I almost laughed in his face for the formality with which he was speaking, but there was something in the anger in his eyes that made me swallow the laughter. "What the hell has gotten into you this week? Even in front of the rest of the management team you have been borderline insubordinate to me since you came back from Edmonton."

"Maybe it's because you barged into my hotel room while I was having sex with my girlfriend!"

His eyes flicked to me, and I tried not to die on the spot from the invisible daggers that glare was shooting.

"Girlfriend...yes, sure, your girlfriend who is not a girl." He shook his head. "You people these days, can't be happy with what you're given."

"Hey!" I shouted, about to step forward when Delilah put her hand out to stop me.

"Dad!" Delilah glanced at me briefly before returning her gaze to her father, who had stood up from the couch. "That was bigoted bullshit and completely uncalled for! You don't get to speak that way to her!"

"I'll speak to *him* however I wish to, Delilah. He's the one who decided to intrude on our family business."

"Gah! I can't deal with you today! I am so fucking done with your bullshit!" She moved then, past me to the right side of the room where her desk sat, showing the view from the other wall of the corner office. She fiddled with her computer for a moment, typing heatedly, as I faced down her father. He smoothed down his crisp suit and ran a hand over the short, very gray hair on his head as if something were out of place that wasn't. Then he started slowly moving toward Delilah's desk, where she bent over, forehead furrowed, as she clicked around the screen.

I didn't move from my spot, unsure what I should do, but right now all I wanted to do was walk up to this bigoted asshole and make him regret what he was saying.

A sound started up behind me and I spun. There was a table along the wall beside the door we'd come through with a handful of heavy leather-bound books lining one side of it and one of those large toner-based printers on the other side. The printer in question started spitting out papers at a good speed. I glanced back at her father, who was staring at the machine with a confused look, paused in his movement.

Delilah stalked over the printer as it finished, collected the papers, then walked back to her father and shoved them against his chest hard enough to make him take a step back.

"Here! Your fucking report! Are you happy now? Pleased with your good little fucking worker drone doing her job again and again at your beck and call?"

As she let go of the papers, he didn't make a single move to grab them. They spilled to the floor and scattered around the two of them as Delilah stared at her father.

"This isn't about the report," he said, his voice the epitome of the calm before the storm. "This was never about the report. This is about you, Delilah, and your poor choices."

"You're telling me that you lied to me to bring me down here so you can yell at me about who I am again? Like you've been yelling at me about it since I was a fucking teenager and knew that I didn't want to touch a fucking man?"

"I brought you down here because of shit like this!" he roared in her face and threw an arm up in my direction.

I gritted my teeth and didn't let myself move, no matter how much I wanted to slap the bullshit out of his mouth. I wasn't sure Delilah would forgive me for that. But I was this fucking close.

"Because you refuse to learn how the world really works and think that *feelings* and bullshit like being able to choose your fucking gender are important to the people who run multi-million-dollar companies like this one. Because you fired a perfectly capable hotel manager all because a couple of the *female* staff decided to get together and start a smear campaign against him!"

"What the fuck? Dad!" Delilah started to say, but he shouted over her.

"The way you act, the way you are, the way you're seen. All of it is judged every moment of every day by the rest of society. The people you work with, the people you pass in the hall, ride the elevator with, all of it. Everyone is constantly judging us and, Delilah, you have been found wanting. People have heard of your proclivities, your inadequacies, your so-called *preferences*, and your refusal to even date, never mind marry, a man. I hear it all the time, how you can't be called to heel, how I cannot run the company because I cannot run my own household! I will no longer be made a laughingstock by you or anyone else!"

I took three steps forward, about ready to throw down no matter how bad that might look, when Delilah spoke. "Heel? Is that what you want from me, Father? To heel? To sit all placidly at your side while you train my so-called husband to run this company that you clearly love more than you ever loved your family?"

"I want you to do what's best for you, for the family, for the company. I want you to stop sleeping around with *freaks* like this one!" He threw his arm out in my direction again and I growled, fingering the collar at my throat to find some modicum of calmness and finding it severely lacking. "Do you even know him? Who he is? What if he's just using you for your money?"

Something in those words made her falter, and I felt my heart sink. Was he getting to her? Was she even considering anything that he said? How deep did this need to please her father go? She cast a desperate glance back at me, and I almost burst into tears that she was actually listening to him. Then he pulled a piece of paper out of his back pocket and unfolded it slowly, a sly look on his face that was nothing like the looks his daughter gave me.

"Sabrina Doyle," he said, looking at the sheet. I panicked but couldn't move. I was frozen in place as he read from this page of information that I had no idea where he got it from. "Thirty-two years old. No recorded father—that explains a lot, doesn't it? Mother, Camille Myers, unemployed and living off disability in a halfway house for addicts. Born T—"

I snapped. Suddenly I found my feet and they were moving right toward the man. I brushed past Delilah, who was looking at me with wide eyes as my arm swung almost of its own volition and I slapped her father, right across his stupid, ugly, gray-mustached face. My mind was too busy processing what I'd done when the return blow came. His backhand took me across the cheek hard, his knuckles connecting with my upper jaw and throwing me to the floor. The sheet he'd been reading from joined me, crumpled up and landing on me like he'd thrown it, though I hadn't noticed.

"Fuck you!" I spat at him from the floor.

"You *freak!*" he shouted, raising his hand to strike again. I prepared myself to stave off the blow as I considered my ways out of this. I could run. It would be better to run. Just leave this all behind. But I couldn't. I couldn't leave Delilah here with him. I couldn't abandon her like her family clearly had to this fucking asshole. As I expected the blow to fall I closed my eyes, but then nothing happened.

I opened my eyes and saw Delilah holding her father's arm back, stopping his blow from falling. He turned to look at her as if something was confusing when she wound up and sucker punched him right in the belly, then a second blow to his face sent him to the floor amongst the scattered pages of her report.

"Dad," she said, and I'd never heard her voice more dangerous, "I quit."

CHAPTER TWENTY-EIGHT

W hat?" He stared at her from the floor.
"I quit." Delilah stepped over to me and offered me a hand,
which I gladly took. She pulled me off the floor with a strength I was
becoming accustomed to. "And if you need it in writing, consider it on
the floor with you."

"What the hell are you talking about?" he sputtered.

"Do I really have to spell it out for you? I quit. I quit this job. I
quit this company. I quit your fucking family. If this is the way you
treat the woman I love, I swear I will never have contact with you ever,
ever again."

I blinked and stared at her. Love? Where the hell had that come
from? Was she saying it because of what he was doing? What he had
said?

"You don't know what you're saying! You're hysterical!"

"No, actually I'm quite calm. Far calmer than I thought I'd be in a
situation like this. I think you're the one in hysterics, Father."

"You can't just quit!"

"Watch me," she said, clutching my hand as if for equal parts
comfort and strength. I tried to give her an outpouring of all the
strength I had left in me, making sure she went through with this. She
stepped forward and I followed, albeit a little behind her. "And if you
ever say anything negative about my girlfriend again, I promise you
will regret it."

She turned around and headed for the door. I faltered for a moment,
looking at her father still on the ground. I almost turned around to give
him a kick of my own, but her hand wasn't about to give up mine, and I
found myself pulled with her. She kept her head up and walked briskly

enough I had a bit of trouble keeping up but slowed as we reached the elevator bank. She pressed the button, then rested her forehead against the hard, marble wall.

"Fuck," she swore softly. "What the fuck?"

"Delilah?" Her grip on my hand tightened at the word.

"Yes, pet?" she said, but there was none of her usual sultriness or enjoyment in the pet name.

"I…I love you too."

She pushed herself off the wall slightly to look at me. "Don't, Sabrina. I know what I said in there, and it's true. Completely true. But I don't want you to feel like you have to say it back."

"But I do love you. I have since we figured out what we wanted, what we were doing. I love you. Everything about you, everything I've seen and heard. All of it. I love you, Delilah."

She smiled, but it didn't quite reach her eyes. "Are you sure? There's a lot of baggage here to love."

I pulled her close and wrapped my other arm around her. Her body tensed at first, then softened against me. "I'm sure," I whispered in her ear. "I love you for exactly who you are. And I'm so proud of you."

She shook her head. "I should've done this years ago. I should've seen the writing on the wall, should've known some shit like this was coming. I—"

"Shh, it's okay." I stroked her face softly. "It's okay."

"It's not. The things he said to you. The shit he pulled out of nowhere! I can't believe he would invade your life like that!"

"It doesn't matter. He doesn't matter anymore. He doesn't have to be in your life if you don't want him to be, okay?"

She started to shake in my arms as the elevator bell rang and the doors at the far end opened. I managed to pull her with me through the doors and hit the parking garage button before returning my attention solely to my Mistress in my arms.

"I don't know how to do this, Sabrina."

"How to what?"

"How to not be…here. Not be…him…"

"You are nothing like him. Never once have you been anything like him. This apple has fallen far, far from the tree."

"But what if I—"

I shook my head. "No buts, no ifs. It's just us here and we're going to be honest with each other, yeah? You are nothing like that man. And you won't be, because you have a fucking heart. You always have, even if you don't necessarily believe me. You care about people, not some company, not money. You care about your friends, and you care about your sister. And you care about me."

"I love you, pet."

"I love you too, Mistress."

I pressed a soft kiss to her lips, and she reciprocated, her touch soft but desperate against me. I gave in to her and let her take whatever she needed from me. I always would. The elevator continued descending. I held Delilah to me like she was the most important thing in my world, and right now she truly was. I couldn't say what was going through her head as she continued to kiss me, but slowly it became less intense, more soft and comforting, until the elevator slowed and came to a stop.

"Thank you, Sabrina." She whispered the words against my lips as the doors slid open to reveal the parking garage. She pulled away, taking my hand and leading me out of the elevator and back toward her SUV. I hesitated climbing into the passenger seat as she moved around to the driver's side.

"Are you sure we should just leave like this? What if he calls security or something?" I realized that we were already in the car park, and if he had called someone they'd probably have found a way to stop us by now, but I knew I wasn't really thinking clearly after everything that had happened. All I could focus on was Delilah and making sure we both were okay.

She shook her head as she started the engine. "We'll be fine. He won't do anything. He'll be too embarrassed about everything to do much of anything."

"What about you?" I asked, rubbing a finger against my jaw and flinching from the pain. The adrenaline rush of the—brief—fight and the speed-walking back to the elevator was coming down now and I was beginning to feel the ache in my cheek where her dad had backhanded me.

"Honestly? I think I need to make a clean break from this. I'm not coming back. I have nothing here that I would lament missing, and there's no way I want him to see me slink back into that office to grab some random, impersonal object that came with the office anyway." She approached the exit, and the door loomed large in front of us. She swiped her card with a confidence I wasn't feeling and I half expected it not to work, but the door slid upward quickly enough, and we exited the car park without an issue. "I won't be seeing him again, and you won't have to either."

I pressed my hand to my cheek in a vain attempt to dull a little of the pain. She didn't seem to notice, and I didn't want to tell her, but I was hoping she would take us back to her place and I could put some ice on my jaw. It really hurt.

We reached the top of the ramp out of the garage and Delilah stopped and watched the traffic for a moment. I watched out the window and tried not to distract her from what she was doing. But then an opening came and went. Then a second. After the third I glanced at Delilah to find her eyes no longer on the road but staring downward, her mouth open and slack, her hands loose on the wheel.

"Delilah?" I said softly. She jumped in her seat and glanced at me. Her eyes were wide, slow to focus, and she looked like she was about to burst into tears any moment. I needed to help her. Give her something to focus on. But what?

"Sabrina?"

I worried at my bottom lip, unsure of what to say. "Um, we can... we can go now."

She looked to the empty street in front of her, then shook her head. "I don't know where to go."

I closed my eyes for a moment. She needed me as much as I needed her. And I wanted to help her. To take care of her, even if it wasn't the same way that she did me. I loved her. I needed her. "Um, I could really use some ice, if that's okay."

Her gaze sharpened and she frowned. "Ice? Why..." Her eyes went wide with realization. "Oh fuck. Your cheek. Sabrina, I'm so sorry. That asshole. I can't believe what he did. I should—"

"You should take me back home, Delilah. Back to your apartment. Where we can talk about what happened and I can ice my jaw. Okay?"

She faced forward again. "Right. Home. I can do that."

"Thank you."

She nodded but didn't look my way. We stayed in our spot for a moment longer before there was another gap in traffic large enough that Delilah could pull out, and she headed toward the apartment. I rubbed my cheek a little more, then dropped my hand to my collar and played with the O-ring a little. It was a comforting little fidget for me, and I was sure I would miss it if I wasn't wearing the collar.

The silence in the SUV felt deafening. Both of us were lost in our own minds about what had happened. The fact that he knew about me, had found out so much. Why would he do such a thing? How did he even know where to look? The more worrisome question was if this was going to affect things with Delilah. Would she be able to handle this schism between her and her father? What about her stepmother? Where would she stand in the face of this? I'd never heard Delilah even speak of her. What kind of woman was she?

My mind spun as much as my jaw ached. I couldn't seem to get a clear thought through. My memory went back to the moment my hand landed across his face, the look of complete surprise that quickly turned to rage when he realized what I'd done. I didn't even hit him that hard, I just had to slap the words out of his fucking mouth. I wasn't about to let him deadname me to Delilah. Not like that. Not if I could help it. And the stuff about my mom. I didn't even know that. I hadn't had contact with her in years. But a halfway house? How did he find her? How did he find any of that information?

I started to wonder what I was getting into with Delilah. Would her father be a constant thorn in our sides? Or would he limp away and leave us alone? I could only hope for the latter.

I jolted out of my thoughts as we came to a stop in yet another parking garage, this one I recognized as Delilah's apartment building. I looked to her first, making sure she was moving again, but she already had one foot out the door. A woman on a mission, it seemed. I'd barely gotten my door shut before she took my hand a little tighter than I would have liked and pulled me toward the elevator bank. In the elevator she turned me around until I was facing her, then put her other hand under my chin and raised it, as if she were examining me.

She swore and shook her head, both her hands gripping me a little tighter than before. I gasped and her hands disappeared, and she gave me an apologetic look.

"I'm so sorry, Sabrina."

"It's okay. I—"

"It's not okay. That asshole really could have hurt you. Could've broken something, the way he hit you. I was so mad I...I couldn't think straight. I couldn't let him do it again. I couldn't."

"You didn't," I told her and took one of her hands in both of mine, wrapping my fingers around hers. "You didn't let him touch me, Delilah. You protected me. You did everything you could."

"It wasn't enough."

"It was. You don't work for him anymore. He has no say in your life anymore. That's the important thing here. Yes, he's an asshole, but he got what he deserved, and now you get a chance at a whole new life." I glanced away for only a second as my brain decided to slip into negative territory. "A life with me, I'm hoping."

She put her other hand softly on my shoulder. "I plan on having plenty of time with you. If you still want to after all this."

"I mean, I don't really want to see him again any time soon. But you, I can't get enough of."

She gave me the first real smile that I'd seen since before we even entered her office. "I can't get enough of you either, pet."

We made it back to her apartment mostly unscathed. I let out a deep breath as the door closed and Delilah locked it behind us. We were safe now. A wave of exhaustion hit me then, and I leaned against the wall for a moment to breathe.

"Go sit, pet. I'll get you some ice for your cheek."

I sluggishly followed Delilah into the kitchen, wanting to be near her. When she turned around from the freezer and found me standing right behind her, she frowned.

"Sabrina? Are you okay? I said you should go sit."

I shook my head. "I want to be near you."

She gripped my shoulders and forced me to look at her. "He can't hurt you again. Okay, Sabrina? I won't let him ever hurt you again."

I stared at her. I could feel myself shaking but I couldn't seem to stop it. Like all that adrenaline, all that energy that had built up was gone now and I was barely standing under my own power.

"I'm okay," I said, looking down. "I'm okay."

"You're not. And that's okay. I don't expect you to be okay after all that." She picked up the bag of ice she'd prepared, then gently led me back to the living room, pushing me down onto the couch. She softly pressed the ice to my cheek, and I hissed as the coldness chilled the pain until my entire cheek was numb. "I know you're not used to it, but let me take care of you right now, okay?"

I nodded dumbly as she kneeled in front of me, keeping the ice against my face.

"I'm so sorry. I know I sound like a broken record at this point, but I can't say it enough. I am so sorry that you got dragged into this... family bullshit." Delilah shook her head. "He never should have done what he did, invading your life like that. It was way too far. A step I never knew he would take. Like I know he disapproves of, well, everything that I am. But to do that to the woman I'm dating? The woman I love? I mean, what the actual fuck is wrong with him."

I stayed silent as she spoke. She seemed to need to get the words out more than she needed me to comment on them. I kept my eyes on the floor, unsure of what to do, what to even say to her. How was I supposed to make things better? That's what I wanted to do, to help her feel better, to help her forget what happened. That's what I wanted. A distraction. A way to forget the pain in my cheek and what caused it, even if only for a short time.

My hand came up and started playing with my collar again, something the sharp eyes of my Mistress noticed.

"Did you want it off?" she asked softly. The question was said innocently, but my brain malfunctioned the second it was out of her mouth.

"What?" I almost leapt up from the couch except I remembered her order to sit. "No! No! Never! I never want to take it off!"

Delilah let out a shaky breath. "That's good. That's good. I was afraid for a moment that…that this was all too much."

"No." I resisted the urge to shake my head and kept my cheek pressed against the ice despite the fact that it was getting number than numb by now. It was starting to hurt in a different way. "I…it hurts."

She shook her head "I'm so sorry. I can't apologize enough for what happened." She pulled the ice back.

I shivered a little, missing the coolness of the ice. Missing the touch of her skin. I stood up abruptly. "I need…I need…um, washroom."

"Do you need help?"

I shook my head and walked away from her, refusing to look back. I needed a moment. A moment to collect myself, a moment to see the damage. A moment to talk myself into being calm for my Mistress. I didn't want to worry her.

I didn't close the door. Only hit the light switch, then found myself standing over the sink. I wasn't sure if I felt like I was going to hurl, or if I needed a moment to breathe. I ran the water. Cold. I wanted it cold. I looked up in the mirror and winced. My cheek was already showing the bruise in the faint shape of the back of a hand. I let out a little gasp that could've been mistaken for a choppy laugh. It'd been a while since something—someone—hit me that hard.

"I…I shouldn't have hit him," I told myself in the mirror. "I shouldn't have done it. I can't believe I—"

I shook my head and splashed the now almost freezing water on my face. The cold was a shock everywhere except my cheek, where it felt a little warm compared to Delilah's ice. I let the water drip from my chin as I stared into the mirror.

It'd been a while since looking at myself gave me more than an inkling of dysphoria, and I was usually able to ignore it well enough to continue on with my day. But right now, I felt nothing but the pain of not being enough. Pretty enough. Womanly enough. Trans enough.

I splashed more water on my face, trying to ignore the fact that there were tears mixed in with it as it sluiced downward. I was reaching for a towel when hands suddenly appeared around my waist, and I glanced up to see Delilah in the mirror. I sniffled and tried to hide the tears from her, but she wrapped her arms around me and pulled me in close to her. I hung my head.

"I'm sorry."

"Why would you be sorry, pet?" she asked, her voice soft in my ear.

"I shouldn't have hit him."

"Maybe not, but next time you'll do better."

"I'm hoping there's no next time with your father."

"Well, he's not invited to Thanksgiving."

The words were said in jest but made me freeze up for a moment. Thanksgiving? That was in October, still a few months away. Was she already making plans for us then? A part of my brain wanted to melt into the wave of happiness that rolled through, but then there was the other side that was more frightened of the idea. She wanted to be with me for that long? What if I screwed it up? What if she realized she missed her family, and I was the one who'd come between them?

"Don't do that, pet."

"What?"

"I know what you're thinking. I can see it all over your face."

Curse my emotive face.

"This has been a long time coming. I don't even know how I managed to last with him controlling my life for so long. Every bit of rebellion he criticized. Everything I wanted was wrong. Against what my life should be according to him. You are not responsible for all of that. You happen to be the straw that broke the camel's back, you understand?"

I lowered my head and wouldn't allow myself to look her in the eye. "Yes, Delilah."

Her fingers found my chin and lifted my head until I could see her reflection in the mirror. "I don't think you believe me, pet."

I bit my lip. Hard. "I never want to be someone who breaks up a family. I know what it's like not to have one, to lose who you do have as an adult, because of so-called *choices*. I never meant to do that to you as well."

"It was inevitable. He brought it on himself. And my stepmother isn't much better, let me tell you. She's always agreed with everything he said. You are *not* to blame for what happened today. But I was glad you were with me."

"What? Why?"

"Because you gave me the strength to finally stand up for myself. For you. For something I loved. Some*one* I loved."

The tears came unbidden, but I couldn't lower my head with her fingers holding my chin up. She let me cry, putting her other hand against my unhurt cheek.

"Oh, darling, I'm so sorry."

And she let me cry. She didn't tell me to stop, she didn't act frustrated by it. She simply kept her arms around me and held on tight. And I cried.

CHAPTER TWENTY-NINE

I was long out of tears by the time I stopped sobbing. Honestly, I couldn't remember the last time I'd spent so much time dry sobbing. Delilah had led me from the bathroom and curled up with me on the couch, snuggled together with her strong arms wrapped around me as I tried not to choke on my own snot. So fucking sexy.

"Easy, darling," she cooed as I coughed up tears and phlegm and shuddered with the pain that was coming back from my cheek. "Come back to me when you're ready."

"Is this like aftercare?" I asked.

"I think we can just call it care, my pet."

"I like it. It feels nice."

"When was the last time someone took care of you?"

"Besides you?" I did my best to shrug while lying on the couch. "Cori's always been really good to me."

"You deserve all the care and love in the world."

I snuggled deeper into her and sniffled. "Far be it from me to argue with you."

"Good pet. You know better than to argue with me. Some subs take a while to learn that lesson."

I couldn't help but smile at the joking in her tone. I closed my eyes, wanting this moment to last forever.

Then I remembered that I had to go back home tonight. I groaned and fidgeted against her until her hold loosened and I was able to slowly, regretfully, pull away.

"Sabrina? You okay?"

"Remembering I need to return to my regularly scheduled life in a few hours."

"Hey, there's plenty of time left with me," Delilah said, holding out her hands to me. "Come back to me? Come rest?"

I wanted to. I so wanted to. But now that my emotions were spent and I felt like little more than a hollowed-out husk, I wanted to move, to find something menial to focus on and deal with. Packing sounded like something I could handle right now. And it needed to be done.

But on the other hand, I really wanted to lie down with my Delilah. Just cuddle with her and ignore the world for as long as we can. But I'd never had that luxury before. Why should I have it now? What were we even going to do from here? Without a job, would Delilah still make trips to Edmonton? Would she find a new job here in Toronto? Neither of us wanted the relationship to end, but I couldn't quite figure out how we might make it work.

I looked to her on the couch again and wanted to ask the hard questions, but the look in her eyes stopped me. She was still hurting. Still recovering. Of course she was. She'd changed her entire life on a whim to protect me. Maybe now wasn't the best time to try to figure out what we were going to do.

"Fine," I agreed. "Another hour or so. Then I have to get packed and ready to go."

"Agreed."

Delilah sat up on the couch and nestled into the corner, then patted her lap. It was so reminiscent of the puppy play we'd had that I couldn't help but smile, then climb onto the couch and rest my head in her lap as I lay down. She dug her fingers lightly into my hair, and massaged my scalp gently as I closed my eyes and breathed in the scent of her. It was better than wearing her sweater—the one I still hadn't given back.

I don't know when I fell asleep in her lap. I don't know how long I slept for either, but I woke up to Delilah gently trying to extricate herself from the couch—and my head.

"Huh? I'm up, I'm up," I said as I raised my head so she could slip out from underneath it. I let it fall back down to the cushion, but the angle was awkward, and I didn't last long before I pushed myself up into a sitting position. I blinked blearily at Delilah. "What's up?"

"It's been a couple of hours, pet."

I yawned. "Oh, right. Packing. Plane ride." I glanced away from her. "Missing you."

She offered me a hand and I took it. She pulled me to my feet and led the way to her bedroom. "Well, I might be able to do something about that last one."

"What does that mean?"

"What if I gave you something to think about on that lonely plane ride back home?"

I faltered. "I don't think we have time to play before I need to be at the airport."

Delilah said nothing, only kept pulling me into the bedroom.

"Delilah, Mistress, I'm serious. I need to be there soon, and with traffic, I—"

My words ended abruptly as she spun and covered my mouth with her hand. I had to take a quick breath through my nose as she pushed me to the bed and let me fall onto it. I tried to squirm my way off the bed, but her hand moved down to my throat, and she gripped it tight enough to be a warning, making breathing a little more difficult. I stared at her, already feeling the arousal flowing through my body along with the anticipation of what might come next.

"Stay, pet."

I froze in place without even needing to think about doing it. Like she could command my body without it going through my mind at all. Not that my mind was going to argue. It rather enjoyed the game too.

She returned with a ream of rope, one she put to quick use. She had me kneel at the foot of the bed and lean against the footboard, then started wrapping the rope around me and through the bars until I was well and truly tied to the bed. I stared at her, then at the clothes I should have been cleaning up so I could be ready to get on a plane.

"Mistress, I—"

"Did I say you could speak?"

"No, Mistress, but I—"

"Then do I have to gag you?"

I shook my head. "I really need to—"

I don't know where she pulled the ball gag out of, but the next thing I knew she was shoving it in my mouth, and I had to bite back my words. I bit down on the heavy rubber and tried to plead with her to let me do my packing with my eyes only. Was her plan to keep me here until I missed my flight? Because that…admittedly, wouldn't be so bad in a lot of ways, but I did have a job to get to in the morning.

But instead of playing with me more, she left me tied to the bed, the gag in my mouth, and started picking up our discarded clothes and packing the small suitcase I'd brought with me. I made a noise, and she only turned to glare at me before continuing what she was doing, even folding the dirty clothes nicely so they fit well into the case—

something I certainly wouldn't have bothered with. I struggled against the ropes, only making myself more aroused as I did, but I wanted to be doing this. It wasn't her job to pack up for me. I was the one leaving her. As much as I didn't want to leave.

She zipped the suitcase, then turned back to me. "Would you say you're sufficiently packed?"

I grunted and nodded. She hadn't missed a thing that I could tell. Even my new books were packed neatly in with my clothes, adding to the weight of the suitcase. Was it going to be too heavy?

Why the hell was I worrying about that when I was currently tied to a fucking bed and potentially going to miss my flight? I struggled more and my Mistress looked at me and sighed.

"Don't you trust me, pet?"

I stopped moving. Of course I trusted her.

"Then I need you to listen to me."

I gave her a bit of a stink eye because she knew damned well I wasn't going anywhere and couldn't even speak to argue.

"Don't look at me like that, pet. Or maybe I won't let you go to catch our flight."

I grunted and struggled at the ropes a little more, but they were taut and well-secured. Wait. *Our* flight?

"Huh?" I managed to make the noise through the gag.

"Oh, caught that, did you?" She smiled as she pulled the queening chair up in front of the bed and sat down as if it were a throne. "Yes, I said *our* flight."

I lipped and bit at the ball gag but there was no give. I couldn't form a word at all. Instead I looked at her, confused.

"I was busy while you were napping. I figured, why stick around here when the person I want to be with most is flying hours away? And as much as I'd rather you stayed here with me, I know you can't. Not that easily, anyway." She reached out and caressed my non-bruised cheek. "So I thought, why not?" She went to her closet and pulled out another suitcase.

I made another grunting noise, and she stopped in front of me. She gave me a sigh, then worked the buckle of the gag at the back of my head. My jaw hurt from the size of the gag as she gently removed it from my open mouth.

"Better, pet?"

"Thank you, Mistress." I glanced at the restraints but figured that might be too much to ask. "May I be candid with you?"

"Of course, pet."

"Do you have any idea what you're doing?"

She blinked. "I'm sorry?"

"You have a life here! An apartment. A job—well, okay, not a job anymore, but I mean you have friends and people that you like and people that you spend time with. Look at the ladies at Velvet Desires! Do you really want to leave Randi behind?"

"Well, no, I don't. But they're good friends. They'll understand, and it's not like I'll never see them again. I can always come visit. But *you're* in Edmonton. Therefore, I want to be in Edmonton. Because I want to be with you, Sabrina. Everything else is secondary."

I shook my head, the only thing I could do in this situation. "I can't do that to you, Mistress. I can't be the only thing connecting you to a place or something. You need more than only me in your life."

"Oh pet, I have that. Remember that Tiffani lives out there, and I own several businesses. It's not like I don't have anything going for me out there. You are the best part of the icing on a very decadent cake."

I didn't know what I could say to that. I mean, I could try to talk her out of it, but it was far too late. And besides, I really didn't want to talk her out of it. I wanted her to come home with me. I wanted her to stay in my apartment. I wanted her with me every day and night.

I sighed. "Did you really need to tie me up to tell me this?"

She laughed. "No, but I also know that if I hadn't, you wouldn't have let me pack your bag for you."

"Why did you?"

"Because I told you I was going to take care of you. It's simply one way I could do that." She glanced away for a second, then back to me. "I mean, was it too much?"

"No. Honestly, you probably did a better job of it than I would have. I might not have fit all the books in there with my packing skills."

"So, if I untie you, you're going to promise not to be mad at me?"

"Mistress, I don't think I could ever be mad at you."

"Oh, live with me for a little while, I'm sure I'll find a way to make it happen."

I grinned. "Ditto."

"Are you asking me to move in with you?"

The heat from my arousal decided to take a detour up to my face. "I…I mean…you can't really stay at the hotel this time…right?"

"No, not really. Not without paying, anyway. And I really don't want to stay in one of my—I mean, my father's hotels."

"That's going to take some getting used to, isn't it?"

"Gimme more than a couple hours and I'll be all right."

"Are you sure, Mistress?"

"I'm certain. It's the right decision to make. I'm sorry it took me so long and involved you being hurt to make happen."

"It's okay. I'm okay. I'll survive. And with any luck we won't have to deal with your father again."

"One can only hope."

"I love you, Delilah."

"I love you too, my precious pet. My Sabrina."

Her words sent a thrill through me, and I fidgeted against the ropes a little, wanting so badly for something more, just a little bit more. But I was tied tight and at my Delilah's whim on when she would release me.

"You know we do have a little bit more time before we have to leave, right?" I said, trying to drop a hint.

"I think there's enough time to give you something you want."

I blinked at her. "I'm sorry, what?"

"Now, pet, are you going to be good for me?"

"Yes, Mistress."

"And are you going to continue to talk back?"

I shook my head. "No, Mistress."

"Good, I didn't want to have to gag you again." She stood up and stalked toward me, then grasped my chin with her hand, taking care not to hurt my cheek with her fingers. "I want to hear the pretty moans you're going to make."

I could only watch as she opened her armoire and pulled out a padded blindfold. She looked to me, and I kept my mouth shut. I wasn't about to safeword out of whatever she wanted to do to me. She put the blindfold on me, then all I heard was rustling around the room. I had to trust that she wouldn't leave it too long.

At least that's what I thought until she had me with my dress flipped up and my leggings pulled down and her strap-on halfway into me, when suddenly her phone started to ring.

"Shit," she groaned. "I think that's the taxi."

I couldn't turn around to stare at her even if I tried. "Are you kidding me right now?"

"Care to continue this later?"

"No! I want to finish this now!"

"Pet…"

"Fuck!"

EPILOGUE

Six months later

I walked in the front door of Delilah's house—*our* house, as it had been for the past month. I had moved in after my lease ended on my apartment. We'd chosen a good time to move my stuff over, avoiding the heavier snowfall that came as winter deepened. As it was, I kicked snow off my boots at the entranceway and unzipped the heavy sweater I was wearing over my dress and leggings to beat back the chill.

"Delilah?" I called out, but there was no reply. I hung up my sweater and left my boots to melt on the mat, then stalked into the living room. I heard voices coming from somewhere and tried to follow them. I checked the main floor first but didn't find anyone. The bedrooms and office upstairs were empty as well.

I smiled. She must be in the basement. My favorite area of the house these days. While our bedroom upstairs was certainly equipped for play enough to satisfy any couple, the real fun toys were in the basement. I could almost live down there, if my Mistress would let me.

I still couldn't believe how lucky I'd gotten the day Delilah had asked me to help her out. It seemed like a lifetime ago. I fingered the collar around my neck. It wasn't the leather one Delilah had gifted me with that weekend in Toronto. No, this was my day collar, a necklace with a heart bound in a Celtic knot that was a little less obvious than the full-on leather collar for my day job at the bookstore.

I was still working at Oracle Books, though I had quit my job at the Emerald Lounge so I could spend more time with Delilah, even if I spent a fair number of nights there with her as her girlfriend instead of as an employee. It was weird, not working to live like I'd been doing for so many years, but it was a lot nicer to have something else to live for. Someone else to live for.

I made my way down the steps slowly, quietly, and listened to the voices as they grew louder.

"I think it's all ready, Mistress." I recognized Randi's voice immediately and couldn't stop the little happy dance I did in place. I hadn't seen Randi since I was in Toronto six months ago, and I'd wanted to see her again so badly. Delilah had invited her to come visit a time or two and was even trying to convince Randi to come here and open up a workshop in the back of Vibe Check, but so far the answer had been no.

I reached the bottom of the steps and walked down the short hallway that separated the utility room and storage room from the rest of the finished basement, the room that was quickly becoming our pride and joy. I stepped through the doorway and stopped, unable to look away from the sight before me.

Randi was on her knees on the floor beside the newest toy she'd put together for us. I didn't realize she'd finished it already. The spanking bench looked deliciously perfect. Red cushioned leather covered the top and the leg and arm supports for comfort, while heavy-duty straps would be used to keep the victim pinned. Delilah looked like she was about to strap Randi to the contraption, which I would've been more than happy to watch, but she glanced over her shoulder.

"Sabrina," she said with so much warmth it easily broke through whatever chill the winter months had tried to instill within me. "Come here, pet."

She crooked a finger at me, and I moved immediately to her side. She put a hand on my shoulder and pressed down hard and I went to my knees, right beside Randi.

"Pet, you should see what Randi made for you," Delilah said.

I turned to the spanking bench, all new and set up and looking at home in our little dungeon. "It looks amazing."

Delilah laughed. "No, pet, not that."

I blinked. What else was there?

Delilah turned to a large box I hadn't noticed on one of the end tables we had scattered around the room. "Randi was kind enough to bring not only the pieces of the bench for us, but also a gift for my beautiful pet."

I looked to Randi, who was still watching my Mistress, her cheeks a little red. When I turned back to Delilah, she was holding a leather garment that my mind took a moment to realize what it was.

"Is that…is that a straitjacket?"

Delilah beamed. "Yes, pet." She lifted the garment and pointed at a couple of the numerous tie-off points that adorned the straitjacket. She picked up an enclosed sleeve and waved it at me. "It's perfect for a wonderful little bottom like you."

I couldn't stop the heat rising up my face until I was sure I was as red as Randi was. Delilah laughed and put the garment to the side. I couldn't help the small whine that came out of my mouth with the idea of not getting to wear it.

"Patience, pet," Delilah said. "I have one more gift for you today."

"Why?" I said quicker than my brain could tell me not to.

"Do I need a reason to dote upon my precious pet?"

I resisted the urge to hang my head, something I'd been working on these last few months despite how much I enjoyed the touch of her fingers on my chin. "No, Mistress."

"That's right," she said, and picked up a small bundle of leather straps that I recognized immediately.

"The…the harness."

"You thought I forgot, didn't you?"

I opened my mouth, but the words didn't come. Delilah took that opportunity to shove the ball gag attached to all those straps into my mouth, with the puppy muzzle covering it. She worked the straps to the back of my head and cinched the harness on, then adjusted the slim leather ears so they sat just how she wanted them to.

"Good girl." Delilah laughed. "Both of you are such good girls."

"Thank you, Mistress," Randi said, smiling at me as I echoed her words as best I could through the gag.

"Do you like the new gifts our doll has made for us, pet?"

I nodded.

"Do you think we should reward her for all her hard work?"

I gave her my best attempt at a bark and felt so proud when it came out pretty well.

"Very good, pet. Very good."

Delilah smiled at both of us, then held out her hands. We each took one and stood up from the floor. We spent the rest of the afternoon together in that room, breaking in the new toys and breaking in Randi as well. I really hoped we'd be seeing more of Randi after this.

I couldn't believe how lucky I was. To have found Delilah, to have found this life. All thanks to be being late, being clumsy, being unable to stop myself from saying yes to this complete stranger. That she took a chance on me and was willing to give me this new life.

When we finished, my Mistress escorted Randi upstairs and tucked her into the bed in the guest bedroom. They took their time up there, but sometimes aftercare took as long as it needed to. As Delilah came back down I waited for her at the bottom of the steps, still wearing the harness around my head. She smiled at me, and I tried to match it with one of my own. It was so easy to smile at her, to be with her. I didn't fully understand it myself, but I could feel it every time I caught her eye.

"Oh, pet, there was some mail for you." She put her arm around my shoulder as we walked back toward the living room and kitchen. On the island counter was a large envelope addressed to me, from the government of Alberta.

"What is it?" I tried to say, and was surprised when she seemed to understand exactly what I said through the gag.

She shrugged. "I'm not about to open your mail."

I ripped open the top and pulled out a small sheaf of papers. I quickly scanned over the top one, then did it again, then took a deep breath and read the whole thing as quickly as I could without skipping any words.

"What is it, pet?" Delilah asked. I looked at her and shook my head, then gestured to the harness. She was quick to remove it, setting it on the island beside us.

"It...it's my surgery. It's all the paperwork. I should get a phone call soon to confirm everything with the clinic. And then...I guess we're going to have an actual date." I stared at the papers in my hand, then looked up at Delilah, who had a smile on her face but looked a little worried.

"Are you okay?"

I nodded. "It's...it's amazing. It's what I've been dreaming of for years. What I've been waiting for." I put the papers on the counter before I could drop them and lose them on the floor. "I'm...surprised. I've been waiting so long, jumping through so many hoops. I'd almost lost hope."

"But you didn't tell me that."

I shrugged. "It didn't seem important."

"Oh, Sabrina. It's always important if it has anything to do with you."

"I love you," I said, stepping up and wrapping my arms around her. I pulled her in tightly, trying to convey every emotion I was feeling to her as best I could.

"I love you, pet. I truly do."

I let go and we both turned back to the paperwork on the counter. I wasn't sure what to do with it. Wasn't sure even how to handle it. It was Delilah who stepped up and took care of it, filing away the paperwork for when we needed it. Then she returned to me and took hold of my arms, so I was looking at her and not the empty spot on the counter where the paperwork had been.

"What do you need from me, my love?"

"What do you mean?"

"I mean I want to support you however I can. How can I do that?"

I melted into those arms and looked into the eyes of my amazing lady. I wanted to spend forever with her. The rest of my life. If she'd have me.

Goddess, I hoped she'd have me forever.

"Just love me, Mistress."

"You make that easy."

We went to bed that night wrapped in each other's arms, on the bed that our dear friend had made for Delilah. Delilah was willing to do all of that for me. With me. She wanted to be with me. She was willing to support me in everything I did. I couldn't ask for a better lover, better dominant, better partner.

I couldn't love her any more than I already did. But I was going to spend every day trying.

About the Author

Elena Abbott is a trans woman, parent, and voracious writer and reader of sapphic literature. She believes that every book can be made better with the inclusion of at least one trans person and multiple lesbians. She writes everything from contemporary and paranormal romance to sci-fi to fantasy and whatever comes into her mind at any given moment. She enjoys playing video games and watching cooking shows, hoping to learn to cook through pure osmosis. She lives in Edmonton, Alberta. Elena uses she/her pronouns. Connect with her on Bluesky @writerprincess.bsky.social or email her at writerprincess8@gmail.com.

Books Available From Bold Strokes Books

Discovering Gold by Sam Ledel. In 1920s Colorado, a single mother and a rowdy cowgirl must set aside their fears and initial reservations about one another if they want to find love in the mining town each of them calls home. (978-1-63679-786-1)

Dream a Little Dream by Melissa Brayden. Savanna can't believe it when Dr. Kyle Remington, the woman who left her feeling like a fool, shows up in Dreamer's Bay. Life is too complicated for second chances. Or is it? (978-1-63679-839-4)

Emma by the Sea by Sarah G. Levine. A delightful modern-day romance inspired by *Emma*, one of Jane Austen's most beloved novels. (978-1-63679-879-0)

Goodbye Hello by Heather K O'Malley. With so much time apart and the challenges of a long-distance relationship, Kelly and Teresa's second chance at love may end just as awkwardly as the first. (978-1-63679-790-8)

One Measure of Love by Annie McDonald. Vancouver's hit competitive cooking show *Recipe for Success* has begun filming its second season, and two talented young chefs are desperate for more than a winning dish. (978-1-63679-827-1)

The Smallest Day by J.M. Redmann. The first bullet missed—can Micky Knight stop the second bullet from finding its target? (978-1-63679-854-7)

To Please Her by Elena Abbott. A spilled coffee leads Sabrina into a world of erotic BDSM that may just land her the love of her life. (978-1-63679-849-3)

Two Weddings and a Funeral by Claudia Parr. Stella and Theo have spent the last thirteen years pretending they can be just friends, but surely "just friends" don't make out every chance they get. (978-1-63679-820-2)

Firecamp by Jaycie Morrison. Going their separate ways seemed inevitable for two people as different as Fallon and Nora, while meeting up again is strictly coincidental. (978-1-63679-753-3)

Coming Up Clutch by Anna Gram. College softball star Kelly "Razor" Mitchell hung up her cleats early, but when former crush, now coach Ashton Sharpe shows up on her doorstep seven years later, beautiful as ever, Razor hopes the longing in her gaze has nothing to do with softball. (978-1-63679-817-2)

Fixed Up by Aurora Rey. When electrician Jack Barrow and artist Ellie Lancaster get stuck on a job site during a blizzard, close quarters send all sorts of sparks flying. (978-1-63679-788-5)

Stranded by Ronica Black. Can Abigail and Whitley overcome their personal hang-ups and stubbornness to survive not only Alaska but a dangerous stalker as well? (978-1-63679-761-8)

Whisk Me Away by Georgia Beers. Regan's a gorgeous flake. Ava, a beautiful untouchable ice queen. When they meet again at a retreat for up-and-coming pastry chefs, the competition, and the ovens, heat up. (978-1-63679-796-0)

Across the Enchanted Border by Crin Claxton. Magic, telepathy, swordsmanship, tyranny, and tenderness abound in a tale of two lands separated by the enchanted border. (978-1-63679-804-2)

Deep Cover by Kara A. McLeod. Running from your problems by pretending to be someone else only works if the person you're pretending to be doesn't have even bigger problems. (978-1-63679-808-0)

Good Game by Suzanne Lenoir. Even though Lauren has sworn off dating gamers, it's becoming hard to resist the multifaceted Sam. An opposites attract lesbian romance. (978-1-63679-764-9)

Innocence of the Maiden by Ileandra Young. Three powerful women. Two covens at war. One horrifying murder. When mighty and powerful witches begin to butt heads, who out there is strong enough to mediate? (978-1-63679-765-6)

Protection in Paradise by Julia Underwood. When arson forces them together, the flames between chief of police Eve Maguire and librarian Shaye Hayden aren't that easy to extinguish. (978-1-63679-847-9)

Too Forward by Krystina Rivers. Just as professional basketball player Jane May's career finally starts heating up, a new relationship with her team's brand consultant could derail the success and happiness she's struggled so long to find. (978-1-63679-717-5)

Worth Waiting For by Kristin Keppler. For Peyton and Hanna, reliving the past is painful, but looking back might be the only way to move forward. (978-1-63679-773-1)

All For Her: Forbidden Romance Novellas by Gun Brooke, J.J. Hale & Aurora Rey. Explore the angst and excitement of forbidden love few would dare in this heart-stopping novella collection. (978-1-63679-713-7)

Finding Harmony by CF Frizzell. Rock star Harper Cushing has to rearrange her grandmother's future and sell the family store out from under her, but she reassesses everything because Gram's helper, Frankie, could be offering the harmony her heart has been missing. (978-1-63679-741-0)

Gaze by Kris Bryant. Love at first sight is for dreamers, but the more time Lucky and Brianna spend together, the more they realize the chemistry of a gaze can make anything possible. (978-1-63679-711-3)

Laying of Hands by Patricia Evans. The mysterious new writing instructor at camp makes Grace Waters brave enough to wonder what would happen if she dared to write her own story. (978-1-63679-782-3)

The Naked Truth by Sandy Lowe. How far are Rowan and Genevieve willing to go and how much will they risk to make their most captivating and forbidden fantasies a reality? (978-1-63679-426-6)

The Roommate by Claire Forsythe. Jess Black's boyfriend is handsome and successful. That's why it comes as a shock when she meets a woman on the train who makes her pulse race. (978-1-63679-757-1)

The Blessed by Anne Shade. Layla and Suri are brought together by fate to defeat the darkness threatening to tear their world apart. What they don't expect to discover is a love that might set them free. (978-1-63679-715-1)

Seducing the Widow by Jane Walsh. Former rival debutantes have a second chance at love after fifteen years apart when a spinster persuades her ex-lover to help save her family business. (978-1-63679-747-2)